UNDER I

First published in 2008 by

WOODFIELD PUBLISHING
Bognor Regis, West Sussex, England
www.woodfieldpublishing.com

ISBN 1-84683-055-9

Under New Management

The sequel to 'Flagship March' and 'BlueBelles on Parade'

Robert C Bertie

Woodfield

Woodfield Publishing Ltd
Woodfield House ~ Babsham Lane ~ Bognor Regis ~ West Sussex ~ PO21 5EL
telephone 01243 821234 ~ **e-mail** enquiries@woodfieldpublishing.com

Interesting and informative books on a variety of subjects

For full details of all our published titles, visit our website at
www.woodfieldpublishing.com

Dedicated to the memory of the late Albert Barrett
who it was my privilege to call a true friend.

Whatever the situation, he was always there
to lend a helping hand.

In Warrant Officer Bill Barrett
I have tried to recreate Albert's admirable qualities
of firmness, kindness and a sense of humour.

Acknowledgements

To my brother Roy, who gave me ideas from some of his National Service exploits.

To Viv Allison (my heroine), who did so much to spread the word of my first book *BlueBelles On Parade* to the numerous ex-RAF and WRAF colleagues.

To Ted Whittaker, ex-National Service, RAF Regiment, Queen's Colour Squadron, for boosting my confidence after reading my effort and giving it his top marks.

*"What? **You** Write a Book? Don't Make Me Laugh!"*

I would like to tell you what made an 'old barm pot' like me at my age write a trilogy of fictional novels based on my service in the Royal Air Force. The answer to that is… I don't know!

But I can tell you how it started.

As a member of a mixed local Crown Green Bowling Club, I was in contact with bowlers of both sexes who, up here in Lancashire, are well known for their humour. I will give you an example (you must appreciate that our club members are sixty years of age and over).

A lady joined the club and after being chosen for her first competitive game I congratulated her on her win.

This was her reply.

"That man I played against, I don't know if he was being offensive and whether I should have complained, because each time I asked whose 'wood' (bowl) was nearest to the 'Jack' he would call 'Urine'. I didn't know what to think and I half expected him to leave the green to go to the toilet, which he never did, but wasn't it a funny thing to say?"

When I explained that he was calling 'You're in', meaning 'your wood is nearest to the Jack', she gave a half scream and, in a burst of uncontrollable laughter, managed to blurt out, "If I don't dash off to the toilet now I *will* wet myself!"

With that in mind, I decided to try my hand at writing a novel about 'Humour on the Bowling Green'.

I wrote one page then gave it up as a bad job.

Weeks later I got the idea for *BlueBelles On Parade* and my keyboard got so hot I had to have a small finger bowl to hand to cool down my fingers!

I have enjoyed every minute of writing my stories. The hardest part, I found, was trying to come up with that elusive ending.

What am I going to do now? I have not a clue!

Maybe the old grey matter will give me a jolt. I do hope so…

My thanks to all those who took a gamble and purchased my books.

I do hope you enjoyed them.

Bob Bertie, *August 2008*

The Author

Born in 1921 in the West Riding of Yorkshire Robert Bertie's family returned to Lancashire when he was a babe.

An 8th.Army war veteran, he also served for 23 years in the peacetime Royal Air Force.

He has been married for 59 years to Jean, who was a nurse for 39 years.

They have one son, Robert Ian.

CHAPTER 1

The Orderly Sergeant collected the RAF Ensign from the guardroom and marched, with it tucked under one arm, to the parade ground, where he would hoist it, in the presence of the Orderly Officer, on the flagstaff situated at the edge of the parade ground in front of Station Headquarters.

As he came in view of the flagstaff he saw that the airmen and airwomen making their way to the dining room for breakfast were pointing and laughing at something. There, in all their glory, blowing in the breeze atop the flagstaff, was a pair of RAF issue 'passion killers'. He hurriedly hauled them down before the Orderly Officer arrived on the scene, to the cheers of the onlookers. He laughed to himself and thought it was inevitable that it had to happen; it was a ritual on a mixed station.

When the Orderly Officer arrived he nodded to proceed. The Sergeant, who had already attached the ensign to the rope fixtures, blew on his whistle, the sign for anyone in the vicinity to stop what they were doing and stand to attention in respect of the RAF Ensign. Anyone failing to do so received a dressing down. He hauled up the ensign, then blew on his whistle – the sign to 'carry on' – before securing it.

"I heard some cheering on my way here Sergeant, any idea what it was about?"

"These," said the Sergeant as he held up the offending article.

The Orderly Officer laughed. "It had to happen and it will continue to happen... and from the size of them she is a big girl! Shall we go and see if there are any complaints about the food?"

They did a quick inspection of the food kitchen, then watched the food being served, followed by a walk around the tables, asking for any complaints. As they were leaving after their inspection the Orderly Officer announced: "Any lost property can be collected from Warrant Officer Butcher's office," which brought a big cheer from the airmen as the two duty men left the dining room, grinning.

♦♦♦

Warrant Officer Mary Butcher, i/c the WRAF recruit training, decided her office needed brightening up and the best thing for her to do would be to buy some flowers from Sam Brown, the civilian head gardener of the station's market garden. Sam was Mary's fiancé and they were both of the age where retirement was not too far away. When she entered Sam's domain the first person she saw was Corporal Bond, a qualified horticulturist and Sam's right-hand man.

"Hello James, is Sam around?"

"He is in the flower greenhouse Ma'am, shall I go for him?"

"No, I will go and surprise him."

Sam looked up from what he was doing to see Mary come in.

"Hello love, what brings you here?" he said as they kissed, making sure nobody could see them.

"I want some of your lovely flowers to brighten up my office."

"Come on then and choose what you want."

As Mary was doing so, Sam said. "I was actually thinking of you when I was dead-heading some of these flowers."

"Thank you very much, you old rascal! Does that mean my head is due for the chopping block?"

"Don't be daft! You know what it's like when you're doing a repetitive job – the mind begins to wander."

"So where did I fit in your wandering mind?"

"It is something I have been thinking about for some time now and I am having a job to shake it off, not that I want to mind you, but I have to tell you."

"Sam, you have gone all serious on me. Come on love, get it off your chest."

"Mary, you know that this arthritis is playing heck with my knee joints and I have difficulty in bending?"

At this point Mary, being Mary, sent her mind into overdrive, guessed what was coming and gave him a big smile of encouragement.

"Will you marry me Mary?"

She grabbed hold of him in one of her famous hugs. "Of course I will Sam Brown."

For a little while emotion took over the pair of them. When they eventually came back down to earth Mary said, "We had better keep it quiet until we have had a talk about what it entails and what we are going to do. Time is creeping up on us and we want a few years of happiness together before it is too late. Now let me have those flowers, I have work to do, I will see you later love." She was denied a kiss because of James appearing on the scene.

On returning to her office her mind was on the recent event, but she forced herself to carry on with her duties, which helped to take her mind off it for a while. She did toy with the idea of taking Bill Barrett into her confidence but thought better of it; she would talk to Sam first. After duty she ate in the Sergeants Mess then drove to Sam's cottage in the village.

"I was expecting you," he said as they embraced. Sam lived alone; he had been a widower for a few years and had not been blessed with any children and had no family.

"We have a lot to discus Sam and my mind has been racing away with me all day."

"I have been pretty well in the same boat," he said with a laugh "by the time we get to the big day we both will be nervous wrecks."

"Look Sam, as far as I can see we have two options. One is, I leave the service and become a housewife, or two, I stay in the service and retire when you do. Becoming a housewife speaks for itself plus the fact I will receive a monthly pension. The second is, there will be more money going into the communal bank and we should be short of nothing when we retire."

"Both options are very tempting Mary, the big question is, which one do we take? That needs a lot of thinking about before we decide. There is also a third option to consider. If you stay in the service and after a while you decide it is not working out for us, what is to stop you coming out?"

"Sam, it is something we need not worry too much about because we are in the fortunate position of knowing whatever option we take will be alright for us. I will now say goodnight and see you tomorrow."

"But...."

"No Sam," she interrupted giving him a kiss. "I will see you tomorrow."

CHAPTER 2

The Station Commander sent for Squadron Leader Cody and Warrant Officer Bill Barrett.

"I have been to Command to try to sort out this business of having no back-up for our drill instructors and to tell the AOC the position we were in and how we got round it. He was pleased with the method we used but sympathised because he could see no way out of the dilemma until such time as the Drill School is re-introduced and until it is we have to carry on with the method we have just used. I share your disappointment but I can see no way of solving the problem unless we can come up with a blue print. Furthermore, in a matter of a few weeks we will be expanding our training staff. Apparently we are getting an increase in recruits of both men and women to warrant us having a full flight of airmen with potential. The flight for airwomen with potential will now be replaced with an ordinary flight. That means Mr Barrett you will need more staff and some re-organising."

"That is no problem sir I have it already worked out. Sergeant Dixon will have the airmen's flight along with Corporal Harper and Corporal Anders who I would like to be posted in. For the WRAF flight I have chosen Corporal (w) James and I hope to recall one WRAF Sergeant and a WRAF Corporal from the ones we had to let go due to the changeover. These we know will ease back into the role they left plus the fact that it eliminates another browsing stint at RAF Records."

"Well done Mister Barrett, when you have chosen your staff let me have their names and I will rubber stamp them."

"What do you say to that Squadron Leader hasn't it worked out well?"

"Indeed it has sir but that can only be expected when we have a mastermind on our staff."

"Are you happy with that Mr Barrett?"

"I am sir; I hope this little increase in recruiting is a promising sign for us it would be great to have at least one of the two closed down establishments re-opened again."

Bill entered his office with a big smile on his face.

Flight Sergeant (w) Viv Anderson his second in command greeted him with. "And what mischief have you been up to?"

"No mischief, just some very good news. I am getting Corporal Anders posted in to fill a vacant Corporals post."

"We have no vacant posts of any description and that can only mean you are hiding something from me."

"You are quite right; you are to get two more members of the WRAF, a Sergeant and a Corporal." He then told her about the new flights.

Quick as a flash she said. "Two from the ones we had to let go?"

"If that is what you want," he said teasingly. "Give me their names and your wish shall be granted."

"Sergeant Millie Cooper and Corporal Catherine Wheeler, they will be delighted to come back here."

"Have you any idea where they are coming from?"

"No"

"It doesn't matter I will take these names to Wings then he can do the rest."

"So these are your selection Mr Barrett."

"Not really sir, Corporal Anders you promised the first vacant slot that came up and the airwomen were Flight Sergeant Anderson's choice."

"But do they meet with your approval?"

"They do indeed sir."

"Then it is all systems go, I will submit these names to the CO. and no doubt he will contact Records Office. By the way have you informed WO Butcher?"

"I am going to see her now sir, actually I should have put her in the picture before submitting the WRAF names to you…protocol and all that."

"Exactly, you do not want to get in her bad books do you? I would say nothing of this visit if I was you because I don't want her barging in here like Flossy did I don't think I would get the better of our Ms Butcher," he said with a laugh.

"It will be a good man who can," replied Bill.

"Come in Bill, it is always good to see you. Is it pleasure or business?"

"A little bit of both Mary." He told her about the new flights to be formed and of the two WRAF replacements.

"That is good to hear Bill, do you think this is a sign the recruitment campaign is on the 'up'?"

"Could be, we shall just hope it is, now what are your thoughts on Sergeant Cooper and Corporal Wheeler?"

"Good choice, well done Viv, they are the ones I would have chosen."

"I will be getting the Corporal I want. Do you remember Corporal Anders? He was one of those three who competed for the two replacement slots who you and Bob Dixon checked out. Wings promised him he would be first choice to join our team."

"You have got three good lads there Bill, how are the others shaping up who were skating on thin ice during that bit of unpleasantness?"

"I think they have seen the light now and I think Corporals Deacon and Farrow have something to do with that. Well, I had better take these names into Wings for him to start the ball rolling."

"Bill, there is something personal I would like to talk to you about. It is rather complicated and it would take up too much time to discuss it here."

"It sounds serious Mary, would you like to come to our married quarter to talk about it?"

"I will have a word with Sam and see what he says because it concerns him as well."

"Mary, my thoughts are beginning to race ahead of me, if it is…."

He was interrupted. "Keep your thoughts to yourself Bill Barrett, you are getting to know nothing until I have spoken with Sam and remember this is in strict confidence."

"Fair enough Mary, you know from experience how tight lipped I can be."

"Yes I know and that is why I want to talk to you. Thanks Bill."

After dinner in the Mess, Mary drove to the village to speak with Sam. They greeted each other with an embrace and Sam said. "I never expected you this evening."

"I can't stay long because I have a committee meeting at 7 o'clock. I had to come because since your proposal I have been unable to get it out of my mind what is the best thing to do after we are married and I cannot make a decision."

"I am in the same boat as you love I can't come up with a solution either."

"What do you say to us taking Bill Barrett into our confidence?

I am not saying he can solve our problem but he has a wise head on his shoulders and he may be able to help us."

"It is worth a try Mary, he is a good man and who knows?"

"That is settled then, do you want me to have a word with him or would you rather we both did?"

"I will leave it up to you love."

"Alright then, give me a kiss and I will be off."

CHAPTER 3

Bill went to the orderly room to have a word with Warrant Officer Roy Shaw who was Bill's best friend, although anyone not knowing them and hearing the in-fighting between them would think just the opposite.

"Come in," said Roy, "it is open house, where can I go on this station to get some privacy?"

"Hello, who has been rattling your cage, in a bad mood are we?"

"As soon as you walked through that door I said to myself here we go again, here comes trouble."

"Remind me to get you banned from the Mess Bar at the next Mess meeting."

"Come on Bill, you would not go to that extreme for your best friend, would you?"

"Yes"

"So much for friendship and loyalty, now what can I do for you?"

"I came to tell you about the change in training, I am to get a complete flight of airmen with officer potential and the flight for airwomen who had potential is to be discontinued and replaced with an ordinary flight of airwomen. Also I am getting Corporal Anders, a WRAF Sergeant and a WRAF Corporal posted in to supplement my staff and you should be getting their postings-in soon."

"What's going on Bill?"

"Apparently there has been an increase in recruits."

"That sounds promising. Are you coming for a jar tonight?"

"I will let you know later Roy I may have something on, you could say I am on a stand-by duty."

When he returned to his office Viv told him Mary would like him to get in touch with her.

"I think this will be a personal call Viv, would you mind please?" After she left he rang Mary. "You wanted a word Mary?"

"Can we have a meeting in private Bill?"

"Where shall we have it Mary? There is my office, your office or at my house or what about the Quiet Room in the Mess?"

"Yes, I never thought of that, say in half an hour?"

Bill called Viv back in. "I will have to leave you for a little while Viv, any urgent calls I will be in the Quiet Room."

He saw Alan Fell the duty barman. "I have an important meeting with W/O Butcher in the Quiet Room Alan, will you see we are not disturbed unless there is an emergency."

When Mary arrived he told her they would not be disturbed. "I have arranged it with the barman. So how can I help Mary?"

"Sam has asked me to marry him and I have accepted."

He went to her, gave her a kiss and a hug and congratulated her.

"That is wonderful news I am so pleased for you both and so will everyone else when you break the news. I will keep it to myself until you make the announcement."

"I know that Bill. Here are three options we are faced with." She told him what they were.

"Mary, all three are good options you cannot lose out on any one of them. To be frank, the choice has to be yours and Sam's and how you feel about each one. I cannot advise you because there is not one of them I could advise you against. Have you had enough of service life? Does becoming a permanent housewife appeal to you? Will your service pension and Sam's salary give you a satisfactory and comfortable living? That is what you have to take into consideration. When it comes down to the nitty-gritty it is a decision only you and Sam can take."

"Deep down I know that Bill but I had to talk to someone about it and funnily enough it now makes the decision easier. Thanks Bill for talking to me about it, you are a good friend and always will be. She gave him a kiss; I will tell you when we have made the decision. By the way, our ceremony will not be as elaborate as yours but the result will be the same."

When Mary left, Bill went to reception to have a word with his wife Tommy the Flight Sergeant Mess Manager. Jackie a civilian receptionist was on duty and a great friend of Bill and Tommy who had adopted her as her Mum because Jackie treated Tommy as a daughter she never had.

"Hello Bill, you are wanting a word with Tommy, I will go and tell her."

When she came Bill asked her if she wanted a girlie night with their friends Viv and Barbara.

"Why, have your pals asked if you can play out again tonight?"

"If you want to put it like that, yes, Roy asked me this afternoon."

"Are you telling me it is a Hen Pecked Club meeting?"

Jackie who was listening to this dialogue and having a good laugh said. "What are you two like? You definitely do not spoil a pair. Go on let him play out you know how you enjoy your girlie nights."

"Thanks Jackie," said Bill, grinning as he went to leave but was stopped in his tracks by Tommy.

"You can tell those other two crackpots that you are taking us girls to the March Hare on Saturday."

'The March Hare' being the village pub which is their local.

'Crackpots' is the name given to them by the Mess barmen who each in turn get teased and have the Mickey taken out of them by Bill, Roy and Derwent. Although each barman tries to get the better of them, not one has succeeded.

"I will try my best to persuade them."

"Forget any persuasion," retorted Tommy, "just tell them *You Are*!"

Before Sam finished work and left for home, Mary went to see him. He was of course pleased to see her and took her into his office where they could have privacy. Mary then brought him up to date with the meeting she had with Bill.

"He said he could not advise me because the decision had to be made between the two of us. Somehow as he spoke about it I could see it in a different light and now I have made my decision and it is now up to you to agree or not. I want to retire and become a housewife for you Sam."

He came to her, kissed her and said. "That is what I was hoping for love." After a long embrace they sat and talked of the implications from her resignation, the ceremony and the honeymoon.

"If you are in agreement I would like George and Betty Miller to be our witnesses and the only guests will be Bill and Tommy Barrett."

"You know I have no family Mary and they are the closest friends we have and it suits me fine to have a nice quiet ceremony."

"I will not say anything to George yet until I submit my application for discharge. On the other hand I would like to tell Bill discretely of course then he can do a bit of planning with the connections he has to get Viv promoted to replace me. Do you agree Sam?"

"I certainly do."

"I will get back and don my thinking cap and I advise you to do the same. From now on it is going to be rather interesting and exciting."

As she entered the Mess she met Bill and Tommy leaving for home.

"You are a late bird for your dinner Mary Butcher, where have you been until now, working overtime?" asked Bill.

Mary just smiled and gave him a wink. Bill nodded and returned the smile.

"What was that all about?" asked Tommy.

"Something very private my dear of which I am sworn to secrecy and if I guess rightly I should be able to confide in you very soon."

♦♦♦

Here comes the HPC chief, Alan." Alan Fell was the duty barman. "Pull him a drink and fill ours up not forgetting yourself. So you did get permission to honour us with your presence after all, what was your forfeit, a shopping trip to Leeds?"

"Sorry to disappoint you Roy but we three have got a collective forfeit and the message is. 'You crackpots will take us girls to the March Hare on Saturday'. "Cheers" said Bill raising his glass. "Serves you right."

"Well I wouldn't call that a punishment," said Derwent I enjoy going there they are good company better than in here at times."

"Are you incinerating we are bad company?"

"Don't you mean insinuating Roy," corrected Derwent?"

"You know I can't say insinuating."

Alan Fell was laughing his head off. "I was told you were crackpots and I can verify that now."

"You have been listening to ugly rumours about us obviously," retorted Derwent "and I suggest," he said speaking to Roy and Bill. "That we put this bar in the out of bounds category on Saturday."

"Well spoken Derwent," said Bill, "You deserve a drink for that. Fill em' up Alan and put one in for you. That is the drink you would have been getting on Saturday, so make the most of it."

Alan's reactions was to laugh to himself as he pulled the beer shaking his head muttering to himself, what have I let myself in for?

"It is nice to see a barman smiling as he serves us," commented Roy. I think he likes us. Your very good health Alan he said," as he raised his glass with the other two following his example.

"Roll on two weeks' time when I can get back to sanity," was his response.

"What was that item you were telling me about Bill that was on the agenda to be discussed at the next Mess meeting? Refresh my memory."

"You mean about increasing the barman's duty Roy?"

"That is the one."

"It is by popular demand from all the Warrant Officers and Flight Sergeants. It has a good chance of being accepted too because of the good service and dedication the Sergeants are putting into this duty."

"You will be alright Alan you will have completed your duty before it comes into effect," spoke up Derwent as he gave the spoon another good stir.

"Time gentlemen PLEASE." Exploded Alan in exasperation."

CHAPTER 4

"W/O Barrett speaking," said Bill answering the ringing telephone. "Good morning to you Mary, I will be right there. Viv, I will be with Mary Butcher if I am needed."

"I can see by the expression on your face Mary that you have some very special news for me, am I right?"

"Yes and you are going to tell me what it is. Bill, we have been very close for a number of years and I expect you are going to tell me my decision. I have written it down on this piece of paper to prove there is no cheating."

"Mary, next to Tommy you are my favourite Housewife."

"Mary smiled then turned over the piece of paper to show 'Housewife' written on it. "Good old reliable Bill."

"Hold it right there Mary, I will have a bit less of the old if you don't mind," as they both cracked out laughing.

"Now here is what we have planned more or less for the wedding. We are having a civil ceremony with George and Betty as witnesses and we would like you and Tommy to be present. But that is not all Bill, I am going to have to be replaced and this is where you come in. Use your influence to try and get Viv promoted to replace me. You know as well as I do her capabilities and she is thought a lot of at Command. You can then try and get Margaret Roper promoted to replace Viv, all you will need is another Sergeant and you have two waiting in the wings that we had to let go for being surplus to requirements."

"You have this all planned out haven't you? I agree with what you suggest; it is like keeping it in the family. My job now is to convince the

hierarchy that my suggestion is the best option. If we can convince the AOC (Air Officer Commanding) we will have won."

"If you can't convince him no-one else can. There is one other thing I want to bring to your attention, when I leave they are sure to post a WRAF Officer in to take over my post as WRAF Training Officer."

"Whoever it is Mary, she will have to be good, or Officers will be shuttled in and out until one becomes acceptable – and we can rely on Wings to make that happen. No more of the Flossy kind, that's for sure.

When you decide to put in your application have a word to Roy Shaw, he will guide you through any sticky patches you may come up against he knows his job inside out and he will see you are treated right."

"Yes, I will need someone in my corner; I will have a word with him."

"If you have set a date for your retirement and wedding, when are you going to announce it?"

"We are working on it. I suppose the announcement will have to come when I submit my resignation. You can let Tommy know she will keep it to herself."

"You do realise that I cannot make any move until you apply for your discharge."

"I will be as quick as I can Bill," she said with a laugh.

Mary's phone rang. "WO Butcher speaking. Hello Viv, yes he is still here." She handed the phone to Bill. "Viv wants a word."

"Yes Viv, right thanks a lot, bye.

Wings wants to see me, probably about the two new flights. Right then Flower all I have to do now is sit back and wait for you to make your move."

"You sound like you can't wait to get rid of me you young devil."

"What other way can I put it? No, it is getting to the stage where there is going to be a lot of negotiating for changes to suit my purpose and I am eager to get my teeth into them, this is a new challenge for me Mary and I want to win it."

"You will, you have never lost one yet, you mark my words."

"That is where you are wrong Mary I have just lost my first one now *You*!"

"Come here you big lump," she said as she gave him a kiss and said "you will not be getting many more of these so make the most of them."

"Have no fear I know where to find you if I run short."

♦♦♦

"Send him in Marion," said Wings to Sergeant (w) Marion Macken his PA. when she announced WO Barrett had arrived.

"Come and sit down Mister Barrett and tell me how things are on the training front."

"Everything is fine sir, we have no problems, everything is running smoothly but your guess is as good as mine for how long that will last."

"I asked you here to tell you that the recruits to make up that extra flight arrive in two weeks time. I have had no word about the arrival of the WRAF Sergeant and the two Corporals yet."

"I will check on that with W/O Shaw sir, he usually lets me know immediately any postings are due."

"Is there anything of interest coming up in the Sergeants Mess?"

"At the moment I do not think so, I have not spoken to any of the entertainments committee and there is nothing on the notice board. You can come round for a game of Bingo."

"Between you and me Mr Barrett I would enjoy that at least I could have a bit of fun"

"Enough said sir, I understand. I think I will go and have a word with WO Shaw and see if he has any gen on the postings."

Bill knocked on Roy's door, poked his head round and asked. "Are you free?"

"Not from you I'm not and not cheap either. Come in and tell me your troubles."

"None to tell Roy I have just left Wings who was asking if there was any word of our new postings in."

"Nothing as yet Bill but you know I always tell you as soon as I get word."

"He sounds a bit fed up at the moment because there is nothing happening. He asked hopefully if there was anything in the pipeline for the Sergeants Mess, I think he wants a bit of down to earth fun."

"Well he won't get much of that in the Officers Mess that's for sure."

CHAPTER 5

Mary made her way to see Roy Shaw who was surprised when she told him she would like his help with a very personal matter.

"I will do my very best for you Mary but whatever help I can give you there is no guarantee my advice will be acceptable to you."

"It is nothing complicated Roy but Bill told me that you were the best man to help me. I want to apply for a discharge!"

That comment really shook Roy. "I can't believe what you are telling me Mary, you of all people want to leave the service after all the years you have served. It is nothing serious is it?"

"Not in the way you are thinking Roy but it is to me. I am getting married."

"Mary what a relief and what a lovely surprise, to Sam of course."

"Of course"

"Well I am absolutely delighted for you both, he got up from his chair came round and gave her a kiss. Congratulations, you make a grand couple. When he sat down he asked. "Do you want to tell me about it or is it too personal?"

"I don't mind now that I am putting the wheels in motion. You are only the second person I have told, you will have guessed I confided in Bill who has been very helpful and supportive." She then told him the story.

"Thank you Mary and I feel privileged you have taken me into your confidence, so let us get down to the nitty-gritty and get your application made out, it is pretty well straight forward." When that was completed he said. "If you want to know how you will stand monetary wise I suggest you have a word with Jock Webster."

Jock was the Flight Sergeant in charge of pay accounts.

"I was hoping to keep this a very low key but once I submit this application it will become general knowledge."

"Mary, everyone will know sooner or later and you have nothing to hide."

"Thanks Roy, I had better take this to Wings for him to put his seal of approval on it."

"No Mary, it will go straight to the Commanding Officer who will send for you for an interview, he will put his signature to it then it will be forwarded to the Records Office. When everything is signed sealed and delivered so to speak you will then be notified."

"Thank you Roy for your help, I can breathe freely now the application has been submitted. Sam and I can now get ourselves organised."

When she returned to her office she rang Bill Barrett and told him the score. "You can start to make your plans now Bill."

"Thanks Mary but I will have to wait until it is official before I can make any move."

When Group Captain Wildeman the Commanding Officer received and read Mary's application he instructed his PA Helen Fraser a civilian ex Squadron Leader to ask WO Butcher to report to him.

Mary was ushered into his office by Helen Fraser and promptly saluted.

"Take a seat Ms Butcher so you have decided to give up your career, for any particular reason?"

"Yes sir to get married and make a new career as a housewife."

"Are you marrying a serviceman?"

"No sir he is a civilian who works on the station as the head gardener."

"Mr Brown? That is wonderful, my heartiest congratulations to you both. I would like to thank you for not depriving us of his services he has been and still is invaluable to this station. I presume then you will be living locally."

"Yes sir, in the village."

"Then you will still be in close contact with your friends. This station is going to lose a stalwart who has done so much for helping to build up the reputation it now holds and you are going to be a very hard act to follow Ms Butcher."

"Thank you sir but you will find that W/O Barrett is already working on that."

"That does not surprise me in the least. He is a very remarkable man is our Mister Barrett. I will certainly see you before you leave us. Then it will be a sad day for this station and the RAF."

Mary saluted then made her exit pausing outside the door to blow her nose.

After Mary left, the CO. told his PA. "Ask Squadron Leader Cody to report to me Helen."

When Wings arrived he was shown Mary's application form.

"This is news to me sir I had not the slightest inkling she was even considering this action."

"Well it is not one of those applications that has to go through an internal chain of command the next stop for this will be the Records Office."

"Has she given any reason sir?"

"Oh yes, she has only just left me a few minutes ago we had a little chat about it. She is getting married and decided to become a full time housewife. We will miss her because she is a damned good Warrant Officer and a very strong one to boot. When I told her that she would be a hard act to follow, do you know what her reply was? She more or less told me not to worry because W/O Barrett was already working on it."

They both had a good laugh over that.

"I will say this Bill." Bill was the nickname he got in the Officers Mess derived from the name Buffalo Bill Cody. "Whatever he has in mind will be worth listening to."

"I have a good idea what that may be sir."

"That does not surprise me Bill because you know the training staff and have been well trained by them and you are beginning to think like one. Come on then don't keep me in suspense."

"It is Flight Sergeant Anderson sir!"

"By Jove Bill you are right, why did I not think of her? It all makes sense now. With foresight our Mr Barrett has been grooming her since he chose her to help him train the BlueBelles knowing she had the potential to eventually replace Ms Butcher when the time came and he will not let just anyone replace her. Whoever it was would have to be very special. He is very protective towards his staff as you know and that quality comes up perhaps once in our lifetime and I count myself very fortunate to be a part of it. As soon as Ms Butcher's application is accepted he will come knocking on your door then I will be going to Command to plead our case. Fingers crossed as they say, eh Bill?"

♦♦♦

"Bill, Roy here. Your postings are due to report in three days time."

"Thanks Roy that is good news."

"Viv will you get one of the staff to go and tell Corporal Deacon I want to see him?"

When he arrived Bill told him. "Corporal Anders is being posted in and will arrive in three days time. I want you to hand over Bunk 2 and Room 2 to him so have it spick and span.. Now where are you going to put all that cleaning tackle you have stored in that bunk?"

"I will put my 'Plan B' into operation sir which will be to get your permission for me to have an extra wardrobe in my bunk to use for storage."

Bill laughed. "You have it all worked out haven't you? I must admit I like your style. I will see what I can do for you."

"Thank you sir," he said with a smile, "I am looking forward to Corporal Anders arrival, we struck up a friendship the three of us and Corporal Farrow will be chuffed to hear the news when I tell him, you will find Corporal Anders will be an asset to your training staff sir."

After he left he said to Val. "Now that lad has great potential I cannot fault him in any way, he is a damned good NCO and he has a future. Now I will have a word with your financee as Roy would put it."

She laughed. "Do you think Roy puts it on by mixing the words deliberately Bill?"

"Yes of course he does, Roy is too clever a person he knows what he is saying, he is a very clever funny man. Look how he tears into me then with a click he reverts to normal. That is his way of showing true friendship and what pleases him is he knows that I understand him then he doubles his efforts to try to make me squirm."

"But you return the compliments I have heard you."

"You see, it has rubbed off on to me which makes us so close. As I was saying. "I want a word with Derwent."

He picked up the phone. "Warrant Officer Barrett speaking, I would like a word with Warrant Officer Waters please…Hello Derwent, I am on the scrounge for," he told him about the wardrobe and the reason he wanted one. "Have you anything that could substitute for it and be more adaptable? As you know, space in those bunks is limited."

"I will have a look at what we have got in our storage hangar then let you know."

♦♦♦

He then rang Roy. "Have you told Tommy about the WRAF Sergeant being posted in Roy?"

"Yes Bill."

"And have you told Mary about the WRAF Corporals being posted in?"

"Yes Bill and have I told *You* to stop trying to tell me my job?"

"Many times Roy but with knowing what such a demanding job yours is I thought you would appreciate the concern I am showing."

"Sod off you bloody creep," snarled Roy as he slammed the phone down.

"There you go again," said Viv laughing, "what are you two like?" She then answered the ringing phone. "Flight Sergeant Anderson speaking. Oh! it is you Derwent, yes, I will hand you over, Derwent for you Bill."

"Hi Derwent have you had any luck?" Good, I will come round straight away to pick it up. No I am not carrying it I am hoping you can provide me with transport and a driver I will provide the strong men, Okay thanks. He has found a storage item that should suit Corporal Deacon's needs so I am off to rally the troops to collect it."

He approached Sergeant York who was training his flight of recruits. "Can I have Corporal Deacon and a couple of your strong lads for a short while Ron?"

"Of course you can." He called the three out to the front.

"Corporal you go and sort your bunk out to receive some furniture, you two lads come with me." They followed Bill to the hangar where Derwent and the transport were waiting.

"Do you think this will do the job?" asked Derwent pointing to an item of furniture.

"That looks ideal for storage; the lad will be chuffed to bits. Right you two load it up then direct the driver to Corporal Deacon's accommodation. Do you want me to sign for it Derwent?"

"Yes please to make it official then we know where it is if it is ever queried."

"Thanks Derwent I will buy you a pint the next time I get to play out."

Derwent laughed. "Roy and his playing out, no wonder we are called the Crackpots."

CHAPTER 6

Mary Butcher was summoned to see the CO.

When she entered his PA's office she asked Helen. "Is it good news or bad news Helen?"

"Now Mary you know very well I am not allowed to divulge anything from this office, you will have to find it out for yourself."

"Well I tried," she said laughing."

Helen buzzed the CO. "Warrant Officer Butcher is here sir."

"Show her in Helen."

"Come Mary and good luck. WO Butcher sir," she announced as she ushered Mary into his office.

Mary saluted.

"Sit down Ms Butcher, I have the information here you have been waiting for and it is in your favour. You will commence your terminal leave in one month's time and as you know from experience your final discharge takes effect one month later. How do you feel about that?"

"Relieved sir I can now swing into action by making some definite plans."

"I know someone else who is ready to swing into action when you tell him Ms Butcher."

Mary laughed. "Yes sir he is very eager to go and from what I can gather he has finalised his plans and is ready for the word 'Go' to submit them."

The CO. laughed. "We are ready and waiting." He shook her hand. "This is not goodbye Ms Butcher that will come later I am just pleased for you having got what you wanted."

Mary thanked him, saluted then made her exit.

When she walked into Helen's office she said. "You knew all along what the result was."

Helen laughed. "There is very little I don't know that goes on around here, that is my job but you know I could not divulge it."

"True but I had a good idea. Your eyes gave it away Helen." With that she left with a smile on her face that said, you can't fool me Helen Fraser.

As she made her way back to her office she stopped at the orderly room to tell Roy Shaw the news.

He was delighted. "Have you told Bill yet?"

"Not yet, but I will do from my office."

The first person she rang was Sam. "My application has been accepted love I start my terminal leave in a month."

"That is what we have been waiting for, we will celebrate it with a nice bottle of wine tonight Mary."

Bill Barrett was chuffed. "You can start your planning in earnest now Mary."

"Yes and so can you," she replied laughing."

♦♦♦

"Viv, I shall be with Wings if anybody wants me."

He asked Marion the PA if there was any chance of an interview with the Squadron Leader

"I will give him a buzz. Sir, W/O Barrett is here asking for an interview."

She heard him laugh. "Send him in Marion."

"That is funny," she said to Bill, "When I told him your name he started to laugh. You can go in sir."

"Come in Mister Barrett," Wings smiled. "What can I do for you?"

"You will have probably heard that WO Butcher is leaving the service."

"Yes, I am quite aware of that, furthermore I have just had a phone call from the CO. telling me to expect you any moment now and Mr Barrett you have proved him right."

"Bill was flabbergasted and did not know what to say."

"You are looking very puzzled Mr Barrett and to add to your puzzlement I can tell you that the CO. and I know why you are here. You forget that you and the CO. have worked very closely together for such a long time and made some very important decisions together, so much so you can almost read each other like a book. Also, you do not realise what a good job you have done training me. Putting my training and the CO's knowledge of how you both think we got the answer. Your Blueprint to replace Ms Butcher I must admit it was the CO. who came up with the answer that you began to groom Flight Sergeant Anderson when you saw her potential the day you chose her to train the BlueBelles along with yourself, for this eventuality."

"Well I'm damned."

"When the CO. said she would be a hard act to follow, Ms Butcher replied that you were already making plans for it."

"Fair enough she let no secrets out of the bag and I must admit both you and the CO. have got one over on me. I still can't believe it and I do not take defeat lying down. Now I will set *you* a puzzle then I will deliver my ace. You have only solved part of my plan but what is the rest of it sir?"

"Hmm, well, that does pose a problem, we never took into account you had something else tucked up your sleeve, we had no idea you had an ace tucked up there."

"Do you want to confer with your partner in crime sir or hold up your hand in submission that I have upheld my reputation?"

Wings roared with laughter. "Mister Barrett the CO. was right when he said it would take a damned good man to get the better of you. I am holding up my hand then giving it you in congratulations."

"I want to congratulate you too sir, my star pupil has now passed the advanced stage with flying colours. Now here it is. I would like Sergeant Roper to replace Flight Sergeant Anderson with a promotion. She is an excellent SNCO even Flight Sergeant Anderson said when we did the assessments that she would be the one to replace her if ever she was posted and we probably would not notice the difference. Then I would like Sergeant (w) Fields recalled, she was the other Sergeant we had to let go as surplus to requirements and she is fully conversant with our standard of training."

"That sounds good Mr Barrett and you have my full backing on that score. I will get it to the CO. straight away. He has already planned his trip to Command he is just waiting for your recommendations." That brought a burst of laughter from them both.

When Wings reported to the CO what had transpired between him and Bill Barrett the CO roared with laughter. "I wish I could have been a fly on the wall when you told him the reason he had come to see you. You know Bill, you are the first person I know who has literally taken the wind out of his sails, I would have liked to have seen his face."

"It was only momentarily sir; he reminded me who was still in charge by catching me out on the rest of his plan of which I had not a clue."

"That is our Mr Barrett all over Bill. Now let us get back to his recommendations. I endorse completely his choice of Flight Sergeant Anderson because I know from experience her qualities, she will be a good replacement for WO Butcher and I am almost sure the AOC will give his blessings. As for Sergeant Roper, we can only go on the recommendations of both W/O Barrett and Flight Sergeant Anderson. Looking at it logically if he wants Sergeant Roper as his second in command she must be worth it and as for Flight Sergeant Anderson's views, well isn't she a spin off from WO Barrett? Bill, we are going for it." He buzzed his PA. "Helen will you contact the AOC's PA for an interview with him on a matter of some importance as soon as possible?"

After a short wait Helen buzzed. "Sir, the reply message is. 'Get yourself down here for lunchtime tomorrow and we will discuss it over lunch!' End of message sir."

"Now contact my chauffeur Pauline, I want picking up to go to Command HQ at 09:00hrs."

"There we are Bill, fingers crossed we get the result we want." He then laughed and added. "That means the three of us of course."

When Wings returned to his office he phoned Bill Barrett to tell him the CO. had endorsed his recommendations and was off to Command tomorrow to present it to the AOC.

"Thank you sir, I am keeping it under wraps until it gets officially accepted."

"Very wise Mister Barrett we don't want to jump the gun and finish up with egg on our faces. I will get in touch with you as soon as I get the result which the CO said is the one the three of us are looking for."

Bill put the phone down, sat back in his chair smiling and thinking...at least I have got a good back-up team. He then burst out laughing.

As Viv walked through the door she remarked. "Well something or someone is pleasing you."

"If only you knew Viv. By the way seeing it is now official I can tell you that Mary and Sam are getting married."

"Oh, that is wonderful, they are just right for each other, I am so pleased for them. When is the happy event? I should rephrase that shouldn't I?" she said with a giggle. "When are they getting married?"

"I do not know yet, all I know it is to be a civil ceremony with George and Betty Miller as witnesses with Tommy and me as sole guests."

"I expect she will be staying in the service."

"On the contrary, she has applied for her discharge and she leaves us in a month's time."

"That means a replacement for her do you think WO Pam Grant, Mary's old friend who was posted from here will replace her?"

"I doubt it very much Viv, Pam could not cope, you should know what she was like you served with her. We will just have to wait and see who we get lumbered with."

"That is what worries me Bill. The ones I know are not a patch on Mary and I am sure that now they have found themselves cushy little numbers and to be posted back to recruit training would seem like the end of the world. It is a difficult situation but an interesting one and I am not looking forward to it one bit."

"Here is a bit more doom and gloom whoever gets the job will not have the status that Mary holds. Command will have no choice but to send a commissioned officer to take charge of the airwomen in general."

"Not another Flossy saga moaned Viv."

"I don't think so, Command has learned its lesson from that episode it caused a Squadron Leader to lose his rank, they will now make sure their choice meets every requirement. How would a female Wings suit you?"

"If only Bill."

"Don't lose any sleep over it Viv it may turn out better than we think.

We now have to concentrate on the new flights and their instructors. Having said that there will be no problem teaching the instructors our methods they already know them. I wonder what their reactions were when they got their postings to come back here, I hope there will be no hard feelings."

"I would not think so they knew the score that someone had to go they were just unlucky to have drawn the short straws."

CHAPTER 7

At Command the AOC shook hands with Group Captain Wildeman and greeted him as an old friend. "Hello Charles nice to see you again and you are bang on time for lunch. Would you like a little pre-lunch 'snifter'?"

"No thanks sir but I would like a glass of wine with it."

They sat down to enjoy a nice meal and were fussed over by the Mess stewards. After exchanging family news the AOC brought up the reason for the visit. "Have you got a problem up there in March Charles?"

"Not a serious one by any means just a little tricky one."

"Right, we will go and have coffee in my study where we will not be disturbed."

When they had settled down Charles said. "Warrant Officer Butcher is leaving the service to get married."

"Now you do surprise me, I thought she was the type to be married to the service, apparently not. So you are looking for a replacement then?"

"No sir that is the reason for the interview to receive your blessings on a replacement." He then unfolded the whole story to the AOC.

"Well I'm damned exploded the AOC as he slapped his hand down hard on the arm of his leather arm chair. Our WO Barrett has done it again I would have had that man as my aide-de-camp if he would only have taken the commission he was offered. What can I say Charles except you definitely have my blessings I have great faith in Barrett's judgement."

"I can only agree with you sir. Besides helping the rankers he has done a wonderful job on Squadron Leader Cody, he has turned him into a first class Officer and a chip off the old block because he is beginning to think like his mentor."

"That does not surprise me. Tell me and I want an honest answer, in my position would you have accepted WO Barrett's recommendations?"

"Taking into account his record that has proved faultless in all aspects. Yes sir, I would go along with him."

"That is all I wanted to know Charles because I have a bigger surprise for you, far greater than W/O Butcher's replacement, so prepare yourself...I am to be promoted to Air Vice Marshal."

"Congratulations sir but I am not surprised or in a state of shock because I honestly believe you have earned it and it has been a privilege to have served under you."

"That is not the surprise I had in mind Charles. I have recommended you to be my replacement."

"Oh my goodness, what can I say sir I am overwhelmed except thank you, I hope I can live up to the standards you have set."

"That is the reason I want you to have the job. Apart from our friendship you have done a remarkable job in getting March to the position it now holds. I shall be sorry to let go the reins on 'My Flagship' but it remains in good hands. You will hear from me in due course of the result. So now you can return to March to make a lot of people very happy."

"Who will replace me sir?"

"Wait and see Charles. I wonder how your senior staff will view the sudden promotional changes when they wake up early one morning to a New Management?"

"They will probably place the blame on WO Butcher."

That brought a chuckle from them both.

"So, I hope to see you sooner rather than later with good news but for the time being keep it under you hat and tell W/O Barrett to keep up the good work. About Flight Sergeant Anderson, you realise she will not hold the same status as WO Butcher of being officer in charge of WRAF recruit training, I want a commissioned officer to fill that post and before you ask…No! There will definitely not be a re-occurrence of the Florence Nightingale episode, we all make mistakes Charles but that was a blunder of the highest order."

"I think WO Barrett will be aware of that sir and I know he would like one in the mould of young Cody who is willing to be taught from basics as Cody was."

"Leave it with me Charles I will deal with it personally."

They shook hands and sent their regards to each other's wives.

All the way back to RAF March the latest developments were churning around in his head. How will the rank of Air Commodore affect his life style? Will I be a good AOC for Training Command? Who will be my replacement? I would like it to go to Eric. Eric Pilling was the Wingco' his second in command at RAF March. It is going to be a hard wrench to leave March and my staff. Helen Fraser is going to be upset and so it went on until he walked in home and poured himself a stiff drink.

"What is the matter Charles did you have a bad day at Command?" asked his wife.

"On the contrary my dear," he replied, I have had some wonderful news and I needed this drink to calm myself down because my head is spinning."

"Would you like me to get you a paracetamol?"

"No dear it is not a headache it is euphoria."

"Oh, then you have had a nice day."

"You could say that my dear. At the moment I cannot tell you anything but all will be revealed in a few days time, in the modern idiom, watch this space. By the way the AOC sends his regards."

The following morning he sent for Wings and Bill Barrett.

"Good morning gentlemen. We have won! When I told the AOC the story his reaction was. 'Well I'm damned; our WO Barrett has done it again'. He then brought up the question of posting in a commissioned officer. He admitted the Florence Nightingale episode was a blunder but he personally would deal with it."

Delight showed on the faces of Wings and Bill. "Thank you sir for your support in pushing it through, said Bill, "that decision will make some people very happy indeed."

"That is true and there are three of them right here," added Wings.

The CO's intercom buzzed. "Yes Helen what is it?"

"Command HQ on your private phone sir."

"Group Captain Wildeman speaking, Oh Hello sir, yes that is fine I will do that thank you sir. That was the AOC, the promotions have been authorised as from tomorrow. I will send for the two ladies tomorrow to give them the good news. I would like you to be present Squadron Leader but I think it would be inadvisable for you to be here Mister Barrett, apart from the protocol aspect it would be better for you to play a low key. You will receive your reward when they report back to you."

"Yes sir I understand, if I was there it would be giving the game away."

"Precisely"

♦♦♦

The three postings had arrived, been accommodated and now after being issued with arrival chits they were doing the rounds of the station to collect signatures of the various sections which would appertain to their stay on the station. Sergeant (w)Cooper and Corporal (w)Wheeler were welcomed back by Bill Barrett and Viv Anderson.

"What do you think of your postings back here?" asked Bill.

"It was the answer to my prayers," replied Sergeant Cooper. "It was a sad day when I had to leave but deep down I knew I would not be forgotten and for that I am very grateful."

Corporal Wheeler said. "When I was told I was being posted back here I just wept with happiness. The orderly room staff thought I was crying in frustration and did not want the posting. I told them. "Just you try and stop me! Thank you very much for remembering me."

"It was a very upsetting time for us when you had to leave but as you know we had no option. It is solely due to WO Barrett that you are back with us again as a team." She then signed their arrival chits and told them to report tomorrow morning.

As they left Corporal Anders reported in for his chit to be signed.

"Welcome back Corporal " Bill said as he shook his hand. We kept our promise to you which was earlier than we thought."

"Thank you sir I have been living for this day since I was last here, thank you."

"Are you in transit?"

"Yes sir and I have seen Corporal Deacon and he told me about the bunk and the responsibilities that go with it."

Bill signed his chit and told him. "Report here tomorrow morning, your first couple of days will be getting to know the ops' room routine."

"Viv, get one of your Corporals in here I have a job that needs doing."

When a Corporal (w) came in he told her. "I want you to go to each flight, give each Sergeant my respects and tell them I want every NCO to report to me after training."

"I shall have to do a swap round Viv with Farrow and Anders; I want Farrow with Bob Dixon."

When the NCOs had gathered in the ops' room Bill addressed them.

"You know we are to have an extra flight and because of that I have had to juggle with a couple of the Corporals. Corporal Farrow will now join Sergeant Dixon and Corporal Harper in the specialist flight. Corporal Anders will join Sergeant York and Corporal Deacon. Sergeant Cooper, Corporals James and Wheeler will start off as the reserve flight for the WRAF. The new intakes arrive on Wednesday. Obviously you Sergeant Dixon take the new bods and you Sergeant Dean will take the new airwomen. Any questions anyone?"

"Sir, answered Corporal Farrow, "When does the change over come into force?"

"It can be from immediate effect if it is acceptable to both Sergeants Sgt Dixon, Sergeant York, what do you say?"

They both agreed they would go along with that arrangement.

"Corporal Anders you can now skip your stint in the ops' room until the time when Sergeant York and his staff have to do the change over, you will be well briefed by Sergeant York. If there are no more questions you may now drag your weary and tired feet home and do not forget your gargle. I do not care what you use but I do not want you reporting sick with sore throats. Off you go then and I will see you tomorrow for morning prayers."

CHAPTER 8

"Flight Sergeant Anderson speaking, can I help you? Oh Good morning Helen how are you? Yes fine, do you want WO Barrett? Who me, what for? I have to report to your office at 10:00hrs along with Sergeant Roper, what for Helen? Oh I see, right we will be there, thank you."

"Sergeant Roper and I have to report to Helen Fraser's office at 10 o'clock this morning and she does not know what it is about. Do you think it is a posting?"

"Sorry Viv I cannot help you there."

"But why have only the two of us to report Bill?"

"It could be a commendation from the AOC because the CO. has just returned from there. Look, you had better get hold of Sergeant Roper and put her in a similar state of shock as you are in. Go on get away and make yourselves look pretty. I will see you when you come back and try to stop your brain from racing away with you, drop it down a couple of gears; you women make such a fuss over probably nothing."

Viv collected Sergeant Roper who went all of a flutter when she was told who they had an interview with. All the way to Helen Fraser's office both their minds were in overdrive and the nearer they got the more nervous they became.

"Come and sit down the pair of you, you are like two nervous wrecks, just try and calm down it is nothing sinister he only wants a chat."

That eased the tension they were feeling.

"Is that all?" replied Margaret Roper, "silly us were thinking all kinds of things."

"Thanks Helen for calming us down," said Viv, "now aren't we a couple of silly girls?"

Helen buzzed the CO. "Flight Sgt Anderson and Sergeant Roper have arrived sir."

"Send the Flight Sergeant in first Helen."

"Come on Viv he wants to see you first." She announced Viv as she ushered her in.

Viv saluted and saw that Wingco' Pilling and Wings was standing behind the CO.

"Good morning Flight Sergeant, from what I can see of you I think you should take a seat. There is no reason for you to feel nervous I only want your thoughts on WO Butcher leaving the service and the gap she will leave which we have to fill, please speak freely."

"She is a woman I have admired ever since I met her she has those qualities which are very rare these days. She is a disciplinarian without being a martinet, very firm in her manner but gentle with it and also very protective to the ones in her charge. One of her favourite sayings is, 'If you have any problems I have a good shoulder for you to come and cry on anytime and it is a very tear stained one'. We shall miss her very much sir."

"What kind of person would you like to replace her?"

"I would expect her to be protective towards the ones in her charge that is my main concern and if she shows half the qualities of W/O Butcher I can work with her sir."

"I agree with everything you have said about you predecessor Warrant Officer Anderson."

Viv stared at him for what seemed a long time before she realised what she had heard.

She turned her startled face towards the smiling faces of the Wingco' and Wings then back to the CO. and stammered "I..I..I don't believe what I am hearing sir; I do not know what to think. All I can think of right now is to thank you sir."

"You are thanking the wrong person Ms Anderson there is only one man deserving of your thanks."

"Warrant Officer Barrett!" she gasped.

"Yes! Mister Barrett." He shook her hand saying. "Here are your badges of rank congratulations Warrant Officer Anderson we think we have made the right choice and you will be happy to know that Sergeant Roper is replacing you also on promotion."

Both the Wingco' and Wings came forward offering their hands in congratulation. "No-one is better suited or qualified than you to take over the reins from Ms Butcher."

"Thank you, I have a lot to live up to."

"Go out through that door then round to my PA's office, wait until Sergeant Roper has been called in then you can wait for her in there."

She saluted him with a huge smile on her face after coming out of shock.

Margaret Roper went through the same phases as Viv., nervousness then shock followed by delight. The CO. informed her as he did with Viv. "There is only one man who is deserving of your thanks Flight Sergeant."

"It can only be one man," she said excitedly "Warrant Officer Barrett." Both the CO. and Wings shook her by the hand congratulating her. He gave Wings permission to do the honours by pinning the crowns above the three chevrons on each arm. It was a very proud Flight Sergeant who saluted with a big smile on her face.

When the two friends met in Helen's office they embraced and kissed each other. Helen congratulated Margaret saying. "Wait till your boss gets her rank on her sleeve there will be no kissing and embracing then," she said with a laugh.

"I am sorry Ma'am," Margaret still laughing said to Viv.

"I will have more respect from you lady," replied Viv as they both hugged each other again.

Their next call was to Mary Butcher who hugged and congratulated them both. "You both deserve your promotions and if you will excuse me Flight Sergeant, Viv's promotion is the icing on the cake as far as I am concerned and if anyone deserves it she does, I can now retire a very happy woman."

"Thank you for that Mary," said Viv as she responded by throwing her arms around her and giving her a big hug.

"I think you know who is responsible for putting the pair of you on cloud nine."

"Indeed we do and we are going now to love him to bits!"

Mary smiled and said. "That is just how I feel about him. Away with you now, go and put a big smile on his face."

They entered Bill's office with great big smiles on their faces.

When Bill got to his feet they both grabbed hold of him hugged and smothered him with kisses. "Thank you, thank you, you lovely man they chorused."

"Steady on now I am a married man."

"That is the least of our worries."

"Anyway, congratulations you both have earned your promotions.

Now let us get down to business. You Ms Anderson must get yourself

off to the clothing stores to be fitted out with the uniform and insignia becoming of your rank. I would ask for the attention of WO Waters and have your smelling salts handy."

"You mean he does not know?"

"Correct, no-one knew other than the CO. the Wingco' and Wings."

"You certainly kept it a secret Bill."

"We had to Viv, we could not jump the gun before it was clarified and that was for the pair of you. Margaret you are now my second in command, take Sergeant Cooper and introduce her to your flight then hand it over to her. On your return you will be responsible for the ops' room staff and taking care of me."

"Is that my first punishment sir?"

"Just one of many, Flight Sergeant," he said laughing. "Viv, when you have finished at the tailors report to Mary, you will be working with her until her departure to ensure you have a smooth take-over. I will notify her of your coming."

After the girls had left he rang Mary Butcher. "Hello Mary, Bill Barrett here. I have sent Viv to clothing stores and tailor to get fitted out then told her to report to you and work with you prior to taking over when you have to leave us."

"That's good Bill she will have plenty of time to learn the ropes and I will enjoy having her to work with me. I will also groom her for when she takes over the chairmanship of the entertainments committee."

"Will you escort her in the Mess dining room Mary? I think she will feel a bit self conscious going to the top table for the first time, after today she will be alright."

It was late morning before Viv was finally fitted with her new uniform and rank. Immediately she went to see Derwent to show him in her splendour.

"You look just the part and I am so proud of you. What is your next step?"

"I have to report to Mary and stay with her to learn the ropes ready to take over from her when she leaves us. Got to go, I will see you at lunch time."

Before reporting to Mary she went to see Roy Shaw who jumped up from his chair to hug, kiss her and congratulate her.

"What a wonderful surprise, I have just been reading the notification of yours and Sergeant Roper's promotion; I could not believe it when I read it because I did not know a thing about it."

"Bill told me it was only the CO, the Wingco' and Wings, Bill himself naturally who knew about it. He said it was kept under wraps in case it fell through."

"Yes that is understandable and you know Bill more than most, he did not recommend you for that promotion because you are a close friend he did it because he knew you deserved it. Did it never occur to you Viv that when he chose you to help him train the BlueBelles he was grooming you for when Mary would be leaving us?"

"No I didn't Roy, thank you for that information it appears I owe him a greater debt of gratitude than I thought."

"That is between you and me Viv, let us keep it that way please. What role are you playing at the moment?"

"I am understudy to Mary I have to stay with her until she leaves, I have to report to her now but I wanted to see you first."

"What about Derwent?"

"He took charge at the clothing store to make sure everything was done right and he was so proud Roy when I told him. He had to contain himself because he so wanted to give me a hug."

"Your Sergeant Sally Fields is due to report in tomorrow Warrant Officer Anderson she will need accommodating, shall I inform Tommy or you?"

"You just carry on as you normally do Warrant Officer Shaw."

"Yes Ma'am," he replied, as they both burst out laughing.

CHAPTER 9

Group Captain Wildeman and Wing Commander Pilling were summoned to Command HQ leaving Squadron Leader Cody in charge of RAF March.

"Have you any idea what this is all about sir?" asked the Wingco'.

"I certainly have Eric and if things have turned out as I was led to believe would happen we are both in for a promotion."

"You mean you are to become an Air Commodore?"

"Yes, and you my friend will be replacing me as Station Commander."

"My goodness me that has come as a shock and what is happening to you sir?"

"I will become your new AOC."

"Excellent, then I will not feel as nervous when you come to give my station its annual AOC's inspection."

"I have no idea who the AOC has in mind to replace you Eric but you can be assured if he does not fit in with our doctrine he will get his marching orders, It is a pity Bill Cody is not eligible to replace you. By the way you are to get a WRAF officer to be totally in charge of your airwomen and I have been assured the AOC is to choose her personally. Whatever the arrangements are, we shall have to play it by ear."

On arrival at Command HQ the aide-de-camp ushered them into the AOC's office as he announced them.

The Air Vice Marshal acknowledged their salutes, surprise and their congratulations.

"Well gentlemen it has happened, today is the big change round. You Charles will replace me after we have had a few days together with the handing over procedure. You Eric will take command of RAF March with promotion to Group Captain forthwith. After lunch you will both visit our tailor to get togged out in all your finery. You will stay overnight; rooms are already allocated to you. Tomorrow when you are dressed as warrants your status; you will report to me and we will interview the WRAF officer and the Wing Commander who I think will be a good replacement for you Eric. Report here at 11:00hrs. tomorrow morning, enjoy your lunch gentlemen."

Over lunch they discussed the interview.

"That was a quick promotional interview Charles don't you think?

"Now you see what life is like at the top Eric, we Brass Hats have very little time for niceties," he said with a chuckle.

"What I am concerned about Charles is what happens if we do not approve of the two replacements will we get demoted if we disapprove?"

"He will certainly ask our opinion and we should be truthful about it but we should put our views in a non-offensive manner, hopefully it will not come to that."

After lunch the pair visited the tailor who did all that was necessary. He assured them their uniforms would be ready for 09:00 the following day. They spent a quiet evening in the Mess bar chatting to members. There were a few anxious looks directed towards them but when the word got round of the status of one of them the anxious looks quickly turned into smiles, greetings and offers of drinks, which were politely refused.

Eric said quietly. "You have got a load of toadies here Charles, you had better watch your step or they will turn you into a p…head."

"Don't you worry Eric; I am clocking the faces of the ones who are most persistent."

At the appointed time the following morning they were shown into the office of the AVM.

"Ah gentlemen that looks better and more appropriate you now look the part, congratulations to you both," he said as he shook their hands. "Did you enjoy our hospitality last evening I heard you had a quiet drink in the bar, how did you find the company?"

"On the whole very friendly, then they became a little over friendly when the word got out who I was."

"Charles, the higher in rank you become the more little toadies you pick up on the way but you are too long in the tooth to be impressed with them. Now it is time for our interviewees and before we start I want nothing less than an honest opinion."

He pressed his buzzer and instructed his aide-de-camp to send in the WRAF officer.

She entered and gave a smart salute. "Flying Officer Georgina Grable sir." she announced. She was a pretty little thing about five feet six in height with a fair complexion.

"At ease, what is your age?"

"Twenty five sir"

"I understand you have recently graduated from RAF Cranwell and are now waiting for a posting. Tell me about yourself."

"I am a single person and I am a graduate of Oxford University where I read English Literature, Maths' and Sociology. While I was there I joined the Oxford University Air Squadron and enjoyed the camaraderie so much that I decided that a career in the RAF was for me."

"Do you want to become a pilot?"

"No sir, I think I will be more use with my feet firmly on the ground."

"Have you any questions you wish to ask Group Captain Pilling?"

Charles just checked himself from answering by forgetting his new rank.

Eric addressed her. "Flying Officer Grable, I am Station Commander of a Recruit Training Establishment. The recruits are airmen and airwomen, what do you know of hands-on recruit training? For example if you were posted to my station would you be capable of instructing a flight of airwomen?"

"No sir I would not but at Cranwell I saw a video of a flight of airwomen out-drill a flight of experienced servicewomen from both the Royal Navy and the Army. I was so proud to see that marvellous exhibition it brought a lump to my throat and I said to myself I want to do something like that. I may know nothing about instructing but I am willing to learn giving it my best shot to do so and enjoy doing it. I do not want to become just a figure head sir."

"Any more questions gentlemen? No? Thank you Flying Officer Grable wait outside please."

"Well gentlemen don't you think I have chosen you a winner in that young lady?"

"You certainly have sir, you have really made up for that Flossy incident," said Charles.

"Who on earth is Flossy when she is at home?"

"Florence Nightingale that was WO Butcher's pet name for her."

"I could not have given her a better one," he said with a roar of laughter.

"Then that is settled, Eric you have now got the WRAF officer of your dreams."

"Don't tell my wife that sir."

"I will call her back in." He buzzed his aide. "Send Flying Officer Grable in."

She entered and saluted.

"How would you like a posting to RAF March where they trained those airwomen you saw on the Video? Incidentally they were called The Blue-Belles."

"Thank you sir I could not have wished for anything better."

"Have you got your own transport?

"No sir"

"Before you do leave take this authorization chit to our Clothing Store Flight Lieutenant Grable, now go and pack your bits and pieces then wait for your Commanding Officer, he will give you a lift in his transport to RAF March."

With a look of amazement she could only stammer a "thank you sir."

"I would like you to meet your Commanding Officer Group Captain Pilling."

"Eric stood up shook her hand then said. "I welcome you to my Station, Flight Lieutenant Grable."

"She was still in a daze as she said. "Thank you sir"

"Well we could not post her to the Flagship as a mere Flying Officer could we?"

"Hopefully there goes Wings 2," said Charles.

"What do you mean?" asked the AVM.

"Squadron Leader Cody is known affectionately by the training staff as Wings because of the Pilot Wings he wears on his tunic. That young lady is a female reproduction of him. He gained the respect of all the staff by doing a mini-course in instructing with the staff doing the teaching and I may add, with no holds barred and I can see young Grable doing exactly the same. If I am wrong which I do not think for one minute I will be, when young Grable settles in to our doctrine, the training staff will want to nominate you for, and I quote one of WO Barrett's little sayings. A Blue Peter Badge."

The AVM roared with laughter. "I like that at least it will be something for them to remember me by."

He pressed his buzzer. "I hope this next candidate is received with as much enthusiasm. Send in the Wing Commander."

A tall and very smart looking officer entered the room, saluted and announced. "Wing Commander John Robert Hopwood sir."

"At ease Wing Commander, I have a feeling we have met before."

"Indeed we have sir and so have Group Captain Pilling and myself."

"Oh I see, then would you prefer he withdraws from this panel?"

"No sir, his integrity is beyond reproach, I would be happy for him to stay."

"If my memory serves me right you were his replacement at RAF Chatworth, am I right?"

"You are sir"

"This is becoming interesting. Tell us about your relatively short stay at Chatworth, Wing Commander."

"When I received the posting I tried to visualise what it was going to be like and if I could make a success of being the Station Commander. I remembered what it was like when I was a raw recruit and I honestly shuddered at the thought. I said to myself John; you are going to need some help here if you are to make the grade. I have a motto, if you do not know ask someone who does; it matters not if he or she holds a low or a higher status. As it turned out the welcome and help I received from the Station Commander and training staff was beyond my expectations. I quickly settled down and had a very good relationship with the Officers and staff. All went well until I began to lose some of the key figures from my instructing staff. If I am allowed to point the finger at the people responsible I would point at you three gentlemen unfortunately the fourth who was the chief instigator is not present."

Here he was interrupted by bursts of laughter by the three members of the interview panel.

When the laughter had subsided the AVM asked the Wingco' to wait outside.

"Well gentlemen, what do you say to that? Is he the man you would want as your number two Eric?"

"Definitely sir, I will welcome him with open arms. He thinks like us and he is very approachable to his staff, there are no airs and graces with John Hopwood he is a straight talker."

"Charles?"

"I endorse everything Eric says; I think he will be an asset to us."

The AVM buzzed his aide. "Ask the Wing Commander to come in."

"I want a straight and honest answer from you Wing Commander Hopwood, are you prepared to accept the position of Group Captain Pilling's Number 2 at RAF March?"

"It would be my pleasure sir."

"Good man," was the AVM's response.

Both Charles and Eric offered their congratulations with handshakes.

"Welcome to my staff John," said Eric. "I am returning to March this afternoon so shall we say I will welcome you the day after tomorrow. You can understand I will be so busy tomorrow but you can be sure of a good welcome."

He saluted and said. "I hope to live up to your expectations sir, thank you."

"That closes the interview gentleman. I will let you get on your way Eric to surprise your staff," he shook his hand saying." You will make a fine Station Commander, good luck. You Charles are going to be lumbered with me for a week or so for the change over."

"Good luck Eric, I will be in touch and will be seeing you soon to vacate my quarter and of course the official handing over of the reins."

When Eric left the room he made his way to a telephone and rang the Officers Mess at March.

"Officers Mess the Chief Steward speaking."

"Group Captain Pilling here, yes Group Captain Pilling I am now the new Station Commander of RAF March. As of now I want you to have a room ready to permanently accommodate Flight Lieutenant Grable of the WRAF and make sure it is one of your best rooms or you will have to answer to me. Have you got that?"

"Yes sir"

The steward lost no time in spreading the word around about the new Station Commander. He then gave instructions to two airwomen stewardesses to clean the room he had chosen.

"I want this room to be squeaky clean," he ordered, "or you will be relegated to the Sergeants Mess."

CHAPTER 10

Eric contacted Flight Lieutenant Grable to say he was ready for leaving. He spoke to a receptionist and asked her if she would supply a steward to carry the luggage to his car. The luggage mentioned being the property of Flight Lieutenant Grable. When he approached the car Pauline the CO's driver was waiting after staying the night at Command. She saluted in amazement to see her Wingco' wearing a Group Captain uniform.

"I apologise for the shock I have given you Pauline but you will have to get used to it, I am now your new CO. Your old CO. is now our new AOC."

Georgina was listening to this scenario with amusement. Pauline supervised the loading of the luggage and was then introduced as Pauline the official driver to the Station Commander. "Flight Lieutenant Grable is your OC.WRAF. Pauline promptly saluted her.

When they were all seated the CO. said. "Take us home Pauline."

By the time they reached their destination the young Flight Lieutenant felt she would know all the important training staff except by sight.

On arriving at the Officers Mess a steward who had been posted to watch for their arrival gave the warning as soon as the car came in sight. Two stewards advanced to the car to off load the baggage and carry it into the Mess.

"Leave mine in the car," said the CO. "Wait here for me Pauline, you can run me round to my quarters in a few minutes." Inside the Mess were a group of his officers waiting to welcome him back and to offer their congratulations.

"This is Flight Lieutenant Grable the new OC. WRAF." He then asked the receptionist if she would have someone to escort her to her room and enlighten her to things appertaining to the Mess and someone to carry her luggage. This was carried out immediately. "Now if you will excuse me I have a wife to see and I do not want to hear 'Your dinner is in the oven' as soon as I show my face."

That funny coming from the CO. brought loud laughter and cries of "Enjoy your dinner sir."

He got in the car saying. "I got away quicker than I expected." When he arrived at his residence he thanked Pauline. "Go and have a good rest now, you deserve it."

At dinner that evening Georgina Grable was the centre of attraction simply because everyone wanted to hear the details of what went on at Command and what had happened to Group Captain Wildeman? When she told them he had been promoted to Air Commodore everyone cheered. She followed that statement up with "And he is now our AOC." That announcement brought about more cheers.

"That calls for a toast," someone shouted. The stewards were then asked to fill the wine glasses and a toast was then drunk to the new AOC and their new Station Commander.

After dinner Wings singled her out took her to a quiet corner where they swapped experiences and he informed her of what his status was regarding recruit training.

She surprised him by saying. "I know quite a bit about you sir."

He interrupted her by telling her to call him Bill. "That is the name I am known by in the Mess, you may or may not have heard of Buffalo Bill Cody, that is the reason but all the training Staff affectionately call me Wings. You were saying you know quite a bit about me how come, I am not notorious am I?"

She laughed. "Not at all, I knew nothing at all about you until the CO gave me a running commentary on all his training staff."

"Did he give my ego a boost?"

"I don't remember him mentioning your ego but what he did say impressed me now that may boost your ego."

They chatted on for a long time enjoying each other's company until Georgina said. "Good gracious look at the time I must fly, I have a busy schedule tomorrow. Goodnight Bill."

"Goodnight Cinders." He was sure he saw a sight blush come to her cheeks. He then retired for the night a rather happy young man looking forward to what tomorrow may bring.

♦♦♦

At 09:00hrs. Helen Fraser replied "Come In" to a knock on her office door. She jumped to her feet in amazement to see Group Captain Pilling enter. "What a wonderful surprise and many congratulations sir."

"Would you like a bigger surprise Helen? You are now my PA because I am now the Station Commander."

She stammered. "What has happened to Group Captain Wildeman sir?"

"Oh you mean Air Commodore Wildeman."

Helen gave a gasp.

"He is now our AOC." continued the CO.

"Then it will be a long time before I see him again," she said with emotion beginning to show.

"He will be returning in about a week's time to clear up, hand over and vacate his residence, so you will be seeing something of him then. You did not think he would leave without seeing you, did you?"

"I must confess that came to my mind the instant you said he is our AOC. Excuse me asking sir but is anyone going to replace you?"

"Have no fear Helen we are getting Wing Commander Hopwood, he replaced me as CO. at RAF Chatworth and I can assure you he is a really nice chap and Flight Sergeant Page is a very lucky lady to be his PA. There is no doubt about it she will like him and so will most people who come in contact with him. He arrives here tomorrow. Will you tell her the CO would like a word with her please?"

When Barbara arrived she asked Helen." What does he want me for?"

"Probably to say hello and give you the latest information concerning RAF March."

"Why should he do that Helen?"

Helen buzzed the CO. "Flight Sergeant Page is here sir."

"Show her in Helen."

"Come on Barbara brace yourself," she said. "Flight Sergeant Page sir," she announced as she ushered Barbara through the door hearing a stifled scream as she closed it.

Barbara saluted and her mouth dropped open. "Oh my goodness it is you sir," she gasped, emotion then took over.

"Sit yourself down I am sorry it has been such a shock to you."

"But it is such a wonderful shock sir and I have to come to terms with it."

"In the present circumstances that is understandable. I did not know myself until I was told going down in the car and that was only a possibility, so I can understand every ones surprise because that is what I went through myself. Now I would like to put you in the picture because you are obviously concerned as to your position now that I have been elevated up the ladder. The AOC has been promoted to AVM and our Group Captain Wildeman has replaced him as AOC with a promotion to Air Commodore. Are you clear on that point?"

"Yes sir"

"We now come to you and your status. Tomorrow, Wing Commander Hopwood arrives to replace me and you are to be his PA. I do assure you that you will like him, he is a fine man and he will fit into my old slot perfectly. As a matter of interest he replaced me as CO. of RAF Chatworth. He is a straight talker with no airs or graces and he can talk to anyone without talking down to them."

"What if he thinks we are not compatible sir?"

"Then I shall have him certified," he said with a smile. "Without appearing to be egotistic, we both have a very similar disposition. To let you know what a character he is. Do you remember WO Barrett submitting names he wanted for his training staff? They were all key instructors at RAF Chatworth and they were commandeered by us. At his interview he said the three of us were responsible for him losing them and the main instigator, alluding to WO Barrett, was not present. We all had a good laugh about it but that shows what type of officer he is."

He observed that Barbara was smiling. "Does that smile indicate you are looking forward to meeting him?"

"The way you put it sir sounds as if he is a very interesting person."

"Have no fear you will enjoy working for him."

"Thank you sir" She saluted then left and had a chat with Helen telling her all about the chat she just had.

The CO. buzzed Helen. "Will you ask Squadron Leader Cody to report to my office then contact Flight Lieutenant Grable and ask her to report to me?

If they arrive together send the Squadron Leader in first."

Wings saluted his new CO. on entering his office. "Congratulations sir this is the first chance I have had of doing so," they both then shook hands.

"Sit down Bill and I will fill you in of the events during the past few days" which he did and surprised Wings of what had happened. "So you see Bill, the new Wingco' is no stranger to recruit training and he certainly knows all about the training language. I can guarantee you and he will get on fine together. Now here is what I want you to do. You will take charge of Flight Lieutenant Grable and guide her through the training programme with the training staff you did when you arrived. I tell you that because she is very willing to learn and has a similar enthusiasm as you had. She too wants to be able to talk 'recruit training' on the same level as the instructors. I see those instructions have put a smile on your face and a twinkle in your eye, shall I as they say, 'watch this space'?"

"She is a very intelligent and attractive young lady sir. Yes, you can watch this space."

"Well done Bill and I wish you the best of luck. Incidentally I would think it advisable to accommodate her in your office, as you know there are no vacant offices available and I understand yours is large enough to accommodate the two of you."

"That is a good suggestion sir I will make arrangements for her to have her own desk and fittings."

The CO. answered his buzzer. "Thank you Helen, show her in please."

Helen ushered her in announcing, "Flight Lieutenant Grable sir."

Georgina saluted smartly.

"Come Ms Grable I would like to introduce you to Squadron Leader Cody."

"Thank you sir we have already met."

"Oh good, are you settling down in the Mess and do you feel comfortable there?"

"Oh yes sir everyone is so kind and the staff are very attentive. I like the Mess very much."

"The reason you are here is to tell you I have nominated the Squadron Leader being your immediate superior officer to chaperone you. Besides you being OC to the WRAF he will guide you through all the training programmes and your responsibilities until such time that you can put any flight, men or women through their paces and can converse with the senior training staff in their parlance on all recruit training subjects. When you attain this standard you will become the first WRAF officer to do so. I should warn you that during the training the instructors will teach you with no holds barred, they will tell you straight if you make a goof but rest assured it will be said with respect. Have you any questions or queries?"

"No sir it is only what I would expect and I promise you sir I will not disappoint you or the training staff."

Wings took her to his office. "This is the office you will be sharing with me for some time because of the shortage of office space."

"It is very roomy all I need is a desk, telephone and incidentals."

"Wings buzzed his PA. "Can you come round for a minute Marion?"

When she entered Wings said. "I want to introduce you to your new WRAF OC. Flight Lieutenant Grable, this is my PA, Sergeant Macken." They shook hands and pleasantries were exchanged.

"The Flight Lieutenant will be sharing this office for some time, can you manage the two of us?" he asked with a smile.

"That is no problem sir it's a privilege."

"Thank you Marion, will you get Tom Hardcastle on the phone for me?"

“Very good sir”

“She seems a nice girl,” said Jean.”

“One of the best, she certainly looks after this office.” He picked up the ringing phone. “Hello Tom, Wings here, I need a new desk with all the trimmings to accommodate Flight Lieutenant Grable our new WRAF OC. who is to share my office and can you do the necessary please? Yes I am available you can come round, thanks Tom… Tom is the MoD manager and he is a very helpful friend, he will have you fixed up in no time. When he has been I will take you to meet some important people who you will have contact with.”

There came a knock on the door. “This will be Tom. Come in.” Tom walked in. “Good morning sir”

“Good morning to you Mr Hardcastle. I would like you to meet Flight Lieutenant Grable she is now the OC. to our WRAF.”

“I am very pleased to meet you Ma’am. So you are taking up residence in here I understand? A desk fit for a lady plus a very comfortable chair and a telephone extension.”

“Just a minute,” interrupted Wings, “My chair is not comfy and I did not get any preferential treatment.”

“That is called the luck of the draw sir.”

“Georgina burst out laughing. “You go ahead with your plans Mr Hardcastle you obviously know what is needed.”

“If we move this old desk a foot or two it should give you more room Ma’am.”

“Just hang on a minute,” said Wings, “do you mind telling me whose office is this Mr Hardcastle?”

“From what you told me over the phone sir you are both sharing it.”

Georgina was having a good laugh at the banter between the two men.

“I just don’t understand you young officers, here you have the chance of sharing an office with a nice young lady and you are trying your best to drive her out I would report sick if I was you sir!”

“It sounds as if you are trying to drive me out of my own office.”

“I will be back later on with your desk and comfy chair Ma’am, by the way would you like a nice fancy padded chair or a very nice padded swivel chair?”

“I think I will go for the padded chair Mister Hardcastle.”

“Very well Ma’am you can always change it if it does not feel comfortable enough.”

“Thank you Mister Hardcastle I get the drift,” said Wings pretending to be resigned to the fact that he was the loser.

Tom left the room muttering to himself but loud enough to be heard. And I thought he was a gentleman.

After he left, Georgina said. “Isn’t he funny?”

“He certainly is,” agreed Wings, “but a good friend to us.”

“You know Bill I am beginning to like it here, everyone is so friendly.”

"You are only touching the tip of the iceberg Georgina, wait until you meet the training staff; they are the salt of the earth."

CHAPTER 11

Wing Commander Hopwood arrived at RAF March booked in and was given a room. After sorting himself out he made his way to SHQ and found Helen's office. He knocked and entered. "Good morning I am Wing Commander Hopwood; I believe the CO. is expecting me."

"One moment sir I will contact the CO." She buzzed. "Sir, Wing Commander Hopwood has arrived he says you are expecting him."

"Show him in please Helen."

"This way sir," Helen said leading him towards the CO's door. "Wing Commander Hopwood sir," she announced."

"Ah, good morning John good to see you," he welcomed shaking his hand. Come and sit down, have you settled yourself in at the Mess?"

"I have sir and I must compliment you on your staff they were very helpful."

"They are a legacy from my predecessor and yes they are a good bunch. There is something we should have asked you at the interview, are you married and in need of a quarter?"

"Yes on both counts sir and I have a boy and girl twin teenagers who are studying at Durham University."

"Unfortunately John we both have to wait until the AOC moves out from his house for me to move in then you to move into mine which from what I can gather will be a week or more until he has taken over Command HQ. Once that happens it should only be a matter of a day or two before we can both begin to settle down."

"That is no problem sir we will get ourselves sorted out sooner than later."

"Now would you like me to take you to your office and introduce you to your PA? She is Flight Sergeant Barbara Page and she is good, intelligent and very loyal. You will find her very protective to you as her boss, she certainly was to me and I can tell you she has a wicked sense of humour. So far as compatibility goes you have no fears there, you and she will get on very well I can promise you that."

"Fine sir she sounds a very interesting young lady."

The CO. buzzed Helen to tell her he will be with Barbara for a few minutes.

Helen immediately rang Barbara. "Visitors are on the way Barbara, the CO. and your new boss."

As Barbara put the phone down there came a knock at the door and in walked the CO. and the Wingco'. She immediately got to her feet.

"Barbara, I want to introduce you to Wing Commander Hopwood who is now you new boss."

The Wingco' walked towards her saying. "I am very pleased to meet you," as he shook her by the hand. "Would you object to me calling you by your Christian name?"

"No sir, not at all, I wish you would. If the CO can I see no reason why you can't follow suit."

Both men laughed. The Wingco' said. "You were right sir she has a sense of humour."

Then with a wink and a slight nod to Barbara the CO. said. "I will leave you both to get to know each other."

♦♦♦

"We have a new Station Commander and a new second in command Margaret," Bill said to his second in command, Flight Sergeant Roper.

"Yes, I have been hearing rumours about that and also the WRAF have got a new OC."

"Then we must be on our best behaviour for we will be getting visitors soon and they will want a tour round the flights escorted by our illustrious leader Wings."

♦♦♦

Wings meanwhile, was taking Georgina to meet Mary and Viv. When they entered their office both rose to their feet when they saw who it was.

"Ladies, I would like to introduce your new OC. WRAF Flight Lieutenant Grable. These two ladies are WO Butcher who sadly is leaving us to retire in a too short a time and WO Anderson who is her replacement." They all shook hands with the usual pleasantries.

"I must warn you that you are now in the presence of Training Command's elite. Ms Butcher was responsible for the discipline and care of the two BlueBelles teams and Ms Anderson was the trainer and team leader of the victorious and famous BlueBelles."

"Georgina gave a gasp of delight. "I must shake your hands again it is such an honour to meet you. I saw your video when I was at Cranwell and that gave me the inspiration to try and follow in your footsteps, little did I know I was going to meet the wonderful people who made that possible. Your signature tune was great, days later I was still singing it I could not shake it off."

"She intends to do a mini-course as I did when I first arrived," said Wings.

"That is pleasing to know Ma'am," responded Viv, "because we were hoping whoever we got would not be just a figurehead, we have had our fill of those in the past."

"There is no fear of that Warrant I am not frightened of getting stuck in, I want to be able to talk and understand your language."

"Good on you Ma'am," interrupted Mary. "But you have still yet to meet the man who is totally responsible for the BlueBelles and the Flagship status RAF March has become."

Georgina turned to Wings and said. "I am on cloud nine because it is just getting better and better."

"Come on then let us go and leave these ladies in peace you can float on your wonderful cloud to the sharp end to meet '*the*' man himself."

♦♦♦

The Wingco' settled himself down and both he and Barbara had a long talk covering the duties, their families and the service. He soon found out that besides having a good sense of humour Barbara was also very quick witted. Both of them realised that they were indeed compatible much to their relief.

"After lunch I will be paying a visit and to run my eye over the recruit training, you can contact me there if I am wanted. I want to meet the man who has been a thorn in my side for some time."

"I don't understand sir," queried Barbara.

He told her how some of his key recruit training instructors were commandeered from my station on the orders of Command HQ with immediate effect and this person was the chief instigator.

"I hope it will not be, a 'pistols at dawn' scenario sir."

"No. nothing like that, I have a sneaking admiration for the fellow for what he has done for this station."

"Do you mind if I make a suggestion sir?"

"Go ahead Barbara I am always willing to listen."

"Go and see Warrant Officer Mary Butcher and ask her to tell you the Warrant Officer Barrett saga. I promise that your sneaking admiration will get a massive upgrade."

"Now that has really whetted my appetite, I will certainly do as you recommend thank you Barbara I will give you the result later. My first stop will be with WO Butcher before I go and confront my arch enemy," he said grinning.

♦♦♦

Mary and Viv were discussing Flight Lieutenant Grable.

"She seems a nice girl said Mary and very enthusiastic about doing a training course I hope she is not just a flash in the pan."

"I agree Mary; at last there is a light at the end of the tunnel for us to be blessed by some-one who is going to take some interest in our training and the personnel. I have a gut feeling as Bill Barrett would say that she will be a spin-off from Wings."

"I sincerely hope so Viv."

The phone rang and Mary answered it. "Hello Barbara what can I do for you? Yes, oh really, of course I will it will be a pleasure, thank you for letting me know, bye. We are to have a visitor after lunch none other than the new Wing Commander and he would like me to tell him the WO Barrett saga. Barbara suggested it to him before he meets Bill because he terms Bill his arch enemy for poaching his key instructors from RAF Chatworth when he was OC."

"I would love to be a fly on the wall when they come face to face," said Viv. When he arrives I will disappear while you tell your story."

It was late in the afternoon when the Wingco' made an appearance. After the initial introductions Viv asked to be excused.

"I have come here on good authority Ms Butcher to ask you to tell me the WO Barrett saga."

"For any particular reason sir?" she asked.

"Apart from a personal reason I am given to understand that WO Barrett and WO Anderson are toasted in most Sergeants Messes throughout the service and in some very high places too."

"Yes sir and I may add with some justification."

"Tell me about it."

Mary began with the birth of the BlueBelles at RAF Chatworth and continued in detail to the present day.

"You have opened my eyes to the man I dubbed my arch enemy, only in fun though for poaching some of my key instructors when I was OC.RAF Chatworth. He certainly has great foresight and it is to his credit that officers of all ranks have listened to him. It will be my pleasure to meet him. Thank you Ms Butcher that was an eye opener of a story."

"One last thing sir, he has earned respect from the highest to the lowest but you will never hear him boast about it. He is the same Bill Barrett I knew at Chatworth but he has become very much wiser."

♦♦♦

"Bill, Roy here your posting has just checked in, Sergeant (w)Fields and before you ask. Yes, I have informed Tommy and Mary Butcher and yes she has been accommodated. You don't mind if I tell her to report to me tomorrow to collect her arrival chit do you? I am allowed to do so you know it is called privilege of rank."

"Roy you are bringing tears to my eyes, what can I do for you to restore faith in me?"

"Buy me a pint tonight!"

"I will ask Tommy for a sub'."

"And ask her if you can play out at the same time," he hung up the phone laughing his head off.

"Bill rang Tommy. "Do you want a girlie night tonight love?" he asked.

"Yes of course if you are playing out with your pals I will ask my pals as they come into the Mess."

After the day's training Bill walked Margaret Roper to the Mess at the same time to collect Tommy. "You will be getting re-acquainted with your old colleague over dinner," he said, "and won't she get a surprise?"

"Yes but it will be lovely to meet her again."

When he collected Tommy he said. "You should have an entertaining evening with the girls especially Barbara, I understand her boss the new Wingco' reported in today."

♦♦♦

That evening in the Mess Bar Bill was welcomed by Roy, Derwent and Alan Fell the duty barman. "We don't see you much in here Bill," said Alan as he served them drinks.

"Cheers everybody," said Bill. "No, once you get back to your married quarter, had a good meal, put your feet up, the contentment does not make you feel like moving. Well you will know what it is like being in quarters yourself."

"Don't believe a word he says Alan that is a load of flannel he can't get over here for a drink with the boys because she won't let him play out."

"Wait until you get married and in married quarters," replied Alan, "you will be singing a different tune then."

"Has anyone seen the new Wingco' and OC.WRAF?" asked Derwent.

"I have heard she is a little doll," interrupted Alan "and, gentlemen I have the privilege of knowing the Wingco."

"Alright point taken," said Roy, "get the drinks in then give us earache."

"This will be interesting especially to you Bill; Wing Commander Hopwood is only the ex-OC. of RAF Chatworth."

"That is interesting Alan he should know all about recruit training but what I want to know is he a know-all?"

"Just the opposite Bill, he is a right nice chap he doesn't talk down to anyone and he is a good listener. We are very lucky to have had him posted here."

"Listening to your assessment Alan I will look forward to meeting him with all the changes that have occurred this station will probably still be run on the same lines as it was when our ex-CO. was in the chair but having said that I am really going to miss the old boy."

"Fill em' up Alan this man is getting morbid," exclaimed Roy, can't we find something more cheerful to talk about?"

"Such as what?" asked Derwent?

"Who will be replacing me next week as duty barman?" said Alan.

"That is more like it I get fed up of seeing the same old face behind the bar for a month said Roy. "Some are boring some inhospitable some serve us as if we are from a different planet."

"What category do I come under Roy?" asked an indignant Alan.

Roy ignored him and turned to Derwent. "What was that you were saying about us going to the March Hare on Saturday?"

"Oh yes, we are going to ask Ann if she will hire a smart good looking barmaid to keep the local's minds off us?"

"You are bloody crackers you lot; I don't know how you put up with these two Bill."

"That is a very serious subject Alan and needs careful consideration, how can we have a serious conversation in the March Hare if there is no attractive barmaid behind the bar?"

"We weren't talking about ruddy barmaids I asked under what category does Roy assess me?"

"Don't you think it is about time it was Fred Fox's turn again Roy?" asked Bill seeing the state of frustration Alan was getting into "now there is a barman and half, if he takes over from er, er. What's his name?"

"Chalkie?" queried Derwent.

"No him here."

"You mean Alan?"

"That's the one. As I was saying if Fred was to take over I would be in here every night he was on duty."

"Hear hear," the other two agreed.

"Roy turned on Derwent. What are you hear hearing about? You have never met Fred."

"Well he must be a good one and better than most for you to keep papping on about him."

Bill was watching Alan's face while this was going on; it was looking grimmer and grimmer.

"Cheer up Fred; sorry I mean Alan, don't let it worry you because you will be handing over the duty soon."

"The sooner the better, I don't think I can stand you crackpots much longer."

"I'll tell you what to do er. Never mind, just put in a written complaint to the Mess Chairman," suggested Roy.

"That's him there," Alan said pointing to Bill.

"Right, you see, you do have a friend on the committee."

Alan spluttered into his drink. When he got his breath back, he said. "If he is a friend thank goodness he is not an enemy."

CHAPTER 12

Sergeant Sally Fields reported to Bill Barrett.

"Welcome back Sergeant Fields," Bill said as he shook her hand.

"It is good to have you back Sally," responded Margaret Roper.

"Congratulations on your promotion Flight, it is good to be back here amongst friendly faces and it was a nice surprise to see Millie was back here as well."

"For the next two days you will be in the ops' room then you will replace Sergeant Cooper. That will become your permanent flight with Corporals Morgan and Banks."

♦♦♦

After Tom Hardcastle had re-arranged Wings' desk to the satisfaction of Georgina Grable and Wings' frustration, he announced. "There you are Ma'am you have got everything you need, if there is anything else you can think of just give me a bell and I will do my best for you."

"Thank you Mister Hardcastle that is very sweet of you and thank you very much for all the trouble you have taken to make me comfortable."

As Tom was leaving, Wings said. "Do you happen to have a spare bucket I could have Mister Hardcastle?" He mimed sticking a finger down his throat.

Tom laughed, "I think you will need more than one before you are finished."

"Are you ready to go and meet the man who is going to change your destiny Georgina?"

"Oh yes that is what I am looking forward to."

"Then do not prostrate yourself at his feet in supplication he would probably stride over you to greet me."

"Silly beggar," was the reply.

Bill Barrett and Margaret Roper got to their feet when Wings and Georgina entered.

"Mister Barrett I would like to introduce Flight Lieutenant Grable OC to the WRAF contingent."

Bill held out his hand. "I am very pleased to meet you Ma'am and in turn I would like to introduce my second in command Flight Sergeant Roper." They promptly shook hands. "I am pleased to meet you Ma'am."

"Won't you please sit down," offered Bill "and would you like a brew?"

"A brew?" asked Georgina looking at Wings with a puzzled look.

"It is our training phraseology for a drink of tea, no cups but in the old fashioned mug and it will be your initiation to attending a mini-course on recruit training."

"In that case Mr Barrett I would love a brew," she said with a giggle.

Margaret said. "I will go and arrange one, milk and sugar Ma'am?"

"In a mug, milk and two sugars please." She looked at Wings with a how am I doing look.

He returned the look with a smile and a nod.

"Mr Barrett, I have heard all about how you put the Squadron Leader through the mill to make him proficient in drill instructing and I am led to believe that he can converse.... here she was interrupted by the arrival of the brew. After taking a drink she continued. "You are right sir they do make a good brew here and it is better than yours. As I was saying, I understand the Squadron Leader can converse on the same level as your instructors. What one would call clever clogs."

She was interrupted again by laughter from everyone.

"Mr Barrett, please will you make me clever clogs?"

"Ma'am, after you have settled yourself down in your role as OC. and when you have the time and think you are ready to be plunged in at the deep end then we will welcome you with open arms."

“Do you hear that sir? Look out for some competition. Thank you Mr Barrett and you too Flight Sergeant.”

As they were leaving Wings turned, looked at Bill, smiled then raised his eyebrows.

Margaret said. “I would never have believed it, the difference in their ranks and she has him wrapped round her little finger already.”

“That was my impression too and she is willing to get stuck in and learn. There is something else I picked up Margaret, I may be wrong but I have that gut feeling there could be a budding romance in the wind.”

“You could be right Bill, there must be something in this March air, look how it affected you three Warrant Officers, it makes you think doesn’t it?”

“I think I will go and have a shufti at the flights and see how Bob Dixon and Dot Dean are getting on with their new flights.”

He stopped for a chat with Sergeant Joe Franks one of his best instructors.

“How is it going Joe happy in your work?”

“As well as I can be Bill.”

“What’s up Joe? You sound browned off.”

“It is all these promotions that are getting me down everything here is in favour of the WRAF. Here’s me with all my service and promotion for me is static or should I say non-existent Bill.”

“Until they re-open the other recruit training establishments Joe you are stuck with your present rank. Would you like a posting from here?”

“No way, this is the best posting I have had and likely to have.”

“Then think about this. If you got your crown you would be posted for the simple reason we have no establishment for a Flight Sergeant then where could you go? As far as I see it there are two options, re-open another establishment or upgrade our set-up. Recruitment has taken a slight turn for the better that is why we have got an extra flight we shall just have to hope it keeps increasing. All is not lost yet Joe, our ex CO. had a bee in his bonnet concerning the lack of quality replacements and as AOC he has got a damned sight more authority than he had as a Group Captain and if I can get the chance to have a word with him I can bring that subject up again. But! It is getting that chance, he is not as accessible to me now but I will keep trying.”

“You are right in what you say Bill I will just have to come to terms with it.”

He left Joe Franks then had a word with Bob Dixon who was training the airmen with officer potential.

“How are these lads shaping up Bob?”

“I have a good flight here Bill they are responding very well and they have a natural rhythm when they are marching.”

“You are not thinking of organising a BlueBoy flight are you?” Bill said with a laugh.

"You can laugh all you want but these lads with intensive training would have given the BlueBelles some stiff opposition and they have only been here a few days, what will they be like in six weeks?"

Bill stayed for little while watching their reactions to every order given which reminded him of the BlueBelles in their infancy especially the rhythm and balance in their marching. If I had this flight at the time I was training the BlueBelles, it would have caused a sensation if I had joined forces and made them a mixed flight.

He wandered over to where Dot Dean was putting her flight through their paces.

"How are they shaping up Dot?"

"They are hard work but we cannot expect much else in the short time they have been here. I have picked out the ones who are not trying so they will be getting leaned on pretty heavily if they do not brighten up their ideas."

"I have just met your new OC.WRAF and I am impressed with her, she is keen on doing a mini-course similar to what Wings did. There is going to be a friendly rivalry between them and believe me she is going to give him a run for his money."

"I will be looking forward to seeing her in action," laughed Dot, "I am delighted we have at last an officer who is going to take an interest in us."

♦♦♦

On returning to his office Margaret informed him he was to contact Flight Sergeant Page.

"Hello Barbara I have just got your message."

"Can you make yourself available to see the Wingco' in half an hour Bill?"

"No problem, any idea what it is about Barbara?"

"Now Bill you know better than that, my lips are sealed. I think it is only a chat to get to know you although Mary has given him your life story and he is impressed."

"Thanks Barbara I may even get to like him," he said with a chuckle."

He reported in to Barbara who buzzed the Wingco', "Sir, WO Barrett is here."

"Then show him in Barbara."

"Come on Bill, I think you will like him he is a nice guy. WO Barrett sir," she announced as she ushered Bill into his office.

Bill saluted.

The Wingco' rose from his chair offering his hand saying. "I am very pleased to meet you at long last Mister Barrett, please take a seat. I asked you here because it was time you and I got to know each other. Having said that I now know more about you from your biggest fan WO Butcher who left no stone upturned and did not glorify you in any way but told me the story straight. When I returned to my office I sat here and thought, what is there about this man who I have never met but respect, yet when I was OC.RAF Chatworth I regarded him as my arch enemy and why you may ask Because you, Mister Barrett were responsible for poaching some of my key instructors. After I heard your story from WO Butcher I understood your motives. You Mr Barrett are blessed with foresight and you used that foresight wisely the proof of that being RAF March becoming the Flagship of Training Command. I hope we can continue with the same partnership you had with my predecessors and like they, my door will be always open to you."

"Thank you sir it will be my pleasure to work with you as a team and can we now kick that arch enemy into touch for good?"

The Wingco' laughed. "Indeed we can Mr Barrett there never was any enmity in the first place."

As he was leaving through Barbara's office she looked at him and just asked, "Well?"

He smiled and answered. "You were right Barbara, he's a good un'."

"So are we back to being one big happy family then?"

"You could say that."

"I just did," she said with a laugh.

"Have you met your new OC.WRAF yet?" Bill asked.

"No," she replied "but I hear she is likeable."

"Ah well, I must be off and back to the grind."

"Keep me posted with any more juicy tit-bits if you come up with any," she said with a big grin."

CHAPTER 13

Saturday night saw the three couples enter the March Hare Pub to a great welcome from the locals and from Tim and Ann Wilson the landlord and landlady who were great friends. While everyone was seating themselves at a table Bill went to the bar to give his order.

Tim shook him by the hand saying. "It is good to see you all again Bill, have you been busy up at the camp?"

"We certainly have we have quite a bit of news to tell you there has been some big changes just lately but we will tell you when you are quiet and have chance to sit with us for a bit." He then shouted to Derwent to come and give him a lift with the drinks.

There came a loud sound of coughing coming from where the locals were sitting.

"You all sound in a bad way do you want a drink of water to ease your throats?"

"That is just typical of you Captain Bligh." That was the name they christened Bill when he plays the hard man with them. "I'll bet it was you who kept those good people away from here by forcing your authority on them. You should be learning to show respect for us poor old pensioners like those two gentlemen in your party do."

"I notice you soon supped up when you heard me ordering the drinks."

"Yes well that was to help clear our throats but we did not have enough drink left so we will most likely be coughing all night. We hope it will not disturb you good ladies and gentlemen."

"For goodness sake Tim, fill up their glasses or we will have no peace."

Upon hearing, that the locals began conferring together in loud whispers. "He is a gentleman there is no doubt about that, he has always got a soft spot for us pensioners."

"Do you think we should all club together and buy him a drink in return for his generosity?"

"Can we afford that much? After all he is a gentleman and he would appreciate it more if we just put our hands together, besides it would cost us nowt'."

Bill spluttered in his beer. "I give up I just cannot win against them," he said to the rest of the party who were killing themselves laughing.

When things had calmed down Ann asked. "Now what is fresh from the camp have you any news of any kind?"

"We will wait until Tim comes then we do not have to repeat it."

"Now that sounds very ominous," Ann replied. "Come on Tim," she shouted, "you are holding us up I am getting excited already and impatient."

"Be there in a few minutes," Tim shouted back.

"Can't you tell me a little snippet to be going on with," said an impatient Ann sensing the news was going to be very important.

"No" they all chorused laughing at Ann watching for Tim.

"I wish he would get his skates on. Do you want me to come and give you a hand Tim?" she shouted in exasperation.

"Will you give her some breadcrumbs to stop her twittering, Bill?" Tim responded.

"I'll twitter you when you do eventually come over here," snorted Ann.

"Attaboy Tim," shouted the locals, show her who the boss is."

"Do you want me to stop your tap?" Ann asked of the locals. "Carry on like that and I will bar the lot of you."

All she got in response were Boos and hisses.

The place was in an uproar with laughter. Roy said. "I have not had such a good laugh for ages, it has been well worth coming here tonight."

Barbara said. "Just look over there at those faces, aren't they enjoying it?"

Ann replied. "It is a good job we have not got any strangers in or they would fly back out through that door in a flash wondering what they had come in to. Talking of strangers, we had a young couple in during the week and I am sure I recognised the young man. I have not seen the girl before but I think they are from the camp. They were very nice and polite and I am almost sure he called her Marion. I could not quite catch what she called him she was so soft spoken."

Roy quick as a flash asked. "Could it have been Chris' by any chance Ann?"

"You know Roy; I do believe it was; now you mention it I am sure it was."

"Well the young devils," laughed Roy, "you know who they are Barbara don't you?"

"Chris' Graham and Marion Macken."

"Chris is my Sergeant," explained Roy, "he got the BEM when I did plus a promotion. Marion was my Corporal she got the PA's job to our Squadron Leader and she too was promoted to Sergeant. Well folk that is a very nice bit of news and I'm sure we are all delighted for them."

They all agreed especially the three ladies because they each had a soft spot for Chris'.

"I will not let slip that I know," smiled Roy, "I will bide my time and surprise him when I think the time is ripe."

"Ah, here is my long lost husband," said Ann giving him a peck on his cheek. "Come on now, you have made me wait long enough, who is going to be the spokesman to put me out of my misery? I will nominate you Bill because you always appear to be in the centre of things, so take a good swig of your beer and let t' battle commence."

"You know that Mary Butcher and Sam have become very close, well they have decided to get married. As you can guess it was a huge surprise to everyone and Mary is retiring from the service to become a housewife. She said 'We want to have as many happy years together as we can'. Her application was approved and she goes on terminal leave in about three week's time."

"So she will need a replacement," said Ann, "have they chosen one yet?"

"They have and she is now sitting-in with Mary ready to take over the reins the day Mary leaves."

"Well, and what is your verdict on the new WO? Will she fit in with your system?"

"If she doesn't I will see she is posted back to where she came from," said Bill, "and I am adamant about that."

"Where has she come from do you know?" asked Ann. She looked at the group who were having a good laugh. "Have I said something funny?"

Bill replied. "Will Mary's replacement please stand up?"

As Viv rose to her feet Ann gave a scream of delight then grabbed hold of Viv with a huge hug and a kiss. "Oh you lovely, lovely thing congratulations, if anyone deserved that promotion it was you Viv."

"Tim then got into the act giving his congratulations along with a kiss and a hug. He then went to the bar and returned with a bottle of champagne and glasses. "We cannot let this occasion go without a toast."

At this stage he was interrupted by very loud coughing from the locals.

"You are very noisy this evening said Ann, I hope you remember this is not a singing room."

"We are really sorry about that landlady but we hope you don't mind us just sitting here quietly watching you young people enjoying yourselves and treating yourselves to expensive drinks to celebrate some great occasion. It reminds us when we were your age but then everybody joined in the celebrations. We will not disturb you again landlady will we?" There came a unanimous noise of coughs mixed with inaudible No's.

"Oh get them a bottle Tim they are bringing tears to my eyes," said Derwent.

There was an immediate bellowing of cheering followed by. "There is a real gentleman brought up to respect the elderly and infirm, thank you young man you are a credit to your upbringing."

"That's enough from you lot," spoke Ann, "I will confiscate your begging bowls if you bring them in here again."

There was a lot of muttering and one voice was heard to say. "If I knew where she kept her broomstick I would smother it with woodworms."

When Viv's promotion was duly toasted they settled down for Bill to continue with the rest of the events.

"Margaret Roper replaced Viv as my second in command with a promotion of course. Wing Commander Pilling who you knew from Chatworth days was promoted to Group Captain and became our Station Commander while Group Captain Wildeman was promoted to Air Commodore and is now our AOC. The WRAF have now got their own OC. and she is a grand lass and we also think the March Air has performed its miracle once more because we sense a budding romance between her and Wings."

"Don't forget Chris' and Marion, Bill," interrupted Roy.

"There you are Ann; you are now up to date."

"You forgot Wingco' Hopwood," said Barbara. "He is my boss Ann he replaced Wingco' Pilling."

"So RAF March in now under new management," said Ann "and do you think you will have new brooms sweeping clean?"

"We don't think so," replied Bill "it will be the same as it was before the changes."

"Where is Mary getting married?" asked Ann.

"She is having a civil ceremony; I suppose the nearest place for that will be Leeds."

"Are you all going?"

"I'm afraid not Ann, George and Betty Miller are to be the witnesses with Tommy and me as the only guests. They want a quiet wedding with no fuss."

"That will be because you and George served with her at RAF Chatworth and are her oldest friends. I expect they will live in Sam's cottage; it is a lovely little place too with a beautiful garden as you can well imagine. Mary will settle down very well to village life, I think she will be good for the community. Sam may bring her in here for a quiet evening out sometime although we do not see him as often as we used to."

"Come on you men, time is getting on so drink up and lets be off.

It has been a great night Ann we have not had a good laugh like that for a long time, and those locals are priceless," enthused Tommy.

"They only act like that when you are here but they think the world of all of you."

As they were leaving, Bill told Tim to give them a drink after we leave.

"I am glad your coughs are much better, when you have drunk up Tim has some more cough medicine for you."

They grinned and thanked them all asking. "Will we see you again soon?"

"If my pension will stretch to it you will." They left all of them laughing with "Good night" ringing in their ears.

CHAPTER 14

The newly promoted AOC rang Group Captain Pilling to say he was arriving at March to complete the changeover of both station and married quarter and it would be a very informal visit.

Never the less Flight Sergeant Tom Bridges of the RAF Police was notified to keep a sharp look out for the AOC's arrival. He in turn tipped the wink to George Miller the Station Warrant Officer and word soon spread round the station of a visit from a VIP namely the new AOC. That caused some hustle and bustle of smartening the station up.

George Miller and Tom Bridges were standing outside the guardroom as the staff car entered the station. The AOC ordered the car to a halt, wound down his window and called. "A word Mister Miller." George came forward and saluted. "I just want to thank you for the excellent service you gave me as Station Commander, you know Mister Miller it feels strange returning here as a visitor yet on the other hand it is like coming home." He put his hand through the open car window and shook George's hand. "Thank you Mister Miller and Good Luck."

"There goes a true gentleman Tom you won't find many like him."

"If any," replied Tom.

The staff car pulled up outside the CO.s quarter and the AOC and his wife were greeted as old friends by the CO and his wife. They chatted for a while over tea and biscuits until the AOC said. "We have to leave you ladies because we have some very important business to attend to. In the meantime you could be packing our possessions ready to be transported off."

"There will be two stewards and two stewardesses to help you," said the CO. He then rang the mess and instructed the chief steward to send the helpers to the CO's residence. "That leaves us free Charles to get our jobs done. By lunch time they had completed the handing over of the station.

"After lunch Eric, can we use your office for me to say my farewells to the personnel who I unofficially call my friends because of the long association we have had together?"

"I think we can expect an emotional scene from a couple of ladies."

"Yes, I know, that is the hardest part of it Eric."

Helen Fraser was taken completely by surprise when they both entered her office. She sprang up from her chair and came forward to greet and congratulate the AOC.

"I have come not to say farewell Helen because in my official capacity I will be returning from time to time to make sure you are all keeping up with the traditions we have already set. I would like to present you with this photograph as a memento for your support you gave me while I was in office here." It was a signed photograph of him in full Air Commodore uniform, mounted in a silver frame.

Helen was delighted with it.

"Thank you sir it will now stay as a permanent fixture on my desk."

The AOC shook her hand, kissed her and said. "Thank you Helen for all your help and loyalty. Now would you please ask W/O Barrett and W/O Butcher to report to the Station Commander's Office?" He and the CO then withdrew to the latter's office.

Helen buzzed the intercom. "Warrant Officers Barrett and Butcher are here sir."

"Show them in Helen," replied the CO.

They both entered and saluted.

The AOC addressed Mary. "I kept my promise to see you before you left us Ms Butcher how are you feeling about it now?"

"Naturally I have mixed feelings sir because I have served for so many years and will miss the friendship and comradeship I have been fortunate to have shared with so many lovely people especially here at RAF March where we have been more like a family. Then of course with getting married which I am looking forward to there is another life ahead for me to enjoy. If you were to ask me what I would consider will be the hardest part of terminating my service, without hesitation I would say, going through those gates and leaving my family behind." Emotion then took over and she broke down in tears.

Bill put his arm round her saying. "Come on old girl I am only too happy to have *your* tear stains on *my* shoulder."

In between sobs she replied. "And I will have less of the 'old girl' if you don't mind, Bill Barrett!" This brought a peal of laughter from everyone and relieved any embarrassment.

The AOC came to her shook her hand and wished her well and a long and happy married life. "I will not forget you Ms Butcher because I have our photograph taken with the BlueBelles' famous victory hung on my office wall and I am very proud of it. Thank you for all your help and dedication."

Mary left that office a very proud but tearful lady.

"This is not farewell either Mr Barrett because I will come back here as often as I can to make sure you are not giving Group Captain Pickering a hard time."

"There is no fear of that sir," said the CO. "There will be no changes my door will still remain open for Mr Barrett just as it was with you."

"I am going to miss our little chats Mister Barrett I will have to pass that pleasure on to your new CO."

"Could I impose on you sir if we could have a tiny one now?"

"Go ahead Mister Barrett give me my first problem as AOC. I am giving you that honour."

"Thank you sir I will write that in my memoirs. Do you remember getting rather uptight because there was no back-up for us when we needed replacements?"

"I will interrupt you there Mister Barrett. I have already logged that in my diary, I had not forgotten. Anything else?"

"Just one thing sir. At the last AOC's inspection Sergeant Franks one of our longest serving instructors explained to your predecessor the reason why promotion at his level had come to a grinding halt due to the closing down of the two training establishments. Flight Sergeants and above are still holding their rank for recruit training but are now sitting on some cushy little number blocking promotion to what they are paid and trained for but not doing."

"That is a bad one to solve Mr Barrett. I fully agree with what you say and I promise to do my best to sort it out. In the meantime if you can come up with an idea of how to solve it pass it on to your CO. and he will get in touch with me. It would I think need some drastic action and I intend to investigate those cushy little numbers. Thank you Mr Barrett for bringing that matter to my attention, I remember that incident well."

Bill saluted and left feeling very happy with himself.

"Well Eric shall we go and see how the ladies are getting on with the packing?"

Everything was organised when they arrived at the house. "I will send a small van up tomorrow if you will see to it loading Eric, fortunately we have no large pieces to take. It is all yours now old friend we will set off back now, no we will not stay for dinner. We will keep in touch of course, we have to that goes with the job." They all shook hands and away they went both women dabbing their eyes as they did so.

♦♦♦

When Bill left the CO's office he made his way to the orderly room to have a word with Roy Shaw.

"Come in Bill I expect you want me to sort out your troubles."

"No troubles Roy but advice and help if you can."

Roy called through the hatch. "Two teas please, take note William; I have lost none of my hospitality."

"This is the place to come for the best brew on the station."

"Alright, alright you have made your point I am just looking for the bucket I keep handy when I am told that I am God's gift when my superior knowledge is required."

"Roy, don't you think that is a bit over the top?"

"Bill, you have found the solution to why the bucket is missing, it must have been overflowing! Ah! Here comes the brew," he thanked the airman who brought it. "Now we can get down to brass tacks what's on your mind Bill?"

Bill told him of the chat he had with the AOC. About the senior NCOs blocking promotions. "The AOC has promised to do something about it and he will welcome any ideas concerning it."

"That is a dodgy one Bill. The first thing that comes into my head is not only are they blocking the drill instructor's promotion but they are doing the same with the personnel whose trade they have slotted themselves into. Now let us think this over. Option one, they do a trade test equivalent to the rank they are now holding. If they fail that they take another test equivalent to a lower rank, if they fail that it is goodbye Mister Chips, or if they refuse to take the tests then it will be services no longer required. Option two, they choose the trade tests or request their discharge. I have your gut feeling Bill that Warrant Officers and Flight Sergeants will opt for their discharge because of a drop in status by serving in a lower rank."

"Roy, you are a genius."

"Yes I know, can you pick any flaws in it?"

"I will tell you what you can do if you will Roy. Get in touch with your pal at Records Office and find out how many Senior NCOs and Warrant officers we have in the trade and if they are substantive or not."

"That is a very good idea Bill I can see my genius is rubbing off on to you at last I will get on with it right away." He rang his friend who told him to ring him back in a couple of hours.

"I will ring you as soon as I get the gen Billy Boy then we will run through it together."

"Thanks Roy that is another star on your card."

Bill was having a word with Sergeant Joe Franks about the measures they were hoping to take regarding the promotion blockage when he heard a tannoy message requesting him to report to the orderly room.

"That will be Roy with the list of Warrant Officers and senior NCOs', fingers crossed Joe."

When he reported to the orderly room Roy asked. "Where the 'L' have you been I have been ringing round the station and had to resort to the tannoy to get hold of you?"

"I was in the field checking up on my flights."

"Right, we have got the list and it is looking good in our favour, sit yourself down and pin your lugs back. One Warrant Officer is to be retired in a month's time. Three Flight Sergeants, one commences his terminal leave in two weeks. One has requested to re-muster to store-man and the other one has requested to re-muster to education. That is them taken care of. We now come to the Sergeants, there are ten of them and they all hold acting ranks."

"Brilliant," said Bill. "It could not be better. If you have a list of the Sergeant's names there Roy will you run me a copy?"

"Sergeant Graham," Roy shouted, "run me a copy of this please," as he handed over the list.

"What do you intend doing Bill?"

"Sergeant York will know most of these from when he was at the drill instructing school and he can give me his assessment of the ones he knows so will my three new Corporals, they are sure to know some of them."

"But why do you want to know their capabilities Bill?"

"Firstly I am going to make sure that Joe Franks gets his crown. I will then get Corporal Farrow promoted as Joe's replacement. I then want the best of the Sergeants who when he reverts back to a Corporals rank will replace Corporal Farrow."

"You have it worked out to a tee."

"Roy, in my position and responsibility I have to be ahead of any eventuality. We have to keep up a very high standard of training and I want the very best of instructors on my staff and if they do not live up to my expectations I replace them until I find the right one."

"Then are we agreed, when you have sorted the wheat from the chaff you are going to the CO. with your findings?"

"Don't worry Roy your part in this will not go unsaid, I will get you a star for your card from the CO."

♦♦♦

When the instructing staff reported in after training Bill asked Sergeant York, Corporals Anders, Farrow and Deacon to stay behind. When the rest had been dismissed he said. "I have here a list of ten Sergeant Instructors and I would like you to give me an honest opinion of the NCO qualities of the ones you know and who you think would fit in here. I do not know any of them that is the reason I am asking you."

After much deliberating it was decided that out of the ten only two were good instructors and NCOs.

"Thank you very much gentlemen you have been a great help, time will tell of the reason I needed this information."

CHAPTER 15

Mary and Sam had made all the arrangements for the wedding plus a honeymoon cruise. They had asked Bill and Tommy's thoughts on what it was like when they had cruised and from the enthusiastic response they agreed it had to be a Caribbean Cruise. They managed to book an early marriage ceremony which was to be held in Leeds to coincide with the flight which would take them to the cruise ship. They would be driven to Leeds by George Miller and his wife Betty the two witnesses and Bill and Tommy would take the luggage and also meet the newlyweds at the airport on their return to drive them back home.

Mary apologised for not providing a wedding feast. "But we may have time to snatch a quick brew at the airport. We will compensate for that by inviting you to dinner at home where you can enjoy my cooking."

♦♦♦

Bill Barrett phoned Roy Shaw. "Stand by for panic stations Roy."

"What are you on about and what is going on?"

"We need a Sergeants Mess meeting for Mary to be dined out!"

"Oh bloody Nora, I had forgotten all about that, you are right Bill it is panic stations we had better get cracking ASAP I will put a Tannoy message out for tomorrow for 14:00hrs. and I will tell Mary she is exempt from attending."

"I will let Wings know the reason we are having one Roy."

There will be an extraordinary meeting to be held in the Sergeants Mess tomorrow at fourteen hundred hours. All Warrant Officers and Senior NCOs are required to attend. End of message.

Bill Barrett as Mess Chairman waited at the Mess entrance to escort Wings in who held the post of Sergeants Mess President.

Bill saluted him on his arrival. "You left this meeting a bit late Mr Barrett."

"We certainly did sir we nearly dropped a clanger."

As they entered the meeting Bill announced. "The Mess President." Everyone got to their feet in respect.

When they mounted the rostrum Wings said. "Please be seated Ladies and gentlemen."

"Are you ready Barbara?" asked Bill.

Flight Sergeant Barbara Page was sat at the rostrum to take the minutes of the meeting. "I'm ready sir"

"I have called this meeting to arrange a dining out night and a presentation for Warrant Officer Mary Butcher. I apologise for this short notice and I take full responsibility, it was a very bad oversight on my part. To the ones who do not know the reason we are dining Mary out I will tell you. After many years in the service she is leaving to get married. You all know Mary and we all have great respect and admiration for that motherly instinct she showed not only to her charges but also to us her peers and we wish her well in her future new role as a housewife.

Here is a point of interest aimed at you single men and women which you should think about. RAF March has now acquired a reputation which those of us who have succumbed to it call the 'March Air' and that is romance. Since I arrived on this station this March Air has brought together four couples which include me and as it swirls around the station I can distinctly hear it whisper 'I have caught two more'."

For a moment there was silence then a burst of laughter and applause.

A voice called out. "Dear Uncle Bill, will it happen to me?" causing an eruption of laughter.

Bill replied. "Are you eligible?"

"Yes sir"

"Have you any aspirations"

"Who hasn't sir?"

"Then you have answered your own question.

We digress; let us get back to business. It is customary to present a parting colleague a gift showing the respect we have for them. I want suggestions we can vote on."

George Miller stood up and said. "Mary Butcher along with you Bill were founder members of the famous BlueBelles. What better than to present her with a similar one we gave to Jim Ball?"

There were many cries of 'Hear-Hear'."

"Are there any other suggestions Ladies and gentlemen? If not can we take a vote on it? Those in favour?" The response was unanimous.

"Thank you, I would like to say you could not have voted for a better gift for such a lovely colleague."

This brought a round of applause.

"The other item is the function will take place two weeks on Friday.

Finally the new chairman of the Entertainments Committee will be Warrant Officer Anderson." This announcement also brought applause.

Viv announced. "I am following Mary's example by taking the names of those who would like me to arrange a baby sitter and remember the first eighty two names on the list get seats, names below that will be reserves for anyone who has to drop out for any reason."

"Has anyone got any questions or queries? Asked Bill "No? Then I call the meeting closed."

"That subject on March Air was very interesting Mr Barrett, how did you come to that conclusion?" asked Wings.

"I know for certain the four couples I mentioned indeed was love at first sight because I was the first one you might say who started the ball rolling."

"And all four are Sergeant Mess members?"

"Yes sir" Bill knew what this was leading up to so he put himself on guard.

"And you say there are two more couples who have been caught up in this phenomenon, any clues to who they are?"

"Sorry sir I cannot confirm or disclose anything at this stage it would not be ethical. We shall just have to be patient and wait until they show their hand."

"Quite right Mr Barrett I agree but it still is a very interesting theory, I can just picture some of both sexes standing out in the open under a starry sky hoping this March Air will take affect on them," he said smiling.

Barbara Page was sat there listening to this conversation and smiling to herself. She could not resist the temptation to add support for Bill.

"Excuse me sir, sitting here I could not help but overhear your discussion concerning the March Air. I support everything that WO Barrett said because I am one of the four couples and believe me it indeed was love at first sight and if you want further proof sir ask WO Anderson."

"No, I will take your word for it but don't you agree it is a strange phenomenon. Keep me posted to how the two latest couples fare or is March Air a figure of the imagination? Thank you for a very interesting chat on a very spooky subject."

"When you are out on some starry night sir just pause and listen you never know what you may hear," warned Bill.

"The only thing I will hear in those circumstances Mr Barrett is 'Halt! Who Goes There'? from someone on guard duty," he said with a laugh.

"Come on sir I will show you out."

When they got to the Mess entrance Wings asked. "Do you really believe in this March Air lark Mister Barrett?"

"Indeed I do sir and so do WOs. Shaw and Waters and the ladies involved. It is not exclusive to the Sergeants Mess it can happen anywhere so long as it is on the station. It leaves room for thought don't you think sir?"

When Bill came back into the Mess and met Tommy, Viv and Barbara they all burst out laughing. "That is the funniest thing I have heard for ages," laughed Barbara. "How I kept from bursting out laughing I do not know."

"He is worried," added Viv, "he is wondering if we have found out his little secret. Wait till we tell Roy and Derwent."

"And wait till he tells his lady-love," said Bill, "I wonder what her reactions will be?"

"She is a girl who would not care who knows," added Viv. "But watch this space they will slip up, you'll see."

♦♦♦

Bill asked for and got an interview with Wings.

"What can I do for you today Mister Barrett?"

Bill explained about the interview with the AOC.

"I complied with his suggestion to come up with an idea and to give it to our Commandant. So I am going through the chain of command to make sure there will be no hiccups or treading on any toes."

"Hm! I see what you mean Mister Barrett and you want me to pass it on through the chain if I approve it?"

"Yes sir, that is the what chain of command is all about, if it is not approved it goes in the rubbish bin and hopefully I will get the reason why then get back to the drawing board and start all over again."

"Very well Mr Barrett I will have a look at it then I will inform you of its progress."

Bill saluted then left to go over to see Roy Shaw.

"Hello Bill what brings you here?" He paused and saw that Bill had a troubled look on his face. "Has somebody been upsetting you old friend?"

"I have just left Wings and he is changing Roy. I told him about the idea the AOC asked for and he gave me the impression of why are you bothering me with this and I will glance through it when I have the time. He appears to have lost that cavalier attitude and wants to distance himself away from us. I have a feeling this stems from the Sergeants Mess meeting."

"Ah,ha! Barbara told me about that, she said he appeared perturbed because you would not commit yourself in disclosing the names of the two couples."

"I think it goes deeper than that, it is not in his character to change so dramatically so quickly. Maybe it is because they are living in each others pockets by sharing the same office. Why don't you have a word with his PA Roy? If he has changed she will be the one to know."

"You know Bill I might even do that, good thinking, I will do that right away." He picked up the phone and rang Marion the PA to Wings. "Marion, Roy Shaw here, are you free for me to come over for a little chat with you? You are? Good, then I will be right over. You stay here Bill until I come back with the gen, if any,"

When he settled himself down in Marion's office he began. "Bill Barrett had some business to discuss with Wings a little while ago and he is very concerned because he thinks Wings is acting out of character and appears to have lost that cavalier carefree attitude we have all come to associate him with. Bill thinks it stems from the arrival of Betty (Grable). I am not asking you to tell any tales out of school but I am asking you if you know any reason for it or do you think there is no foundation in Bill's assumption?"

"I honestly do not know anything Roy but I have a similar feeling as Bill Barrett. Wings is definitely not his sparkling self and totally against his character he has spoken quite sharply to me on several occasions of late and I agree with Bill it has only happened since Betty arrived. Initially they were very lovey-dovey but I am not sure about that now."

"How do you get on with her, what is she like?"

"Deep down I am sure she is a very nice person but I think she has begun to realise her rank holds a lot of power and it is showing. My opinion for what it is worth is, Wings is trying his best to guide her the right way and she is being obstructive. I know he thinks a lot about her even romantically but he is not putting the pressure on her which he should be doing as her senior officer in case she rebuffs him permanently."

"Poor sod, he is letting his heart rule his head. It looks like we are going to have a try to get him out of this mess, we do not want to lose the Wings we know and respect. Thanks very much Marion I am sure you have solved the problem for us. I will now go and report to Bill, he is in my office and could be biting his nails."

"It looks like we have a problem on our hands Billy Boy." He then repeated what Marion had told him.

"I knew it I knew there was something wrong with the lad he just acted out of character. I put it down to infatuation Roy and she is taking every advantage of him and he does not know what to do about it and neither do we. Once I could knock on the old Commandant's door and we could talk it over. I think I could do the same with our present Commandant but this new Wingco' is the stumbling block and I am not quite sure how he would receive me criticising a commissioned officer. If we could get him out of the way so that I could by-pass him and see the CO. directly I would get no kick-back about going over his head."

"A desperate situation needs desperate measures Bill we have to save Wings from himself."

"I am going to have a word with Mary and Viv to put them in the picture and see if they have any fuel to add to the fire. In the meantime get in touch with Barbara and find out if the Wingco' has any outside commitments coming up soon."

♦♦♦

When Bill entered Mary's office he was greeted with. "Ah, just the man we want to see."

"You are going to tell me you have trouble in t' mill aren't you?"

"How have you come to that conclusion?" asked Mary.

"Because that is why I have come to see you two ladies, I am suffering from the same symptoms."

"Who is your culprit?" asked Viv.

"Wings and who is yours?"

"Betty Grable"

"Sit down Bill," said Mary "and we will swap experiences."

"Ladies first."

"We had Betty in here a little while ago and oh boy has she changed. No longer is she the nice reticent little thing full of enthusiasm to please every-one by trying to keep in step. That attitude has gone right out of the window with a mighty crash. "She then explained what had transpired.

'Ms Butcher I am not too pleased with how the airwomen are being treated disciplinary wise, I find they have an attitude towards authority. Their living accommodation is filthy which to my way of thinking shows it is never inspected. From now on I will hold a weekly parade to inspect them and their accommodation and you two Warrant Officers will also be in attendance. I intend to smarten this station up, is that clear?'

"I asked her. Would you define the filth in the accommodation?"

'I needed to wear gloves to check for dust left on some of the lockers and some of the bed packs were a little askew.'

"Did you inspect the toilets," I asked?

'Well sort of, when I saw the toilet rolls were of unequal length that was enough for me.'

"And that was enough for me." I said. "And you call that filthy? I'll bet it is no different to your accommodation unless you have skivvies to do your dusting and cleaning up after you. And let me tell you this madam, when *we* inspect the airwomen's accommodation they certainly know it has been inspected without us wearing white gloves or yielding a feather duster."

'I do not like your attitude Butcher.'

"And I do not like your attitude Grable. Now you just listen to me madam, you have not the slightest idea of how to treat airwomen under your command, you got your promotion far too soon only because the situation merited a Flight Lieutenant 's rank and you do not know how to handle this sudden rise to fame. If you will accept my advice you should take a good look at yourself because if you insist on carrying on with your present attitude you will lose any chance of a career in the RAF. Now get out of here and try to act like an officer and earn some respect, at present you are not a fit person to be in charge of airwomen."

'I will have you charged for insolence.'

"I could not help but use that old cliché; you could not charge a battery madam." She left my office in tears. "What have I got to lose Bill if it helps to get rid of that little upstart, if she is not stopped she will turn into another Flossie."

"Phew! That was some telling off you gave her Mary and it was more than justified. I am proud of you old girl."

"Bill, how many times have I to tell you?"

"Alright I'm sorry Mary, less of the old."

"That's better. Now what have you to tell us?"

He told them of his meeting with Wings and Roy's chat with Marion and that he wanted to get to the CO. without having to go through the Wingco'.

"Your brush with madam should help to solve it if the top brass give her the boot and I am sure our CO will certainly do that. Now it is a case of wait and see for further developments. I will go and report back to Roy and he will be chuffed. By the way Viv are you learning anything?"

"I am indeed Bill but I have such a long way to go to get anywhere near to Mary's standard. I can see me knocking on her door in the village asking her what do I do now Mary?"

They all had a good laugh over that.

"I am off now and thank you ladies I feel over the moon with what you have told me."

When he told Roy he could not believe it.

"She has played right into our hands Bill. This is going to end up with the AOC and she won't have a leg to stand on with him, he will not tolerate such behaviour. I will ring Mary to give her a bit of advice. Hello Mary, Roy Shaw here, thank you very much, Bill has just told me. I am ringing you because I advise you to write everything down that was said while it is fresh in your mind then let me have it and I will personally run two or three copies off for you.

We can sit back now for a little while Bill and wait for things to happen." Roy answered the ringing phone. "Hello Marion, what's that? I am not surprised Mary Butcher has given her what you might call a motherly talking to I will fill you in when I see you and thanks but be prepared for fireworks.

Marion said Betty came in yelling, screaming and then sobbing as she was opening her heart to Wings while he just listened to her very quietly she hardly heard him say anything. They both have now left his office more than likely they have gone to see the Wingco'."

"Things have started to move, put it there old pal," said Bill shaking Roy's hand both wearing a big grin.

CHAPTER 16

"W/O Shaw speaking, Hello Mary what's up, you have? Well good luck and report in later please. Mary has been summoned to see the Wingco' Bill."

"Then I will hang on here until she comes back."

Barbara whispered "Whatever it is, Good luck Mary" as she ushered her through the door into the Wingco's office.

Mary saluted and saw Wings and Flight Lieutenant Grable standing behind the seated Wingco'.

"Warrant Officer Butcher I have had a very serious complaint against you."

Mary interrupted him. "Excuse me interrupting you sir but can I have this interview in private?"

He turned to Wings and the Flight Lieutenant "Would you mind leaving the room?"

"I certainly would mind sir I want to hear the lies this woman is about to make snapped the Flight Lieutenant "

"Then I want this interview with the Station Commander, sir and if that is not possible I would like it with the AOC."

"I am afraid the Station Commander is not available and will not be for some time, would you care to withdraw your request?"

"Most definitely not sir."

"Then I will submit your request immediately Ms Butcher and inform you when you can proceed to Command HQ."

"Thank you very much sir." She saluted smartly then left.

As she left through Barbara's office she whispered. "Roy will tell you later," then gave her a wink.

Mary went to see Roy and Bill. "Bloody great," said Bill she is going to have a few sleepless nights you can bet."

"Do you realise," Roy suggested, that the Wingco' must have tumbled to her because why did he not object to Mary going to the AOC instead of insisting he dealt with it himself? Of course he would have had to refer Mary to a higher authority if he could not have come up with an answer."

"I have just had an idea," said Bill. "When you get notification to go to Command Mary will you ask the Wingco' if I can escort you? If I can manage a few words with the AOC I can tell him my idea of the promotion blockage."

"But what about the proforma you gave to Wings?"

"It is my guess he is still sitting on it. If he refuses to return it to me then it is no skin off my nose I know what I have written off by heart. I will tell the AOC somebody is sitting on it and knowing how he thinks he will probably say. 'When, or if it is forwarded for my attention it will be too late because I will have put it into action as my idea then there will be no repercussions. Of course they will know at this end but will be unable to prove anything."

“You have got it all mapped out haven’t you Bill?” said Mary with admiration.

“It is a matter of keeping one jump ahead of the so called experts Mary. Of course I have a good partnership with Roy here, we make a good team don’t we old pal?”

“Bill, do you want me to do a Mary on you? A bit less of the old if you don’t mind.”

“See what I mean Mary, give him a little praise and it brings out the prima-donna in him.”

“Look, do you mind clearing off I have work to do....I will let you know if Barbara can tell us anything more.”

“The next day the Wingco’ sent for Mary. You are to report to Command tomorrow Ms Butcher. I have heard only one side of the story so I cannot judge but tell me one thing please. Were you insolent to the Flight Lieutenant?”

“No sir not to an Officer but I did retaliate and give a stupid girl some sound advice. I am sure you would like my side of the story, well I have here my version written down and witnessed by Warrant Officer Anderson and you can take my word for it every word is true. I have held nothing back and what you read is what was said. Please accept it I have another copy I shall take with me.”

“Thank you Ms Butcher for your honesty and I would expect nothing else but that from you. Incidentally Flight Lieutenant Grable will also be seeing the AOC but I doubt very much if you two will meet.”

“Can I ask you something sir?”

“Ask away Ms Butcher.”

“Would you consent to WO Barrett chaperoning me to Command sir?”

“Why”

“We are great friends and have been comrades for a very long time and it would be comforting to have him by my side, win or lose he will be my comfort.”

“That is a strange request Ms Butcher but I would never think of depriving you of a friend’s support.”

“Thank you very much sir, you are a good man.”

Bill got an interview with Wings. “What can I do for you Mr Barrett?”

“That proforma I gave you to read sir hoping you would give it your blessings and forward it through the chain to the Commandant.”

“What about it?”

“Have you read it sir?”

“Indeed I have not; it will be in my in-tray under more priority documents. You must realise Mister Barrett not only am I a very busy person I have no intention of giving you priority with every bit of scrap paper you bring to me. Do I make myself clear Mr Barrett?”

“Perfectly clear sir. I now wish to withdraw my bit of scrap paper sir.”

“Why would you want to do that?”

"Because for some reason known only to yourself sir you intend to conveniently forget about it."

"And why should I want to do that Mister Barrett?"

"God only knows and he will not split on you. Before I leave I would like to say, as far as we the training staff plus one or two more of our friends are still supportive of you, Wings!"

With that he saluted and turned to leave but at the door he was stopped.

"Mr Barrett. Thank you."

♦♦♦

On arrival at Command HQ Mary and Bill were shown into a waiting room by the AOC's aide-de-camp.

"I will return when the AOC is ready to receive you, can I offer you a hot drink?"

"Two teas please," replied Mary. "It looks very nice here Bill how would you fancy a posting here?"

"No way Mary I would have to be watching my back all the time, no it is not my scene."

A stewardess arrived with the tea, as she went to pour the tea Mary said. "It is alright dear I will play mother."

The girl smiled. "Let me know if you want anything else Ma'am."

After an hour of a wait the aide came and asked Mary to follow him. He knocked entered and informed the AOC that W/O Butcher was here.

"Show her in man."

As Mary entered and saluted, the AOC said. "Welcome Ms Butcher how nice to see an old friend again, how are things at RAF March? and you will be getting closer to leaving the service. Now you have asked for an interview and knowing you it must be of a serious nature, tell me about it. Forgive my bad manners I was so delighted to see you, please take a seat. Now what is this serious problem?"

Mary told him the story of when Flight Lieutenant Grable came to RAF March and the sudden change of attitude and the reason she wanted an interview.

"I have made a statement witnessed by W/O Anderson and every word that is written is exactly what passed between us. I have not covered over anything sir what you read is the truth." She passed the statement over for the AOC to read.

"Ms. Butcher this is incredible, I cannot pass any judgement at the present until I have interviewed her but what stands out is your honesty in its entirety and I can understand your reactions to that situation. He buzzed for his aide. "Take W/O Butcher and hide her in your office until I have finished my next interview but do not let the two interviewees meet at any cost."

"Very good sir and what should I do about W/O Barrett sir?"

He looked at Mary. "Did he come with you?"

"Yes sir I got permission for him to chaperone me but it was a means to see you, he said you and he had some business to discuss regarding a promotion blockage."

"Bai Jove so we have, tell him I will see him after I have sorted this nasty business out. That will really make my day seeing that old rascal again. Take the two WO's into your office," he told his aide.

Mary saluted as the aide escorted her out.

When Mary met up with Bill again she told him what had been said.

"Well he has to hear the other side of the tale but from what you tell me I think the Flight Lieutenant is in for a very rough ride. "Thanks Mary for putting a good word in for me."

"He is looking forward to seeing that old rascal he said, I think seeing you again will make his day."

Flight Lieutenant Grable was shown into the AOC's office and promptly saluted.

"You were sent to be interviewed by me on a very serious breach of discipline."

"Yes sir"

"Well get on with it then and I do not want any fancy jargon just tell me straight and in detail what happened."

"I had reason to visit WO Butcher and WO Anderson because of the lack of discipline and respect shown by the airwomen towards their superiors. Their dress was untidy and their accommodation was filthy.

I advised the W/O s to rectify the problem. That is when W/O Butcher became abusive and accused me of not knowing what I was talking about; I was meddlesome, over ranked and unfit to be in charge of airwomen. When I told her I would take disciplinary action against her for insolence she resulted to the use of barrack room language to order me out of her office."

"Then what happened?"

"I reported it to Squadron Leader Cody sir and he took me to give my report to Wing Commander Hopwood. He sent for that woman but she would not listen to him but demanded an Interview with you sir."

"Were you in the Wing Commander's office when Warrant Officer Butcher came in?"

"Yes sir along with Squadron Leader Cody."

"Did you say anything during the short interview?"

"Not a word sir, I was not allowed."

"Prior to W/O Butcher becoming abusive and insolent were you disrespectful to her even though she was holding the rank of Warrant Officer?"

"Not at all sir I used her title all the time."

"Flight Lieutenant Grable I served with W/O Butcher for a long time and I found her loyal, trustworthy and above all honest. I have here a signed statement from her and she has detailed every word that was exchanged between the two of you. You have besmirched the reputation of a lady and you madam are not fit to lick her boots. She has served in the RAF for many years and her loyalty has been rewarded with a BEM. She was wearing the rank of Warrant Officer when you were probably wearing a Monitor badge at school. You even accused her of lying in the presence of Wing Commander Hopwood and Squadron Leader Cody. You are a despicable liar and you have no place in the RAF. You will now remove that extra bar from your shoulder and I shall commence discharge procedures against you immediately. I have now the onerous task of apologising to WO Butcher for choosing you for the RAF March position in an error of judgement and you betrayed that trust. You will return to RAF March to collect your possessions then report back here to collect your discharge papers. Now get out!"

The AOC then told his aide to bring in WO Butcher.

Mary saluted smartly.

"Sit yourself down Ms Butcher. You are now minus a WRAF officer and once again we have fallen by the wayside in that department. How are we going to find someone suitable to head your WRAF personnel?"

"Flight Lieutenant Grable could have become a good officer in time but the power she gained on promotion was too much for her ego and she could not control it. I do not know what she said to you sir but she thought with her rank she was untouchable. It is a pity because she has thrown away a promising career but who can say in time when she had more power to her elbow it would not happen again with more serious results not for her but her victims. We don't need any more Flossies sir."

"Thank you Ms Butcher you have saved the reputation of RAF March and me having to take paracetamol every time I heard her name." He came round from his desk to shake her hand. May you have many years of happiness in your married life Ms Butcher, thank you and God Bless you."

Mary saluted then left with tears of emotion running down her face.

When Bill was called he entered giving a big smile as he saluted the AOC.

"It is good to see you Mr Barrett you are a sight for sore eyes," the AOC declared as they shook hands. "Sit yourself down and tell me what has been going on up there. You know I miss those little chats we used to have we did a good job of putting the world to rights. We have just had a nasty bit of business where W/O Butcher's name was dragged in the mud and I was adamant nobody was going to get away with besmirching her character. Anyway Grable has got her marching orders; we will not have the unpleasantness of her company again but we have to find a replacement and it is becoming very difficult to do so, have you any thoughts on the matter?"

"I would think the best person to ask sir is WO Butcher, she may be able to recommend someone she knows from way back, a more mature person perhaps."

"Yes I think you are right, we certainly made a mess of that choice I will call her back in to ask her."

When Mary entered the AOC asked. "Do you know of any serving WRAF officer who from your experiences would fill the role as your OC.?"

"I had the greatest respect for one sir, Flight Lieutenant Macfarlane a mature person and a good disciplinarian, when she said Jump! you leaped but she had a heart of gold. I have no idea where she is or even still in the service sir. Apart from her I cannot help you."

"Thank you I will get my staff to chase that up, do you happen to know her Christian name?"

"It is Heather sir.

The AOC buzzed his aide.

"I want you to find for me the details of a member of the WRAF – Flight Lieutenant Macfarlane, H – and I would appreciate you doing it quickly.

"How is the new Wing Commander settling in up there?"

"He is a good man," said Mary I can see him being good for the station."

"I agree," added Bill he appears to be on the same wave length as we are, he has a good head on his shoulders."

The AOC called "Come in" to a knock on the door.

His aide entered, handed some paperwork to the AOC saying. "I hope this is the person you are seeking sir." Included was a thumbnail photograph.

He showed it to Mary asking. "Is this the person you told me about?"

Mary looked and nodded. "That is her alright sir."

"Thank you very much," he said to his aid. "You have done us a great service."

He began to read, "Yes, she is still a Flight Lieutenant and has been for a number of years, she must have been passed over in the promotion stakes, if she fits the bill I can soon rectify that. She is serving in Germany and has been for the last three months. Her records assessments are first class too. Excellent, I will have her here for an interview within a day or two. Ms Butcher you have triumphed once again, can I persuade you to change your mind to stay in the service?"

"I am flattered and honoured by that sir and I thank you but my future better half would challenge you over that. I will be living in March village and can be easily contacted if you want any further help; if I am AWOL I will be on my honeymoon."

They all had a laugh over her response.

Mary then saluted and left with the AOC's thanks ringing in her ears.

"Right Mr Barrett let us get this promotion blockage unblocked."

Bill told him his idea which impressed him.

"Very good I like it. Are there any snags to go with it?"

"There is every chance now you may be getting the proforma sent to you sir. Can I suggest you reject it in favour of your idea if you know what I mean?"

"Mr Barrett as the Air Chief Marshal has always said. 'You are still a crafty bugger' and what do you hope to get out of it?"

"The satisfaction of Sergeant Franks receiving a long overdue promotion sir."

"That is very commendable Mr Barrett." He then rose from his chair with hand outstretched. "Thank you for coming to see me I do miss our little chats, I keep repeating that but I do."

"And so do I sir I wish we could do it more often."

He saluted and as he got to the door turned and asked. "No comments sir?"

"Not this time Mr Barrett."

Bill met Mary in reception and told her he was ringing Tommy to tell Roy I will see him tonight.

"Ask her to tell Viv I will see her tonight too Bill."

"Would you like to have a girlie night with Tommy then you could include Barbara?"

"Good idea Bill, you are not as daft as you look are you?"

"Not if you say so Mary." When he returned from making his phone call he told Mary. "She is very excited and is going to round up the girls."

CHAPTER 17

At the Sergeants Mess reception Tommy told Jackie "That was Bill on the phone' he is playing out again tonight." This comment always caused a laugh. "But I have a girlie night with a special guest Mary Butcher who will be giving us the news from Command and I think it is going to be very interesting indeed."

"Is it about the Betty Grable affair?" asked Jackie. Betty was the nickname Flight Lieutenant Georgina Grable had been given by most of or even all of the staff.

"Without a doubt," replied Tommy "my money will be on Mary coming off best. I had better phone' Roy to tell him his playmate can play out tonight."

"W/O Shaw. Oh hello Tommy what can I do for you?"

"Nothing Roy it is what I can do for you, I am going to put a smile on your face."

"Why, have they decided to keep him on permanent staff at Command because the AOC is missing him so much?"

"Roy, now would he run away without telling you?"

"Yes"

"Here is the smile for your face. He is being allowed to play out tonight, now don't get too excited it is only because I have a girlie night on and I am entertaining besides Viv and Barbara a V.I.P."

"Aren't you going to tell me who it is Tommy?"

"No way Jose, wind your neck in, you don't tell me what goes on in that macho world of yours."

"I'll ask Barbara!"

"Ask away Roy Boy, Barbara has been sworn to secrecy."

"You are a hard woman Tommy Barrett, I used to like you."

"Flattery will get you nowhere I am not a member of your HPC, Ta ra Roy."

"Thank God for that," he exclaimed, "because nothing is sacred where you women are concerned." All he could hear was laughter as she hung up.

At dinner that evening in the Mess, Roy and Derwent were sat together on one table while Mary and Viv were sat at the other.

"I see you are back Mary." Spoke up Roy.

"Yes"

"Did you have a good day at Command?"

"Yes"

"Did everything go according to plan?"

"Yes"

"How did Bill get on?"

"Alright"

"Did he manage to see the AOC?"

"Yes"

"It appears I shall have to get any information from Bill when I see him tonight."

"You will."

During this exchange Viv and Derwent were enjoying every word and struggling to contain their laughter.

"It's a bloody mad house," Roy exclaimed as he jumped up from his seat and stormed out.

Derwent and Viv waited while Roy had cleared the dining room then let out the emotions they were feeling, even Mary joined in the laughter.

"You know I should never have done that to Roy because he has been so helpful and supportive to me. I will apologise when I next see him."

As soon as Bill entered the bar Roy was waiting for him. "Who is this VIP guest at the girlie night?"

"I did not know there was to be one."

"Tommy rang me this afternoon to tell me the reason you are playing out tonight is because they were having a VIP at the girlie night."

"Why did you not ask Barbara?"

"Because she was sworn to secrecy, what is going on?"

"Tommy never mentioned anything to me so I am as wise as you Roy."

While this was going on Derwent was hiding his feelings with some effort.

"Pull me a pint Ron," Bill said to the barman Ron York one of his training staff who was the duty barman. "It is coming to something when I walk in and have to buy myself a drink, I must be losing my popularity."

"I will get that Ron and fill the rest up including yourself," offered Derwent."

Roy was paying no heed he was busy trying to puzzle out who the VIP could be.

"Aren't you going to ask me how I went on at Command Roy?"

"Hang on a minute I am thinking of something."

"Derwent spoke up. "It is Mary Butcher Roy."

"How do you know that?" snapped Roy.

"Viv told me."

"Then why did you not tell me that in the first place instead of keeping it to yourself?"

"Because you never asked me that is why not."

Turning to Bill Roy asked. "How did you get on at Command Bill?" I have been dying to know ever since you returned."

Derwent and Ron looked at each other and grinned as much as saying, what is this man like.

Bill told his tale and Roy was chuffed because the AOC had accepted their joint idea for the promotion blockage. He then told them about Betty Grable how she had lied to the AOC while he had Mary's statement in front of him and then tore into her verbally and then made her remove that second bar. She was then told to return here to March collect her gear then report back to Command to collect her discharge papers.

"She had only herself to blame," spoke Roy, that quick promotion did it. She was too young to handle the responsibility, it went the wrong way and she became power crazy. So what happens now?"

"The AOC was at a loss and asked Mary's advice. She recommended a Flight Lieutenant (w).Macfarlane that she knew way back but did not know if she was still serving or where she was posted. In less than ten minutes the AOC had the information on his desk. She is serving in Germany and if she is accepted I think she will come here with a promotion. From what Mary told us she is in the same mould, firm but fair."

"I wonder how Wings will be affected with Betty getting the push?" asked Derwent. "Will he have seen the light and let the romance fizzle out if there was any romance in the first place?"

"All the signs led to him being keen on her," said Roy. Do you realize we will have a problem if we get this Squadron Leader?"

"Such as what?" asked Bill.

"Finding her an office, I have just been thinking about it and I cannot come up with one, and I cannot see her wanting to share with Wings."

"There is a wall map of the station on the wall of the SWO's office, maybe you could find something on there or else get in touch with Tom Hardcastle he is the man who can tell you where there is a room which could be converted into an office."

"I will have a word with him tomorrow."

"Have you got any extra stock in for the dining-out night Ron?" asked Bill.

"I have started making my order out Bill, some sensible barman has made a guide line list of what will be necessary for such a function so I am following that."

"Have you done a function before Ron?"

"No I haven't"

"Well if you need any help don't be afraid to call me, Tommy will sort out the stewards you will need. "Don't get yourself in a flap; help is not so far away."

"Good evening gentlemen" greeted George Miller as he walked into the bar.

"Well this is a surprise," was the response. "Give him a drink Ron he looks to be in need of one," ordered Bill. "What brings you in here tonight George has someone been upsetting you?"

"No, I just felt like wetting my lips with this good beer it is a while since I was enjoying my last one. Have this lot been behaving themselves Ron?"

"Only as well as they can be, you are lucky to find them in one of their better moods because there are times when it is sheer hell behind this bar."

"That is no surprise Ron but why don't you try wearing earplugs?"

"They are no use to me I can lip read."

"Stop moaning and get these glasses filled up and you had better have one or we will get earache all night said Roy."

"Anything new in the wind George or are we going through a quiet spell at present?"

"If only, I had a meeting with the Wingco' today, he has decided that Admin' wing and Tech' wing are due for a work parade. I hope you two have remembered your parade ground routine," indicating Roy and Derwent. "Have you a drill manual you can loan them Bill?"

"Thank you George, retorted Roy, "I hope that is a voice of confidence I am hearing."

"It looks like I will be borrowing that Class 'A' drill sergeant of yours Bill, he is number one in my books, he did a great job with the AOC's parade, they don't come any better than Joe Franks. Unfortunately there will be no practice parades for this one and if it is not up to scratch I think you will be in for a hard time. Well I must be off I told the wife I would only be an hour."

"Before you go George, did you know we are likely to be getting a Squadron Leader (w) Admin' someone with quite a bit of service in?"

"She will be a damned sight better than the last one. Goodnight all."

CHAPTER 18

Flight Lieutenant Heather Macfarlane reported to Command HQ as instructed from her Germany posting. The AOC's aide-de-camp buzzed him to report that Flight Lieutenant Macfarlane had reported in.

"Show her in at once."

"She saluted smartly giving her rank and name.

He saw before him a well built woman about forty years of age five feet ten inches in height and who carried herself well. First impression very good he thought.

"Sit yourself down Flight Lieutenant Macfarlane. You will be wondering why you have been brought from Germany. How do you like your posting there, I know you have been there only a short time but have you settled down?"

"It is not a bad posting sir, I have had worse and I have had better. The downside is it is too cushy a posting for me I find myself looking for something a bit more constructive to do I appear to have too much time on my hands which I find boring."

"Good." he saw a puzzled look at that remark. "Do not get me wrong Flight Lieutenant I mean good from my point of view. Look, I will tell you why I sent for you in particular. I have a post vacant which I think you are well qualified to fit the bill." He then told her about RAF March. "I want you to go there as Officer Commanding the WRAF. If you decline you will return to your cushy little number in Germany or would you like some time to think it over?"

"No sir that is the kind of posting I have wanted for years."

"Have you given thought to why you have been singled out for this post?"

"Yes and I would like to know sir."

"You were highly recommended to me personally by someone who served under you quite some time ago. Do you remember Warrant Officer Mary Butcher?"

"I certainly do, in my eyes she is or was the perfect WRAF Warrant Officer and I owe a lot to Mary she nurtured me when I was pretty green and she taught me such a lot. It is a long time since I saw her, is she still serving sir?"

"She is but you are not going to get much time together because she will be leaving the service in about two weeks time to get married."

"So she is at RAF March sir, now that news is the icing on the cake for that posting, I will get there as quickly as I can."

"Then I shall not delay you Squadron Leader."

She looked at him not believing what she heard.

"When you leave my office go to our stores where you will be issued with that extra bar for your shoulder then nip in to the tailor to have your new rank sewn on your sleeves, both the store man and tailor are expecting you."

"You had this planned out already sir, what if I had not been suitable or refused the posting."

"Would you if you were in my position have rejected Ms Butcher's recommendation? I think not."

"Definitely not sir".

"Well congratulations Squadron Leader Macfarlane" he said as he shook her hand. "You are going to a good station, while I was there as CO. I could not have wished for a better staff. Good luck."

♦♦♦

"Roy Shaw paid a visit to Tom Hardcastle at the MOD site to tell him what he was looking for. Tom got a detailed map out and the pair of them began to pore over it looking for that elusive spare room which could be converted into an office for the new OC.WRAF.

“There is definitely no spare room in SHQ” said Tom. We could however convert a classroom in the Education Section but as you know they are wooden huts and not very salubrious for the rank of Squadron Leader especially a woman.”

“Another thing we must take into consideration,” said Roy. “The Squadron Leader and Viv Anderson need to be working close together we cannot have them at opposite ends of the station and we cannot have them sharing an office.”

“I have an idea,” said Tom. “Move the Squadron Leader into Mary Butcher’s office and I guarantee to convert a classroom into an office with everything Viv will need. It will be just a spit and a stride from SHQ almost within shouting distance and when it is finished everybody will want one like it, have no fear Roy I will do Viv. proud. Shall we go and have a shufti? Better still can we get hold of her to explain the situation and let her choose which room she would like?”

“I like the sound of that Tom I will go and see her now and explain the situation then phone you when we are ready to go.”

Mary and Viv were surprised when Roy entered their office.

“Now that has made my day seeing you here Roy Shaw can we help you in anyway or is it a social call on two of your biggest fans?”

“On the contrary Mary I have come mainly to help Viv.” He told them what he and Tom had in mind due to the shortage of office space.

“That makes sense said Mary and we know of Tom’s expertise in these kinds of situations. When he has finished your office Viv you will want to move your bed in it. You had better get cracking and not keep the man waiting then he can get on with the job.”

Roy and Viv met Tom at the education section.

“There are four rooms you can choose from Viv and I will advise you which would be best suited for your needs.” After much deliberation Viv was satisfied with the one Tom advised her to have. “The Education Officer is in the next office and the dividing wall is soundproofed. The ablutions are at the end of the corridor segregated of course for male and female. If you tell me the colour of paint you would like for the walls and ceiling you need not worry about anything else, when you see the finished product you will not recognise it, I promise you will be delighted with it and you will be able to move in within a week.”

“Thank you Tom I have no fear of not liking it I am just eager to move in but I would like a picture hook for my BlueBelles’ photograph please.”

“No problem there Viv, when you come to see the finished job I will have a hook with me and I will place it where you want the photograph to hang. If there is anything else you can think of I am only at the end of a phone.”

“Thank you Tom I appreciate that.” Turning to Roy she exclaimed. “Isn’t it exciting? I can’t wait to move in.”

“We are very lucky to have Tom in our corner Viv. We would never have got this service with that plonker Mister Smythe your predecessor Tom and a nasty piece of work to boot. Any idea what happened to him? Bill Barrett told me the Air Chief Marshal booted him back to the MoD."

Tom grinned. "He got posted to some remote staging post up in the Shetlands for his sins and it couldn't have happened to a nicer man."

♦♦♦

Squadron Leader Cody was stood at the head of the parade waiting for the arrival of the inspecting officer Wing Commander Hopwood.

When he arrived the parade went through the usual formalities and the inspection of the personnel began. Right from the start Wings had a premonition things were not going at all well because of the number of faults that were found with dress, shoes and haircuts. The Wingco' told each culprit his faults who then had his name taken by a SNCO who would make sure the fault was rectified before any subsequent inspection.

The flight of airwomen did not fare any better.

At the completion of the inspection the Wingco' told Wings. "I am not satisfied with this turnout I am not nit picking but every one of the faults I drew attention to was well founded. It draws my attention to the fact that the SNCOs are not carrying out their duties. From now on each section will carry out an inspection on the daily work parade under the supervision of a SNCO and not leave it to the junior NCOs and I want you to make sure that is carried out. I am not taking a knee jerk reaction but the next time I call for an inspection I want a good one or heads will roll. March them off to their places of work."

Wings saluted then called the Warrant Officers to him then told the SNCO left in charge of each flight to march them back to their places of work. He then gave them the message from the Wingco'. "Get your houses in order or face the consequences. You cannot deny that the faults were well founded and should not have been allowed to happen. You will ensure that every airman whose names were taken have their faults rectified and you *will* carry out an inspection on your daily work parade I personally will check on that. Further more if I find an airman not wearing denim working clothes when he should be his feet will not touch the ground and the NCOs in charge of that person will find themselves facing the Wing Commander. That also applies to you and the airwomen W/O Anderson. That is all."

They saluted and marched off.

♦♦♦

Tom Hardcastle phoned Viv. To say her new office was ready for her inspection.

"Come on Mary we have our new office to inspect and Tom is waiting there for us."

The first thing that took their eyes was Viv's name on the door. "Well you can't expect my name going on there with me having just days left in the service," remarked Mary.

On entering they were amazed to see the transformation from what it was before. “My words Tom,” said Mary. “You have excelled yourself here; it makes me feel like withdrawing my application to leave the service. There is everything you will need here Viv except a couple of big ‘shadow boards’. Do you supply them Tom or have we to get our people to make them?”

“What is wrong with the ones you already have?”

The new Squadron Leader will need those Tom that is why we need some for here.”

“That is your responsibility Mary, your ‘Chippies’ will knock them up for you in no time. Now where do you want that photo’ hanging Viv? A few minutes later the job was done. “There you are it is now ready for you to move in,” he said as he handed her the key. “By the way your desk came from Wings’ office; he does not need two in there now.”

Viv was delighted and was profuse in her thanks. “You are a good man and friend to us Tom Hardcastle.”

“Come on Viv. let us go and have a word with George Miller to see if he can lend us a couple of his men to help move us over then we can clean our old office ready for Heather to march in to.”

“Who on earth is Heather?” asked Viv.

“If I guess right and I’m sure I am, she will be your new OC. Flight Lieutenant Heather Macfarlane and you mark my words, she will arrive here with a promotion.”

“Do you know her then?”

“Heather and I go back a long way, when she was just a Flying Officer and my boss and that is going back a few years and I have not seen her since then.”

“What is she like Mary?”

“A very good officer who looks after her staff and cannot tolerate incompetence, cross her and you are in trouble. Ask her for help and she will go all the way for you. I cannot visualise her changing her attitude over the years that is not in her make up.”

“So are we going to have another Mary Butcher then?”

“That remains to be seen Viv, between you and me, Heather was not too proud to come and ask for advice which she was always grateful for. I can honestly say we made a good team in those days.”

As they entered SHQ they met George Miller in the corridor. “Just the man we were coming to see,” said Mary.

“Why what have I done now?” asked a startled George.

“Nothing you great lummox,” she said laughing. “We would like the loan of two of your lads to help us move offices.”

“Where are you moving to?”

“Into the Education block and we would like to move today, there is not a lot to take over.”

“What time do you want them?”

“Two o’ clock if that is alright by you?”

♦♦♦

Squadron Leader Heather Macfarlane booked into the Officers Mess at RAF March. At reception a male steward was summoned to carry her luggage to the room already prepared for her. The steward asked if she would like any refreshments.

"I would love a beaker of tea please"

This was brought to her on a tray with an array of biscuits by a stewardess. When questioned, the girl informed her of the Mess routine and the number of resident Mess members. "You will find it rather a quiet Mess Ma'am and the resident members very nice and easy going."

"From what you tell me I assume you like it here too."

"Oh yes Ma'am it is a very happy station and I would hate to be posted."

"Thank you that is very interesting I shall look forward to finding that out."

"When you have finished with the tray Ma'am place it outside it will be collected. On behalf of the stewardesses, welcome to RAF March."

"Why thank you, that is most kind of you."

At dinner everyone introduced themselves and welcomed her to the Mess. She gave a brief summary about herself and the reason for being posted here. She put everyone at ease by announcing. "In the Mess I am usually addressed as 'Mac'," much to the relief of the junior officers and a delight to the senior ones most of them had either nicknames or shortened names, like in Mac' for Macfarlane.

Wings caused a laugh by announcing. "I am an exception to the rule, I have two nicknames, 'Bill' for Buffalo Bill Cody which I am known by in the Mess and 'Wings' by my staff, so I can say I top the leader board."

In the lounge where they were being served coffee Wings approached Mac' and asked if he could have a word.

"Certainly, sit yourself down what do you want to tell me?"

"I just want to introduce myself properly because we will be working in harmony together. I am the Squadron Leader OC. Tech' Wing, Admin' Wing and Recruit Training, as such I sincerely welcome you to RAF March and hope we can make a good team."

"Thank you Bill that is a very nice and genuine welcome and I most certainly will do my best to make it a good and amicable partnership. Now what can you tell me about the training staff I have heard they are the best in the business."

"They do not come any better Mac' and personally I have a lot to thank them for."

"It sounds very interesting will it take some time in telling Bill? The reason I ask is couldn't we continue it this evening over a drink?"

"That would be ideal because there is so much to tell and I promise not to bore you. There is another more interesting story to tell but you must hear that from a WRAF Warrant Officer. You are very fortunate in that respect because she is the only one who can really cover that story and she will be leaving us in a few days time."

"Mary Butcher," she surprised Wings with.

"You know of her?" he asked

"Know of her," she exclaimed, "I know her, we served together years ago and I have a lot to thank Mary for."

"What a small world, we have more in common than we thought," exclaimed delighted Wings. Good, then we will meet in the bar, will eight o' clock do?"

"That will be fine and I am now really looking forward to the Saga of RAF March," she laughed.

Wings was waiting outside the bar to escort her in. After getting the drinks he began his tale from when he first arrived at March and of his meeting with W/O Barrett and how he guided him from knowing nothing about recruit training and with his encouragement plus a mini-course on instructing he was able to talk to them in their own language. "He was solely responsible for me getting such a rapid promotion." He told of the incident when he was thought to have been replaced by a Squadron Leader. "The reaction when I walked into the CO's office sporting my new rank was amazing, he shook my hand then emotion took over the pair of us and we embraced like brothers in front of the Commandant who had the biggest smile on his face I have ever seen. As long as I live I will never forget what that man has done for me."

"That is some story Bill, I want to meet your W/O Barrett, you are a very lucky man to have had him and Mary Butcher in your corner that was some combination, I wish I could have been here then."

"That story is nothing compared to what is widely known now as the Saga of Bill Barrett and Mary simply loves telling it and you had better believe that every word she tells you is true. That man is respected by an Air Chief Marshall right down to the lowest ranks and it has not affected him in the least. Mary maintains he is the same Bill Barrett she first knew long ago but a much wiser one."

"Thank you Bill I realise from what you have told me I was very fortunate in getting this posting and that was only because Mary Butcher recommended me to the AOC. So we do have something in common. You have your Bill Barrett in your corner and I have Mary Butcher, unfortunately not for long. I will bid you goodnight, you have given me a very interesting evening and as you know tomorrow will be a busy day with interviews etc. Thanks again Bill and Goodnight."

CHAPTER 19

Bill Barrett was summoned to Wings' office.

"Mr Barrett I want to apologise for my bullish and inexcusable bad behaviour towards you the last time you were in this office and it was only when I was brought down to earth with an almighty bump with that unfortunate incident which was fortunate for me because it brought me to my senses."

"There is no need for an apology sir because your staff is more world wise than you and having been through similar situations have been right behind you from the word go."

"Thank you Mister Barrett those words mean a lot to me. Now tell me, have I beaten the March Air phenomenon?"

"I do believe you have sir, congratulations."

"Thank goodness for that, I have been a bit silly by falling for a pretty face but it has taught me a lesson, one that I will not forget in a hurry."

"Falling for a pretty face is not exclusive to you sir."

"It baffles me Mister Barrett how you have come to deduce all these happenings, it sounds very weird to me I am beginning to suspect you have the blood of a warlock running through your veins."

"Just leave it to nature and the March Air will do the rest sir."

"Right, let us get down to business. The proforma you gave me to pass on through the chain as you put it was forwarded as you requested. It went through the stages after being approved at each one and finished up on the AOC's desk. Do you remember me saying at one time that you and our ex CO had worked together for so long that you both thought along the same lines?"

Bill smiled to himself because he knew what was coming next, the plan he and the AOC had concocted had worked.

Wings continued. "The AOC has beaten you to it, apparently he has already formulated a similar plan to yours and it had already been progressed, you have been pipped at the post Mister Barrett."

"At least I have the satisfaction of knowing sir that great minds do think alike I would have liked to have seen his version."

"You will Mister Barrett when it comes into operation."

"I assume you read my version sir."

"Indeed I did and I was impressed with it as were the Wingco' and CO. it was a good solution to the problem of freeing blocked promotions. You had an interview with the AOC when you escorted WO Butcher to Command I understand."

"I did sir, when she told him I was her escort he wanted to see me. He said, 'It is like old times, I miss those little chats we used to have.'

"Thank you Mr Barrett. It will soon be the dining-out for WO Butcher and I am looking forward to it."

Bill saluted and as he got to the door Wings called. "Mr Barrett our ex-CO. was fond of the saying the ACM used to make concerning you."

"What was that sir?"

"You are a crafty bugger Mr Barrett."

They both smiled each knowing what the other knew.

♦♦♦

Squadron Leader Macfarlane was received by the Commandant who welcomed her with the history and development of the station and what it had achieved. "You will find the staff is among the best in the service.

Like any other station we have had our ups and downs but still remain a happy one."

"Squadron Leader Cody gave me a very interesting insight to the training staff

last evening and I was most impressed with what he told me."

"Ah! Squadron Leader Cody, a very remarkable young man who has become very knowledgeable with instructor training and has become very popular with the training staff to the extent where I think they have adopted him. He will have told you that you will be working together where you will be responsible for the administration, welfare and discipline of the airwomen he is responsible for their recruit training. Your Warrant Officer is Anderson she is replacing WO Butcher, she was an excellent choice and is well respected. Incidentally she trained the BlueBelles team under the guidance of WO Barrett and was their leader who took them to that famous victory."

"Then I have a lot to live up to sir."

"I would not put it like that, you will find they have their feet firmly on the ground and never flaunt their successes but they are very protective towards their staff but at the same time being very firm. Have you been made comfortable in the Mess and is everything to your satisfaction?"

"Indeed I am sir and I find everyone so friendly."

"Your next stop is with Wing Commander Hopwood." He stood up shook her hand saying "Welcome to RAF March I am sure you are going to be a good team member."

She thanked him, saluted, then made her way to see the Wingco'.

There she was welcomed and was put in the picture of what her duties were and who would be responsible to her. "I suggest you go to see Squadron Leader Cody now and he will show you around to meet the people who are in charge of the various sections. I strongly recommend you have a good chat to Warrant Officer Butcher who is unfortunately leaving us very soon."

"We served together some years ago sir and I have a lot to thank her for regarding service life. I am looking forward to meeting up with her again albeit for only a short time."

"Yes, she is a very remarkable woman and she will be sorely missed, I understand she is thought of very highly by the rank and file as a motherly figure. I am relatively new here myself and I think it is a good station, mark my words you will enjoy it too."

She saluted and made her way to see Wings.

♦♦♦

Margaret Roper answered the ringing phone'. She handed it to Bill saying. "Helen Fraser wants a word."

"Hello Helen, what can I do for you? What, right now? I will be there in a few minutes, thanks Helen. The Commandant wants to see me, I do not know what for but I will see you in a bit Margaret."

"Come on Bill sir is waiting for you. "Warrant Officer Barrett sir" Helen announced as she ushered Bill in.

"Ah, Good morning Mr Barrett, sit yourself down." He said in response to the salute.

"Mr Barrett, we are going to open an NCO training school. All newly promoted airmen with the rank of Corporal will attend a monthly course on the responsibilities required from an NCO. That also includes Corporals who have not done the course. What I want from you are the numbers we can accommodate and what extra training staff we will need."

"I have an empty barrack room which will accommodate twelve personnel and a room for an NCO. The NCOs' room I would like the senior Corporal on the course to have that. For the instructors I would like a Flight Sergeant and a Sergeant from my staff. I would like Sergeant Franks promoted to Flight Sergeant and Corporal Farrow promoted to Sergeant. I would then want a Sergeant to replace Sergeant Franks and a Corporal to replace Corporal Farrow."

"Do you really expect you will get those men promoted and replacements for them posted in Mr Barrett?"

"I do sir that is why the AOC has pushed his idea through to get rid of the promotion blockage. Sergeant Franks is a very senior Sergeant and Corporal Farrow a very senior Corporal. With respect, sir, you will find that the AOC is working on those lines and has only to rubber stamp it."

"Wait in my PA's office Mr Barrett while I get in touch with the AOC."

"Anything exciting happening Bill?" asked Helen.

He told her the tale.

"That is a foregone conclusion because you and the AOC are as thick as thieves."

"Give the CO time to settle down to his promotion, Helen. He is new at it yet."

"Send Mr Barrett in Helen," said the CO over the intercom.

"In you go Bill. You know the way."

He knocked, entered on command, then saluted.

"Well Mr Barrett, it seems you have got what you wanted, the AOC verified what you told me. The promotions will come through shortly and the course will start in three weeks time. Records Office will detail the Corporals when they receive the details from Command HQ. Is there anything else we have not covered Mr Barrett?"

"Catering and clothing stores sir."

"Why clothing stores Mr Barrett?"

"Because sir I have a gut feeling they will need to supplement the No1 dress head gear. The Corporal training instructors are prone to slash the peaks thinking it gives them the macho guardsman look to scare recruits. Now they are not training recruits peaked hats should not be worn, as a matter of fact they should not be worn at any time with their working uniform. Therefore sir I can see our stores doing plenty of trade in peaked caps."

The CO laughed. "It looks like someone is due for a shock when they attend their first parade."

"Especially, with Flight Sergeant Franks in charge sir, he is a stickler for correctness."

"Very well, if there is anything I should know or you have a problem with and you want to discuss with me, contact Helen."

"What about chain of command sir? I do not want to go over any ones head."

"Leave that to me I will put the Wing Commander and Squadron Leader in the picture."

Bill saluted and left.

He made his way to the orderly room to see Roy Shaw.

"Here comes trouble," Roy greeted him with. "What nefarious activities have you been up to this time?"

"Now could you not phrase it better to greet a bearer of good news?"

"I get the message. Two teas please" he shouted through the hatch.

"Now Hermes, what is the message the gods have trusted you with?"

"Our plan for unblocking the promotion has been accepted by the AOC and is now in practice."

Roy leaned over and shook his hand. "What a team we are!"

"There is more Roy. We are opening a school for junior NCOs in three weeks time and guess who is in charge of it? Flight Sergeant Franks and Sergeant Farrow."

"Bill Barrett, remind me never to upset you or it would be the kiss of death. Congratulations old friend," he said as he shook him by the hand once more. "That is really good news and worth a celebration. Two biscuits with the tea please," he called through the hatch.

"You should be receiving the notification of the promotions any day now."

"Do you think Wings will take the huff when he gets to know all this? He will know it was all your doing."

"He knows there was some underhand dealing between me and the AOC regarding our plan but he cannot prove a thing. He told me so in a round about way coining the ACM's phrase 'You are a crafty bugger Mr Barrett'."

"I don't think he will repeat that when he hears about this little lot it will be something a bit riper."

"He will be more upset when he finds out I am allowed to jump the chain of command to see the CO if necessary."

"The plot thickens. I should tread very carefully if I was you Bill you may be thought of as a threat and a danger to their position."

"Thanks Roy but I have the bigger advantage they have not got you in their corner. Thanks for the brew I will now go and pass the glad tidings to Joe Franks and Cpl Farrow."

When he got back to his office Bill sent for Joe Franks and Cpl Farrow.

"I have some good news and some bad news and I am not giving you the option of which you want first I will give you the good news. We are to open an NCO training school for newly promoted Corporals and for Corporals who have never attended one. It will become operational in about three weeks time. The bad news is you two are posted!"

There was a look of dismay on their faces.

"Why?" asked Joe Franks, "when you will need extra instructors for the school, that does not make sense. Whose idea is that Bill?"

"I plead guilty Joe, a Flight Sergeant and a Sergeant have already been assigned to that post and I am expecting your promotions coming through any day now."

Bill smiled to see the look of incredibility on their faces.

Joe broke the silence with. "You have bloody well cracked it you crafty bugger," as he came forward to give his thanks in a firm handshake followed by Jim Farrow.

"How on earth did you manage that Bill?"

"Do you remember when we were discussing it and I said if I could get to see the AOC I would remind him of how we wanted to put an end to the promotion blockage? I saw my chance by getting Mary Butcher to ask for me to chaperone her to the AOC. I had formulated a plan and he accepted it and put it into practice straight away. Today our CO sent for me to tell me about this school and when he instructed me to take charge of it I recommended you two to take it over and when I told him the reasons he contacted the AOC to confirm it which he did. Of course if you do not want to accept the responsibility, fair enough."

The delight on their faces said it all.

"Keep it to yourselves for the time being. We will get together later and plan an itinerary of sorts."

Joe shook Jim Farrow's hand saying. "I am glad to have you as my partner Jim."

"By the way Joe, I told the CO to instruct stores to get a stock of No1 dress caps in because there will be a few slashed peaks that will have to be replaced."

Amid the laughter Joe said. "I can't wait to see their reaction when the drill instructor elements have to wear berets instead."

CHAPTER 20

Squadron Leader Macfarlane reported to Wings. He immediately introduced her to the 'Brew'. "This was part of my indoctrination into the world of recruit training." He then told her of his arrival knowing nothing and how the training staff took him under their wing to train him to the level where he could instruct and converse with the staff at their own level of training language. "I have a lot to thank these people for especially Warrant

Officer Barrett, he and he alone is responsible for me being in the position and rank I now hold and this little beauty here," showing her the model of a silver pace stick in pride of place on his desk, "was presented to me as my badge of office."

"I had a similar experience with Warrant Officer Butcher a few years ago when I was a very green Pilot Officer, she steered me in the right direction and do you know Bill, she was responsible for me getting this posting."

"Are you ready for a tour of the station?"

"I would like to go and pay my respects to WO Butcher first if you don't mind Bill, if you will point me in the right direction I would like to go and see her now."

On the command 'Come in' she entered Viv and Mary's office.

On seeing her Mary gave a scream of delight, after they embraced Mary introduced her to Viv.

When they had exchanged greetings Viv said. "If you will excuse me I will go and have a word with Bill Barrett and leave you two ladies to have a good chin-wag."

"Hello" said Bill what brings you over here, are you missing us?"

"Surprisingly no," she said with a smile. Mary has a visitor, her friend Squadron Leader Macfarlane, so I came out leaving them to have a chat.

How are things over here? Things seem pretty quiet just now, have you anything new?"

He told her about the NCO school and the AOC curing the promotion blockage.

"You had something to do with that if I remember rightly."

"Roy Shaw helped me formulate it. Are you ready for the take-over from Mary?"

"Yes, surprisingly I have everything under control the only thing I have not got is her experience."

"That only comes with time Viv, how are the arrangements coming on for the dining-out?"

"Everything is under control but we have not got anyone to do the presentation, have you any suggestions?"

"That is a difficult one, off the top of my head the only one I can think of is our Commandant because he was CO at Chatworth with Mary when the first BlueBelle team was formed. Other than him there is Ann Wilson who led the BlueBelles at Chatworth but I would have to ask Wings to find out if that was permissible. Leave it with me and I will see what I can come up with."

They were interrupted by the ringing phone. "WO Barrett speaking, yes Mary I will tell her. Mary has given you the all clear, your OC has left."

The phone rang again. "WO Barrett, Hello Marion, yes I will be over right away thanks. I will walk over with you I have to report to Wings he must have got word about the NCO school and the promotions and he is going to ask questions, namely why he was not informed."

"Well the best of luck Bill if you get the boot I can always find you a job as my PA." she laughed as she left him shaking his fist at her in mock anger.

♦♦♦

"I have been summoned to see sir, Marion."

"I will give him a buzz to see if he is free. WO Barrett is here sir."

"Send him in Marion."

Bill entered and saluted and saw that Squadron Leader Macfarlane was present.

"I have sent for you..."

Hey up Bill, he has got his knickers in a twist, no Mister Barrett and no take a seat. Looks like I am not the flavour of the month.

"Because I am very displeased with the present situation and I have brought you here to answer to it."

"I am sorry sir but I do not know what you are referring to."

"You know damn well what I am referring to, this Junior NCO school, the two promotions, the two replacements and ignoring the chain of command."

"With respect sir what is the problem?"

Wings banged his desk with his fist. "You! You are the problem Barrett and I want an explanation."

"Where would you like me to start sir?"

"At the bloody beginning man, where else?"

"It will take a little time to tell sir and I would like your permission to stand easy."

"Permission refused."

"Then I request the Station Commander to witness my explanation Sir"

Wings was taken aback and was at a loss for a reply.

After regaining his composure he asked. "And why should the Station Commander be interested in bearing witness?"

"Because sir it is he you should be questioning and demanding an explanation from."

That came as a shock to Wings' system.

"You are being insubordinate and you know I can take disciplinary action against you."

"Indeed you can sir and I also can enter a redress of grievance against you."

"Get the hell out of my office."

Bill saluted and withdrew. Outside he smiled and thought, he has lost and he knows it.

After Bill had left Wings banged his desk in frustration. "That man is so frustrating Heather, what do you make of him and his insubordination?"

"Can I speak frankly Bill?"

"Please do."

"He was not insubordinate he was trying to stop you digging deeper in the hole you had made for yourself. You told me he was a good friend to you and I think he showed it. You will not lose his friendship he is too big a man to let a little burst of self pride spoil it."

"You are right Heather I was a damned fool and went in with both feet before I knew my facts. Give the man his due, whatever he did it could only have been for the good of the station. The Air Vice Marshal calls him a crafty bugger but it is with respect. The only thing WO Barrett gets out of it is the satisfaction that other people gain from his efforts. I owe that man a great big apology."

"From what Mary Butcher told me about him and from what I have just seen of him you are a lucky man Bill Cody to have him as a friend."

Bill went to see Roy. "You have come to enjoy my hospitality haven't you or you would not have come to see me at this time of day and why are you smiling?"

"Is being threatened with discipline for insubordination worthy of a pot of your delicious nectar?"

"I like the sound of that and it is worth a biscuit. Two teas and biscuits please," he shouted through the hatch. Well get on with it, what happened?"

"Wait until I see the tea and biscuits I don't want you to renegade on me."

"Give me a clue then."

"Wings"

"That does sound intriguing, is he bearing a grudge about Betty Grable?"

"No, besides that was nowt' to do with me."

An airman brought in the brews. "Anything else sir?" he asked Roy.

"Don't you think it is worth another biscuit?" smiled Bill.

"No it is not, be satisfied for small mercies. Now get on with it."

Bill told him what had occurred

"What is the matter with the man?" exploded Roy. "You have nursed him along from knowing nothing and this is how he repays you I would kick the ungrateful little sod into touch."

"He has got hold of the wrong end of the stick and without knowing the facts he jumped in with two feet. I will lay bets he is cursing himself right now for being such a ruddy fool. As I have already told you he had the WRAF Squadron Leader in the office no doubt as a witness, I wonder what she thought of his attitude.

"If my advice counts for anything Bill," said Heather Macfarlane, "go and explain to the CO what has transpired then more than likely you will be told the full story."

"You are right I will get on to it right away. Marion, will you get me Helen Fraser?"

"You are through sir."

"Helen, Squadron Leader Cody here, can you arrange an interview for me with the CO please?"

"I will call you back sir."

"Helen Fraser is on the phone for you sir."

"Hello Helen, that's fine thank you."

When he arrived at Helen's office she told him. "You can go straight in sir."

Wings saluted.

"Hello Bill what is on your mind? Sit yourself down you are looking a bit harassed."

"More likely embarrassed sir." He then told the full story of what happened.

"I don't believe what I am hearing Bill, you have really made a faux pas."

"I do realise that sir, I lost control and it just got out of hand.

What made it more infuriating was me knowing all along that he was in the right. I started something I could not finish."

"In a way I suppose I was to blame for not putting you in the picture sooner. I received the information of the Junior NCOs course from the AOC with the instructions that W/O Barrett had carte blanche for choosing the staff. This he did and I received confirmation from the AOC that it was acceptable. Also, W/O Barrett had my permission to ignore the chain of command and report directly to me if he has problems with this project. Are you quite clear on that score?"

"Yes sir"

"Then off you go and if you have more problems think about them first before getting on your high horse and having a tantrum."

Wings saluted and left feeling very chastened after that rebuke from the Commandant.

CHAPTER 21

"Bill, Roy here. Your two promotions have come through with affect from tomorrow."

"Thank you Roy that is what I have been waiting for especially for Joe's sake. I expect he will want to take us for a drink to celebrate."

"Then you had better ask Tommy if you can play out. Ta ra Bill," he laughed as he hung up.

"Margaret, will you get one of your staff to go and ask Sergeant Franks and Corporal Farrow to come to my office?"

When they arrived he told them. "Tomorrow we shall have a powwow concerning our new project if you have any ideas on how you are going to run it I would like to know then the three of us can discuss them on their merits. That should take up most of the morning. I want you Sergeant to hand over your flight to your Corporals for that period and you Corporal give my compliments to Sergeant Dixon and tell him I want you for tomorrow morning. The reason for all this is, tomorrow will be the official congratulations day that is when your promotions come into force."

"Two beaming NCOs' faced Bill with "Thank You sir".

"The first thing tomorrow morning is to get your authority from the orderly room, report to clothing stores for your new ranks, report to the tailor give him my compliments and ask him if he can make it a priority job. Finally, report here as new members of my staff in all your grandeur. Keep mum and give the rest of the staff a nice surprise later on."

Bill went to have a word with Corporal Deacon who was in charge of the flight while Sergeant York was duty Mess barman.

"How is Corporal Anders shaping up Corporal?"

"He is very competent sir."

"Could he be left in full charge say for a morning?"

"That would be no problem sir I have every confidence in his ability."

"Good. Now tell me have you got two good airmen I could count upon to do a job for me for half a day then be rewarded by getting the rest of the day off?"

"When do you want them sir?"

"Tomorrow morning and I want you to take charge of them. I want them to clean the spare dormitory to a squeaky clean standard and then lock the place up until I order it to be unlocked. Have all bedding ready to be picked up by the bedding store personnel. I will have it replaced when the time comes and if any mattresses or covers need replacing do so through the bedding store. Do you think that is a too big a task for two airmen?"

"If they knuckle down to the job they should have it finished by lunchtime but I will make sure they do not cut any corners sir."

"Good man I will go and organise the bedding store people."

He then went to see George Miller who took him to the bedding store where Bill explained to Corporal Hermett what he wanted.

"So your little empire is being extended, remarked George, well it can only be a good thing for the station."

Bill told him about Joe Franks' and Corporal Farrows' promotions.

"Now that is good news and Bai gum' but Joe deserves his promotion, I have a lot of time for Joe he is one of the best Drill Instructors I have met in all my service career. You can count on one hand the number of instructors who are or have been on a par with Joe.

You will be getting replacements for the two of them, how are you going to sort them out to your standard?"

"I have got two on my list who Sergeant York and Corporals Farrow and Deacon recommended and I am now going to see Wings to get them posted in ASAP."

"Well I hope you are lucky with them Bill."

♦♦♦

Bill went to see Marion Macken asking for an interview with Wings.

"Sir, W/O Barrett is here seeking an interview."

"Send him straight in Marion."

Bill knocked walked in and saluted.

"I am pleased you came Mr Barrett because I owe you…"

"You owe me nothing sir as far as I am concerned things are the same as they always have been between us."

Wings shook his hand. "Thank you Mister Barrett, I have learned my lesson. Sit yourself down and tell me about this NCO school."

"Actually sir, that is the reason I came to see you. You will already know the two promotions come into effect tomorrow. I am calling them to a round table conference tomorrow on what I expect from them regarding the school and strict discipline tops my list and with Flight Sergeant Franks in charge I have no worries there. I do need replacements for them both and with insider knowledge from Sergeant York, and Corporals Farrow and Deacon they have given me two names they say will fit in with our training methods. That is the reason I came to see you to ask if you will sanction their postings to us."

"What if they do not meet with your approval Mister Barrett, what next?"

"There is always that chance but those three are so reliable I cannot but go along with their judgement. The alternative is to go through that nausea at Records Office again "

"Yes, I see your point and I can see other alternative Mister Barrett but give me the two names and I will push them through."

"Sergeant Wilcox, P. and Corporal Thomas, J. By the way sir could you contact Records Office who I understand will be detailing the Corporals for this course to insist they come with full kit I would like a full kit inspection each week and would you do the honours sir?"

"That is more like it I will do it with pleasure. Talking of pleasure Mister Barrett it will soon be time for the dining–out night I am going to enjoy it but in another way it is going to be a sad one losing W/O Butcher but keep me posted Mister Barrett."

♦♦♦

At 10:30am the following morning Joe and Jim reported to Bill in his office. After congratulating them Bill said. "Right, let's get down to business, sit down while I get a brew organised." He went into ops' room and asked for three teas.

"Here is what I want from you both. Discipline, that is paramount, dress and cleanliness and I want a kit inspection every week which will be inspected by Wings. After the introductory address they have the first day preparing their kit for their first inspection and you are to make sure it is fit for inspection. That is where your famous bonuses will most likely come into force Joe. Have you anything to add to that or do you disagree with any of it?"

"How many are on the course?" asked Joe.

"Thirteen, twelve will be in the dormitory and the senior Corporal will be in the bunk. Don't forget that slashed peaks are taboo and are to be replaced by new headgear. That is going to hurt a few I can tell you. Corporal Deacon with two lads are cleaning the dormitory today and changing bedding, mattress covers and mattresses if need be, then the dormitory will be locked until the personnel arrive. Until that happens you will have to carry on with your own flights. Now go out there and give the staff a surprise."

"Are you coming to the mess tonight for a drink Bill? We both would like to celebrate our promotion in the time honoured fashion and in appreciation of what you have done for us. We will ask the other Mess members after they have stopped taking the Mickey out of us. Will you also ask the other two crackpots for it will not feel the same without them? I will gen up Jim here as to what he will be in for."

"Put him in the picture as to what his duty will be when we dine Mary out."

♦♦♦

The dining- out night was a huge success. The presentation to Mary was made jointly by Bill Barrett and Viv Anderson; who made up the famous victorious BlueBelles threesome. It was a very emotional presentation not just for the BlueBelles connection but for the esteem in which Mary was held and the sadness of her departure from the service, many tributes and toasts were given in her honour. In a few days time the tears will flow yet again as Mary is escorted through the gates into civilian life.

♦♦♦

The day arrived when Mary had to leave the station. After saying goodbye and thank you to the Mess staff she made her way to the exit where she was met by George Miller and Bill Barrett her two oldest friends who led her between them through two ranks of Warrant Officers and Senior NCOs who then commenced to escort them to the station entrance. As they came in sight of the Station gates Mary gasped to see the number of personnel who had lined the route to see her off. She paused then linked arms with George and Bill.

"I need your support more than ever now," she whispered.

"Come on old girl put a brave face on," encouraged George.

"Now I will tell you both for the last time."

The three of them chorused. "Less of the old," then burst out laughing as Mary squeezed their arms with affection.

Waiting lined up outside the guardroom were the Station Commander, Wingco' Hopwood, Squadron Leader Cody and Squadron Leader Macfarlane.

"We leave you here," said George and Bill.

She embraced each one in turn and kissed them. "I will see you both later."

The officers in turn shook her by the hand, Wings kissed her and Heather Macfarlane presented her with a bouquet then kissed her saying. "This is from the Officers Mess Mary, Good luck and God Bless."

There was applause and cheers from the personnel as Mary walked through the gates where Sam Brown was waiting for her. Mary turned and looked back at everyone with tears running down her face. Her lips formed the words 'Thank You'. When she entered the car she said. "Take me home Sam," then gave a regal wave as they moved off to a new life.

Early Saturday morning George and his wife Betty, Bill with his wife Tommy drove independently to collect Sam and Mary. George drove the Bride and groom to where their civic ceremony was to be held while Bill carried their luggage in his car. The ceremony was short but very nicely conducted. George and Betty signed the marriage certificate as witnesses. The two couples then congratulated a very happy and smiling Mister Brown and an absolutely glowing with happiness Mrs Brown.

"Come on," said Mary laughing. "We have plenty of time to have a celebration brew before we go to the airport."

After booking-in at the airport they found seats where as soon as they were seated they were confronted by Roy Shaw with Barbara and Derwent with Viv. Everyone was taken by surprise and of course the congratulations and kisses were the order of the day.

"How nice of you to come to see us off, on behalf of my husband and I we thank you very much." This statement brought howls of laughter from everyone.

They heard a voice from behind them saying, "Will you please keep your voices down."

They turned and saw with astonishment Squadron Leader Wings Cody and Squadron Leader Heather Macfarlane. "We could not miss coming to see you both off," said Wings, as he and Heather offered their congratulations, along with a handshake and kisses. "What does it feel like, Mary, being an old married woman?" he said laughing "...and I know what is coming next," as they all joined in with. "Less of the *old!*"

"Come here young man, let me give you another kiss for your cheek," she said, as she grabbed hold of him.

When the time came for boarding they departed a very happy couple, carrying with them the wishes of the friends who came to see them off, all waving madly as they went through into the departure lounge.

"Wasn't that kind of them to take the trouble to see us off Sam?"

CHAPTER 22

Flight Sergeant Joe Franks unlocked the door to the dormitory which would house the Corporals on the JNCO course. He entered and inspected the accommodation which was to his satisfaction. He then pinned a notice to the notice board which stated.

> *'Corporal Anders is the NCO i/c this room. Your bed space and layout will conform to the poster displayed on your notice board. You will stand by your beds for a daily pre-parade inspection of this room. The first morning of arrival after the initial room inspection you will parade in your best uniform outside the Barrack Block at 09:00.*

Signed by. Flight Sergeant Franks'.

After locking up he made his way to see the SWO George Miller.

"Hello Joe, what can I do for you this lovely morning?"

"You know about this NCOs school George, I am expecting them to arrive on Monday. Will you ask your staff to direct them to Block 'C' Room 4 please? I have just had a shufti at the room and it is spick and span your lads have done a good job with the clean bedding. If you want to run your eyes over them they will be on parade Tuesday morning at 09:00 in their best bib and tucker."

"I will make it my business Joe I would like to see what shape they are in before you get to work on em'. I hear you have got a phobia on slashed peaks just like your boss Bill Barrett."

"That is true George, there are going to be some very unhappy Corporals when they have to buy a new cap, the culprits of course will come from the Corporal Drill Instructors contingency as you can expect. I am looking forward to that I can tell you."

♦♦♦

"Margaret, send someone to tell Corporal Anders to report to me please?"

"You wanted to see me sir?" asked the Corporal as he faced Bill.

"Yes, you are a member of Sergeant Dixon's staff as from now. I want you to vacate your bunk, leave it clean and habitable because we will have a new Corporal Thomas who will take it over. Move into the empty dormitory bunk 4. The empty dormitory will be occupied by all Corporals who will be attending the NCO school and you will be in charge of that room. This is your chance to shine and remember the occupants of that room toe *your* line. Hand your bunk key to Corporal Deacon. I will explain to the Sergeants about the staff changes."

He then visited the flights to put the Sergeants in the picture.

He asked Joe if he had the key to the bunk and explained why.

"I have it here, said Joe I will send one of the lads with it to Corporal Anders. Have you thought Bill that we will now have one Corporal too many? The thirteenth Corporal was moving into that bunk remember."

"I had better see Wings straight away to get Records to cancel one Corporal thanks for reminding me Joe."

Off he went and asked Marion if he could have a quick word with Wings.

"Go right in sir."

Bill saluted.

"You have a problem Mister Barrett I can sense it a mile away."

"It is a slip-up on my part sir." He then told his tale.

"If I can get Records to do that all well and good otherwise we shall have to put our thinking caps on. Stay there while I check with Records.

"Hello, this is Squadron Leader Cody of RAF March. I would like to speak with the Officer in charge of delegating Junior NCOs to report to RAF March for Junior NCO training please. Hello, yes, good, you are just the man I would like to speak to. I am Squadron Leader Cody of RAF March and the NCO school comes under my jurisdiction. I have a problem which only you can remedy. We have over estimated by just one the total we can accommodate at any one time. Yes, just one and I am hoping you would cancel one from your total of thirteen. I am sorry this is short notice for you and I indeed do apologise for any inconvenience it will cause you.

You can do that? I say, that is awfully kind of you, if ever there is a chance for me to return the favour please do not hesitate to contact me. Who is that Corporal Williams? Good and thank you once again.

There you are Mister Barrett it was no problem."

"Listening to you putting that across how could anyone refuse?"

"That is in the curriculum of instructor training, I can recommend a good training school Mister Barrett!. No, I really cannot take any credit because when the person who you want a favour from realises that it was RAF March that produced the BlueBelles it is like a having a Golden Key that opens any door...." he was interrupted by the buzzer on his inter-com.

"Yes Marion"

"Warrant officer Shaw is on the phone sir."

"Put him through Marion."

"Yes Mister Shaw what can I do for you?"

"The two replacements Sergeant Wilcox and Corporal Thomas arrive on Monday sir."

"Thank you Mister Shaw that is good news, I will inform W/O Barrett he is here with me."

"Is he bumming a brew from you sir?"

Wings laughed. "Not yet Mister Shaw but I am thinking of offering him one."

"That would be a grave mistake sir he will never be away from your office if you do."

"Thank you Mister Shaw, point taken, stand by I will send him over for you to give him one. Mister Shaw invites you to have a brew with him."

"Aye and pigs might fly sir." He saluted then left to have a word with Roy.

"Come in friend," Roy responded to Bill's knock. You are just in time for a brew. Don't look so gob smacked Wings said he was sending you over for one and I don't want to go against his wishes."

"Bloody creep," Bill muttered under his breath.

"You will be pleased to know your replacements arrive on Monday. The Sergeant is married and will probably want a married quarter."

"You can also strike off Corporal Williams from the Corporals list we find we can only accommodate twelve."

"So who has dropped that clanger?"

"No clanger Roy, just a little oversight. How do you want the Corporals to report for their arrival chits? Joe is going to fall them in at 09:00 outside the Barrack Block."

"Sergeant Graham will be there to give them their chits to save them cluttering up SHQ and my orderly room. When they have collected all the necessary signatures have one of them return the chits to the orderly room."

"I'm now going to see Joe Franks to put him in the picture about the arrival chit business. Thanks for the brew."

"Don't thank me thank Wings, when my master speaks I obey."

"Bloody Creep!"

♦♦♦

"How are you settling down to your exalted rank Joe?"

"Feels like I have had it for years Bill."

"Aye and it should have been too. When you parade your bods on Tuesday morning, Sergeant Graham will come and dish out the arrival chits, when they have collected all the relevant signatures get one of them to return them to the orderly room."

"I like that Bill it means I can march them to each port of call just like raw recruits and they are going to hate me for it but it will help to knock the swagger out of them."

"Yours and Jim's replacements arrive on Monday, Sergeant Wilcox and Corporal Thomas,"

"If it is Pete Wilcox I knew him when he was a Corporal he was a good lad then, you might have struck lucky Bill."

"Let's hope so."

♦♦♦

George Miller paid a visit to the market garden to find out how Corporal Bond was coping with the situation of being on his own with Sam Brown being away. He found the Corporal in one of the greenhouses attending to the vegetables.

"Are you working without any help Corporal?"

"Yes sir and I find it difficult to sort out the veg; for all the Messes and getting it delivered which takes up a lot of valuable time."

"We can't have that, how many bods do you want until Sam gets back?"

"I could manage with two, sir."

"Well you choose the ones you want and let me have their names as soon as you can and you will have them first thing in the morning."

"Thomson and Davidson sir, they will be fine, they are good workers."

"Good, you can keep them until Sam returns."

"Thank you sir," he said with a smile of relief.

On his return to his office George sent for his runner. "I want you to find Thomson and Davidson and tell them to report to me on the double."

Ian Roberts, George's second in command told the runner where he should find them.

They arrived puffing and panting.

"You two are right out of condition don't you do any exercises? Young lads like you should be as fit as a butcher's dog. How do you fancy doing a job for three weeks, excused duties and work parades?"

Their faces lit up. "Yes please sir."

"I have chosen you two because the report I have got is, you are very good workers and you have no time for skivers, those are my sentiments too. Tomorrow morning you will report to Corporal Bond, you know he is a good man and he will look after you. All I ask of you is to give him your full support."

"We will do that sir and thanks for choosing us."

"Away you go then and take the rest of the day off."

"Thank you sir," they said gleefully.

♦♦♦

W/O Viv Anderson received a telephone call from Squadron Leader Macfarlane saying she would inspect the WRAF Barrack rooms at 09:00 tomorrow and all Corporals in charge of rooms would stand by for the inspection. "You and Flight Sergeant Roper are also to be there."

Viv was quick to pass the message on to Margaret Roper who in turn would break the news to the WRAFs.

The permanent staff would be included in the inspection. Viv informed them of what to expect and they would have to conform along with the rest of the WRAF. That meant that they would be confined to their accommodation to carry out a 'Bull night' and could only stand down when the NCOs in charge were satisfied the dormitories were fit for inspection. That news brought a flutter of panic from all concerned. After their evening meal the airwomen made straight for their accommodation to get stuck into the 'Bull' having had to put their dates on hold with the airmen for that evening. It was quite a hive of activity with the Corporals in the thick of it cajoling the ones who were getting stuck into the cleaning and threatening the lackadaisical ones who weren't. As always the thought of having to do it all over again in their own time if it was not acceptable was a good inducement. When the Sergeants came to do an inspection, apart from a few niggly little things the accommodation passed the first inspection. As soon as they got the all clear there was a mad dash to go and meet up with their boyfriends in the NAAFI.

"We would have been here sooner but for Dotty Dean (Dot Dean), Mini-Minor (Millie Cooper) and Gracie Fields (Sally Fields)."

"What's betting we get an inspection now you are having one?" said the lads, "at least we know what to expect from our lot. You have got an unknown quantity to contend with."

"Yeah! If she is worse than old Butcher we will be in for a rough time."

At 06:30 reveille was sounded and the Corporals in charge of the dormitories entered and made sure everyone was awake. After breakfast everyone was kept busy to make sure there would be no faults found therefore getting in the good books of the inspecting officer. Viv and Flight Sergeant Roper arrived to give the accommodation clearance for inspection.

"Open all your windows and get some fresh air into the rooms," ordered Viv. "I don't want any nasty smells lingering about. What do you think Margaret, are you satisfied?"

"It looks alright to me; if the OC can find anything wrong it can only be about something and nothing."

"Fall in outside in your respective flights. March them off SNCOs."

At precisely 09:00 Squadron Leader Macfarlane arrived and was greeted with salutes and "Accommodation ready for inspection Ma'am."

"Good morning ladies let us hope it is a good inspection."

In most of the rooms she found beds not quite in-line otherwise the cleanliness and neatness was very good. The ablutions did not equal the room's standard. She found rings missing from most of the shower curtains and some of the curtains had not been washed down. The toilets needed more elbow grease and the woodwork needed more attention. There were hairs in the drain holes of the wash basins and dust on the water pipes beneath the wash basins.

"The ablutions have let them down Warrant. I cannot understand why they do not pay more attention to the hygiene in the ablutions, for young women that should be paramount. I will not punish them by having another Bull Night," she said with a smile. "Give them a good talking to about the hygiene angle they will remember it next time and remember to get those missing shower curtain rings replaced too. Thank you ladies I will see myself out, I will leave you to have a talk with the corporals to put them in the picture."

CHAPTER 23

In dribs and drabs from Sunday to Monday the JNCOs arrived at RAF March and were directed to their accommodation. As each read the notice board in the dormitory various ribald comments were passed especially from the Corporal Drill Instructors.

"It looks like we are back to recruit training."

"They are not going to treat me like a bloody sprog."

"We will probably be able to teach this lot a thing or two about instructing."

♦♦♦

Sergeant Wilcox and Corporal Thomas booked in at the orderly room and were given arrival chits. When they reported to Bill Barrett he shook hands with them and welcomed them to the training staff.

"I understand you will be needing a married quarter Sergeant. Have you any family?"

"Yes sir, a girl."

"Excuse me a minute". He phoned Roy Shaw. "Roy, Bill here."

"I know, you want a quarter for your new Sergeant Well I have beat you to it this time, he can take one over tomorrow at 10:00 hrs."

"Thank you Roy, once again I am in your debt."

"You are never out of it, my trouble is I am too soft hearted and generous."

"Well that is another step to you getting the Blue Peter Badge."

"Sod off Barrett I don't know why I tolerate you."

"I am pleased to tell you Sergeant Wilcox that you can take over a married quarter at 10:00hrs tomorrow. As soon as you take it over get yourself off to your family to hand over your present quarter and I want you back here on Monday morning."

"The Sergeant was gob smacked. "I just do not believe it but thank you sir the wife will be over the moon when I tell her."

"We look after our staff and that makes them contented and we are repaid by their loyalty." He then signed his arrival chit. "I will see you on Monday then Sergeant "

"Thanks again sir, I still can't believe it."

"Flight Sergeant Roper will you send someone to tell Corporal Deacon I want to see him?"

When he arrived he asked. "You wanted to see me sir?"

"Yes, I want to introduce you to Corporal Thomas our new instructor. He is moving into the bunk that you hold the key to. I want you to take him there now and put him in the picture of what I expect and get from my NCOs. Corporal Deacon here is in complete charge of all the Barrack Block which includes the Corporals and you will responsible to him regarding the airmen and dormitory which you will be in charge of. You are also assigned to Sergeant York's staff Corporal Deacon being the other Corporal and as from now you two will be working in harmony." He signed his arrival chit. "Off you go. Give him a hand to move in Corporal Deacon and report back to your flight after lunch."

♦♦♦

After the evening meal Corporal Ron Anders was approached by one or two of the class who had more to say than the rest and demanded to know what all the rubbish on the notice board was about.

"What it says is what you do and if you do not conform you will find yourself in trouble."

"But it is treating us like sprogs. We are NCOs we have not come here to do square bashing we teach that ourselves."

"Where do you teach it? This is the only station that teaches recruits, so why are you masquerading as Drill Instructors?"

They had no answer to that.

"I will tell you what this course is all about, it is to teach you how to become NCOs and from your attitudes your instructors have got a lot of teaching to do. I am in charge of your dormitory and don't you forget it and you *will* adhere to the instructions on the notice board. One more thing you should know, my rank is substantive and I am a damn sight senior to any of you lot."

At 08:45 the following morning Sergeant Farrow entered the dormitory and ordered, "Stand by your beds." He inspected each individual and his bed space passing comments of a minor nature. He came to one Corporal and asked. "Why are you not wearing your best uniform?"

"I did not bring it with me"

"I repeat, why are you not wearing your best uniform?"

"And I repeat I did not bring it with me."

"When the flight falls in outside you will fall in four paces to the left of it. Do you understand?"

"Yes"

"Yes what?"

"Yes I understand."

He carried on with his inspection and some instinct made him turn round quickly to find the previous Corporal sticking two fingers up at him.

"What is your name Corporal?

"Hammond"

"Corporal Hammond I am placing you under close arrest for gross insubordination. Corporal Anders carry on with the inspection then fall them in outside, when you have finished wait with them until Flight Sergeant Franks arrives. You two Corporals picking two who he had already inspected and you Corporal Hammond fall in outside. He then gave the order. "To the guardroom Quick March."

At the guardroom he reported to Flight Sergeant Tom Bridges of the station police. "I want this Corporal placed under close arrest Flight for gross insubordination to myself. Report back to the flight," he told the escort.

When he filled in the charge sheet Tom said. "Shoe laces, belt, tie, Off! Now empty your pockets." The contents were tabulated then placed in a bag. "Welcome to the Hotel Splendide, put him in suite one. Well done Jim, Joe will be proud of you. Hey-up speak of the devil," as Joe entered the guardroom smiling.

"Corporal Anders has just told me, he is standing by while Sergeant Graham dishes out the arrival chits. Is everything in order now Tom?"

"It is and you can both get back to try turning that lot into NCOs."

"Thanks for your help Flight," said a grateful Jim Farrow.

"No problem, I have more suites vacant when you want to fill them."

On returning to the flight Joe thanked Corporal Anders for his help. "Report back to W/O Barrett and tell him why you are late reporting in."

He then marched the flight on to the parade ground and made them open order so he could inspect them. "Stand at ease! Before we go any further I will introduce myself. I am Flight Sergeant Franks and my second in command who you have already met is Sergeant Farrow. I will now tell you why you are here. Command in its wisdom wants the newly promoted Corporals who besides being trade qualified need to be taught how to become qualified NCOs. Then suddenly Command discovered that the majority of Corporal Drill Instructors although competent in their trade are a big let down as NCOs. I will even go as far to say, from my experience that when we have had interviewees here to fill our vacant posts as NCOs they were found to be brain dead. Our job if it is at all possible is to turn you into NCOs the results of our findings will be sent to your parent unit. I understand some of you object to our character building programme commencing with our Barrack Room Rules. Take a step forward those of you who object." Five stepped forward. "You five will face our Station Commander Group Captain Pilling who will very likely relieve you of your acting rank then return you to your units as Leading Aircraftsmen."

He turned towards Jim Farrow to tell him to take their names and saw Jim grinning. He turned back to see what he was grinning at and saw that the five objectors had stepped back into line.

"Very well it is good to see we have a happy and contented flight. Front rank Atten...Shun. He began his inspection saying nothing until he had completed his inspection. "Who gave you permission to slash the peaks of your headgear?"

Corporal King who was obviously their leader replied. "It is the done thing with Drill Instructors Flight Sergeant."

"I asked who gave you permission to slash the peaks of your headgear?"

"Well no one did Flight Sergeant."

"Then why have you done so?"

"It gives us status over recruits."

"You are not instructing recruits are you?"

"No Flight Sergeant."

"Then who are you trying to impress, yourselves? You five will be marched to the clothing stores to purchase replacement headgear and count yourself lucky I am not taking disciplinary action against you for defacing the Queen's uniform. Now about this inspection, you are a disgrace to the rank you are holding. Brasses, shoes, sweat marked collars and uniforms that have not seen an iron for yonks. There is quite a catalogue of faults which you are going to rectify sharpish. The order of the day is...Sergeant Farrow will march you to each section where you will need a signature on your arrival chit. One of you will return the completed chits to the orderly room and the 'Famous Five' will be marched to clothing stores for replacement headgear. Tomorrow morning you will have a full kit inspection by Squadron Leader Cody. You have the rest of the day to get your kit up to scratch because from what I can see of it you will need all that time to prepare it. After the kit inspection you will put your gear away then change into working blue uniforms then fall in outside the Barrack Block. Have I made myself clear?"

He received a very week acknowledgement.

"I said, HAVE I MADE MYSELF CLEAR?"

"YES FLIGHT SERGEANT." they shouted in reply.

"March them off Sergeant."

Joe went to clothing stores and asked to see W/O Waters to tell him about the headgear. "Be prepared for more custom after their kit inspection tomorrow."

Derwent laughed. "We will try our best to oblige them Joe."

Joe then reported in to Bill Barrett and put him in the picture of the first morning's actions.

"You have got a good man in Jim Farrow, Joe and I think you are not going to be the flavour of the month. That reaction from the Corporal drill instructors I had foreseen, they think they are God's gift. I can't help laughing over the quick return to the ranks by the objectors; you certainly put the wind up them."

"Will you contact Wings Bill and ask him to do the kit inspection tomorrow morning?"

"He rang Marion and asked to speak with Wings.

"Hold the line sir."

"Squadron Leader Cody. Ah Mister Barrett what can I do for you?"

"Can you give Class 1 a kit inspection tomorrow morning sir?"

"I have a charge sheet on my desk relating to one of the Corporals What is going on Mister Barrett?"

Bill repeated the tale Joe had told him and the reason for the close arrest of Corporal Hammond.

"It appears those characters have to be re-educated and from what you tell me Flight Sergeant Franks and Sergeant Farrow are the right men to do it. Indeed I will inspect their kit Mister Barrett and they had better put on a damned good show or they will not know if they are on this Earth or Fuller's. Tell Flight Sergeant Franks I will take that charge tomorrow morning at 11:00hrs."

"Sir, it is getting better and better, thank you."

Bill repeated to Joe what Wings had said.

"Roll on tomorrow."

CHAPTER 24

There was pandemonium in the Barrack Room when they discovered nobody had an iron for pressing their uniforms. Irons were not a general issue it was up to the individual to provide his own. Nowhere could they borrow one because their reputation had already spread and nobody was daft enough to lend them one. They finally came up with the solution to club together to buy one from the NAAFI shop. Then the squabbles began accusing each other of hogging the iron. For a pressing cloth each man used a pillow case. By the time they had finished preparing their kit it was the small hours before some were climbing into bed.

At 09:00 Wings arrived at the Barrack Block to be received by Joe Franks.

"Good morning sir," greeted Joe as he saluted.

"Good morning Flight, are we ready to do battle?"

"As ready as we will ever be sir."

"Come on then let us go and make their day," he said with a glint in his eyes.

Jim Farrow was waiting at the room entrance. He saluted when Wings arrived.

"Good morning Sergeant Farrow, I am taking that charge at 11:00hrs. and I say, well done."

Joe entered the room and yelled. "Stand by your beds, Officer present. STAND... at... EASE you will come to attention when the officer approaches you then give him your rank, name and trade."

Wings approached the first man who came to attention obeying the instructions.

Wings looked him up and down. "Your brasses are clean but you left some residue of the polish on your tunic. Is this your full kit?"

"No sir."

"You were told to bring your full kit with you were you not?"

"Yes sir."

Wings looked down the two lines of men and said. "Raise your hand anyone who has a full kit."

Six hands were raised.

He went to the first one. "Corporal Jameson sir, MT Fitter."

"A good lay out. You can put it away."

"Corporal Norman sir, Store man."

"Practice more tying a decent knot in your tie. Put your kit away.

"Corporal Philips sir, Airframe Fitter."

A bit more work on you footwear would not go amiss Corporal. Put your kit away."

"Corporal Leonard sir, Officers Mess Steward."

"A good turnout Corporal. Put your kit away."

"Corporal Grace sir, Clerk."

"Trousers need only one crease in each leg Corporal not two, work on it. Put your kit away."

"Corporal Fielding sir, Armourer."

"More work is needed on your footwear. Put your kit away. You six Corporals after you have put your kit away make yourselves scarce to the NAAFI until you are called for."

"Corporal King sir, D.I."

"What is your excuse for not bringing a full kit when you were told to Corporal?"

"I did not think it was necessary for only one month sir."

"You wilfully disobeyed an order Corporal. Take his number, rank, name Sergeant Farrow."

"Corporal Smith sir, D.I."

"What is your excuse Corporal?"

"I too thought it was unnecessary for so short a period sir."

"Take his number, rank, name Sergeant."

Each Corporal D.I. made the same excuse, consequently Sergeant Farrow took their particulars with a view to disciplinary action being taken.

Wings then addressed the five.

"Your kit, what little there was of it, was pitiful and for you to have the effrontery to offer it for a kit inspection was an insult to me as the inspecting officer. What I cannot understand is you come from different units yet you all have the same excuse for not complying with the order that full kit was to be carried. I have a gut feeling there is a conspiracy between you five and when I find the ringleader I can assure him he will serve a long term in detention. I am personally taking disciplinary action against each one of you five.

Flight Sergeant Franks, a word please."

They left the room and Wings told Joe. "They are off this course as from now can you keep them occupied until I can sort this mess out?"

"There is one thing you can do sir which they will not enjoy. Can you square it with the Education Officer to give them some education lessons and tests because none of those six have passed the Education Test Part 2."

"Excellent! That is a good idea. Maybe that will help to knock the cockiness out of them. Keep 'em busy until you hear from me, I have to see to this charge now. Tell Sergeant Farrow to report to the Station Warrant Officer."

Joe returned to the Barrack Room and told the Corporals, "Put away your kit and change into your working blue uniforms, leaving your bed spaces neat and tidy, then fall in outside. You have five minutes starting from NOW!"

He made his way outside, smiling to himself and thinking 'they thought they could get away with it. I wonder if mothers ever get a letter from their wayward sons these days saying, 'Dear mum, sell the pig and buy me out.'

He stood and watched them hurrying to fall in on parade. He called them to attention and saw they were all wearing their peaked caps.

"Each one of you is improperly dressed, why are you not wearing your berets?"

"We did not bring them with us, Flight Sergeant," was the reply.

"Then we must rectify that oversight, don't you think?" I asked you a question. Don't you think we should rectify that oversight?"

"Yes Flight Sergeant."

"Then return to your Barrack Room, remove your cap badge, put it in your pocket for safe keeping then leave your peaked cap locked away in your locker. You have two minutes to be stood facing me bare headed starting from NOW! MOVE YOURSELVES," he roared.

Within the time they were stood to attention facing him.

"Now we will make our way to the clothing stores Quick March!"

At the clothing stores he left them stood at ease while he went inside to see WO Waters.

"I have the same five outside and this time can you fix them up with berets?"

"Bring them in one at a time and we will do our best."

Joe called the first man in. "When you get fixed up put your cap badge in and place the beret on your head then adjust it as per regulations in that mirror then send the next man in."

When they were all fixed up Joe thanked Derwent. "I will go and give them a bit of exercise now."

He marched them to the parade ground and stood them at ease while he went into the NAAFI to bring out the six Corporals who had already changed into their working blue uniforms. When they fell in on the left of the other five he called Corporal King to his side.

"I want you to assume this is a flight of raw recruits and you are to teach them basic drill movements and you have ten minutes to show me your technique."

♦♦♦

Meanwhile Corporal Hammond was facing Squadron Leader Cody and listening to the evidence given by Sergeant Farrow. When the Sergeant had concluded his evidence the Corporal was asked if he had any questions to ask Sergeant Farrow.

"No sir, whatever I say would be ignored because the verdict is already cut and dried."

"So how do you plead, guilty or not guilty?"

"Guilty"

"I am remanding you to appear before the Station Commander to receive his verdict. You will remain under close arrest until such time as the Station Commander wishes to see you. Do you understand Corporal?"

"Of course I understand do you think I am thick or summat?"

"March him back to the guardroom Mister Miller."

"Marion, will you get me Helen Fraser on the line please?"

"You are through sir."

"Helen, Squadron Leader Cody here can you get me an interview with the CO. please? It concerns a charge I have just taken."

After a short wait Helen replied. "You can come right away sir."

When he entered Helen's office she told him to go straight in.

"Come in Bill," said the CO. in reply to the salute. "What's the problem?"

Bill told him the tale. "I had no option but to remand him to you sir."

"You did right Bill he sounds to be a nasty bit of work. You say he is one of the Corporal Drill Instructors. No wonder the AOC wants a school for Junior NCOs. Bill then told him the story concerning the Corporal Drill instructors and the kit inspection.

"I am taking disciplinary action against the remaining five, sir."

CHAPTER 25

On the Parade Ground Corporal King was putting the flight through the basic drill moves. Most of the faults came from the six tradesmen and King's temper had a short fuse so much so he resorted to swearing at the culprits when his orders were not carried out to his satisfaction.

Before things got out of hand Joe called. "That is enough Corporal King your time is up," Rejoin the flight."

Each one of the drill instructors was given ten minutes to show their skill. Two out of the five were good instructors the other three were prone to bullying if things did not go right.

"That is enough for today," Joe told them. "Raise your hand the ones who have completed and passed Part 2 education test." Six hands were raised belonging to the tradesmen. "Sergeant Farrow will be in charge of you tomorrow. You five will spend the day being educated and will fall in at 08:50 and I will take you to school via the Lollypop Lady. Make sure you are equipped with a pen of sorts, I will check to see if you have got one I don't want to hear the excuse I did not bring one because I thought it was not necessary for one month." That quip started the six Corporals laughing but only scowls from the Famous Five. "At 08:40 you will stand by your beds for the daily inspection. Flight, Atten…Shun, Dis…Miss!"

Back in their Barrack Room arguments began among the Famous Five blaming King for getting them disciplined and probably being stripped of their rank by the CO.

"If that happens God help you Kingy," was the threat.

♦♦♦

Wings was summoned to the Wingco's office.

"I understand you are with the CO. at 10:00hrs with a charge Bill, I would like you to make yourself available for 11:00hrs? I want to take your charges can you give me a brief on what transpired."

Wings told him everything.

"What do they hope to gain with this so called Macho style? It is apparently only found in the junior NCOs of drill instructors. There is no place for that kind of imbecilic behaviour in this modern Air Force more so when they have raw recruits at their mercy."

"I have a gut feeling that Corporal King is the ringleader sir and used his seniority and bullying tactics to force the others to back him up."

"Right-ho Bill I will hear what they have to say for themselves, see you at 11:00."

♦♦♦

"You have already pleaded guilty to the charges that have been brought against you Corporal Hammond. Do you wish to change your plea?" the Station Commander asked.

"No sir"

"Then I will ask you again Corporal Hammond, do you plead guilty or not guilty?"

"Guilty"

"How you were ever accepted to train recruits beggars belief I have a feeling you are trying to work your ticket. Am I right in my assumption?"

"Do you think I am daft enough to admit that?"

"I thought so. With the authority of the Air Officer Commanding I then Sentence you to be reduced to the rank of Leading Aircraftsman and to serve 28 days in detention and the title Drill instructor will be erased from your records. March him back to his cell Mister Miller."

"I can do that standing on my head," he yelled, as he was being marched out.

"March him back in Mister Miller," called the CO.

"I am charging you Lac Hammond with gross insubordination to a senior officer, namely myself. I hereby sentence you to 28 days detention to run consecutively with your previous sentence."

That shook Hammond to the core and knocked the cockiness out of him.

"That will give you extra time to decide how you are going to carry out that sentence. March him back to his cell Mister Miller."

♦♦♦

Joe went to see Sergeant Arthur Bell in Education and apologised for wanting the Famous Five excused from class. "They have a date with the Wingco' at 11:00 Arthur for being naughty boys."

Arthur laughed. "I am not surprised Bill I would have my work cut out trying to teach them anything. I just hope this is the last time I will see them."

"I'll see what I can do for you Arthur. Fall in outside and make it snappy the headmaster wants to see you."

He left Arthur having a good laugh at him as he marched them to the SWO's office and handed them over saying. "These five have been recommended to be expelled from school sir and have now to see the headmaster."

"I will want you Joe to stay outside to keep your eyes on the rest while I march them in one at a time with the escort."

George addressed the five. "Leave your headgear here and you should know the ropes by now and I want it done smartly." He lined them up in the order they were to appear before the Wingco'.

"Excuse me sir," one of them asked, "What happened to Corporal Hammond?"

"He was reduced to LAC and 56 days inside!"

Shock appeared on their faces.

A look of unconcern showed on Corporal King's face although inwardly he felt like he wanted to go to the toilet.

George marched them to the CO's office and waited for the command to march the first man in. When the order came Corporal Smith was marched in first.

He acknowledged his number, rank and name.

"Squadron Leader Cody will now give his evidence."

On its conclusion Smith was asked if he wanted to question the Squadron Leader

"No sir"

"Do you want to present any witnesses on your behalf?"

"No sir"

"What have you got to say for yourself?"

"We were misled sir."

"Cpl, you are here to speak for yourself only."

"Sorry sir. I was misled by Corporal King who used his seniority to bully me into following his example."

"In what respect Cpl?"

"I did bring my full kit with me sir but was persuaded to hide most of it."

"Where and for what reason?"

"Inside the spare lockers in our room, sir. Corporal King said that we were too senior as Corporals to be treated like bloody little sprogs and to follow my example if you know what is good for you."

"I am remanding you for the Station Commander. March him out Mister Miller and keep him separate from the others."

The next three more or less told the same story and were also remanded for the Station Commander.

After the preliminaries Corporal King was told to explain his behaviour commencing with his lack of kit.

"When I was chosen to attend this course I thought well it is only for a month and I would not need it because I was sure there would be no 'Bull' and if there was we would..." He was stopped at that point.

"You are here to state your case Corporal not others. I want to hear 'I' and not 'we'. Do I make myself clear?"

"Yes sir, sorry sir."

He continued. "I would be exempt with being a senior Cpl and Drill Instructor."

"So you expected preferential treatment."

"In a manner of speaking yes sir."

"Corporal this course has nothing to do with your trade it is a Junior NCO course to train you to become NCOs and from what I can gather neither you nor your compatriots have reached that standard. In fact Corporal as an NCO you are a complete waste of time. You think because you have two protection stripes on your arm and that is all they are and strut around with slashed peaks imitating guardsmen and frightening the hell out of recruits that is being an NCO. I have news for you Corporal never in this wide world will you ever make the grade as an NCO.I am remanding you for the Station Commander. March him out Mister Miller."

The five were then marched to the SWO's office to retrieve their head gear.

Flight Sergeant Roberts answered the ringing phone. "Yes sir he is still here he mouthed the word Wingco'."

"W/O Miller speaking, yes sir I still have them here, will do sir."

He went outside and told the five to remove their headgear.

"You are to see the Station Commander in half an hour. Stand easy but if I hear you talking I will take you for a few laps round the parade ground at the double. Do you read me?"

"Yes sir," they replied nervously thinking about what will be in store for them when they come before the CO.

When the time came for the Famous Five to face the music they were not very happy to do so. George halted them at the CO's door and waited for the command to march them in.

The first four were taken in one at a time and each one pleaded guilty to the charges.

The CO. told each one. "Because you gave the name of the ringleader and I welcomed that, I shall lessen your punishment. With the authority of the Air Officer Commanding you are to be demoted to the rank of Leading Aircraftsman and title of Drill Instructor will be erased from your records. You will now be returned to your unit and have escaped being sent to detention by the skin of your teeth, remember that."

Corporal King was marched in, the charges were read out to him and the CO. asked. "How do you plead, Guilty or not Guilty?"

"Guilty"

"I have sifted through your testimony and come to the conclusion you have been telling a pack of lies. Your kit which you said you had not brought with you has been found along with the rest of your little group's, it has now been placed on your beds. As the senior Corporal you used a bullying technique with threats to force the other Corporals to join your evil scheme which puts you in the role of ringleader. You played a dangerous game and lost, not only that but your rank and liberty too. With the authority of the Air Office Commanding you are to be reduced in rank to Leading Aircraftsman and sentenced to 28 days detention. After serving your sentence you will be dishonourably discharged from the Royal Air Force. Until you are transported to your place of detention you will stay under close arrest. March him out Mister Miller."

"Well, well, well, what have we here sir," asked Flight Sergeant Bridges of the Station Police. "Another guest for the Hotel Splendide? We have just lost one guest who said he preferred the 'Holiday Camp'. Empty your pockets and when I have tabulated them you will check that I have missed nothing out then sign here to that effect. Off with your tie, belt and shoelaces. Put him in suite one," he ordered his police Corporal "I think that is our guests favourite it must be a comfortable room."

"What's the gen on him George?"

“He is an evil little sod.” He told him what had happened. “You would have had five guests but the other four shopped him and just got demoted to LAC. I think they did right otherwise they would have ended up in the ‘Holiday Camp’ as well. Looks like our camp tailor is going to be busy, make sure his tailoring is done Tom.”

♦♦♦

Back in the Barrack Room Joe was organising the remaining four by making them remove the Corporal chevrons from their uniforms. “I want two volunteers,” he pointed to two of the airmen.

“You and you pick up Kings’ kit and come with me to the guardroom. I have brought King’s kit Tom for him to remove his clothing to be sent to the tailor and I will also need his uniform blouse. You two go into the next room out of sight.”

King was brought out and told to remove the clothing for tailoring and essentials for an overnight stay.

“Right you two, back to the Block with this lot.” You two, pointing to the remaining airmen in the barrack room will remove the chevrons from Kings’ uniforms, you two sit this one out, when you all have finished fall in outside.”

“Excuse me Flight Sergeant, but we will be improperly dressed,” suggested one airman.

“Has the fall in grace from such a high and exalted rank made you brain damaged? You have two choices, number one, wear your uniform blouse going and return in shirt sleeve order. Number two, shirt sleeve order both ways. Any more questions?”

Two of the airmen said. “I am wearing braces Flight Sergeant.”

“What are the rest of you wearing to stop your trousers from falling round your ankles?”

“Belts, Flight Sergeant.”

“Have you two been issued with belts?”

“Yes Flight Sergeant.”

“Then will somebody show these two Brains of Britain how to transfer from braces to belts? No wonder you never qualified as technicians. So you have decided to wear your uniform blouses with no rank of any kind on the sleeves. With the mentality of some of you that is how it should stay. Come on fall in outside and let us get back here as quick as we can before anybody sees us.” God help us if the next batch we get is as intellectual as this lot he said to himself.

On their return Joe addressed them. “You will pick up your uniforms at 16:00hrs. In the meantime you will busy yourselves making this room clean enough to live in and I will be back at that time to inspect it and take you to collect your uniforms. Carry on.”

CHAPTER 26

Both Wing Commander Hopwood and Squadron Leader Cody were summoned to the Station Commander's Office.

"We got ourselves in a bit of a pickle when we got rid of those seven undesirables. Fair enough it was justified but that does not alter the fact we have lost half of the JNCOs class. I would like your views on if it is going to be viable to continue with it and what is to say that the next batch of Corporal Drill Instructors is going to be any different to this last lot?"

"There should only be a handful of them left sir and I think it would do the service good if we assessed the remainder. If they failed our assessment we will rid the service of as you call them, undesirables. I say go ahead and have them report here and as before with full kit."

"You have a good point there John but where do we draw any replacements from if need be?"

"If it turns out we have to get rid of the remaining Corporal D.I.s then we scrap the JNCO course and turn it into a Drill Instructor School as it used to be then we can train our own replacements sir."

"I think that would be the more sensible thing to do what do you think Bill?"

"I think it a great idea sir I have a gut feeling the remainder of the Corporal D.I.s will be in a similar category to this first batch. Remember sir we did get rid of five as unsuitable when we interviewed them for two replacements and I am sure they will turn up here again. I suggest we weed out these characters while we have the chance sir."

"I am in full agreement with what you both tell me, I will go to Command HQ to put the AOC in the picture and hear what he says."

The CO. was ushered into the AOC's office by the aide-de camp. He saluted as the AOC rose to shake him by the hand in welcome.

"Come and sit down Eric, it is good to see you." They chatted about their families then Eric told of the latest news from RAF March.

"That JNCO School is not proving to be a success is it Eric? Where have we gone wrong?"

"We have not gone wrong Charles it is due to bad training in the past. The emphasis has been solely on drill and nothing else consequently when the Corporal chevrons were handed out the recipients suddenly fancied themselves as RSM Brittain and could not wait to show off their new given power to recruits which was obviously never checked. The closing down of the two training establishments has shown up the faults in the training methods along with bad management and we are left to pick up the pieces."

"You are so right Eric thank God we have RAF March where sanity prevails. Look, shall we discus it further over lunch? I don't know about you but I am ready for something to eat."

At lunch the subject was never mentioned they chatted about everything but that.

"Have you settled down here Charles?"

"Surprisingly yes, I thought when the job was handed over to me I would be shouting for help I was really pleased with myself by getting to grips with it much easier than I thought. I have been helped along the way by a few good officers; unfortunately there are a few whose cards I have already marked ready for me showing them the exit sign. Come on then let us go and have a coffee in my personal lounge we can talk in private there."

When the steward arrived with coffee Charles told him. "I do not want to be disturbed unless there is an emergency."

"Now Eric let us see if we can sort your problem out."

Eric told him what Hopwood had suggested. "I am inclined to agree with him. If we can return the Corporal tradesmen back to their units then bring the remainder of the Corporal Drill Instructors to RAF March we could sort the wheat from the chaff if that is at all possible and if they do not meet our criteria they will be demoted and returned to their parent units. If you remember Charles while you were CO at March five were rejected as unsuitable and as WO Barrett put it, 'they were brain dead'. So there cannot be many more to assess. Once they are sorted out Drill Instructing could be readmitted to the choice of trades. If there is a good response to that we could perhaps re-open a Drill Instructors school."

"I must say Eric you have certainly put up a very good option to the present situation because it looks like that one is not going to get off the ground. The beggar of it is we *do* need back-ups that *is* essential and we must try every avenue of possibilities and personally I cannot better your suggestion. Let me sleep on it and I will tell you tomorrow on what I have decided. How is Squadron Leader Macfarlane getting on with the staff, is she fitting in?"

"Very much so, she has made her mark and is earning their respect." He then told Charles about the send-off W/O Butcher got from the station personnel; it was very emotional as you can well imagine, she is now honeymooning in the Caribbean."

"What about our friend W/O Barrett, what has he been up to?"

"Where the JNCO School is concerned he has kept very much in the background and left it in the hands of Flight Sergeant Franks and Sergeant Farrow. He certainly knows how to pick his men because they have done an excellent job. Flight Sergeant Franks especially, he is a stickler for discipline and I must give him credit it is the right kind of discipline. He has the qualities of the kind you and I appreciate. in other words he is a good understudy to WO Barrett."

"Ah ha. You have given me the answer Eric. That is the reason he wanted him promoted, cant' you see? He is repeating what he did for W/O Anderson he is grooming him to take his place for when the time comes for his retirement." He stood up and held out his hand to Eric. "I am sorry I must leave you now Eric I have work to do and also some thinking about your problem. It has been grand to see and speak with you again, give our best wishes to your wife and I hope to see you again before too long."

The following day Wing Commander Hopwood and Squadron Leader Cody were summoned to the Station Commander's Office.

"Good news gentlemen, the AOC has accepted our recommendations to scrap the JNCO's course and revert back to a Drill Instructors course."

That news brought smiles of satisfaction to the two faces.

"But before that comes into effect we will be receiving the last of the Corporal Drill Instructors for a JNCO course and it is predicted they will fail it and here is what we have to do. Return the Corporal tradesmen to their respective units as from now and instruct the Education Section to re-enter in the choice of trades list for the recruits' benefit, 'Drill Instructors male/female'. The AOC has already told Records Office of our plans, will you put W/O Barrett in the picture John?"

"Do you think sir there may be a chance of re-opening one of the training schools?" asked Wings.

"The AOC has thought of that and if there is a good response of applicants for Drill Instructing he will take the message to the top. It will be our job to convince the recruits that the days of the slashed peaked brigade is now a thing of the past and to become a Corporal Instructor you will be taught how to become a respected NCO. So gentlemen there will be some extra classroom lectures for the recruits who will be ready to choose a trade of their choice. If we want another recruit training establishment we will have to work damned hard for it. The AOC has sent a signal to all Training Command Stations stating that the course for training Drill Instructors has now been re-opened."

Bill Barrett was called to see the Wingco'.

"Is there anything exciting to report, Barbara?" he asked the Wingco's PA.

"I have heard nothing Bill and if I had I would not tell you."

"I was only teasing Barbara."

"Come on I will take you in then you can tell *me* what is going on."

"That would be more than my job is worth."

"Daft beggar," was her reply.

"W/O Barrett sir."

"Come in and sit down Mister Barrett," acknowledging Bill's salute. "There has been a change of plan concerning the JNCOs' course. As from now the remaining Corporals are to be returned to their parent units. It has been sanctioned by the AOC to change it to a Drill Instructors School once the remaining Corporal D.I's have been assessed by you. There are only a few of them left and it is thought you may be able to sort them out leaving us free to adopt the Drill Instructor course. I understand you have previously categorised five of them as brain dead and if the rest fall into that category it will be in our favour."

"I get your drift sir at last we could be heading in the right direction.

"The Education Section will be instructed to place on the choice of trades list for the recruits, Drill Instructor male/female. Also, you are to provide lectures to give the recruits who are ready to pick a trade, the insight to what is required to become a good NCO besides becoming an

Instructor. Install in them Mister Barrett the bad image of the slashed peak strutting bully has gone to be replaced by honest discipline. What are your thoughts Mister Barrett?"

"We here are in the right place where we hopefully can get the recruits interested in becoming a Drill Instructor. In the past we have had some very bad incidents concerning bullying attitudes from both junior and senior NCOs and those experiences will take a long time to heal. We have to convince them that bad image has gone for good and I will do my utmost to ensure my staff does just that sir."

"You cannot do more than that Mister Barrett; I shall watch your results with interest. By the way, I am impressed with your choice of Flight Sergeant Franks and Corporal Farrow."

♦♦♦

Bill carried on from there to the orderly room to have a word with Roy Shaw.

"Before you ask they are to report here in two days time and there are ten of them."

"That is what I call efficiency of the highest level Roy."

"Of course it is and stop your creeping you are still not getting a brew."

"Then I will take my custom elsewhere."

"I will have you blacklisted!"

"Alright then you are not Mister Efficiency, otherwise you would have given me the list of names."

"I was saving those to hear your reaction. How do these strike you for starters? Corporals Benson, Young, Norton, Ingham, Robinson. You might say are the Return of the Prodigals."

"It is what I expected Roy little do they know they will be coming to meet their Armageddon."

"Do you mean they have to do battle with Corporal Alice Springs? The very mention of her name will have them pleading to be locked away for safety."

"Who are the other five?"

"Corporals Fletcher, Robertson, Williams, Green, and Croft."

"Give me a list of that five Roy I will ask my Corporals if they know them and also we want to get the remaining six away before that lot come in."

"They are already going round with their clearance chits, everything is organised as always in my domain."

"Thank you Roy I must leave you wallowing in your self glory, I need some fresh air."

"The next time you are here in SHQ do me the favour of carry on walking past my door."

♦♦♦

Back in his office he asked Joe and Jim to come in for a chat.

"We have that brain dead five coming back to be assessed Joe."

"That will not be difficult, have you the names of the others?"

"There are only five more, do you know any of these Jim?" as he showed him the list."

"I certainly do, they are on a par with the other idiots."

Bill laughed. "Then it looks like their visit is going to be short but not very sweet. I want a word with all NCOs after training today. Go round the flights and notify everybody Jim."

When they all had assembled in the ops' room Bill addressed them.

"I want to put you all in the picture of some changes which concern us all. You know the NCO school idea has never got off the ground so it has been decided to scrap it; instead we are to try and establish another Drill Instructors course. There are reasons for that, the main one being we have no reserve of instructors with the proper NCO qualifications for a back up when we need replacements to our staff. To rectify that is why a Drill Instructors course is needed but where are we to get the trainees from? From the recruits of course and that is where every one of you comes in. You are required to try and make the recruits interested, talk to them by telling them of all the good points and how rewarding to see the end product at the end of training. Reassure them that the days of the bullies are over. At the end of the day the more trainees we can get to opt' for the course the more chance we will have of re-opening one of the training establishments that was closed down. You can tell them they will do their training here at RAF March. Incidentally the course will also be open to any airman or airwoman that wants to re-muster from their present trade. Has anyone got a question?"

"When does the first course start sir?" "As soon as we get enough applicants, then once that gets under way we hope they will snowball."

"How long will the course last sir?"

"That has not been decided yet because training to a high standard of NCO efficiency will be incorporated in the course."

"From our point of view" said Sergeant (w) Dean, who will instruct the airwomen on the course? Will you mix the trainees or will they be in separate flights?"

"That too has to be discussed I suppose it will depend on the number of airwomen who want to join the course. If there are just a few they will most likely be held in transit to wait for a full flight to be formed, or as you said, join ranks with the airmen. Do not take that as gospel it is just my assumption. All your points will be ironed out when the subject comes up for discussion."

"What happens if any of us Corporals do not meet your criteria sir?"

"If you did not meet my criteria you would not be on my staff but that is not to say you are not under constant surveillance. Thankfully you are a damned good staff and I foresee no problems there. If that is all away you go. No, hold on a minute. As from now the daily Barrack Room inspection stops."

That was greeted by cheers.

"I thought that might please you but remember it can always be reintroduced. Away you go and don't be late for prayers in the morning."

"No Father Barrett," was the reply as they left laughing.

"Roy, its Bill here. I showed that list to Jim Farrow and he classed them in the same mould as the other idiots. I have been thinking could we give that particular five their first test by having your Corporal Springs take their particulars when they book in.? You what? You have been thinking on those very same lines yourself, what do they say about great minds? What do you mean who is the other one besides yourself? Sorry Roy I will have to hang up I have no time for quizzes. Yes Roy I am sodding off."

CHAPTER 27

Roy Shaw called Corporal Springs into his office. "Do you remember those two Corporals you made to face the wall like naughty children?"

"I certainly do sir."

"Well they will be visiting us again along with eight more who are thought to be of a similar mentality. Would you agree to put yourself in the same position when they book in here?" He told her it was to be their first test. "Sergeant Graham and Corporal Barton will be in my office and we will be keeping a watchful eye on their behaviour. If they start acting up give them their arrival chit then send them round to my office."

"That is no problem sir I think the idea to test them is a good one."

"If more than two come in at any one time ask them to wait outside. Thank you Corporal "

Very soon two slashed peaks and four highly bulled up boots entered the orderly room. A quick look round to see what staff was present then a thump on the counter. "Let's have some service in this dump."

Alice Springs approached the counter and asked. "Was that necessary?"

"Well somebody had to wake you lot up."

"What is your name?" asked Alice.

"Give us a kiss and I'll tell you." said big mouth.

"I would not give the likes of you the time of day, now I want your name!"

He turned to his partner. "You know David I think she likes me."

"Like a cat likes mange." Alice retorted. She then asked the other Corporal for his name.

"Corporal Robertson."

"Here is your temporary arrival chit."

"What about mine?" asked big mouth.

"You give me your name and I will give you your chit."

"Then I will jump over this counter and get it myself," he said with much bravado.

"Then you will end up in Sick Quarters," warned Alice.

He let out a guffaw and asked. “Who is going to stop me,” as he leaped onto the counter only to receive Alice’s fist in his face knocking him backwards off the counter to the floor with blood from his nose dripping on to his uniform. He leapt to his feet mouthing obscenities at Alice and as he reached forward to grab her she quickly lifted the counter flap and smashed it on his outstretched arm making him scream with pain.

At this point Roy and Graham rushed through the door and grabbed hold of him.

“I am placing you under close arrest for attempting to physically assault Corporal Spings.”

“What is his name?” Roy asked Corporal Robertson.

“Corporal Fletcher, sir.”

“Sergeant Graham phone SSQ then Flight Sergeant Bridges asking him to send over a police escort.”

When the Sergeant Medic arrived he attended to Fletcher’s face. “Walk into a door Cpl?”

“What do you think? Ouch that hurt,” he complained after the medic put a little extra pressure on his nose.

“I asked you a straight forward question Corporal ”

“Not wanting more pain he answered. “That bloody crazy WRAF Corporal did it.”

“What about the arm then?”

“She did that too, is it broken? And what about my nose?”

“No just bruised, so is your nose, but the M.O. will have to examine it. The Corporal must have pulled her punches not wanting to hurt you but you are going to have ‘Two Lovely Black Eyes’, I notice she has not a mark on her, was she too big an opponent for you?”

“Ha bloody ha, she caught me off my balance that’s all.”

“Don’t you mean she knocked you off the counter,” added Roy. “Anyway here come your escorts,” as two Station Police Corporals entered.

“Escort him to sick quarters,” Roy instructed, “then to the guardroom where I will be entering him on the charge sheet.”

By this time the corridor had filled up with the rest of the Corporals waiting to book in.

“Back to normal,” Roy told his staff. He then addressed the waiting Corporals “You will book in two at a time and the rest of you will remain quiet until it is your turn.”

When Roy re-entered the orderly room he asked Corporal Springs if she was alright and could carry on.

“No problem sir I am fine.”

“Well you had the cavalry to back you up. Take good care of her Sergeant Graham she is worth her weight in gold. I am now off to the guard room if anyone wants me then I will be reporting to the Squadron Leader ”

At the guardroom he told Flight Sergeant Tom Bridges what had happened.

"It sounds as if another Corporal is going to bite the dust Roy; I would have given anything to have witnessed it, that young lass is certainly not one to be trifled with that's for sure. Hey up, here comes the horizontal champ'. Right Corporal I want you to empty your pockets, I will list them and you will sign that all is correct. Now off with your belt, tie and shoe laces. Warrant Officer Shaw!"

Roy addressed the Corporal "Corporal Fletcher I am charging you with attempted assault and using obscene language to Corporal Springs and you are being placed in close arrest to await your charge being taken."

He let out a stream of obscenities at Roy then turned on Tom bridges with. "And you can shove your crummy little cell where monkeys shove bad nuts."

"Tom replied. "Now that was very naughty of you Corporal because you have missed out on being shown into Suite One a big favourite with my guests. You have now talked yourself into Cell three where all naughty boys are put. Bang him up Staff," he ordered one of his police corporals. "That show of bravado means he will want to change his underpants soon. Roy."

"Thanks Tom I had better go and report to Wings now."

Wings was not pleased when Roy reported the incident.

"What on earth has got into these chaps Mister Shaw? It appears to be endemic with Corporal Drill Instructors. Surely it could not have been like this when the other two training establishments were operational or was it bad management that turned a blind eye to this kind of behaviour? I totally agree with W/O Barrett it is time these people were sorted out once and for all. Now we have them here it is up to us to do just that and your Corporal Springs has set the ball rolling with a vengeance, tell her from me, well done and thanks. Mister Shaw I will take the charge tomorrow at 10:00hrs. Have Corporal Springs made available."

"Very good, sir."

After Roy had left Wings rang the SWO. "Mister Miller I will be taking a charge concerning a Corporal Fletcher, who is in close arrest, at 10:00hrs tomorrow."

George rang Tom Bridges. "Tom, who is this Corporal Fletcher you are playing nursemaid to? Wings is taking his charge tomorrow at 10:00hrs."

Tom explained the incident.

"Well can you credit it? And she is only a slip of a lass too. I am looking forward to seeing her handiwork. Aye it does look like Joe Franks has got his hands full again, but who better to sort them out? Cheers Tom."

There were no further incidents in the orderly room the message had got through to the macho men, even Ingham and Robinson the bad boys from the last time were very subdued when booking in.

As each Corporal reported to Bill Barrett he warned them of their conduct. "There are regulations concerning you pinned to the notice board in your Barrack Room, you will adhere to its instructions. Corporal Anders is the NCO in charge of your room and you will toe his line."

They had already read the notice board instructions when they moved into the room with similar reactions to the previous Corporal D.I.s.

"I am a qualified D.I. not a flaming sprog.

"This is going back to recruit training and we are the bloody recruits."

"Why are we here anyway we can teach this lot a thing or two about drill."

"If they want co-operation from me they will have to squeeze it out."

And so it went on each trying to outdo the other with the best excuse for not complying.

When Corporal Anders introduced himself he told them. "You are required to carry out the instructions on the notice board to the letter. Also each and every morning bed packs will be made up and laid out as per diagram on the notice board. At 08:45hrs. each morning you will stand by your beds for the SNCO's inspection."

That statement caused a right uproar of what they would and would not do.

When it quietened down Corporal Anders continued. "You will have no excuse for not complying because I have given you the instructions verbally and if you have any ideas concerning me and my rank I am senior to any of you lot and *my* rank is not acting. I will give you one bit of advice, if you have not got an electric iron you should see about getting one for you are certainly going to need one, enjoy your course."

At 08:45hrs. the following morning Sergeant Farrow entered the dormitory to see no bed packs were made up and all the Corporals were dressed in their working blue uniforms and wearing their slashed peaked hats.

He asked each one. "Why is your bed pack not made up and why are you not wearing your best blue uniform in accordance with the orders on the notice board?"

Each one gave the obviously rehearsed reply. "Because we are NCOs and not raw recruits."

"Do you realise you are laying yourselves wide open to disciplinary action?

"Yes Sergeant."

"He ordered them to stand at ease then waited the arrival of Flight Sergeant Franks.

When Joe arrived he saw Jim in the doorway and asked. "Why are these Corporals not on parade?"

Looking into the room he saw the reason why.

"They say they are NCOs and not raw recruits."

Joe approached the first Corporal "I know you don't I?"

"Yes Flight."

"I said I know you, don't I? AND STAND TO ATTENTION WHEN YOU SPEAK TO ME!"

"Yes Flight Sergeant."

"That is more like it. Your name?"

"Corporal Benson Flight Sergeant."

"I have just cause to remember you and the other four. Now tell me Acting Corporal Benson why you have not complied with my orders pinned up clearly enough to read, on that notice board?"

"We...."

"Are you the spokesman for this lot? Because I asked you for your reason."

"No Flight Sergeant we have not got a spokesman."

"Well I suggest you nominate one to speak for you all because each one answered Sergeant Farrow like a bloody parrot, word perfect. I shall now leave this room for just two minutes and in that time you *will* elect a spokesman." When he withdrew he told Jim to go and bring Wings, stress that it is very important. You can report back to WO Barrett Corporal Anders, tell him I will report in when this lot has been sorted out. You will earn a pint or two from your mates telling them about this incident." Joe then waited until Wings arrived.

"This sounds very serious Flight; at what stage are you at?"

"Choosing a spokesman sir."

"Shall we go and see if they have done just that?"

Joe entered ahead of Wings and called them to attention.

"Have you chosen your spokesman?" asked Joe.

"Yes Flight Sergeant it is me," answered Corporal Benson.

"You have the temerity to call yourself an NCO. When an officer is present you answer sir, or was that not taught you at recruit training?"

"Sorry sir"

"Now let us hear what you have to say Mister Spokesman."

"We have come to the conclusion sir that we have made a very grave mistake in not conforming to your orders. Our reactions were made in the heat of the moment when we surmised we were to be treated like raw recruits."

Wings took over. "You mean you have panicked because you now realise that your actions are akin to mutiny and that could put you away for many years in prison not a 'Glass House'. You have been very foolish and you are not going to get off Scot free. Each one of you will be charged with wilful disobedience in not complying with orders given and I see each one of you is sporting a slashed peaked hat. You will also be charged with defacing the Queen's uniform. Do you understand the charges?"

As one they all answered "YES SIR" with relief showing on their faces.

"Flight Sergeant, march this lot to the Clothing Store I want to see them wearing proper issue headgear for my kit inspection."

Outside the room Wings spoke to Joe and Jim. "It could not have been better they have done us a favour by shooting themselves in the foot. Unfortunately we cannot put them under close arrest because of the lack of cell space. Give them a stern warning Flight that they had better be on their best behaviour or they will get the book thrown at them. Take all their particulars and fill in the charge sheets I will have a word with the Wingco' because he will have to take the charges. Speaking of charges I have one coming up in a few minutes."

When they returned to the room bed packs had been made up. "I hope you are counting yourselves very lucky; the thoughts of being on a chain gang would not go down very well. Normally you would have been placed under close arrest but we have not the cells to accommodate you all. The Squadron Leader has kindly put you on your honour to be on your best behaviour but remember this, we do still have two empty cells begging to be occupied, make sure none of you fill them. You know the charges so give your details to Sergeant Farrow. Tomorrow morning you will have a kit inspection make sure it is up to scratch and this room squeaky clean."

♦♦♦

Corporal Fletcher appeared before Wings. After evidence had been given by Corporal (w)Springs and W/O Shaw Fletcher was asked if he wanted to question them to which he replied. "No sir"

"Do you want anyone to speak on your behalf?"

"No sir"

"Corporal Fletcher do you plead guilty or not guilty?"

"Guilty "

"Corporal Fletcher I remand you to the Station Commander for sentencing and you will remain in close arrest until you are called to see the Station Commander. March him out Mister Miller."

At 11:00hrs. Corporal Fletcher was stood facing the Station Commander.

"You have already pleaded guilty to the charges but I will ask you once more, do you plead guilty or not guilty to the charges brought against you?"

"Guilty."

"On the authority of the Air Officer Commanding you are to be reduced in rank to Leading Aircraftsman and sentenced to fifty six days detention. After serving your sentence you will be dishonourably discharged from the Royal Air Force. March him out Mister Miller."

And so followed the pattern of the last course, the remaining Corporals were reduced in rank and returned to their parent units with Drill Instructor erased from their records.

Bill Barrett was very pleased with the outcome it meant that he could now train airmen to become Drill Instructors and NCOs. The positive results he was also getting from recruits who were choosing to become Drill Instructors was very encouraging.

CHAPTER 28

Bill Barrett asked Flight Sergeant Roper his second in command. "Can you remember the three Corporals we had to lose due to the big change over what are their names?"

"Olive Branch, Marjorie Dawes and Carol Liner. Why do you ask Bill?"

"I am thinking about the Drill Instructor School we hope to get off the ground now we have got rid of that load of nut cases. From the feed backs the airmen's interest is very encouraging thanks to the efforts the staff are putting in to promote it but the response from the airwomen is not. What I am planning is for a Sergeant (w) with two Cpl (w) s. who are competent to teach to Drill Instructor level, this is between you and me Margaret. I would like to give Dot Dean and her team the chance to fill that slot and Cpl (w) James with promotion and two of our old Corporals to replace Dot and her team and one to replace Corporal James that takes care of the three we had to let go."

Margaret answered the ringing phone. "Yes he is here. Helen Fraser wants a word," she said as she handed Bill the phone.

"Hello Helen, yes 14:00hrs I will be there, thank you. By the way will the Wingco' and Wings be there? I know what it will be about. See you later Helen."

"The Commandant wants to see me, it will be about the school and when can we have the first course attending. It is a good job we sorted our staff out when we did Margaret, the Wingco' and Wings will be there as well so it looks like it is decision time."

Sure enough the subject was the Drill School.

"Gentlemen, we are now at the stage where we can go ahead with the Drill Instructor and NCO course providing we have enough applicants to get it off the ground. Over to you Mister Barrett, have you any figures for us?"

"There has been a good response to the efforts of my staff in promoting the course to the recruits. Ten airmen have applied for the course and six airwomen which is quite an achievement. I have had no indication of any other applicants from outside the station, having said that those applications will not come to me direct, I do not know who will receive those."

"I think that is an excellent start, hopefully we should be able to open the school within a very short time. Have you two got anything to add or suggest?"

"I would like to ask Mister Barrett what are his staffing provisions for the school? It is obvious he will need more staff to run it."

"I have already sorted that out sir providing it meets with your approval. For the airmen I will need one Corporal to assist Sergeant Farrow. We do not have any in reserve as you well know but I would like to take Corporal Deacon from Sgt York's flight leaving him with one Corporal on a temporary basis....."

He was interrupted by the Wingco'. "What do you mean by a temporary basis?"

"As I said sir, we have no reserve Corporals my idea is to dangle a carrot to our first intake by selecting the best trainee passing the course to be posted to our staff."

"In the meantime Mister Barrett your Sergeant York will be working with one Corporal "

"Indeed he will, sir and if any of my Sergeants cannot carry out his duties with one Corporal for a short period then he is not worth his salt. Sergeant York has already proved his worth by running his flight I'll admit for a very short period without any Corporals "

"Point taken Mister Barrett."

"Now this is where you gentlemen have the upper hand. For the airwomen's course I need a Sergeant and two Corporals. What I would like to do is use Sergeant (w) Dean and her two Corporals, she could be replaced by a promoted Cpl (w) James and three of the Cpl (w)s we had to let go because of the big change over."

"Mister Barrett, you still continue to amaze me with your forward planning. From my point of view I can see nothing wrong with that scheme. What do you think about it gentlemen?" asked the Commandant.

"I could not better that sir," answered Wings "It is a good one."

"Wing Commander?"

"I have to hold up my hand to Mister Barrett he is way ahead of me with his organising, he has my full backing."

"Congratulations Mister Barrett all we need now is confirmation from the AOC about that promotion and the replacements. I shall be in touch when I get the word from the AOC, Thank you Mister Barrett."

Bill saluted then exited.

He went to give Viv the good news. She was delighted. "Once again you have come up trumps and that is nice getting our old girls back with us and with them knowing our system is half the battle but do you think Dot's two girls are up to teaching Drill Instructing, it is much different to teaching recruits basic drill I think they might feel a bit pressurised."

"I have thought of that but their experience should stand them in good stead. What I intend doing when we get our replacements and they take over from Dot I will have Joe Franks take them under his wing until we commence with the first intake."

"That is more like it Bill I would feel happier with them doing just that."

"How are you getting on with your OC?"

"She's nice, got a good head on her shoulders and takes an interest in her girls. She often pops in here for a brew and a chat. She tells me how when she was a young green officer how Mary took her under her wing but all during that time Mary never took advantage of their service friendship and never once lost her respect. I can see Mary in her attitude Bill, at last we have got someone who cares and she is so easy to talk to."

"Well I must be off and report to Margaret, she will be chuffed to know the results of the meeting. Have the entertainments committee got anything planned for the near future Viv?"

"We are working on having a dance but have not decided on when."

♦♦♦

The next day Bill was summoned to the CO's Office.

“Good morning Mister Barrett,” he said in reply to Bill’ salute. “It is good news from Command HQ. The AOC has sanctioned everything we asked for. The postings have already gone out to the three WRAF Corporals and that promotion will take effect tomorrow. He likes your scheme very much and he sends his congratulations. When the time is ripe I have to open the school but you and I will work together for when it can be put into operation.”

“I would like two more airmen and six more airwomen to apply for the course sir but we could get it off the ground with ten of each, once the course starts I do not think we will have any trouble getting more applicants because we have brought a new look to recruit training and our prestige must be spreading by the recruits who have passed through our hands.”

“That is what I want to hear Mister Barrett. You can go now and have the honour of breaking the news to your new Sergeant (w).”

“Thank you sir,” then saluted.

Returning to his office he asked Margaret to send someone to tell Corporal James to report to me.

When she arrived she asked. “You wanted to see me sir?”

“I most certainly do Sergeant James.”

She looked at him not believing what she thought she had heard.

“That is right what you hear, as from tomorrow you will be addressed as Sergeant.”

She was speechless; she looked across to Margaret Roper as if to say. Is this a leg pull?

Margaret came to her congratulated her with a kiss and said. “You have deserved that Marion.”

Accepting that it was not her imagination running wild she gave a great big smile and thanked Bill. “It was only you sir who could have got this for me I promise you will not regret it.”

“The first thing tomorrow morning report to the orderly room where you will receive confirmation to go to clothing stores to be issued with your chevrons then visit the tailor. While he is busy sewing away you can collect your gear from your accommodation and book in to the Sergeants Mess where you will find a room all ready and waiting for you to move in to. Margaret will escort you to the Mess and will show you round and introduce you to the staff and whoever is in the Mess at that time. The rest of the day is yours to enable you to get used to your new environment.

I will save my congratulations for when I see you in all your splendour. You may as well have the rest of today off to sort out your gear ready for the move.”

“Who do you recommend to take over the dormitory from you Marion?” asked Margaret.

“Corporal Wheeler.”

"Good, then that is taken care of you can tell her later but she must keep the dormitory up to your standard. Off you go then and start packing. I will go and have a word with Sergeant Cooper and put her in the picture Bill."

Bill answered the ringing phone. "Hello Roy what can I do for you? Good, I have been expecting them, no I do not need to write their names down I know who they are and yes I know about the promotion too. No I would not like to take your job over you do a better job than I could ever do. I can't help it if I get the information first hand what am I supposed to say, tell W/O Shaw first then he will tell me? You have the consolation of being in good company Roy, I think the Wingco' and Wings will have only just been informed. Now here is something you will be the first to know and are getting it straight from the horse's mouth. I am going to the Commandant to tell him we can open the school after this next passing out parade, the recruits who are to attend this course will return here from leave. Are you happy now? Good, I will report to you after I have seen him."

He then rang Helen asking for an interview with the Commandant.

"He will see you in an hour's time Bill."

"Thanks Helen."

He than rang Viv. "Hello Viv, Corporal James' promotion has come through she puts her third stripe up tomorrow. Will you inform your Squadron Leader? because she will want a word with her about her duties and what is expected from her as a Senior NCO. I am seeing the CO soon to tell him we can open the school in a couple of weeks."

♦♦♦

"Well Mister Barrett what progress have we made is everything going to plan?"

"It certainly is sir the replacements arrive in two days time then everything will be geared up to opening the school. I would like to suggest we open it when the applicants return from leave that will be two weeks after the passing out parade. We will have ten airmen which is enough to make a start with. I am thinking if we do not accept the airwomen for the first course they might go and change their minds if they are kept waiting until we have enough to form a full course."

"I see your logic and I am agreeing with it. Go ahead Mister Barrett, full steam ahead we have to make this work. I will sound out the AOC to see if the recruiting figures have improved and if there are signs of another Training Establishment re-opening. That is what we want Mister Barrett to ensure the success of our school."

CHAPTER 29

Bill called to see Tommy as he was making his way into the dining room for lunch which he had to pay for due to him living in married quarters. Jackie was on duty at reception.

"Hello Bill, you will want to see Tommy of course."

"I certainly do Jackie, if you would be so kind and tell her."

Tommy came out from behind the scenes and gave him a kiss.

"See what we have got this morning?" as she held out a picture postcard from Mary and Sam. "They are having a great time according to Mary. I like the bit where she says she could get used to this life."

"Well it will soon be over because we have to pick them up on Saturday."

"My goodness, that three weeks has really flown by I was expecting them being away another week at least."

"Can I take this card to show Roy and Co?"

When he entered the Mess for lunch he saw Roy and Co. already sat at the WO's table.

"Just the man I want to see," said Roy. "I have been trying to get hold of you all morning, where have you been skiving off to?"

"Roy, like you I head a very important section therefore I am always in great demand. My personality must have some bearing on it you know everyone does not have greatness thrust upon them."

"I don't think I can finish my lunch Derwent, maybe if I go and sit at the other table I could finish it without choking."

"Should I go and leave you in peace then Roy? Asked Bill.

"Don't bother you can't ruin my meal any more than you have done. Although I shall propose at the next Mess meeting that you living-out personnel who come in here for a meal should be segregated from us living-in personnel."

"Thanks very much Roy for dropping the rest of us in it," Derwent said angrily.

"What do you mean dropping you lot in it?" demanded Roy.

"Well what do you think is going to happen when Bill tells Tommy about your mean streak by wanting him segregated from us? That will be the end of any invitation to the Barrett's married quarter." Giving Bill the wink he continued. "On behalf of my fiancée we disassociate ourselves from your outburst."

Viv trying to keep a straight face nodded in agreement. "I shall have to report this to Barbara; goodness knows what her reactions will be."

"Alright, alright so I am not the favour of the month."

"Don't you mean flavour Roy?"

"So I can't say flavour, just typical of you lot to kick a man when he is down. Anyway I am going, I'll see you in the bar tonight Bill if Tommy will let you play out. What about you Derwent?"

"It depends on Viv."

"Here we go again, the dreaded HPC raising its ugly head, can he play out tonight Viv?"

As Roy got up to leave, Bill said. "Hang on a minute I thought you wanted to see me."

"I'll tell you tonight if a free drink will tempt you out." He left having a good laugh.

"I still cannot understand that man and I don't think I ever will," exclaimed Derwent. It is times like this when I could throttle him."

"C'mon Derwent it is about time you had him weighed up you have known him long enough now," said Viv.

"I will never know him."

"Here is a post card we got this morning from Mary we thought you would like to read it. Their time is up now I have to pick them up from the airport on Saturday morning."

"Their three weeks has passed quickly and from reading this card they have had a really nice honeymoon. So after the weekend Mary will be sorting her stall out for the beginning of a new life as a housewife and she will make a good one. Sam is a very lucky man to have found her" said Viv.

Derwent reached for her hand. "That puts me on a par with him, I feel very lucky to have found you."

Viv was taken aback and did not know how to reply.

"Go on, give him a kiss I don't mind watching and I am sure if anyone in the room is watching they will only feel a tinge of jealously," encouraged Bill.

"No, I will save that for later because it is too personal."

"Well I am off to the TV room to catch up the news. I don't know about tonight Derwent but if you think of a good excuse to have a girlie night Viv it would help."

"I will see what I can do Bill, I will have a word with Barbara."

♦♦♦

"Flight Sergeant Roper speaking, yes he is here. WO Shaw for you Bill."

"Hello Roy, what can I do for you?"

"Your three (w) Corporals are due to report in tomorrow. Corporals Branch, Dawes and Liner."

"Thank you for that information I can start my organizing now."

"Hang on a minute Bill I have further news for you which has come as a surprise.

Jock Webster has got his Warrant Officer promotion."

"Has he been informed yet?"

"Of course and as you can guess he is chuffed to bits and also because he is staying here at March. Then there is the matter of Tim Harris who has got his crown with an overseas posting to Seletar, he is delighted with that, he told me his wife is over the moon because she is going to Singapore."

"I am not surprised it is every ones favourite posting. I must go and congratulate both

Jock and Tim. There is no chance of you getting a posting is there Roy?"

"Perish the thought Bill, how would you survive without me to keep you on the straight and narrow? Besides if that was to happen you would be down to Command HQ to see your pal the AOC to put a stop to it. After all he would not want his pride and joy Under New Management to get scuttled would he?"

"Roy.... that would put me in a very awkward position, if I went with cap in hand he would term it as favouritism."

"You ungrateful wretch, after all I have done for you. Me, who has sacrificed a brilliant career to train you in becoming respected throughout the RAF only for you to trade me in for a handful of silver, you can buy me a pint tonight for your sins...Judas!"

"Thanks for all the information pal, I'll see you tonight."

♦♦♦

"Margaret, will you send someone to tell Corporal Deacon to report to me please?"

When he reported in he asked. "You wanted to see me sir?"

"Corporal Deacon, how would you like to support Flight Sergeant Franks and Sergeant Farrow in the. Drill Instructors School we are starting? It means you will be their only Corporal "

"What does it entail overall sir?"

"At present and until we get more applicants you will be in charge of twelve airmen in Barrack Room accommodation, that means you will have to move from your present accommodation."

"Do I have a choice sir?"

"Let me put it this way, I would like you to fill that post because you have the qualifications and experience that is needed for that post. I could of course detail you but I want a willing enthusiast who can be relied on to give one hundred percent. The school has yet to get off the ground and I want the best team to make sure it does and I want you to be part of that team."

"The way you put it sir makes it very difficult for me to turn it down but I will willingly accept the challenge with my one hundred percent."

"Thank you Corporal you will not regret it for you are joining a great team. Now here is the situation regarding the accommodation. You will know that rooms one and two in Block C' have just been refurbished after being closed for various structural reasons. You will take charge of those two rooms and you will move into Bunk 1 tomorrow. At the same time Corporal Anders will move into your Bunk. Do you think he can take over your role of being in charge of the complete Block and the Corporals? If he cannot then the other Corporals will have to be responsible for their own dormitories. Take tomorrow off to do your change over then report to Flight Sergeant Franks. I will have a word with Sergeant York and Sergeant Dixon. Rejoin your flight after sending Corporal Anders to me and give Sergeant York my compliments and tell him I would like to see him after work."

When Corporal Anders reported in he asked. "You wanted to see me sir?"

Bill filled him in with the relevant details.

"You will take tomorrow off for your change over. Tell me what do you think about taking over Corporal Deacon's role regarding the Block or would you prefer the other Corporals to be responsible for their own dormitories?"

"I would prefer each Corporal to be answerable for his own dormitories sir."

"Fair enough so it shall be, rejoin your flight and give Sergeant Dixon my compliments and tell him I would like to see him after work. When you report back for duty after your move you will report to Sergeant York."

When training was over for the day the two Sergeants reported in to Bill.

"Due to this school project I am afraid I have got to do a shuffle around with Corporals Deacon and Anders. Deacon is going to Joe Franks' team and Anders to your team Ron. You Bob will be left with Corporal Harper only." He told them of his plans regarding the school and choosing the best student from the first class to join our staff.

The two Sergeants agreed the changes were necessary and would co-operate fully with Bill on all accounts.

"Thank you, if all the changes prove to be as satisfactory and loyal as the staff I already have I will count myself a very fortunate and happy man," he said as he shook each of them by the hand."

CHAPTER 30

Bill Barrett received a call to report to the Station Commander immediately.

"Hold the fort Margaret I'm off to see the big boss; it must be very important because I have to report at once, see to the new Corporals arriving will you? I don't know how long I will be."

"Is there a panic on?" He asked Helen Fraser the CO's PA.

"Now how would I know that William, you forget I am just a secretary and in your parlance I know nowt'?"

"You mean you are not going to say owt," he replied with a grin. "Come on show me the way."

"You have been in there often enough to find your own way, there are times when I do not know whose office it really is, his or yours. Come on then and I want to see a big smile on your face when you come out." she knocked and opened the door and announced. "W/O Barrett sir."

"Come in and sit down Mister Barrett," the CO said in response to Bill's salute. "I have asked you here to congratulate you; your plan of getting your staff to spread the word to the recruits is working as is also the AOC's message to all stations of the Command. We have received a further twelve applications from airmen and nine from the WRAF. Command has also had a good feedback from Recruiting Offices to the effect that Drill Instructor is in a favourable position in the top ten of the most popular trades."

"That is the best news we could have wished for sir. Now it is up to my staff to deliver the goods and show the hierarchy we mean business."

"My sentiments entirely Mister Barrett, we have had an uphill struggle to get this far thanks to you and your staff and Bai George we are going to make some Brass Hats sit up and take notice of RAF March. If there is anything or anyone you need to make this a roaring success Mister Barrett my staff will support you all the way."

"Thank you sir, the support from your staff is already first class and I cannot ask for more than that."

"Go and break the news to your staff I am sure they will receive it well."

Helen Fraser was delighted to see him emerge with a great big smile on his face.

Bill went to her, gave her a kiss and said. "That is the best bit of good news I have had for a long time."

"Yes, wasn't it wonderful, is RAF March going to make the headlines again Bill?"

"I sincerely hope so Helen. By the way, if I want to know owt' in future I will by-pass you and go straight to the horse's mouth."

She laughed "Be off with you, you ungrateful man. I will still tell you nowt'."

To his assembled staff Bill told them the good news of how their efforts to educate the recruits in Drill Instruction had paid dividends. "The Station Commander is really chuffed to how you have rallied round but not as much as I am. Thank you all very much and I am proud to be part of your team. Will Flight Sergeant Franks' and Sergeant Dean with their teams please stay behind I would like a word?

We have just less than two weeks to set our stall out before the course students arrive. Your first priority is to get their accommodation ready for occupation. Check everything and report to me immediately you find any faults, any rectifications will get top priority. Sergeant Dean, your staff will receive some expert tuition from Flight Sergeant Franks to boost your confidence in your new role. Have you any questions?"

"Yes Sergeant Dean."

"Accommodation, can I suggest we move into the overflow block and take over Rooms 3 and 4 which are only partially occupied plus the Cpl's.Bunks. They will have to be thoroughly inspected and cleaned and with the short space of time we have before the course students arrive, I say the sooner the better."

"I will take that point up with W/O Anderson immediately.

"Yes Corporal Deacon."

"Sir, with the extra mouths to feed I doubt if there will there be enough room in the Mess to seat everyone in one sitting. Will the catering staff be able to cope when the permanent staff, the school and the recruits descend on the Mess all at once or will staggered meal times be the answer?"

"Good point, I will take that up with WO Jackson the Catering officer."

"Yes Flight."

"With drilling areas being in short supply and I want to keep the Drill school and the recruits well apart, I would like to suggest that we the Drill School have the Parade Ground for our instructing."

"I will have a word with the Station Warrant Officer and I can foresee the pair of us arguing it out with the Station commander.

"Any more questions? Remember, if you have a problem or not happy with anything or even a suggestion please do not sit on it, come and see me this School has to be a success and we will have only one shot at it. I know you can succeed because you are the best. Thank you for your time and suggestions. Margaret, I have to leave you for some very important business concerning the Drill School I know I am going to be away for some time so if you need me I will be with W/O Anderson, W/O Jackson and the SWO in that order. I will probably end up in the CO's Office."

He knocked and entered Viv's office on her command of 'Come in.'

"Ah it is you Bill, sit yourself down and tell me what it is you want from me?"

"Good old Viv you know I am after something don't you?"

"I have worked with you too long Bill, now what is it?"

He told her everything about the school from seeing the CO up to the meeting with his staff.

"I see Dot's point and it is a good one but I'm afraid I shall have to put it to Squadron Leader Mac', shall I ask for an appointment for the two of us to see her because I will be given the job of sorting it out if she approves."

"Yes, go ahead I want to get it sorted out too."

They stood in front of Squadron Leader Macfarlane while Bill explained about the Drill School and the WRAF accommodation.

"I see your point Mister Barrett and I also am concerned about the accommodation. I see the logic of Sergeant Dean wanting to keep the course students separate from the recruits and the permanent staff and I am in full agreement. As you say time is short for getting all these changes implemented and I suggest Warrant Officer Anderson you give it your top priority. I have spoken with the Station Commander who stressed how important this project is for the good of the Command and the Royal Air Force. Mister Barrett I will keep my eye on your progress with interest and I hope you are very successful."

"Thank you Ma'am for your co-operation and good wishes."

"That is the first hurdle cleared Viv. Now I am off to see Harry Jackson to see what he suggests about catering for the multitude."

"Hello Bill it is good to see you, I can't remember the last time you were in my office, sit yourself down because I sense it is something important you have come to see me about."

"You are right Harry." He then told him about the Drill School and how it could affect his Messing programme.

"Thanks Bill for coming to put me in the picture and giving me advance warning of more hungry mouths I have to seat and feed. At present you say you will have a total of thirty seven which is going to increase as time goes by. Right then, we have the permanent staff and your recruits. I suggest I split the meal times into two separate sittings; the permanent Staff will have the first sitting and the recruits along with the course students the second sitting. That I think will balance it out pretty well but hang on a minute I will get Flight Sergeant Cook who is in charge of the Messing, a good name for a Catering SNCO. I think it only fair to put him in the picture. Hello there Howie, can you pop round to my office?"

"Hello Bill," he said when he saw Bill sat there. "He has not brought trouble for us has he Harry?"

"A little bird told me things were getting a bit slack in the Catering Section so I thought I would come and put a bit of business your way," grinned Bill.

"If you have a couple of hours to spare I could tell you just how busy we are, our noses are well and truly on the grind stone, we have not the time to go swanning round the station getting our britches arse shiny having brews."

"Howie, if I had a beer in front of me now I would be crying into it."

"If you two can stop complimenting and patting each other on the back for a few minutes I would like to put you in the picture Howie of why I sent for you. I want your thoughts on what I am about to tell you then you both can get the hell out of my office because you are doing my head in."

"Harry then told him what he and Bill had been discussing.

"I thank you for including me in making the final decision and what you are suggesting Harry is as far as I am concerned the only right one. The two sittings will not put the cooks under any pressure as opposed to a mad stampede to get in there first. I heard about you opening a Drill Instructor School Bill and for the other things you have done for this station I applaud you and here is my hand on it. You know where I am if ever you need me."

"So there you are Bill, you have the full backing of the Catering Section."

"Thanks to both of you, what more could I ask? That is my second hurdle I have cleared, now the last one is with George Miller and the Station Commander."

"Hey up Ian we have a stranger in camp, have you come for one of our famous Sergeant Major brews Bill?"

"I'm afraid not George I am on an errand of mercy and to grovel at your feet."

"Hear that Ian? Fame at last, it has taken it's time to come but it looks like I have cracked it."

"Don't you mean cracked up George?" Offered Ian.

"Well everyone is entitled to his own opinion Ian, are you looking for a posting or summat?"

"What is the favour you want Bill?"

"He told about Joe Franks' problem with a shortage of area to drill his course students away from the recruits and he suggested if he could have the Parade Ground it would solve his problem."

"There is logic in his thinking Bill and I think it would work but he takes second place to formal parades."

"He is well aware of that George but I had to come and put the problem to you and if you had objected which would have been fair enough, we would have had to fight it out with the Station Commander as referee."

"You crafty bugger, you know damn well I would not have had a leg to stand on."

"What did you tell Ian a few minutes ago? Fame at last. Well I am honoured to have the privilege of standing by your side in that hall of fame."

"You are a smooth talker Bill Barrett and I would like to shake you by the hand because you still uphold that Barrett tradition of not losing an argument. How are you getting on with applicants to join the course?"

"Very well George we have thirty seven in total, twenty two airmen and fifteen WRAF, so that is a good start for Class1."

"If the school gets off the ground which is hoped it will, what happens then are the facilities here going to be expanded or what."

"We have not thought about that yet George but it could mean that one of the Training Establishments which was put in 'Care and Maintenance' could be re-opened.

By the way I am off to the airport on Saturday to pick up Sam and Mary we had a card from Mary who I think would like to do an extended tour on the cruise."

"Aye, we had one too, they are certainly enjoying it, now she has got the civilian type of foreign travel bug there will be no keeping her at home."

"I must be off now and break the good news to Joe and the rest of his staff."

At the end of the day's training Bill asked all his staff to stay behind for a few minutes.

"I wanted you here to give you the latest update on the Drill School and how it will affect us all. The airmen course students will be accommodated in 'C' block rooms 1 and 2. The WRAF will be accommodated in the WRAF overflow Block in Rooms 3 and 4, WO Anderson is arranging that and it has number one priority. There are to be two sittings for meals in the Airmen's and Airwomen's Mess. Permanent Staff will have the first sitting and the recruits and course students the second sitting, you will be notified of the change on Station Orders. The Drill School only can use the Parade Ground for drill purposes except when the Station holds formal parades. I must remind you that the school will open in less than two weeks time so we have quite a lot of organising to do before then. Has anyone any questions? No? I will keep you all updated when any or if any changes come about. One last word, I want to thank you for the part you have played in getting the recruits interested enough to make them want to apply for the course. The Station Commander too is very pleased with your efforts. Thanks for your time, go now and enjoy your dinners and don't be late for prayers in the morning," he said with a big grin.

"Margaret, just a second, did you sort out the three Corporals?"

"Of course, no problem I told them to report here first thing to be detailed for their flights."

"Thanks Margaret, I don't know why I asked, sorry, see you in the morning."

He than rang Wings' PA. "Hello Marion are you locking up for the day?"

"In a few minutes I will be why can I help you in any way?"

"I would like to book an appointment with Wings first thing in the morning can you do that for me please?"

"No problem any particular time?"

"How about 09:30 give him chance to settle down?"

"09:30 it is sir."

"Thanks a lot Marion."

♦♦♦

"Good morning Mister Barrett." Wings greeted in response to Bill's salute. "What is it you want to see me about?"

"I have come to give you my report on the progress made regarding the Drill School."

"You made all the necessary arrangements and now you want me to give it my seal of approval."

Hey up Bill, watch your step he is up on his high horse again.

"I don't know what you want to call it sir I am just here to tell you everything that needed to be done has been carried out and I can safely say from the training side of it we are ready to receive the first batch of course students."

"And I can safely say from my point of view as OC Training I am not satisfied with the way this project has been carried out behind closed doors."

"There has been no secrecy whatsoever sir about this project and I take umbrage that you have accused me of such."

"You can take what the hell you want, I am your OC and I will decide whether the arrangements are satisfactory or not."

"I was given total responsibility to get this project off the ground which I have done but because of your king sized ego you want to sabotage the work that has been done because you were not given the job in the first place. Very well sir I will officially hand the whole project over to you."

"Who the hell do you think you are? Talking to me in that insubordinate manner."

"I am talking to what was a damn fine officer who has suddenly lost his way."

"I will make sure it will be you who will lose your way."

"Make that a promise sir and I will apply for a posting, I cannot work with you any longer."

"You had better get out of my office before I lose my temper with you."

"You have already done that sir." He saluted and walked out.

From there he went to wind down in Roy's office.

"What's up Bill I have never seen you look so frustrated. Don't tell me, Wings is behind it. Sit down and I will get a brew organised."

Roy could not believe what he was hearing from Bill.

"You are right Bill he has lost his way, what has got into the man? I think he got that promotion far too soon. I'll bet when you said you would apply for a posting he made a sudden dash to change his underpants after you left. What are you going to do now?"

"Nothing, I will wait until I am summoned to see the CO. You know something Roy I have a gut feeling all is not well with Wings. There is something that is triggering off these outbursts which he cannot control and my gut feeling tells me it has something to do with the reason he was grounded from flying."

"If that is so Bill surely he would have had to have medical check-ups and we would have sussed it out before now if he had been for any. I know this much Bill it will be sooner than later before you get a summons to see the Commandant and I can't wait to hear the outcome so be sure to come here afterwards."

CHAPTER 31

On returning to his office Bill welcomed the three WRAF Corporals "Before we start will you remind me of your names please?"

"Corporal Olive Branch sir."

"Corporal Marjorie Dawes sir."

"Corporal Carol Liner sir."

"Thank you, you have already been interviewed by Flight Sergeant Roper and been told what is expected of you. You have also been detailed to various flights and being ex-staff you know the ropes." He shook each one by the hand and saying. "It is good to have you back." While he was chatting to the girls the telephone rang and Margaret answered it.

"It is for you sir."

He dismissed the girls telling them to report to the Sergeants in charge of their respective flights.

"W/O Barrett, oh hello Helen yes of course 14:00hrs thank you. I have a very important appointment with the Station Commander after lunch Margaret don't let me forget it."

"She laughed. "As if you would. Is it serious Bill?"

"I am afraid so, I will tell you about it afterwards."

♦♦♦

Meanwhile, Wings was with the Station Commander trying to explaining his actions.

"He entered my office telling me he had organised everything regarding the Drill School and as far as his staff were concerned they were ready to receive the course students and he had the audacity to expect me to rubber stamp the project. I, as OC Training have been kept completely in the dark and I told him in no uncertain terms that I will say whether it is satisfactory or not. He retaliated by saying he had been given the responsibility of the project and I was trying to sabotage it because of my king sized ego that I had not been offered the job. Then came the crunch, I now officially hand the whole job over to you. According to him I was a damn fine officer who had lost his way. I replied I would make sure he lost his way. Make that a promise and I will ask for a posting because I can no longer work with you was his last words before I ordered him out of my office."

The CO listening to this felt himself getting uptight and had to control himself. When he eventually calmed down he told Wings to return to his office and wait to be sent for. After Wings had left he asked Helen to contact the Wingco' to drop everything and to come to my office.

When he arrived he asked. "Is there an emergency sir?

"You could say that John, sit down for I find this rather distressing and I want your views on the subject."

He then repeated what Wings had told him.

"Have you had W/O Barrett's version sir?"

"No, and I don't need to after Cody's statement. I do not know what has got into the lad because this is not the first time I have had to drag him over the coals for slighting Mister Barrett. The beggar of it Cody is always singing Barrett's praises who in turn is like a big brother to him. I think Barrett had something there when he said Cody has a king sized ego."

"WO Barrett as far as I can see is doing all the ground work, wrapping it up and presenting the finished product to Cody who has taken umbrage because he has not been top dog to be in total command of the project. You also said you have had a similar incident between the two. Now this is supposition sir, Cody was medically grounded from flying and we do not know what those grounds were but could it be he may be having a reoccurrence of the same symptoms?"

"You may have something there John I will ring the MO and ask if Cody is subject to regular medical checks. Get me the MO Helen please."

"You are connected sir."

"Doc', the Station Commander here, can you tell me if Squadron Leader Cody is subject to regular medical checks due to him being grounded from flying duties?"

"Hold the line for a minute sir while I check my records.....sir... he is due to take a medical every six months to be held at the RAF Hospital."

"Thank you Doc'. You were right John he has to take a medical every six months."

"So where do we go from here sir?"

"I think I will have him back and try to get some information out of him and I would like you to stay John.

Helen, ask Squadron Leader Cody to come to my office."

"I have asked John to stay because we are not happy with your attitude concerning W/O Barrett. This is the second time within a very short period you have stood before me over a similar situation. I echo W/O Barrett's summing up of you that you are a damn fine officer who has suddenly lost his way. There must be a reason for your uncontrollable outbursts which I am not going to put up with or let any of my staff suffer from them. Squadron Leader Cody you will tell me the reason for these outbursts right now."

"It stems from my flying days sir. Like now I began to have sudden bursts of uncontrollable anxiety which made me feel very irritable. The MO sent me for various tests and they found a nerve of sorts which reacted to certain pressures. Naturally that resulted in me being permanently grounded. I was to have a medical check up every six months and at the last one I was given clearance to report only if it showed signs of re-occurring. On my posting here everything was great, I was happy and relaxed until I found myself infatuated with Flt Lieutenant Grable which turned out to be one big disaster. That is when that nerve reared its ugly head again. As you rightly said sir WO Barrett bore the brunt of it. I could not believe how I treated the man who had done more for me than anyone else and he has been the target once more. After the first incident I should have reported for my check-up but I thought I could beat it.

It is now necessary I should have that medical. I truly apologise sir for everything."

"Thank goodness for that, and thank you for being so frank, I must admit I was quite prepared to throw the book at you if it had been an ego trip you had been on.

Tomorrow morning you will report sick Bill and there will be transport laid on to take you to the RAF Hospital. Our wishes are they can do you some good with a view to a full recovery. About WO Barrett I will have a word with him, you are so very lucky to have such an understanding friend."

"What amazes me sir about him is, as much as I have maligned him he pushes my apologies aside and just carries on with our friendship as if nothing had happened."

"When they made him they threw the mould away, don't you agree John?"

"Indeed I do sir…he never fails to amaze me."

"I suggest you now go and have a word with our MO for him to see when it will be convenient with RAF Hospital for you to attend."

"Thank you sir I will do that and also for being so understanding." He saluted and left.

"You certainly came up with the answer John, well done. You know it must have been a burden for Bill knowing all the time what he was doing but could not stop it."

"My admiration is for W/O Barrett who knew there was something wrong with Cody's behaviour, he used his head by retaliating to whatever Cody threw at him hoping it would bring him to his senses. In a way it worked because it made Cody come to you to explain his behaviour and not to take action against W/O Barrett. You of course sent him on his way with a flea in his ear not knowing the cause of his outbursts."

"That is so true John, the reason had to come out one day he could not fight it for ever. Anyway, shall we have W/O Barrett in and explain the situation? Helen, please ask W/O Barrett to report to my office."

"W/O Barrett sir,"….Helen said as she ushered Bill in.

Bill saluted and noted the Wingco' was there. Looks like he has a back up of the big guns he thought, tread warily Bill. "You wanted to see me sir?"

"I do indeed Mister Barrett. I have had Squadron Leader Cody in to tell me about some disagreement between the two of you. Apparently you both exchanged harsh words in respect of the organising of the Drill school. Tell me about it."

"I carried out the order you gave me sir in organising completely the Drill School to make sure it would get off the ground. I have completed the task from the training point of view so I asked for an interview with the Squadron Leader to tell him the organising had been carried out and we were ready to receive the course students. He blew his top because he had not been given command of the project. I must add sir this outburst is very much out of character and I suspected all was not right, but I realised I had to be firm in retaliation even to the point of being insubordinate to try and bring him to his senses. The last time this happened Squadron Leader Macfarlane was present and I heard from good authority she calmed him down and made him realise he was responsible for the situation getting out of hand. I hope you don't mind me saying sir I think he should be seeking some medical advice, it is like a Jekyll and Hyde syndrome and I would hate it to spoil such a promising career."

"Thank you Mister Barrett, the Wing Commander and I read the situation before hearing your toned down version. You were right in your assessment that it was totally out of character and the cause of it is connected to him being grounded from flying."

"That figures sir."

"You do realise Mister Barrett this is strictly confidential."

"Indeed I do sir and I will still continue giving him my full support."

"You cannot give him any more support than you have already given and still giving Mister Barrett, he is a very lucky man to have you as a friend.

"Now what is the status regarding the Drill School Mister Barrett?"

"As far as the training is concerned sir we are ready. The accommodation has been sorted out for both airmen and airwomen. The meal times are being readjusted and Flight Sergeant Franks has the sole use of the Parade Ground except for formal station parades. All that is needed now is a curriculum drawn up for education and physical training classes and time sir is running short."

"Will you attend to that Wing Commander?"

"I think that just about covers everything sir."

"Very well Mister Barrett if anything else does crop up come to see me immediately."

Bill saluted and made his exit.

He went to see Roy as had been arranged to tell him the verdict.

"Before you say a word Bill take a seat. "Two teas and biscuits please," he called through the hatch. After an airman had brought it round and left he asked. "Well?"

"Close the hatch Roy it is confidential."

"Roy went to the hatch and called to Sergeant Graham. "Chris I am closing the hatch for confidentiality, make sure all 'ears' are kept away."

"What I am about to tell you is so confidential only The CO., the Wingco, myself and now you know about it so let us keep it that way Roy." He then told him what had been said in the Co's office and the action taken.

"So that gut feeling of yours did not let you down, well at least we have got to the bottom of the problem. I hope everything turns out alright for the lad and his career not affected, we do not want to lose him."

"We will just have to wait and see what the result will be after his trip to the RAF Hospital."

CHAPTER 32

Saturday morning saw Bill and Tommy waiting at the arrivals exit for Sam and Mary to appear. "Here they come," exclaimed Tommy as she began waving to attract their attention. "They have seen us Bill and waving."

Then it was kisses and hand shakes.

"Here, let me take the trolley, you come with me Sam and let the girls bring up the rear, I can hear them chatting away already. Have you had as good a time as it said on your postcard?"

"It has been absolutely brilliant; anything less than three weeks would have been a waste of time."

"Were you like me and Tommy, resigned to relaxing in a deck chair and watching all the young ones having the time of their lives?"

"We had to because it was too energetic for us oldies but we enjoyed watching them. And the sights we saw when we berthed at the different islands were wonderful it made you want to put a deposit down on a house and go and live the life of leisure, it certainly was an adventure with a difference."

"Here is our transport, lets get this luggage stored away then wait for our passengers. Just look at the pair of them, linked arms and chattering away like a couple of magpies."

When the girls looked to see where they were they started giggling. "Are we holding you up?" laughed Mary.

"Actually we were about to send a tannoy message out for you in case you had lost your way," laughed Bill.

"We will have less of your cheek Bill Barrett, I am back home now and don't try teaching my husband any of your bad habits."

"My apologies Mrs Brown."

"Get in that in that driving seat and get us home I am dying for a good brew."

All the way back to the village the chatter never stopped from the rear seats.

"Did you suffer from ear-ache while you were away Sam? They have only been in the car a few minutes and I am suffering from it."

"You will be suffering from summat' else if you don't concentrate on your driving instead of ear-wigging about what we are discussing Bill Barrett."

"Yes Mrs Brown."

"He is incorrigible that husband of yours Tommy how do you put up with him?

"At times with great difficulty Mrs Brown."

That brought a roar of laughter from the front seats.

"I hope you are not paying attention to this old married couple Sam Brown, because if you are you will be sleeping in the back bedroom."

Bill spoke softly to Sam. "If at any time you want a break from the old battleaxe we can put you up in our spare room."

"How many more time have I to tell you Bill Barrett, LESS of the OLD!"

"Here we are Mrs Brown out you go, Sam and I will bring the luggage while you get the kettle on. I see the milkman has left your bottles of milk in the shade, I expect he daren't do otherwise or you would have him on Jankers."

Mary winked at Tommy. "This garden needs tidying up Sam."

"There you go Sam, see what you have let yourself in for."

Sam just grinned and shrugged his shoulders. "It'll be reight," he said with a grin.

"Are you bringing that luggage in today or are you staying out there gossiping?"

As they entered with the luggage Bill called out. "Where's our brew?"

"Just sit yourselves down and it will be serve to you sir," smiled Mary.

Tommy entered with tea and biscuits. "Here you are gentlemen," she said politely as she poured the tea added sugar and milk then stirred the teacups. "Is that to your satisfaction gentlemen?"

Bill and Sam looked at each other then Bill said. "Go on tell her."

"Mary!" shouted Sam.

"Yes dear." Mary answered.

"This is how I want it every day, got it?"

The place was in an uproar, they could not drink their teas for laughing.

When they calmed down Mary said. "Oh it is lovely having you two for our friends thank you for everything especially for the laughs we have had today, what a homecoming. What is the news from the camp?"

They told her about all the latest developments, how Mac' was settling in, how Viv has filled your position perfectly and the opening of the new Drill Instructors School very soon. Marion James had been promoted and we have all the staff back that we had to let go and the more interesting part for Sam is George Miller gave young Bond two airmen until you returned and they have done a great job between them."

"Come on Bill, we had better get back home to let them sort themselves out. I advise you to go to bed and have a sleep before you do anything else Mary. It will help you get over the jet-lag and I can assure you that you will feel better for it. By the way, when are you due back to work Sam?"

"On Monday, I am not living a life of leisure I have to work for a living."

"No but I am," laughed Mary."

"Then can I give you my order on Friday as usual Sam?" asked Tommy.

"You could have given it me now if you had brought it."

Tommy gave a little giggle and fished her order from her handbag and gave it him.

"Why you crafty little devil exploded Bill."

"That is a sign of good house keeping Bill, forward planning is what they call it," explained Sam. "Your order will be delivered on Friday Mrs Barrett because we are back in business."

Tommy gave him a kiss, "Thank you, you lovely man. Come on Bill, we will be in touch Mary," she said as she gave her a kiss.

♦♦♦

When they arrived home they found a note pushed through the door.

Can't go to the March Hare tonight, Derwent is Orderly Officer all week-end. See you in reception at 8pm. Bingo or the Quiet Room.....Roy.

"Are we going or having a quiet night at home?" asked Bill. "Or should we invite them here? We have drinks in and we could give them supper and it will make a change for them."

"What about Derwent though?" asked Tommy. "Won't he be confined to the Sergeants Mess to be contacted there?"

"So long as he leaves notice where he can be contacted at the guard room and he does not forget his parade at 10pm that will be in order."

"Alright, go and have a word with Roy, you will have time to have a drink with him while I make lunch but I want you back here by mid-day."

Roy was surprised to see Bill when he answered the knock on his door. "What on earth are you doing here?" Come on in.

"Tommy sent me with an invitation for you all to come over for a drink and a bit of supper tonight she thought you might like the change. Furthermore I have not to be back no later than noon, so come on let us go and have a drink."

"That is great Bill it will be a nice change, lets go I have got a thirst on," he said as he slipped his jacket on going through the door in his eagerness.

As they went past the TV room Roy poked his head inside to see Derwent sat watching a Programme.

"Hey up Derwent we have a visitor and he is taking me for a drink, come on he'll buy you lemonade."

"Oh hello Bill what is the occasion?"

"Never mind that now lets get in there I am parched we can talk in there," said Roy impatiently.

♦♦♦

Jock Webster picked up his phone. "Warrant Officer Webster speaking, hello Roy what can I do for you?"

"I have just got Tim's replacement posting in and I think you will be very pleased with it"

"Aye, knowing you there must be a catch in it. Go on tell me the worst."

"There is no worst Jock it is a posting with promotion…"

He was interrupted by a loud groan and "I knew there was a catch to it."

"That is where you are wrong old timer, he is a Scot' by the name of Iain Stuart."

"Oh the canny wee laddie, that has made my day Roy, he must be bright to gain promotion and be posted here and when is he due in? Is he married? What age is he?"

"Steady on Jock, just have a pause to draw breath. Yes, he is married and in his late twenties and before you ask me I am getting in touch with Tom Hardcastle to sort out a house for him. He arrives here on Thursday and I will ask Tom if he can hand over the quarter to him on Friday then you can give him time off to hand over his quarter at his previous station which will take a few days."

"Thank you very much Roy you are a good friend."

"Jock, here at the sharp end our aim is to provide a first class service to please everyone."

♦♦♦

Bill Barrett was in the ops' room checking the wall charts.

"We need another chart for the course students Margaret, I had better get in touch with the Chippies shop to come and measure up for one….he was interrupted by the phone ringing.

"I'll get it," Margaret said.

"You have to report to the Wingco' at your earliest convenience."

"I wonder what that is about."

"Hi Barbara I am expected."

"Yes Bill he wants to see you, I don't think it is anything to get alarmed over. Come on let's go. Warrant Officer Barrett sir she announced."

Bill saluted.

"Sit yourself down. I have called you in to tell you we are now getting quite a few more applications for the Drill Instructor course. How many can you accommodate in a dormitory?"

"At present I have twelve and there is plenty of room for four more in each dormitory without it being cramped. On that basis I can accommodate thirty two bodies in total and it is similar for the airwomen. At present we have twenty two airmen and sixteen airwomen sir."

"It has been confirmed ten more airmen have applied and eight airwomen. I suggest we include those in Class 1 making a grand total of thirty two airmen and twenty four airwomen. I think Flight Sergeant Frank's staff can easily cope with those numbers, don't you Mister Barrett?"

"I do indeed sir; I think they would prefer a larger flight than a smaller one. I will arrange with MoD to update the dormitories with the required furniture. I am still waiting for the list of names of all the applicants' sir I am in the process of requiring more wall charts for the ops' room."

"I will see you get that list Mister Barrett. I think that covers everything for the time being."

"There is a very important item we all appear to have overlooked sir. What is the duration of the course?"

"You have now put the cat among the pigeons Mister Barrett, how could we all have forgotten that? Can we come up with a figure I can take to the CO who in turn will want to consult the AOC?"

"I have a figure of nine weeks in my head sir; remember besides drill they will attend education classes plus numerous lectures on the responsibilities of an NCO.

Then as we get into a routine the length of the course could always be adjusted if necessary."

"I agree with what you say, it sounds sensible. I will take our views and recommendations to the CO. well done Mister Barrett."

"Excuse me asking sir but have you any news of Squadron Leader Cody's progress?"

"Not really only that he is undergoing extensive tests, for how long we have no idea."

"There is one more thing I would like to ask of you sir. Would you be prepared to address the course students on what will be expected of them?"

"Of course Mister Barrett nothing would please me more."

"Thank you sir," he saluted then left.

"Everything alright Bill?" asked Barbara.

"Yes and we have no problems…not yet anyway. See you Barbara."

He immediately went to MoD to see Tom Hardcastle.

"Hello Bill and what can I do for you?"

"Tom I have a big problem. He told him about the accommodation for the course students. I have had to increase the bed spaces by four in each of the dormitories which includes the WRAF making a grand total of sixteen extra bed spaces and we have just over a week to implement it Tom. I am sorry to spring this on you at such short notice but I have just been informed of the extra numbers I have to accommodate by the Wingco'."

"I will try my best Bill as you say it is short notice, so it is large wardrobe, small locker, bed and bedside mat times sixteen."

"If you have any problems getting the items Tom, see our Station Commander and he will get some pressure put on the people responsible for any hold-up."

"There will be no problem Bill I have got plenty of clout."

Bill shook his hand. "Thanks Tom it is appreciated."

CHAPTER 33

Thursday morning Bill had gathered the Drill School Instructors in the ops' room.

"I am doing a final check today to make sure everything is as it should be. As you see we have two new wall charts, one for the RAF and one for the WRAF, they contain the particulars as much as we have got at present of the course students. Next I want you Sergeant Dean to take your team to the accommodation where you will be met by W/O Anderson to inspect that everything is above board. You Flight Sergeant Franks and your team will accompany me to inspect your students' accommodation. The students will begin to arrive on Sunday and we have today and tomorrow to do any rectifications if they are needed....he was interrupted by a ringing telephone which Margaret Roper answered.

"Yes sir he is here." She mouthed, "it is the Wingco' for you."

Bill took the phone from her. "W/O Barrett speaking, ah good morning sir, yes, I see, that is good news, thank you sir I will let my staff know. The AOC has confirmed that the course for Class 1 will be for nine weeks. During that time we can assess if the course needs to be shortened, lengthened, or to stay at nine weeks. Let us go and get these checks done then we can relax until Monday. Take over from me Flight I have thought of something I must ask WO Shaw to do for us."

"You have come to ask a favour haven't you?"

"How did you know o' wise one?"

"Because you were wearing your best smile as you came through the door."

"You never fail to amaze me Roy."

"Less of the old flannel what do you want?"

"I would like five printouts of the number rank names of all the students, two of the airmen and three of the WRAF. Also I would like four printouts of the meal times for the two sittings."

"When would you like them sir would fifteen minutes be too long a wait for such a busy man as yourself?"

"What can I say except please do not put in for a posting or this station would collapse."

"Of course it would I am glad you have finally realised that, it has taken you long enough to accept it." He then called Sergeant Graham to the hatch and told him what he wanted.

"No problem sir, tell WO Barrett not to blink or he will miss his delivery."

"Hear that? That is efficiency at the top level and you are still not getting a brew! Besides you would not have time to drink it."

"Where would I get those I.D. labels that fit in the door of the wardrobes Roy?"

"How many do you want?"

"Sixty four."

"Sergeant Graham send someone to our stores to bring me sixty four wardrobe labels please."

"Is there anything you have *not* got Roy?"

"A knighthood."

"I will see what I can do for you in that respect I will get in touch with my friends at MoD."

"I don't think you will you are up to your old tricks again telling Porkies."

"If I could old friend I would do so and if it came about I would apply to be your batman!"

"If I could get hold of that magic lamp I would make that my first wish."

"Your printouts and I.D. labels sir." said Sergeant Graham peering through the hatch.

"That is what is called service with a smile now sod off I have work to do and I will see you in the bar tonight to claim a buckshee pint."

Bill found his staff and gave the printouts and I.D. labels to Joe and Dot. "You Corporals can arrange the students how you like in the dormitories, you realise that some of them have been in the service longer than the recruits and want to remuster from their present trade. You may have to keep a watchful eye on those who may take advantage of their longer service to lean on the recruits. Any wrongful behaviour, i.e. bullying, will not be tolerated. If anyone does not respond to our code of behaviour inform Flight Sergeant Franks or Sgt Dean. They in turn will report to me if they think it too serious for them to handle. Any questions?"

"Yes Corporal Deacon."

"Does it mean that we Corporals who are in charge of the dormitories will be on duty all Sunday to guide them to a specific bed space sir?"

"Not if you use your loaf Corporal. You have a list of their names and I.D. Labels, write their names on the labels and insert them in the wardrobe where you want each person to go. Put a notice on the room notice board stating…Read the wardrobe I.D. label for the bed space you are assigned to. They will come to you if they want to be next to their chum. Does that answer your question?"

"Yes sir, I should have thought of that."

"Apart from that if everything is tickety-boo with the inspection you may stand down. Remember, the Wing Commander will be addressing them first thing Monday morning so make sure they are gleaming for he does not miss a trick. Enjoy your week end."

♦♦♦

Friday morning Bill went to see Sam Brown to pay his debts for the provisions Tommy orders.

"Have you and Mary settled back in after your cruise Sam?"

"We have that Bill, Mary has been busy sorting everything to how she wants it, I'll tell you what, she is a damned good cook I am going to have to watch my waist line. You and George will soon be getting an invite to dinner she is already making plans for it."

"That is something we are looking forward to. I had word from Tommy that young James had delivered her order so I have come to settle up with you and to give you her next order. I believe George Miller gave young Bond a couple of airmen to help out until you returned."

"It was a good job he did because James could not have managed by himself and the two lads turned up trumps they really worked hard for him. I had a word with them early on and they asked me if I could use my influence to have them permanently assigned to me. I will try my best Bill but I doubt very much if I could get them permanently although I would like to."

"I will be ordering more flowers soon Sam because I have a Sergeant moving into quarters this week."

"Just let me know when you want them."

♦♦♦

Saturday night saw the family at the March Hare receiving the usual good welcome from Tim, Ann and the locals.

Derwent went to the bar to order drinks and as he was chatting with Tim loud whispers encroached on their conversation.

"There they go again," laughed Tim, you have come in and they suddenly find they are thirsty, just listen to them."

"There is that young man who always makes sure we have a drink in front of us. Just watch him closely after he has been served with his order." "He is walking back to his table," said another. Yes but he is not sitting down yet that means he is going back to the bar, now he is talking to Tim." "Sup up, said another he is looking over here." "Hello young man it is nice to see you back again, we do miss you when you are not here."

"Have you got rid of your bad coughs you had the last time we were here?" asked Derwent.

"Some of us have but our wives are still suffering, the doctor said they must always keep their throats well lubricated and not allowed to dry out."

"We'll see what we can do about that then."

Everyone was waiting expectantly.

"Give the ladies a drink Tim it might help them."

They began coughing and muttering amongst themselves. "Look, here is what we will do. Us chaps will get a clean glass from the bar and you can pour some of your drinks into them it will help to prevent us catching your coughs."

"I do not believe what I am hearing," said a flabbergasted Tim. "The tricks they get up to cadge a free drink, it is said you can't teach an old dog new tricks and you are looking at proof."

"Go on Tim give em' all a drink I think they have earned one."

On hearing that a big cheer went up and they began singing 'For he's a jolly good fellow'.

"Have you ever heard the like?" Asked Ann.

"It is worth every penny spent on them just to hear their reactions if they think they are going to miss out getting a free drink," laughed Bill.

“Good health young man,” they said holding up their glasses “and good health to all you other kind and generous people.”

“They never give up,” Ann said. “You just watch when they have drunk up there will be the noise of glasses being put down noisily on the table and the sound of coughs going round the table in turn, they are as crafty as a wagon load of monkeys.

What is the news from the camp?”

They brought her up to date with everything the main topic being the Drill Instructor School.

“Are you trying to get RAF Chatworth or RAF Camberly opened up again?”

“If we can get enough applications for the course and the recruiting figures increase there is every good chance one of them could be re-opened.”

“Then you would lose your school and the training staff that goes with it, have you thought of that?” You could even lose your new Wingco’ as Commandant, think of the implications of it Bill they are far reaching.”

“Now you have got me thinking Ann, you make sense but it will be long term before that materialises, never the less some forward planning is needed or my previous plan of commandeering staff from other stations is going to back-fire on me. I will work on that before dropping it in the laps of the hierarchy. What do you think of that Roy?”

“Ann is right in what she says it will certainly make a big hole in your training staff and you would lose your star personnel because it all depends on recruiting figures. So Merlin the Magician you will need to get that magic wand of yours out of moth balls, give it a good rubbing and see what it can come up with.”

“Why are we talking shop?” asked a disgruntled Tommy, “when we are supposed to be on a night out enjoying ourselves and if the subject is not changed then I am on my way home.”

“Well spoken and we are with you all the way,” Val and Barbara said gleefully.”

“Sorry girls it is my fault, “apologised Ann.”

A round of applause came from the locals “and so you should landlady.”

“Oh hush your faces and get them stuck back in your beer,” retorted Ann.

“We have no beer to get our faces stuck into landlady.”

“Fill their glasses up Tim,” shouted Roy.

There was another round of applause and from the murmuring came. “You can tell he is a gentleman it stands out a mile… Thank you, sir.”

The rest of the evening went well and the ladies were happy.

“Have you had Graham and Marion in lately?” asked Roy, “or Sam and Mary?”

“We have had the two young ones in sometimes twice a week, they usually sit where you are sitting and they are so engrossed with each other they are oblivious to what goes on around them.”

“Looks like it is developing into being serious,” suggested Roy.

"Mary and Sam have not been in since they returned from their honeymoon I expect they are still settling in."

"Sam tells me, Mary is certainly taking good care of him. 'She is a damned good cook', so she must be feeding him well." Bill told them.

"And Tommy must be feeding you well Bill Barrett you look as if you have put a bit of weight on," laughed Ann.

"I am not complaining and I will back her cooking against all comers, when she gets her order from Sam she works miracles with it."

"We will second and third that won't we Roy," enthused Derwent.

"And we will third and fourth it won't we Viv," volunteered Barbara amid a roar of laughter.

Of course that outburst startled the locals.

"We will just have one for the road then we will return to the grind. Same again Tim please," Bill called amid coughs and noise as empty glasses rattled… "All round," he added.

"Three cheers for Captain Bligh," cried the locals.

CHAPTER 34

Sunday was to be a very busy day especially for the M.T. (Motor Transport) section of RAF March who are supplying a shuttle bus to ferry the course students from the railway station and would continue until the last train of the night. The Corporals in charge of the dormitories took W/O Barrett's advice appertaining to detailing each individual to a specified bed space. Any requests from individuals to move bed spaces to be besides their pals or friends if it appertains to the airwomen it can be sorted out later. If any of the airmen arrived at the camp in the early hours of Monday they would be accommodated in transit.

♦♦♦

Monday morning saw Corporal Deacon rousing airmen from their slumbers who had not responded to reveille. In each dormitory he did a head count and found everyone present and correct. The airmen were instructed to read the notice board and check meal times and to be properly dressed and wearing headgear when in uniform outside the accommodation blocks.

After breakfast he supervised the bed layouts which included bed packs being made up, towel draped over the wooden towel rail which was a fixture on the rear of the small bedside locker. Their second pair of shoes with plimsolls had to be lined up between the legs at the foot of the bed. After a few sharp words with a reminder they were not rookies and should not need any supervision he was satisfied with the outcome.

"These bed spaces will stay like this until training finishes for the day. Now you will remain dressed in your best uniform and form up in threes outside the Barrack Block at 08:50 to collect your arrival chits. I advise you to present a good turn-out or Flight Sergeant Franks will want to know why. Until it is time to fall-in I suggest you check each others appearance then read your notice board thoroughly. By the way, if any of you want to exchange bed spaces, do so this evening.... Carry on."

At 09:00 they fell-in outside their accommodation Corporal Deacon called the roll, sized them off by heights then marched them onto the Parade Ground.

The WRAF contingent marched on and formed up behind the airmen's flight to await the arrival of Flight Sergeant Franks

When he arrived he introduced himself Sergeant Farrow, Corporal Deacon, Sergeant (w) Dean, Corporals (w) Peters and Briggs.

"We are your instructors. Your first task is to officially arrive on the station, Sergeant Graham and Corporal (w) Springs from the orderly room will come and hand out your arrival chits. The RAF Corporal and the two WRAF Corporals will then march you to the various sections for your chits to be signed. On completion you will return here and the Corporals will collect your chits and return them to the orderly room. We then wait the arrival of Wing Commander Hopwood who will address you. A word of warning, throughout the course you will be under constant surveillance and any misdemeanour will reflect in your assessments. It will not be a hard or difficult course but if you do find it so it will be due to your own personal attitude. Apart from instructing you we are here to help you, so remember that, our staff is here if you need us but do not expect us to mollycoddle you. If everyone has got his or her arrival chit we will get this show on the road. PARADE...ATTEN....SHUN....Take over Corporals and March them off.

What do you think of them so far?" Joe asked the Sergeants

"The airmen appear to be reacting very well and their turnout was pretty good," said Jim Farrow.

"What about you Dot, any problems with your girls?"

"I wouldn't say problems," she replied "but I think one or two will perhaps need to be leaned on to toe the line, otherwise the turnout on the whole was quite good."

"We have got off to a good start with having no waifs and strays to round up. After the Wingco' has said his party piece I suggest they take the rest of the day to clean up their kit ready for tomorrow's kit inspection. I will have a word with Bill Barrett to ask the Wingco' to stand in for the absent Wings and Squadron Leader Macfarlane will inspect the airwomen's kit. We of course will be there in support. I realise you have not got the week's full itinerary yet but I will see to that now. In the meantime go and relax at our training office we will hear the flights returning. Come on I have to go there myself to see Bill Barrett."

"Hello Joe what can I do for you?" asked Bill.

"You can start by letting me have six copies of this week's itinerary and I would like advance copies each week for my forward planning. I would appreciate you contacting the Wingco' and Squadron Leader Macfarlane to inspect the student's kit tomorrow morning, which I hope is included in the itinerary."

"That is odd, we should have some copies in the ops' room, give Margaret a shout Joe....Margaret have we some copies of the weekly itinerary for the course students? Joe here is complaining because he has not been issued with any."

"We have quite a few but I do not know how you were missed out Joe, how many do you want?"

"Six will be enough but I would appreciate it if I could receive six copies at least a week in advance, the earlier the better. I would feel a right pillock if I was asked by the Commandant. 'What is the agenda for tomorrow? Flight Sergeant?'

"Alright Joe you have made your point, would a brew pacify you?"

"Go on then if you are twisting my arm, Jim Farrow and Dot Dean are out there I fancy they wouldn't say no to a brew either."

"Okay you win, I will go and sort out the kit inspection team after I have had mine then I will see you on the parade ground."

The two flights of students were formed up in readiness for the address by the Wingco'. As he arrived they were brought sharply to attention by Bill Barrett who marched to the Wingco' and announced. "Class 1 course RAF ready for your inspection SIR!"

"Thank you Mister Barrett I will begin with a quick inspection." When he was introduced to Joe Franks he asked. "What do you think of this idea of a Drill Instructor School? Sergeant."

"It is the best thing that could have happened sir, if we can make a success of it and the recruitment improves there would be a good chance of MoD realising their mistake in closing down both Training Establishments plus the fact we would then have back ups for our qualified training instructors."

"I could not agree more Flight Sergeant; personally I would like to see RAF Chatworth re-opened." He then began his inspection of the airmen stopping to speak with a number of them. "I am impressed with their turnout Mister Barrett let us hope the rest of the course makes a favourable impression. After acknowledging Bill's salute he marched over to the WRAF students to be received by Squadron Leader Macfarlane.

"Class 1 course WRAF ready for your inspection SIR!"

Warrant Officer.(w) Anderson and Sergeant (w) Dean were then introduced. After a few complimentary words with Viv he spoke to Dot Dean.

"So Sergeant Dean you are at the sharp end to teach these young ladies, the reports I have had of you and your Corporals have been very good and I am sure you are going to give Sergeant Farrow a run for his money in producing the best all round student. Come on let us go and have a look and have a little chat with them." Turning to Mac and Viv he suggested. "You two ladies sit this one out, Sergeant Dean and I can manage alright," he said finishing off with a wink and a smile.

"I have never experienced anything like that before Ma'am a senior officer with feelings and he is not afraid to show them."

"We are very fortunate Warrant to have an officer with those attributes."

They watched him and Dot walking slowly between the ranks chatting to the airwomen and receiving beaming smiles in return. When the walkabout in lieu of an inspection was concluded, he said. "I don't think you will have any trouble with those girls Sergeant Dean."

He then faced the two flights. "I am Wing Commander Hopwood and my second in command who you will soon meet is Squadron Leader Cody who will not be with us for a few days, that takes care of the RAF contingent. For the WRAF, Squadron Leader Macfarlane is in command. That leaves the Warrant Officers, the senior NCOs and the junior NCOs. I will not bore you by rattling off their names you will be in close contact with them and you will find just how close that contact will be if you misbehave. Respect them and they will return that respect and you will also be surprised to find they are not the 'Drill Pigs' of yesteryear, that name tag has gone forever. We welcome you Class 1 to the new updated Drill Instructors School and you will make us all happy if you set such a high standard that those who follow you will have to work jolly hard to meet. At the end of the course an airman and an airwoman will be chosen as the best all round students and invited to join our training staff here at RAF March. That does not mean you have to walk all over your classmates to achieve that goal, your character will play an important role in the selection. Give your instructors one hundred percent effort and they will be very happy. Give them one hundred and ten percent and we all will be 'Chuffed'. Good Luck to all of you."

The parade was brought to attention and the Wingco' acknowledged the salutes.

"Take over Flight Sergeant," Bill addressed Joe Franks while Viv handed the WRAF flight over to Dot Dean.

Both flights were told the rest of the day was free to prepare their full kit for the kit inspection.

Joe addressed the airmen. "A word about the kit inspection, we expect a good standard from you, this will be the first of many you will have during the course. We do not call it 'Bull' we prefer to see it as character building in potential NCOs. Before the end of the course you will be able to display a perfect kit lay-out with your eyes closed. A word of warning to any who think they know better than us and think that anything will do, do not be disillusioned, we know all the tricks because we were taught the hard way. If any single one of you throws a wobbly it will reflect on the whole flight resulting in a collective punishment and you will become very popular with your fellow students...I don't think. Looking on the bright side I will give you a very helpful tip. Help each other, if one of you struggles with a particular subject help him do not take the attitude of 'Sod you Jack I'm alright' you can put your own version to that, who knows it may come your turn to appreciate some help.

After the inspection you will put your kit away, change into your working blue uniforms and fall in outside the barrack block. Gentlemen, tomorrow will be your first day to becoming a fully qualified Drill Instructor and the first course with a one hundred percent pass. No 1 course, Dis…Miss."

He walked over to where Dot was talking to her flight of airwomen.

"Everything alright Dot?"

"Yes, I was giving the girls a run through of do's and don'ts. Whether it is the way I am trying to put it across to them or they are not interested I can't make up my mind."

"Would you like me to have a word with them?"

"Certainly, maybe you can hold their attention."

"Flight…Atten…Shun. Stand… at… Ease. I see we have a mixed bag of some who respond immediately to an order and some who do not. I will give you the order again and if you drag your feet I will double you round this Parade Ground until you do respond. Flight…Atten…Shun. Very good and that is what you will do until the end of the course respond immediately to orders given you and carry them out smartly.

Stand… at… Ease, very good. I am Flight Sergeant Franks and I am the one who makes this course tick. I do not hide away and leave all the instructing of you to my staff you will see me at times watching your progress and there will be times when you will not see me but I assure you I will be there. You have volunteered to join this course therefore you will accept the rules and regulations of it, if you don't we do not want to know you because you will never make the grade as NCOs. Tomorrow is your first kit inspection of many during this course, we do not class this as 'Bull' but we think it helps in character building. We expect you to show a good layout and before the end of the course you will be able to lay out a perfect kit with your eyes closed. Do not for one minute think you can pull a fast one over the staff, if a single one of you does not toe the line it will reflect on the whole flight and a collective punishment will be enforced in your own free time. To avoid anything like that it is suggested you help each other, someone may be struggling with a particular subject, do not turn your backs on them go to their aid and work as a team then we can hope to avoid any failures at the end of the course and speaking for all the staff we want you all to pass. If you find the course is hard it will be because you personally will have made it so. Good Luck to you all and give the airmen something to think about. Incidentally you will be shown a Video of the famous BlueBelle girls who after only three weeks as recruits were instructed and trained by W/O Barrett and W/O Anderson to wipe the floor with teams with more service experience from the Royal Navy and the Army. If you show signs of promise to become Drill Instructors WO Anderson might even pass some of her expertise on to you. Good Luck to you all. Flight!…Atten…Shun. That movement was quite smart, keep it up. Was that alright for you Dot?"

"Thanks Joe it should have hit home."

"Dismiss them Dot and let them get cracking on their kit."

For the rest of the day the course students were very busy, the electric irons hardly getting the chance to cool down. The airmen were helped by Corporal Deacon who suggested a system by which half the occupants of each room concentrating on using the iron for ironing and pressing while the other half concentrated on blancoing and polishing the brasses of their webbing equipment. That method would eliminate any squabbling to taking turns with the iron. At an agreed time they would swap roles.

"I suggest you make a rota and a specific length of time you think each one of you should use the iron. If some of you have a personal iron all well and good, the ironing table in the drying room can accommodate two of you at a time so re-adjust your timings. But if I hear any squabbling or fighting, beware, if I have to sort you out you will all be grounded and that means, no NAAFI or the Astra cinema."

Over in the Waffery it was pretty hectic, everyone wanted to be at the ironing table at once consequently squabbles broke out, shouting and screaming interspersed with language unbecoming of young ladies.

Corporal Peters went into the dormitory and ordered the airwomen to "Stand by your beds and MOVE yourselves," she thundered.

There was a hasty scramble to get themselves in position and stood to attention.

"You will stay at attention and you will not speak." She went to the next dormitory to see what steps Corporal Briggs had taken and found the airwomen there were stood at attention by their beds getting a right dressing down. She called Corporal Briggs out and told her what action she was taking with her girls.

She returned to face her own charges. "You chose this course because you thought you had the qualities to become NCO Instructors and an easy way to get a quick promotion. Who do you think you are kidding? You did not listen when you were warned about your conduct during your course training. I will not tolerate the kind of behaviour you have just shown. Another incident like this or if you do not toe the line I will make it my business to recommend you being thrown off the course. To make sure you realise I am not bluffing you are grounded. That means after your last meal today you will report back here for a roll call and will continue getting your kit ready for inspection and make sure your dormitory and ablutions are also fit for inspections. That will keep you busy until lights out. Now get on with it."

After that rollicking the girls concentrated on what they were supposed to do although there were quiet murmurs of discontent because they had been deprived of their free time mainly to visit the NAAFI or the Astra cinema.

In the airmen's Barrack block everything was going smoothly thanks to Corporal Deacon's tips. During the afternoon he wandered between the two dormitories he was in charge of to see what progress was being made. In each room he asked for the airmen's attention.

"When you have got your kit up to scratch you will make sure the room and the ablutions do not let you down on the inspection. I suggest you organise yourselves into working parties that way you will find the task much easier. At 18:00hrs you will stand by your beds and if I am satisfied the rest of the time will be yours. "

After breakfast the following morning kit was laid out for inspection under the watchful eyes of the respective Corporals. The airmen had obviously listened well to Corporal Deacon's advice and instructions because he had very little correcting to do.

"You have done well and exceeded my expectations, I can find nothing wrong with your kit layouts, your dress and the cleanliness of your accommodation and if I cannot find any faults I am sure the Wing Commander will not."

That reassurance brought smiles from everyone and eased the nervousness they were feeling.

In the Waffery there was very little harmony. Some of the airwomen with more service were being very disruptive towards the girls who had just left basic training and were concentrating on arranging their kit lay-out as per the diagram pinned to the notice board. Norma Peters beckoned Jean Briggs to ask her if she was having any problems with her girls.

"Two and they are ones with some service in."

"I have three and I am going to mark their card for they are a bad influence especially on the girls who have only just left recruit training their attitude will definitely put the new girls off this course. I'll tell you what I will do and I will take full responsibility. I will charge them with being disruptive then make them put their kit away then fall them in outside. You come with me Jean."

When they entered the dormitory they found three of the new girls in tears and their kit being scattered around .by the three older girls.

"You three, stand by your beds and be quick about it. I am charging each one of you with using bullying tactics to intimidate other course students. You have now five minutes to stow away your kit then fall in outside. Corporal Briggs, stay with them and make sure they do just that. The rest of you girls help your friends to rearrange their kit."

As she went towards the other room she heard raised voices and laughter which she quickly saw was coming from the two disruptive girls who were shaking laid-out kit off beds by means of bouncing the bed rail at the foot of the beds.

"What do you two morons think you are doing?"

The girls drooped what they were doing and scrambled back to their respective bed spaces.

"I am taking disciplinary action against you two disgusting creatures. I am charging you with employing bullying tactics to intimidate other course students. You have now five minutes to stow your kit away then fall in outside. 'MOVE'. The rest of you girls help your friends to rearrange their kit."

When she returned to her own room the three miscreants were tidying their bed spaces, their kit already put away.

"Go and keep an eye on those other two Jean and let me know when they are ready I will take them all outside together. Stand at ease by your beds and I do not want to hear the slightest noise from you."

"Corporal Peters, Corporal Briggs!" shouted Sergeant Dean from outside the rooms.

Norma went to meet Sergeant Dean and saw W/O Anderson there as well.

"What is going on Corporal? the inspection officer will be here in a few minutes."

Norma told them what had happened and the steps she had taken. "I am just waiting for the two to come from Corporal Briggs room Ma'am then I am marching them outside."

"I want you to stay with the inspection party; Corporal Briggs can take charge of them outside. Are your two ready Corporal Briggs?"

"Yes Ma'am."

The WO looked into the room. "You two out here and be quick about it." She went to the other room. "You three get out here on the double. Corporal Briggs take these nauseating females outside and you five will keep silent until I can deal with you. Stay here Corporal Peters while the Sergeant and me go and meet the Squadron Leader."

"Five students absent from the kit inspection Ma'am otherwise all present and correct," said Viv reporting to the Squadron Leader

"Are these the five missing from my inspection Warrant?"

"Yes Ma'am, disciplinary action is being taken against them by Corporal Peters."

"Good, but tell me about it after the inspection. Lead the way Sergeant Dean."

Norma Peters saluted her outside the room and reported. "Room 3 is ready for your inspection Ma'am."

"Corporal Peters?"

"Yes Ma'am."

"We will have a chat when I have finished the inspection."

Sergeant Dean called the room to attention.

"Stand them at ease Sergeant "

"Stand at ease! Then come to attention giving your rank and name to the officer when she approaches you."

On completion she spoke to the girls. "I congratulate you all for a smart turnout it is a very long time since I have had that pleasure, you have commenced your course in fine style and I hope you will continue to do so."

She was equally satisfied with Room 4 and repeated her congratulations to the occupants. Both rooms were instructed to put away their kit then wait for further instructions.

The two room doors were closed while Norma Peters recounted what had happened to make her take disciplinary action against the five culprits.

"Well done Corporal you took the proper action, not only will you have earned the respect of the students but it will be a big boost in creating a good reputation for this NCO Instructing School. Now I want you to bring the girls from Room 4 into Room 3, I would like a word with them all."

When they were all assembled she addressed them. "Don't stand around sit on the beds the inspection is over and this is an informal chat. I have just been put into the picture of what occurred this morning in these two rooms by your Corporal Peters. That sort of behaviour should never happen and we try our best to eliminate it and that is paramount in our curriculum. Unfortunately incidents like that do flare up but believe me we punish the culprits most severely. Carry on W/O Anderson."

Viv called the room to attention as the Squadron Leader left the room.

"Outside she faced the five airwomen. "I will be taking your charges as soon as I receive the paperwork. Sergeant Dean keep these five separated at all times until I have seen them."

"Corporal Peters get the rest of the students out here on parade," ordered Sergeant Dean.

When the students had assembled Dot placed each of the five between two senior airwomen. "You will stay in that position between each two students they are your escorts until you are called to see the Squadron Leader "

"What about visits to the toilet and at meal times Sergeant?" asked one of the escorts.

"You will escort them to the toilets and stay with them and the toilet door must be kept open. At meal times I will arrange for you to be seated at five separate tables, are there any more questions? Very well then, Corporal Briggs take over and March them off to the education block to see the Blue-Belles film documentary. Corporal Peters go to the orderly room and make out the charge sheets."

In the airmen's accommodation everything went according to Corporal Deacon's prediction. The Wing Commander congratulated the students on their kit presentation and also the smartness in their appearance. "It is obvious to me Cpl Deacon has played a big part in you producing such an excellent turnout but not a surprise because you people are being trained by the elite. You have followed your Cpl's. advice, keep on doing so and you will turn out as first class NCO instructors.

W/O Barrett brought the students to attention as the Wingco' left the room. "Carry on Sergeant ," he said to Jim Farrow.

"Well done, now put your kit away, change into your working uniform then fall in outside, we are going to see the BlueBelles documentary film where you will learn a lot about foot drill."

When the Wingco' got outside he found Squadron Leader Macfarlane waiting for him. "Hello Mac' how did your inspection go? This one was a doddle; I could not find a single fault. From the look on your face you have been having problems haven't you?" She then told him about the whole incident.

"Well done Corporal Peters, you know Mac' we have certainly got a great team of NCOs. This is when we show our support for them. I will deal with these charges myself Mac' to stop wasting our time for us to get them off the station as fast as we can. I will have a word with the CO to put him in the picture and remand them to him for his punishment and you can guess what that will be. I want them off the station today because we have not the facilities to keep them under close arrest which is where they should be right now. Leave it with me Mac' I will get in touch with you as soon as I can."

Three hours later the five ex-WRAF were deposited at the local railway station with travel warrants in their hands for transportation to their home town. Their discharge papers to be sent later by post.

The news of the discharges brought cheers from the students. The quote of the day came from one of the student airwomen.... "Thank goodness for that, perhaps we can now get on with what we joined this course for!"

CHAPTER 35

The students now began their training in earnest. Early morning Physical Training was followed by Foot Drill and Education Classes. It was noted by the training staff how much they appeared to be enjoying the drill and they were constantly asked if they could see the BlueBelles film again. When this request was brought to the attention of Bill Barrett he phoned Viv and told her about the keenness the students were showing and would she accompany him to look them over.

"I certainly will it will be very interesting to see what progress our staff has made with them and there is no time like the present Bill. I will meet you at the parade ground in five minutes."

As soon as they stepped foot onto the Parade Ground Joe Franks came over to them.

"There is no problem Joe," said Bill, we have heard the students are keen to see the BlueBelles film again and that gives me the impression they are keen on their drill."

"I can confirm that Bill, they are taking in everything the instructors tell them and it shows in their reactions and they seem determined to improve on themselves. I am not surprised they want to see that film again you could even hear a pin drop they are so intent on watching every movement. Corporal Deacon tells me the lads even practice in their dormitory some of the moves they have seen in the film. That shows how much they are interested."

"That is pleasing to know Joe, why don't you stand with us then we can compare notes. Shall we assess the lads first?"

"They watched for a few minutes whilst Sergeant Farrow put them through their paces.

"Ladies first, what do you say Viv?"

"They have a good body movement and they hold their rank and file very well. I did see two or three moving their heads instead of using their eyes to keep their dressing. They also know they are being watched and some are over reacting by swinging their arms too high causing their shoulders to twist. Those are not faults because of the short time they have been drilling, I would say it is enthusiasm, they just want to please their instructor but in this case…us."

"Thanks Viv that is a very fair assessment. Don't you agree Joe?"

"I could not have made a better one it was a good one VIv."

"What about you Bill?" asked Joe.

"Sorry Joe, I too could not improve on that assessment, I will add, you are doing a cracking job on those lads. Now for the girls and it is my turn to do the honours."

They took a long hard look at the girls in action.

"Oh dear," exclaimed Bill, "I have a feeling our presence has knocked them off their stride. I am not going to be unkind and mark them down for what I believe is sheer nerves instead I will judge them on how they can improve. Remember the Wibbly Wobblies Viv? That is number one fault which will have to be righted. For your information Joe, they are the bouncy bits that bounce about uncontrollably when they swing their arms too high."

The three of them had to turn away from facing the girls to have a muffled laugh.

"Right then let us get back to business. As with the lads they also are turning their heads to keep their dressing and not concentrating on the words of command, their minds are on us. What do you think Joe?"

"They are way behind the boys' standard but as you said, they are conscious of us watching."

"I am not happy about their body movement as they march," added Viv, they have not got into a rhythm and I think they could do with a bit of the old BlueBelle treatment."

"What kind of treatment is that if you don't mind me asking?" asked a perplexed Joe.

"Shall we tell him the magic formula Bill?"

"Aye and why not."

They both began to sing softly…"BlueBelles are we, bouncing up and down like this"

"That is the song that will make them sway their bodies in harmony and we guarantee it not to fail Joe," smiled Viv. "Would you like Bill and me to give you a demonstration?"

"I would indeed and if it works I will buy you a pint in the Mess bar Bill."

"Then go and tell the lads to stop what they are doing and tell them why, they may as well see the BlueBelle magic in operation."

They approached Dot Dean and asked her to sit this one out. "Please do not take umbrage because it does not reflect on your instructing Dot but we think they are a little slow and we hope to give them a little impetus by sprinkling a little BlueBelle Magic on your girls."

"I don't mind because I am sure to learn something myself from you two and maybe if I ask you nicely you will give me that magic formula," she said with a laugh.

Bill faced the flight of girls and ordered..."Atten...Shun. Stand at Ease. You appear to be having a little difficulty in marching to a rhythm so W/O Anderson and I are going to sprinkle you with some BlueBelle Magic. Do you all know the famous BlueBelle song?"

"Yes sir" they all answered.

"Good, because you all will be singing it shortly. Now I want you to visualise you are BlueBelle girls and W/O Anderson who trained the BlueBelles is now going to sprinkle you with some of that magic."

"Viv took over the flight by ordering them..."Atten...Shun. Right...Turn, Quick..March." As they marched she encouraged them to swing their arms midway between waist and shoulder. Bill was marching with them told them to correct their dressing without moving their heads use your eyes only. He then began to whistle the BlueBelles song which brought smiles to the faces of the girls.

"Right girls you know the tune now sing it and let your body move to the rhythm."

The response was weak to start with but when he chided them to sing louder they responded well. Gradually they found they were keeping time with the tune followed automatically by their body movements. Viv marched them round the Parade Ground until she was satisfied the tune was doing the trick. "Stop singing and March to attention" she ordered. When she saw some faltering she told them. "Sing it to yourselves but still concentrate on your marching and I do not want to hear you or see your lips move." After a few circuits she halted them and stood them at ease.

"Well ladies what do you think of your performance now?"

"It was great Ma'am we could not help but March properly to that tune."

"That was the BlueBelle magic working for you, it got us to victory and there is no reason why it cannot happen to you. Listen to that applause from the airmen that should be some encouragement for you."

Joe Franks and Dot Dean could not believe the improvement it had made in such a short time.

"You both have never lost your touch; you are still 'The Best', what a team you two were. I am going to watch that film again as well as this lot are you coming with me Dot?"

"I most certainly am. Thank you for your demonstration I will try to build on that."

As Bill and Viv walked off they did so to spontaneous applause from everyone on the Parade Ground. They looked at each other smiled and responded with a wave.

"That was nice," said Viv.

"Hey-up! Here is George Miller waiting for us, I'll bet he will have something to say he is sure to have been watching."

"Been putting in a bit of practice have you?"

"Not really George just giving a helping hand but I admit it was good to get hold of the reins again especially with my partner here, it felt very nostalgic but enjoyable. We were just saying we would swap places with those instructors if we could get away with it."

"That big victory put an end to the BlueBelles saga that was a one-off never to be repeated mores the pity. Anyway you certainly showed you have not lost your touch I enjoyed watching your performance especially for what it did for those girls. You don't mind if sometime when the film is being showed if I sneak in and watch it."

"George, you would be more than welcome and that film is there for anyone to see."

"Just listen to Joe Franks there," observed George, "he will probably March off singing that song to himself.

"Right, shouted Joe. Parade…Atten…Shun! Carry-On NCOs and remember what you have just been taught but sing it to yourselves and that includes you 'BlueBoys'." Joe's wit brought instant laughter from the whole parade.

♦♦♦

The first assessments covering a four week period were good overall. A few of the students had to be reminded to put more time into private studying if they want to qualify for the RAF education test. Some were told to show more enthusiasm by asking more questions about the roles of NCOs. All were congratulated on their foot drill and from now on they would be taught how to become successful instructors and NCOs.

Joe Franks called Sergeant Jim Farrow and Sergeant (w) Dot Dean to him. "We are now at the stage where the students are to learn how to give orders and have full control of a flight of airmen or airwomen as the case might be. In our case the airwomen are outnumbered so I have devised a scheme where we can even the flights out and that is by having three mixed flights of seventeen personnel. Any questions so far?"

"What parts do the instructors play in these mixed flights Joe?" asked Jim.

"I was coming to that. The three Corporals will take a flight each. Yes I do realise women will be giving orders to men, tell me…what's new? An instructor be it a man or woman should be qualified to teach members of the opposite sex. Who did not have a woman teacher at school? So tell me what is different. And I stress, if there are any instances of male chauvinism among the male students I want to know immediately. Now where were we? Ah, yes. The three corporals will have a flight each and you two Sergeants will be fluttering about between them doing what you know best…supervising. Does that answer your queries and doubts?"

"There is no reason why it cannot fail to work," replied Jim.

"Of course it will work it is my solution to a tricky problem but don't come patting me on the back and calling for three cheers in front of whole assembly please spare my blushes."

"Would one of Bill Barrett's Blue Peter Badges be acceptable as a substitute?" asked Dot.

"Haven't you two got students waiting for you?" retaliated Joe. "Go on hop it."

They both left him laughing their heads off.

"Cheeky bloody kids he muttered to himself," with a grin.

Jim and Dot worked together to form three mixed flights. The girls were spread among the boys to avoid being bunched together. On completion, Joe who had been watching came forward to address the assembly.

"Now that is a grand sight for sore eyes, Roses blooming amongst thorns. I wish that could have happened to me when I was in training. It is no good you lads pulling your faces you don't know how lucky you are, think what these young ladies are going to have to put up with you lot, they have my sympathy. Seriously it will be a big help to you all in character building. I now offer a word of warning to you all, if there is the slightest sign of any chauvinism the culprit will be kicked off the course immediately, there will be no second chance. Have you heard of the word 'Comradeship'? That was the watchword of the BlueBelles you have seen and admired and look where it got them…think about it. Your task now is to take over your flight in turn to learn how to give orders as an NCO instructor. You will be assessed at regular intervals so please remember you are now at a serious stage of your training. You are not being thrown in at the deep end because your instructors are always there to help you. For your own sakes give it your best shot we want you all to pass this course." He turned to Jim and Dot. "Carry on they are all yours."

CHAPTER 36

Bill Barrett was in his office and called "Come in" in answer to a knock on his door. It was opened slightly and a voice asked. "Any chance of a brew sir?" When the door was flung open Bill jumped to his feet sporting a huge grin to see Wings enter with just as big a grin. Bill came forward to shake his hand very warmly.

"What a surprise and pleasure to have you back sir; you are back permanently aren't you?"

"Indeed I am and it feels great to be back."

"Welcome back sir we have missed you terribly," added Flight Sergeant Roper.

"Thank you Flight," he replied as they shook hands.

"I will go and organise a celebration brew."

"Sit yourself down sir and tell me all about it for you have been away for quite some time,"

"Yes and I am given to understand you have been rather busy here during that time. Has it been a case of while the cats' away the mice will play?"

"We have had little time to play I can assure you sir, you will be surprised at what we have achieved."

"I have already had a run down from the Wingco' and he is delighted with your progress, I felt I was on the brink of redundancy."

"No fear of that sir, we could have done with some of your little snippets of ideas you used to spring on us. Anyway are you fit to take up the reins again?"

"I am, I had a lot of time on my hands and I was trying to come up with some ideas but a hospital is not the right environment for that."

"Here is your brew sir."

"Thank you Flight I have waited far too long a time for one of these, Cheers everyone, this has been worth waiting for," he said as he took a good slurp from his mug. "No doubt you are waiting to hear of my hospital experience Mister Barrett."

Bill looked at Margaret who took the hint and said. "If you will excuse me sir I have a bit of sorting out to do in the ops' room."

"Right Mister Barrett here we go. I was in a pretty poor state when I was admitted and it took a few days before it was decided I was ready to go under their microscopes I lost count of the number of times I was under scrutiny and tests. Fortunately from the consultants point of view that damned nerve reared its ugly head sending me into one of those states that you bore the brunt of.. I can never forgive myself for placing you under that ordeal. No, let me finish." he said holding up his hand. "Straight away I was whipped into the X-Ray room so that the normal and abnormal X-Rays could be compared. When I had calmed down and was back to normal I was told I had a ninety nine percent chance of being cured but only after what would be a very delicate operation. I was told that I was a very fortunate young man because one of the top brain surgeons was interested in my case and wanted to know the results at every stage of the examinations. He had been informed of the latest test and we were waiting anxiously for his reply. Two days later I was told he had decided to carry out the operation. The consultants and staff were highly delighted and I might add I was quite chuffed myself. I then had to wait until it was convenient for him to carry out the operation and I tell you Mister Barrett two or three days seemed a very long time. The result was I am now completely cured with no more thin edge of the wedges for you."

"That is the best news I could wish for sir. Welcome home we all have missed you."

"I have now a lot of threads to pick up to get back into the swing of things. Tell me are you satisfied with the way the school is being run and the progress of the students?"

"It could not be better sir it is in the very capable hands of Flight Sergeant Franks who is running it to...I almost said perfection but that would only appertain if you and I was running the show," that brought on a laugh from the pair of them. "We are short on female students; the CO. got rid of five airwomen for being a bad influence and bullying. We do have a full quota of airmen and Joe Franks has used his loaf and come up with a good scheme. I will not tell you about it but I would like you to see for yourself the students in action and it will give Joe the opportunity to introduce you to them'

"Right then I will do that before reporting back to my office and PA.

"I'll bet she has missed you. By the way, where did you get the tan? You did not get that in hospital"

"That is another story Mister Barrett but it can wait. Pop round to my office sometime and I will give you all the gen." As he left he looked in the ops' room "Thanks Flight, all is clear now."

♦♦♦

As Bill Barrett made his way to the Parade Ground to see how the mixed flights of airmen and airwomen were progressing he met George Miller.

"Going my way George?"

"If it is to see your students, yes I am. You know Bill I keep popping out from my office just to watch them performing. Joe and his staff are doing a cracking job instilling confidence into them; you have a damned good team of instructors there."

"When Joe Franks saw them he came over to ask. "Well what do you think of the mixed flights now?"

"I can expect the Training Manual to get overhauled and amended" replied George.

Bill joined in with. "I want it to be a success to show that we can turn out Drill Instructors to a high standard and with the right facilities we could set up a permanent training school here at RAF March."

"How many students have you?" asked George.

"Fifty one."

"When they all qualify as you hope, you will have fifty one personnel qualified for promotion, what is going to happen to them? From information I have gathered the recruitment figures are far from being satisfactory. So how are these fifty one going to be employed? You can't keep churning out NCO drill Instructors willy-nilly can you?"

"George, I don't think that point has ever crossed the minds of the top Brass and it is certainly going to give them a king sized headache. I put myself to blame as much as anyone for not having the foresight to see that this could happen. I think I had better go and place it in the lap of the first chain of command, our friend Squadron Leader Cody."

He went to ask for an appointment to see Wings. "Is there any chance of seeing your boss Marion?"

She buzzed Wings. "Yes you can go straight in sir."

"Ah Mister Barrett I see you have something on your mind haven't you?"

"Indeed I have sir good guess."

"No guesswork Mister Barrett, observation."

"So what else have you been studying during your stay in hospital, trick cyclistism?"

Wings laughed. "I had plenty of spare time on my hands to think about what I call important matters. My favourite was body language, one can learn a great deal from that and I pride myself on being able to read a person almost straight away."

"So will that be another string to your bow sir?"

"I must admit that it can be very useful but I need a few more test flights under my belt. "Now shall we get down to your problem?"

"Not mine OUR problem sir. When the students complete this course what is to become of them and will they be promoted? And will we be able to continue running courses when the students would have nothing to see at the end of them? With no improvement in recruitment we do not stand a chance."

"That is a blow Mister Barrett which we did not foresee and I can visualise our reputation taking a nosedive when this gets to Command. Have you had any thoughts about it Mister Barrett?"

"It is a sticky one sir, I don't think we can cure it but somehow we shall have to find a way out to soften the blow to avoid egg on our faces."

"I agree with you there Mister Barrett and it looks like we all need to pull our fingers out to find a solution."

"Before I leave sir are you going to tell me about that tan?"

"Wings laughed. "Do you remember me asking you about your honeymoon cruise? I followed up that conversation and booked a similar one the difference being it was not a honeymoon one."

"So you went solo?"

"Not on your Nellie, what fun would I have had going alone, I did not fancy the idea of being a wallflower so I took my girlfriend."

"Not the one you told me about was 'just good friends' with no commitments?"

"The very same one and the name of the game has changed us around to being a fully committed couple."

"Well done sir that means the cruise was a success."

"It was everything like you told me except we did not spend all out time relaxing in deck chairs like you did. We young ones do not take too kindly lounging about sat on our backsides doing nothing," he grinned. "We were up on our feet joining in the fun and what a time we had."

"I gather from your enthusiasm you enjoyed the cruise but did you benefit from it?"

"In more ways than one Mister Barrett it did me the world of good and I now feel like a new man. I have you to thank for putting the idea in head in the first instance."

"And what is the situation if I may ask regarding your girl friend?"

Wings smiled and replied. "It could not be better, after all this time we have come to realise that it is what we want for keeps."

"Congratulations to you both." He said as he shook Wings by the hand.

"Thank you Mister Barrett but I think now it is time I went to pass the buck."

"What is on your mind Bill?" asked the Wingco'.

Wings told him the reason for his visit.

"It appears we have dropped a huge clanger then Bill and I don't think it is going to be well received at Command and we want to avoid that if it is possible. What are W/O Barrett's views on it? Are we going to need him to get us out of another mess?"

"At present he has no ideas sir but he is trying to give it his best shot and if he does not come up with something then I will be very surprised. The real answer is in the recruiting figures and W/O Barrett's magic wand has its limitations."

The Wingco' reached for his intercom buzzer and asked his PA to get himself and Squadron Leader Cody an interview with the Commanding Officer.

After a minute or two Barbara buzzed back to say." You can go right away sir."

"Come on Bill let us go and I suggest we throw our hats in first."

"Gentlemen I can see from your faces all is not well, take a seat and let me hear the worst."

"I'm afraid that is all you will hear sir there is no good news." He repeated what Wings had told him.

"By the sounds of it we have got ourselves in a right pickle, how the dickens are we going to wriggle out of this one? The AOC will be reaching for his paracetamol when he hears this. Has W/O Barrett not come up with a solution?"

"Not as yet sir but he is certainly working on it. He says if we cannot find a cure we can try and soften the blow to avoid having egg on our faces."

"Gentlemen I think we have a light at the end of the tunnel, W/O Barrett's mind is working overtime already, what he is saying is, if he cannot cure it he will find the next best thing. Bill, I want to be contacted as soon as W/O Barrett brings his solution to you, I will send for you John then we can pour over it together and hopefully give it our blessings."

On returning to his office Wings rang Bill Barrett. "Mister Barrett I have just returned from a meeting with the CO. and the Wingco'. I am afraid the CO. is depending solely on you to solve the problem because to be honest the three of us haven't got a clue."

"Don't worry about it sir but what I would like from you are the latest recruitment figures. I shall be in the SWO's office if you want to contact me, if I move off I will contact you."

"What a nice surprise, look who has just come in Ian to visit us," exclaimed George. "Take a pew and tell us your troubles."

"I have come for help and I think you are the man to solve a big problem." He then reminded George of the previous conversation they had concerning the fate of the school students.

"It is a sticky one alright don't you agree Ian?"

"It certainly is George but can't we sort it out for him he seems a nice enough chap."

"Aye he is not a bad old stick let us give it a go."

"Just a minute before you start George Miller, can we have a bit less of the old?"

"Have you made any progress yet Bill?"

"Not really because I am waiting for the latest recruitment figures from Wings. We can easily close the school down until the recruitment figure increases but if they don't the school will be a dead duck."

"That does not sound so good to me what say you Ian?"

"I think those kids out there have no chance to qualify with that hanging over their heads. Initially it was a good idea but circumstances robbed them of that. I think the students should be returned to their respective units with the exception of the ones who have just passed out in their basic training, they will have to apply for another trade. The two best students should be as promised posted to your staff Bill then close the school down."

"What do you think of that Bill? I think it will better any solution the Brass might come up with but if they want to brush it aside and leave egg on their faces they will need to take a second look at it."

"It is a good one Ian and I shall put it to the board, it is no use the three of us having a bet on it being accepted because the three of us would make it the favourite." The telephone ringing interrupted any further conversation.

Ian answered it. "It is Squadron Leader Cody for you sir."

"Hello sir, a very small increase, that is bad news it does look like the school; is doomed. I have been given an idea to our problem by Flight Sergeant Roberts he is the SWO's right hand man sir. It is not the happiest of solutions bur we are clutching at straws and I think it is worth looking at. Very good sir I am on my way now."

"He wants to hear about your idea Ian. I hope it puts a smile on his face because when I left him he told me none of the big boys even had a clue where to start. If it is accepted Ian I can see you getting another stripe"

"Hey up, you just hang on a minute I am having no bloody jumped up so called Top Sergeant working in my office, this is The Royal Air Force not some damned Yankee Doodle imitating an Air Force,"

"George is getting peevish Ian he thinks you are going to take over his job."

"Get out of my office," he shouted pointing to the door.

"YES SIR" laughed Bill giving him an imitation of an American salute.

"I will swing for you one of these days Barrett," as Bill went through the door laughing.

Bill told Marion that Wings was expecting him.

"Send him in Marion", he said in reply to her buzzed message.

"Here we are again Mister Barrett up to the neck in it as they say, now give me that glimmer of hope we are looking for."

"When Bill had finished Wings looked very thoughtful then said, "It sounds a bit drastic after all the planning and preparation that has gone into it don't you think?"

"But it was the lack of foresight that let us down sir."

"I agree but is Command going to react by posting us off to RAF El-Adem as a punishment?"

"I doubt it sir but Flight Sergeant Roberts' idea has given my brain a little nudge. I think I can save our faces to a lesser degree sir and also soften the blow for the students."

"Mister Barrett, if we need a life saver now is the time, please let me walk tall into the Wingco's office with a smile on my face and an even bigger one when it is accepted at Command."

"When you think about it, it is quite simple we complete the course and promote the two star students as promised with a posting to us. The rest of the students who pass the course will have 'Qualified Drill Instructor to Junior NCO Standard' added to their personal records. All it would need is a senior officer to explain the reason why the course has to be discontinued and to give their morale a boost they would be on permanent standby. Anyone of them can be recalled as a replacement when needed. How does that sound to you sir?"

"I like it, I think you may have come up with a winner Mister Barrett but I wish I knew how you managed to think of that more or less on the spur of the moment."

"It needed something to trigger it off, in this case it was Flight Sergeant Roberts' contribution prior to that I had not a clue."

"If this is accepted I will have a word with Flight Sergeant Roberts but right now I am going to strike while the iron is hot. You know Mister Barrett I have that gut feeling it is going to work out; it has to because we have no other alternative."

Later in the day Bill received a phone call from Wings telling him the Station Commander was on his way to Command with what he says is the only solution and both he and the Wingco' were chuffed with your suggestion."

"Can you fit me in with an interview tomorrow sir?"

"What is on your mind Mister Barrett?"

"Forward planning sir," he said with a laugh. I want us to keep ahead of the AOC when he rubber stamps our idea."

"You sound very confident I must say and I would like to share it with you."

"I will do you a swap sir, your body language for my self confidence." All he could hear was a roar of laughter.

"Better still Mister Barrett what about a partnership?"

"I thought we already had one."

"Well make this an amendment. O9:30 tomorrow and I will have a brew waiting."

CHAPTER 37

Bill phoned Roy Shaw. "Roy my old friend and buddy do you fancy a gargle tonight?"

"Only on condition you are buying."

"That can be arranged, no problem."

"So you are going to stick you grubby little fingers in Tommy's China teapot again."

"She has a new hiding place now so I need to ask you or Derwent for a sub' and if that fails Fred Fox can put it on the slate."

"Bang goes my quiet reading night."

"What are you reading old pal?"

"Less of the old if you don't mind. A Medical Dictionary."

"You are still not swotting up on Brain Surgery are you?"

"No, just the quickest way to get rid of a Leech," with a loud laugh he put down the telephone receiver.

What is that man like Bill said to himself? He then rang Tommy to ask if she wanted a girlie night.

"I am always ready for one that is my only means of getting up to date news and gossip. Have you got the backing of your crackpot friends?"

"But of course and also permission to stick my grubby little fingers in your China teapot."

She laughed. "Tell Roy that unfortunately it is too heavy with all its contents for me to lift high enough to brain you with but I could always borrow Chef's Sauté pan to sauté you out."

Bill heard her giggling as she replaced the receiver.

When Bill entered the bar that evening he was welcomed by Fred Fox the duty barman.

"Good evening sir what a sight for sore eyes to brighten up this dismal clientele I am suffering with at the moment. Please accept your first drink of the evening from me to welcome you to my bar."

"Thank you Fred I accept your gracious offer and welcome with pleasure which I find very touching. As one gentleman to another thank you and I drink to your very good health."

"Hey! Just a minute what is going on here?" snorted Roy in exasperation. "Who do you think you are serving Royalty? I don't like the sound of this Derwent; does it give you the feeling that our presence in this hostelry is an embarrassment?"

"Take a pause for thought Roy; have you ever witnessed Fred being so gushing with his fingers down throat syndrome to any of us three before? It gives me the impression that Fred is toadying up for a big favour from Bill. Could it be he wants him to use his influence on us to take the pressure off Fred?"

"Now do you think for one moment I would succumb to bribery, me who has one foot in the Palace?"

There was a loud chorus of 'YES' "You would sell your soul to the devil for a free pint," laughed Roy gleefully, "and the only Palace you would step foot in is the Crystal Palace Football Club. By the way you owe me a pint."

"Fill em'up Fred and get one in for yourself, I am feeling flush tonight after raiding Tommy's China teapot."

"Okay chaps, I admit I went a bit over the top when Bill came in but I was feeling a bit cheesed off and I thought to myself go on stir it up a bit and get some life back into the bar because we don't seem to have the laughs as much as we used to."

"It is his fault," moaned Roy, "for getting wed."

"Your turn will come pretty soon." retorted Fred "I can feel it in my water."

"Then you can turn that bloody tap off quick."

"No disrespect Fred but will you excuse us for a few minutes I have something of a private nature I need to discuss with these two."

"I take no offence Bill so long as you give me a print out to barter with. Give me a shout when you want topping up."

Bill led Roy and Derwent to a table far enough away from Fred's sharp hearing.

"What is this all about?" asked Roy.

Bill told them the situation regarding the Training School and brought them up to date as far as waiting for the AOC's decision.

"So another brainwave bites the dust, when are you people going to screw your heads on the right way round? Granted the end result always ends up in your favour, it was always on the cards that recruitment was the making or breaking of its success," Roy pointed out.

"Pity about that," sympathised Derwent, "because you had a damned good system going but to my way of thinking, your idea is the only decent way out. You must keep us posted when you get the result Bill and let us hope it is the right one. Come on let us get back to Fred we need a refill and it is my shout."

"Have you put the world to rights? And can we sleep safely in our beds?" queried Fred.

"How is your good wife keeping?" asked Bill.

"She is fine thanks and she still keeps on about you taking us with you to see the BlueBelles in action. We have a group photo' of you all and each time she dusts it she gives it a kiss and says 'Thank You'."

"You want to keep on the right side of Fred and maybe his wife will put you on her famous Christmas card list Derwent and once you get that honour you can hold your head high, Bill and I are on it. A little tip, ask her for a dance at our next function you could get a tick in your box."

"What would you like to drink Fred?" Derwent asked a smiling Fred as Roy and Bill curled up laughing."

"Don't you think that is the right kind of approach then?" asked a puzzled Derwent.

"It is pathetic," answered Roy as he held his hand to his mouth pretending to stifle a yawn.

"Take no notice of these two silly sods," said Fred in sympathy, you are doing alright."

"Did you hear that Bill? He is encouraging Derwent to buy him drinks taking advantage of his good nature. Why don't you report him to the Mess President?"

Fred let out a guffaw. "He will have a job he is still in dock."

"Are you sure Fred?" asked Roy.

"Course I am and I have three pints here to back up my statement, are you on?"

"We will have to discuss that Fred if there is a danger of us losing a bet."

They moved away from the bar but just far enough for Fred to hear their loud whispers.

"He knows something because he has contacts all over the station who feed him little snippets, I would not like to risk betting against him," said a supposedly concerned Derwent.

"On the other hand if we do not accept his bet word would spread like wild fire that we only bet on sure things which would destroy our reputation."

"I am inclined to agree with Bill's logic, I say we should go for it and sod the consequences said Roy in exasperation."

Fred meanwhile pretended to busy himself polishing glasses and to all appearances oblivious to what was being said but his smiling face gave the game away that he had not missed a single word.

"Right Fred you are on," was what greeted Fred when the trio returned to the bar which was music to Fred's ears. "But how are you going to prove it?"

"Here comes my proof," he gloated, which was in the form of George Miller.

"Good evening George," he was greeted with.

"Evening all and it will be a good one when you serve me with a pint of your delicious beer Fred."

"This one is on me sir because you are the very man I want to see."

"You are not buttering me up to do you some big favour are you Fred?"

"Not at all George I am feeling very benevolent this evening after taking a beer from each off these suckers in a bet."

"Now that is some achievement Fred, you will the first one who has ever won a bet against these three shysters, how did you manage that.?"

"I bet them the Mess President is still in the RAF Hospital."

George spluttered in his beer accompanied by loud laughter from the three crackpots.

"Have I said something out of turn or summat?" queried a bewildered Fred.

"Sorry Fred," said George, "I was talking to him only today and he told me he had been discharged fit for duty and he was on his way to see you Bill, did you see him?"

"I certainly did and honoured him with a brew he had been waiting yonks for."

"When are you going to learn not to bet against these three reprobates Fred, the next one to win a bet against them will be the first."

"Don't take it to heart Fred you deserve a drink and I will be the first to buy you one."

"And I will be first after you Roy," said Derwent.

"Hang on a minute," exploded Roy. "How the 'L' can you be first after me being the first? You mean second."

"No, I know I should be second in reality, but I will still be first after you."

"I need a strong drink this plonker is doing my head in."

"I will be the first to buy you one," said Bill

"And I will be first after you," laughed George.

"Its is a bloody madhouse," exclaimed Fred shaking his head along with the roars of laughter coming from other Mess members sat in the bar shouting 'Good old George'."

"And I will have less of the old from you lot too," retaliated George'

It was some time before sanity returned to the bar.

""Do you think that George can now qualify to became the fourth crack-pot?" asked Bill of Roy and Derwent.

"After that momentary mad rush of blood to the head I think he shows potential. I personally will be the first to nominate him to the madhouse, "announced Roy.

"And I will be the first after you Roy," piped up Derwent.

"Don't start that again," snarled Roy "or I will be the first after you to buy me a drink, now get a round in then sod off and go and see if it is raining outside."

"Why?"

"To make sure I don't get wet going back to my room."

"But you live in the mess here," spluttered Derwent the drink beginning to take an effect on his thinking.

"And so do you," Roy replied, "now sup up and I will take you home."

Fred took the hint from Roy and craftily replaced Derwent's part full glass with an empty one.

"It looks like you have already supped up," continued Roy, "come on now let me get you back to your room. Goodnight all."

CHAPTER 38

At 09:25 the following morning Bill Barrett entered Wings' PA's office.

"Good morning Marion," he greeted the PA.

"Good morning Bill, you are expected I have it down in the engagement book and I have to escort you in with a brew for you both at 9:30."

"How are you Marion and how is the romance?"

She blushed then asked. "How did you know?"

“Marion, we, our little family have known since you first visited the March Hare.”

“Then Roy knows and he has never said a word to Graham about it.”

“Oh yes, we decided not to mention it until you more or less gave the game away but you have done a good job of keeping it under covers. I thought it about time it was brought out into the open to save you playing hide and seek; now you can relax and carry on with your courtship out in the open.”

She laughed. “I must admit it has been rather a strain playing cat and mouse but thank you Bill for lifting the pressure. Graham will have a surprise when I tell him because he thought we were fooling everyone. Come on or sir will be wondering if you had forgotten to turn up.”

“Good morning Mister Barrett, you are late.”

“Sorry sir I was waylaid down the corridor.”

“Thank you for the brew Marion I was ready for this.”

“Now Mister Barrett make my day with what you have got hidden up your sleeve you did mention something about forward planning to keep one step ahead of the AOC. I find that a bold statement but with your reputation nothing surprises me. This I am going to enjoy and if it does not come up to your standard I will admonish you for being late. Fire away I am ready.”

“When the students have been returned to their respective units we will be left with enough accommodation to house two more flights, consequently we will need more staff.” .

“It is getting interesting Mister Barrett and I am curious about the staff adjustments.”

“Your alarm bells are not ringing are they sir?”

“Get on with it man and put me out of my misery,” he said laughing.

Bill smiled. “To pull this scheme off here is what I would need. Two RAF Corporals one WRAF Sergeant and four WRAF Corporals ”

“Spell it out to me Mister Barrett.”

“Sergeant Farrow will have Corporal Deacon and a student Corporal and another student Corporal will join Sergeant Dixon and Corporal Harper. One student Corporal will replace Corporal Peters in Sergeant Dean’s team. Corporal Peters will be promoted and two student Corporals will join her team. I will then put Flight Sergeant Franks in charge of all the RAF flights and Flight Sergeant (w) Roper in charge of all the WRAF flights”.

They recapped until Wings had digested it.

“I think you have come up with a good one there Mister Barrett, I cannot see that being thrown out by the Big Brass, well done. I will now go and put the smile back on our senior’s faces and I will let you know how it was received.”

Bill went to the parade ground to watch the students performing. He wandered over to have a word with Flight Sergeant Franks.

“How’s it going Joe are you winning?”

"It has gone just how we wanted at each step of the way Bill, apart from one or two of both sexes who are not very confident when stood in front of the flight giving orders. We are persevering with them though but can see very little progress I'm afraid we will have a few failures."

"That is not the end of the world Joe because there is going to be a reassessment of this project."

"Don't say this is the beginning and the end of the school!"

"We have no way out Joe, the poor results in recruitment is kicking it into touch. We cannot churn out Drill Instructors if there is no-one to instruct."

"Then what is going to happen to these poor sods? They will have gone through all this for nothing."

"In a way yes, I have put forward a plan to minimise the blow and the CO will now be on his way to offer it to Command."

Bill then explained what had transpired and his plan to soften the blow.

"I can see no alternative Bill and I admire how you have thought a way out of a sticky situation. Whatever you do don't get posted from here."

"So does being in charge of the RAF flights suit you Joe?"

"Thanks Bill, it could not be better that is a responsibility I am looking forward to and you can be sure I will not let you down. When I think back to when I questioned your motives never in this wide world did I think I would be in this position today. You could easily have ruined my prospects but you had faith in me and as long as I live Bill Barrett I will never forget that. Put it there." They then shook hands.

"Can I leave it to you to put Jim and Dot in the picture Joe? By the way we want six students for our teams make sure we get the best."

"You will get the best for the best have no fear."

When Bill got back to his office he was greeted with. "You have to ring Squadron Leader Cody," from Flight Sergeant Roper.

"Thanks Margaret. "You wanted me to ring you sir, sorry I was not available I was on the Parade Ground running my eye over the students."

"No problem Mister Barrett I just wanted to tell you the CO is on his way to Command both he and the Wingco' think your idea is a life saver, all he needs to do is convince the AOC and from our experiences any idea of yours is looked on very favourably by him. I will let you know the result as soon as I get it Mister Barrett."

Bill then told Margaret Roper what was in the pipe line. "You will be fully in charge of the WRAF contingent. How does that appeal to you?"

"I will look forward to that with relish that will keep me busy."

"But it does not mean that I am to be neglected."

"Well if you cannot look after yourself God help the rest of your staff."

"I am just off to have a word with Viv to put her in the picture of what is going on. Can you manage without me for a little while now you are about to get extra responsibilities?"

"I can do that job and yours with my eyes shut given the chance."

"Then I had better look to my laurels or a female battleaxe will be sitting in this chair bossing everyone around. I will have a word with your superior about you madam."

"You will get no sympathy vote from Viv she is our leader and if it comes to 'hey lads hey' you will be out-voted. Now clear off Bill Barrett and let me get on with my work."

♦♦♦

At Command Group Captain Eric Pilling was well received by his old friend Air Commodore Charles Wildeman. "Good to see you again Eric although the subject matter could be more pleasing," he said shaking his friend' hand. "Now put me in the picture of where we went wrong."

Eric started by telling him the findings that had emerged and what it entailed.

"How the 'L' could we have overlooked that Eric, not just you and me but the rest of your staff and the biggest surprise is WO Barrett not picking it up. We have been relying on Barrett to pull us out of the mire too often Eric which is totally unfair of us. The crunch is have you come up with a solution?"

"No sir we have not but W/O Barrett has."

The AOC's face lit up immediately on hearing that, he banged his desk top in delight. "That man has gone and done it again. Eric I can visualise us relying on him right up to his retirement day. Come on tell me his idea."

Eric unfolded Bill's plan in detail to a very happy AOC.

"Not only has he has saved our faces Eric but in a roundabout way he has turned it to our advantage. A very simple but well thought out plan and it has my approval in its entirety. Tell me, has the course been a success and if we had the recruits to train would it have been a success?"

"In one word sir, Yes"

"Thank you Eric and to show my appreciation for what you have all done I will come and take the salute at the passing out parade then comfort them with the reason the school has to close and present any awards they may have earned. Give me the date of the passing out parade I need it to have it entered in my forthcoming engagements. Now about the Queen's Birthday honours list which is due shortly and from the list I requested from you earlier I have whittled it down to six names to put forward for recognition. For the B.E.M. I have chosen W/O Miller and Flight Sergeant Franks. For my Commendation I have chosen Flight Sergeant (w)Page, Sergeant (w)Dean, Corporal Deacon and Corporal (w)Springs. I will present them on the passing out parade day. Does that meet with your approval Eric? I have also added two civilians to the list, Helen Fraser and Mister Hardcastle to receive my personal Commendation; I will present these two privately".

"Excellent, each and everyone has earned their award I am pleased with your choices and thank you very much Charles the training staff and trainees will appreciate and feel honoured you have taken such an interest in them."

"You will stay overnight with us Eric we will enjoy your company and have a good chat exchanging views of RAF March and here at Command, I will just phone the wife and tell her you are coming for dinner and to make up the spare bed for you."

♦♦♦

Viv was very surprised when Bill told her the instructor school was doomed.

"It has to be Bill if we are not getting the recruits there is nothing we can do about it. I like your idea of promoting Corporal (w) Peters, she is a smart and clever girl as she proved with that bullying business and you are giving six of the students a chance as opposed to the original two and getting two extra flights. I like that build up of our training programme but that will be as far as it goes won't it Bill? We cannot accommodate any more can we?"

"No, this will be our lot mores the pity. I think it was George Miller who said. If one of the establishments were to reopen as a training school your present staff would be decimated, they would be needed to staff it. When that time comes which looks like being a long way off it will be pandemonium trying to fill the staff vacancies then promotions will be handed out by the bucketful. At least we are training enough students to fill those roles when the time comes after a refresher course, of course."

"But of course."

"Anything in the pipeline for Mess functions Viv? Is there any chance of a dining in night followed by a dance?"

"We are working on having a Whist Drive for a change but we are short of tables."

"Tom Hardcastle may be able to help you there, sound him out and see what he can come up with."

"Good idea Bill I never gave Tom a thought, and it has been suggested we do have a dining-in night to celebrate the Queen's Birthday, you never know there may be some lucky person who will have cause to celebrate it personally."

"Now that is something worth following up Viv. I know Wings will jump at the chance of dining with us unless the Officers Mess take priority if they celebrate as well. I will sound him out."

♦♦♦

The following afternoon Bill received a message to report to the CO's office.

"He was greeted by Helen Fraser. "Hello Bill, welcome to the gathering of the *Three Just Men*. You three are here that often I often wonder if it is some kind of a secret lodge similar to the Freemasons."

"If I give you our secret sign will you let me in?"

"Come on, I will take you in, you daft beggar, they are waiting for you. Warrant Officer Barrett sir," she announced.

"Ah Mister Barrett, come and sit down," the CO said, in response to Bill's salute.

Bill saw that the Wingco' and Wings were present.

"Gentlemen, you are waiting for the result of my meeting with the AOC. You can now uncross your fingers Squadron Leader Cody, for the decision has been made."

Wings looked a bit sheepish. "There is no harm in calling on the fates to be kind to us sir."

"When I explained the situation to him he was taken completely by surprised and asked how we all could have overlooked it. Oh yes he blamed himself as much as the rest of us and became quite despondent until I told him that you Mister Barrett had come up with a solution. Gentlemen, it meets with his approval and he accepts it in its entirety. Well done Mister Barrett once more you have pulled us out of the…speaking politely….mire! He was so delighted he has decided to visit us on the passing out parade day to take the salute and tell the students the reason of the discontinuation of the school, how it affects them and to present any awards."

"We certainly have come off better than expected sir," said the Wingco' "thanks to Mister Barrett here. Perhaps we can now settle down to a quite and well organised unit and I can fore-see no more changes until the recruitment figures cause us to open up one of the closed down establishments."

"Then it will cause mayhem with our training staff sir," replied Bill, "because we are the only ones able to supply experienced instructors."

"I see your point Mister Barrett, as you say it will cause mayhem we will need our thinking caps on then that is for sure."

"After our present situation has been sorted out I would like to ask Mister Barrett if he will work on a contingency plan for that event happening."

"It will be a huge task sir and the success of it will be in a lengthy notification of it happening. Once we get that, full backing from the highest level will be required. If I was given carte-blanche similar to the one I had when training the BlueBelles team I would guarantee a job well done."

"Mister Barrett I could not give you that power it would have to come from the highest authority, at present all I am asking you to do is draw up a contingency plan. When the need arises the person to put in charge of putting the plan into practice will no doubt be decided by a higher authority. Don't get me wrong Mister Barrett your qualifications are of the highest standard as you have already proved but it is not a subject we can discuss at this present time. That will be all gentlemen, thank you."

"Well I made a right pig's foot of that sir didn't I?" He said to Wings as they walked down the corridor towards Wings' office.

"I'm afraid you did Mister Barrett I think the CO was none too pleased he gave me the impression he thought you wanted to take full command of the situation. I was stunned when you let your tongue do your thinking, very much out of character Mister Barrett. I would put it down to having a mad rush of blood to the head."

"You are right in everything you said sir, I was a complete idiot and I should have known better. I am going back to apologise he deserves that much."

"Good for you Mister Barrett."

Bill turned tail and went back to Helen's office. "Is the CO alone Helen if so will you ask him if he could spare me a minute please?"

"Trouble in t'mill Bill?"

"You could say that, I am hoping he is in a forgiving mood."

"Oh dear, Sir, WO Barrett is here asking if you could spare him a minute."

"Send the rascal in Helen."

She laughed and said to Bill. "I have to send the rascal in," she then held up a thumb for encouragement. "Go on, in you go you know the route."

"I'll see you when I come out."

Bill saluted on entering.

"You have not disappointed me Mister Barrett I have been expecting you. I know you have come to apologise but that is not necessary because it takes a big man to admit his mistakes. I may have seemed abrupt with your little outburst but I could not ignore it in the presence of two senior officers. I put the incident in the category of euphoria we all felt with the AOC's acceptance of your plan."

"Thank you sir for being so understanding there will be no more stupid outbursts and that is a promise."

The CO laughed. "You know Mister Barrett the more we work together the more I find I am following in the AOC's footsteps in understanding you and your logic; let us keep it as such."

Bill thanked him, saluted then left the office a very relieved Warrant Officer.

"Nice to see you with a bit of colour back in your cheeks Bill," teased Helen, "are you back in his good books?"

"I think in future when I come to your office I will enter with a complete shut down of my inner thoughts, that should stop you from reading them, you are too clever by far Helen Fraser but I love you for it." He bent over and kissed her on the cheek.

"Be off with you, you old flatterer," she said smiling.

"A bit less of the old if you don't mind madam."

After training had finished for the day Bill asked all NCOs to stay behind.

"What I am about to tell you concerns each and every on of us." He commenced by giving the reason the school had to be discontinued, then the steps to be taken to introduce two new flights. It will need the addition of one Sergeant , two RAF Corporals and four WRAF Corporals , to supplement our staff. On the passing out day parade the AOC is coming to take the salute, present awards and explain the reason why the school has to be discontinued which hopefully will soften the blow to the students. There you have it in a nutshell. Are there any questions or queries?"

"Who will form the instruction teams for the new flights?" asked Sergeant Fell.

"Sergeant Farrow, Corporal Deacon and a student Corporal. Sergeant Dixon, Corporal Harper and a student Corporal. The other three flights stay as they are. The WRAF flights have still to be detailed. One other thing, Flight Sergeant Franks will be taking full charge of all the RAF and Flight Sergeant Roper will take full charge of all the WRAF and I will be the major-domo. You two being so considerate will be taking the load from my over burdened shoulders. Do I hear murmurs of discontent?"

"No sir" mumbled Joe and Margaret.

"Does an office each go with this exalted position sir?" asked Joe.

"We are getting four new Corporals but there will not be enough bunks to accommodate them," said an anxious Sergeant Dean.

"Flight Sergeant Roper that is your first problem to solve as i/c the WRAF," said a grinning Bill.

"Thank you sir and I can see it being a right problem."

"I think you will have a similar problem on your hands Flight Sergeant Franks."

"And don't I know it, I knew there was a catch to being put in charge of all the airmen," he replied.

"It is tough at the top Flight Sergeant but don't come crying on my shoulder I am not a Mary Butcher. If there are no more queries then off you go for your din-dins. Stay back Flight Sergeant Franks, Flight Sergeant Roper, Sergeant Farrow and Sergeant Dean I want a quick word."

When the rest had left Bill said. "I just want to tell you in strict confidence I have nominated Corporal (w) Peters for promotion and it has been accepted by the AOC. That is the reason I could not nominate the instructors for the new WRAF flight."

"Oh well done Bill" enthused Dot, "she will make a good Sergeant."

The others agreed.

"You appreciate with having two extra flights I have had to increase the number of students to join our staff. Can you find four of them who you think will make the grade with us?"

"From the feed backs I am getting from both Jim and Dot I can see no problems on that score," said Joe. "There are many there with potential and apart from the top airman and airwoman we will have to get right down to the nitty-gritty to select the next three."

"Do you agree with what Joe says?" Bill asked the other two.

"The second airman more or less picks himself," Jim Farrow said.

"Apart from your number one girl what about the other three Dot?"

"Two are definite the other a possible but she needs that extra bit of go in her when standing in front of the flight. A bit of encouragement from Joe would do the trick you know how persuasive he can be."

"We will leave it at that then for you to sort it out between you and you two Sergeants take note of Joe's persuasive powers."

"Off you go, I will escort these two ladies to the Mess. Thanks for your time."

CHAPTER 39

Squadron Leader Cody made his way to the Parade Ground. As soon as he appeared Fight Sergeant Franks called the flights to attention and saluted.

"Good morning Flight Sergeant, I would like a few words with your instructors and students if you would stand them easy."

When this had been carried out he addressed them. "Good morning everyone, as you well know you are shortly coming to the end of your course and now is the time to start putting that extra effort into making sure each and every one of you reach high grades from the assessors. The scenario for the ones who are to be chosen to join our instruction staff here has now been changed. From the airmen, two will now be chosen and from the airwomen four are to be chosen, that is the incentive you are faced with. If you want to join our team here at RAF March you will now need to work jolly hard to win those six places. For a bonus the AOC has decided because you are the first students to take this course he will preside over your Passing out Parade and present certificates of awards.. Needless to say we want to show our appreciation by putting on a good show for him. To make sure we do that there will be a practice run for your instructors to iron out any little flaws but from what I have seen of your drill I would be very surprised if they find any.....Flight Sergeant Franks, will choose when he is ready for this practice run to take place. In the meantime Flight Sergeant you can give them some practice in putting the swank on for Wing Commander Hopwood when he makes his inspection. By the way are you any nearer to choosing the six?"

"We are nearly there sir."

"Good, carry on Flight Sergeant."

Joe addressed the three flights.

"The officers want you to put on a good show for the AOC, shall we give them a BlueBelles style show?"

He got a unanimous "Yes" from the students.

"Very well we will take a tour round the station to find somewhere to train where we can train in privacy and not be conspicuous. NCOs take your posts, I will take the lead and remember to sing that song to yourselves and when we pass the recruits at training put some swank into your marching to show them how it should be done. Quick...March."

Joe deliberately marched them past the recruits in basic training and each Sergeant Instructor stopped their flights to watch the march past telling the recruits to "Watch and learn because that is how it should be done and that is how you are going to do it!"

Joe eventually found a place behind the big hangars now used for storage by various sections of the permanent staff and well away from prying eyes. When he and his staff were satisfied with the situation Joe addressed the students.

"Well done, you certainly made those other flights take notice of you, I am now putting you on your honour not to tell anyone what we are doing in secret and that goes for you ladies who have boy friends on the camp. If I hear from anyone else of what we are up to I will know someone has been naughty and spoiled our element of surprise and then I will definitely find out the person or persons responsible and believe me your assessments will suffer but I am a trusting soul and have a lot of faith in you all. This is our plan of action." He then explained the drill routine he wants. "For the next hour we will discuss it and give it a run through until you are quite sure what you are expected to do. For the rest of the day we will revert to our normal training programme. For the first hour each morning we will come here to practice starting from tomorrow morning. If you have any suggestions I am always ready to listen but at the end of the day which will be the Passing out Parade we want this station to remember the Class 1 with pride. Parade, Atten…Shun, come on now lets give these recruits another eyeful, Quick…March."

After a few days of Joe carrying out the same routine with his students Sergeant Dixon asked Bill Barrett. "What is Joe up to?"

"What do you mean Bob?"

"Every morning for the last week he has marched his students and staff past us and after about an hour he has marched them back again. He is up to summat Bill and none of our recruits know a thing so it looks like his lot have been told to keep it buttoned."

"Thanks Bob for telling me, it does sound a bit odd I think I will go and have a word with our mystery man. Tell the other Sergeants that on no account must Joe be followed and that is an order and whoever disobeys that order will be up in front of Wings tout suite."

"It is not that serious is it Bill?"

"No, it is not serious to us but it could be to him because now I have an idea of what he is doing and I will make damned sure nobody spoils it for him."

After tidying up his desk work Bill went to the parade ground and stood on the edge watching the instructors at work on their students and noticing a big change for the better in their drill. I know what you are up to Joe Franks he said to himself, I did the very same thing myself. Well done old lad I hope you are as successful.

When Joe spotted Bill watching he marched over to him. "Good morning Bill have you come to see if we are doing our job to your satisfaction?"

"Morning Joe. No, that will be the day when I have to come and check up on you but I want to congratulate you on the great improvement the students are showing in their drill. Have you been giving them extra tuition? I have been told you have been taking them walkies for their first daily lesson, which is good it does help to get rid of the cobwebs to make them fresh and eager to carry out their drill in a better frame of mind."

"That is a roundabout way of asking what the hell are you up to Joe?"

"Give me some credit Joe, when I was told you took your charges for an hour's walk each morning I knew exactly what you were doing."

"How could you unless somebody talked out of turn."

"Nobody talked out of turn Joe I knew because I used the same method training the BlueBelles. I hope you are keeping it to yourself and not revealing it until the passing out day to show the AOC and the rest of us what the school has achieved."

"I ought to know better than to try and hide it especially from you."

"And it will stay with me Joe I will not interfere and I will not ask you your scheme I want to be as surprised as everyone else but how are they shaping up for you?"

"Very well indeed Bill they are full of excitement and therefore putting their heart and soul into it I am really proud of them."

"I have sent out an order you have not to be followed by anyone during your morning exercise with dire threats to anyone disobeying my order so you now know that you can practice in peace."

"Thanks Bill that is a relief."

"It is me who is now worried that you are going to steal my thunder."

"Never, no one will ever be able to do that Bill....but I could run you a close second," he said with a laugh.

"Sod off Franks, go and see to your students I've never seen such a sloppy lot."

"Thanks Bill for your support," he said as he went off whistling the BlueBelles theme song.

Bill laughed to himself as he made his way to have a word with Viv Anderson.

"So what have I done to deserve a visit from your illustrious self?"

"I don't see much of you these days and I do not want to lose touch. Tommy was only saying the other day that since the new management took over we don't have a family get together as often as we used to and I must agree with her. I will have a word with her and see if we cannot come up with something. Now are you open for business?"

"I thought there was method in your madness, softening me up then coming up with some problem. I know you too well Mister Barrett, come on lets have it."

"That is where you are wrong Ms. Anderson I came to ask you if you have sorted out the accommodation for the extra Corporals we are getting?"

"It is not easy I'm afraid because we will have more Corporals than single bunks. I am going to call a meeting with all the WRAF Corporals to tell them they are going to share their bunks with another Corporal otherwise the surplus will have to share dormitories with the girls. I remember having to share a bunk with another Cpl in my younger days and providing they are both compatible it will be the answer to the problem."

"Now you mention it Viv I had to do the very same thing, I wonder if Joe Franks has remembered when he would have been in the same position, I will have a word with him but remember Viv because we are short of accommodation the Corporals have no options and we cannot detail them off yet, not until after the parade. They will have plenty of time to come to terms with the move before the new recruits arrive."

"I will definitely supervise that along with Dot Dean because I want the three new Corporals to move in with three of our most experienced Corporals."

"We are a week away from our big day," said Joe addressing the students. "Tomorrow morning we will go through our special routine then for the rest of the day we will practice what the officers think will be our parade for the AOC. I will contact Squadron Leader Cody to say we are ready for his inspection. If he is satisfied we will continue with our early morning session then you will all have your final interview to be assessed. Any questions?"

"What happens to the ones who fail the course Flight Sergeant?" asked an airman.

"We are not expecting any failures but if we are proved wrong 'heaven forbid, the failures will return to their parent unit as such."

"What happens to the ones who pass the course but are not chosen to be posted here?" asked another.

"Unfortunately I cannot answer that question but I am given to understand the AOC himself will answer that. Are there any ore questions? If not then when you are dismissed I expect you all to relax and don your thinking caps and get studying. Parade…Dis…Miss!"

"Sir, Cody here, Flight Sergeant Franks has reported to me that the students are now ready for your review prior to the AOC's visit. Will one hour's time suit you Flight?"

"We are ready at the drop of a hat sir. What will be the dress?"

"That will be fine sir and dress? Good, yes sir I will be in attendance.

It will be working dress Flight."

Joe rejoined his instructors and students. "You have forty minutes to return to your accommodation to put some polish on your footwear and polish your cap badges. The Wing Commander is reviewing you on parade prior to what he thinks will be the AOC's review. Give him a good parade but remember he is not seeing our speciality parade today. I want you to fall in, in front of your respective accommodations in thirty five minutes time. MOVE YOURSELVES!" he roared as they all made a mad dash from the parade ground.

The inspection and march past went down well with the Wing Commander congratulating the students on a good show.

Wait till he sees the big one muttered Joe to himself, I wonder what his reactions will be then.

Before dismissing the parade Joe addressed them. "You did very well on parade.

When you are dismissed you will get your heads stuck into your note books, read them and better read them and test each other on what we have tried to teach you. I do not want to hear of any larking about, if I do I will have you back on the square and you will do your swotting in your own time. We are trying to help you by giving you this concession use it well, we do not want any failures. PARADE! To your studies, Dis…Miss."

He then called his NCOs to him. "You Corporals go and keep an eye on the students to see they don't get up to any mischief. Sergeant Farrow and Sergeant Dean come with me to have a chat with WO Barrett."

"Hello, hello, what have we here a deputation?" remarked Bill Barrett when they entered his office on his answer to their knock.

"Not at all" replied Joe. "Took a vote on whether we should come and see if you had been posted with us not seeing you for yonks, unfortunately the 'Yes' votes won."

"Spare me the sob story and get on with what you have come to see me about then get back to be doing what I pay you for."

"We want a rise otherwise we want a posting to somewhere we will be appreciated."

"Go and collect your applications from the Orderly Room, collect your clearance chits, hand over your married accommodation and say your goodbyes tomorrow. How's that for efficiency? Now clear off I am busy."

"Can we have a brew first? asked Joe, causing everyone to crack out laughing. "We have come to put you in the picture of what we have been up to." He told him about the parade they had put on for the Wingco' and standing the students down to do their final swotting before being interviewed by the board of selectors. "Talking of which Bill have you any idea who will be sitting on the board?"

"Yes. Squadron Leader Cody, Squadron Leader Macfarlane, WO Barrett and WO Anderson."

"Well that is a fair panel, we have decided who we consider the best to join our staff; don't ask who they are because that would be unethical, we will disclose the names at the appropriate time."

"You have it all planned out well which I am pleased with, it is just the pity we do not have any more courses to train for you have done a good job between you. I assume you have everything ready for the big day, you Joe are totally in charge I will be admiring your handiwork from the side lines along with the rest of the training staff and trainees, just make sure you give them something to cheer."

"Thanks Bill we certainly will and there will be some very surprised people watching our display you can bet on that."

When the panel of judges assembled, Wings addressed them. "We have fifty one interviews to carry out and they must be completed today. It would be easier of course for us to split into groups to get through them more quickly. I do not hold with that, they each deserve a fair interview and that is what they are going to get. I would like each of you to write 'Pass or Fail' against each student's name after each interview. Six of them are to be selected to join our staff, two airmen and four airwomen. This is not mandatory but I would like you to number the airmen one and two and the airwomen one to four, number one in each case is the first choice. This exercise is for comparing with the choices of the training staff but their choices stand.

Be free with your questions. Are you all happy with that arrangement? Good, then let battle commence, we will start with the WRAF, will you do the hours please Ms. Anderson? and Mister Barrett will you stand the airmen down and have them report here at 13:15hrs.?"

And so the interviews for the airwomen went smoothly taking them up to lunch time, all the judges acknowledging that the standard was higher than they had expected it to be.

"We will reconvene at 13:30 and if this afternoon goes as smoothly as this morning did," said Wings, "it will have made today well worth while."

As Bill and Viv walked to the Sergeants Mess for lunch they spoke about the reserve back-up the airwomen would provide for the training staff. "The snag is," remarked Viv, it is going to be a long time before most of those girls will get a chance to practice what they have qualified for and it will be only natural the majority will find themselves another trade."

"That may be Viv but if we can keep the interest kindling by recalling them perhaps every six months for a refresher course and the recruiting figures take a turn for the better enabling another school to become operational, who knows. I will have a word with Wings and get him to put a word in the right places or if I can get an interview with the AOC or even an impromptu chat with him on the quiet without our officers listening in and accusing me of going over their heads. I'll tell you what Viv, if you get a chance to get a chat with him before me bend his ear he is a good listener as you well know and he has a soft spot for you."

When they had collected their food they went to sit with Roy Shaw and Derwent Waters, Viv's fiancée, passing Dot Dean who asked. "How are the interviews going Viv?"

"Great Dot, they have certainly made a good impression with us all."

"Well how are the interviews going?" asked Roy. "Got many rejects?"

"You would be very surprised if you had been able to see and hear what went on Roy Shaw," retorted Viv. I will be very surprised if we have a single reject from the airwomen, Joe Franks and his staff have really done a wonderful job with them."

"Do you think you could manage an evening off tonight Bill?" said Roy changing the subject quickly.

"Well you are the smooth talker, I'm sure Tommy would not refuse you knowing her husband would be in good hands."

"Why, are you frightened of asking her?"

"No but I suggest you tread very carefully today be on your best behaviour and put on your best pleading voice."

Turning to Derwent Roy demanded. "Why don't *you* ask Tommy for a change?"

"That is no problem I don't know why you are making a big thing out of it, in fact I will go and see her when I have finished my lunch, now can I have it in peace? All this fuss over nothing."

Bill looked at Viv with a smile which said, "Good lad Derwent he is learning." Viv read the unspoken message and nodded her head.

"Are you coming with me Viv?" asked Derewnt.

"I am indeed," she replied.

"Hello taking your back-up partner in case Tommy gets stroppy."

Derwent snapped back. "Don't be a bloody plonker all your life Roy take a day off," then walked from the Mess.

At reception he asked Jackie the receptionist if Tommy was not busy could he have a word?

"Shan't be a minute Derwent." She returned with Tommy in tow.

"Hello Dewent, Viv, have you a problem?"

"Roy!" He is being his cantankerous self again." He then told her the tale.

"Derwent, we will never change Roy you should know by now it is his way of winding us up, look how he treats Bill you would think he hated his guts."

"I am sorry Tommy I doubt if I will ever get used to him and I can only stand so much from that man and I am not very good at retaliation."

"You will learn with age and time love," consoled Viv."

"Well spoken Viv, now don't you go letting the side down Derwent Waters or you will have me on your back. Now about letting Bill play out tonight, I think we are due a girlie night what say you Viv?"

"I am always ready for one Tommy you know that."

"What do you say to us having the rest of the Mess ladies too I am sure they would enjoy a change from staring at four walls, there will only be nine of us if they all come?"

"Oh that would be lovely I am sure they would enjoy it, I will ask them and let you know Tommy"

"I would like to be a fly on the wall when you lot get together," laughed Derwent.

"Then there would be a competition to see who could swat you first said the girls as they burst out laughing.

"So that is settled then," added Tommy. "Now I will have to think of something tasty to nibble with a glass or two of wine or whatever takes one's fancy. You know something Viv, I am really looking forward to tonight's little soirée."

"Me too Tommy."

"And if Roy starts his antics tonight I will come and join you!"

When Bill entered the Mess Bar Roy was stood there alone.

"Evening Bill," called out Fred the barman. What has happened to the other crackpot?"

"Evening Bill," said Roy. "Pull him a pint Fred, I think I must have upset Derwent at lunchtime "

"On the contrary Roy, he phoned me to give his excuse that he had to go back to work and would be about an hour late."

"That's his excuse," muttered Roy.

"Come on Roy," rebuked Bill. "Give him a break, with your attitude at lunch I'll bet your staff kept clear of you today. What's the matter have you seen your backside or summat? I would not blame him if he did not turn up at all."

As Bill spoke Derwent arrived. "Good evening sorry I'm late chaps, got held up at work."

"Get the drinks in Fred," said Bill, "All present and correct now."

"Was that an excuse to get over a sulk?" said Roy scornfully.

Derwent did a Roy's favourite ploy ignoring him he addressed Bill. "Viv and I had a right good laugh with your Tommy at lunch time. She is having a houseful tonight and the way she spoke they were going to have a great night."

Bill laughed to himself hearing Derwent giving Roy a taste of his own medicine. "Yes she told me all about it; I had to get the drinks lined up in preparation of the stampede. I tell you what she is putting on a nice looking buffet for them, have you ever thought of doing the same for us Fred?"

"There are some tasty morsels in the fridge here which will not cost you an arm or a leg I can recommend them, mind you they can't be compared to summat' home made."

"Who is taking over from you Fred? Your time is nearly up," Roy asked.

"I have no idea, pity because I am enjoying this stint behind the bar, I would do a double turn but my Warrant Officer would object."

"What about the wife?" asked Bill, "surely she would not like it.?

"She would not mind she knows I am in good company."

"And what is all this that is happening at the Barrett residence this evening," asked a curious Roy.

"Tommy decided she would invite all the living in WRAF Mess members to a social evening."

"I would like to be a fly on the wall," said Roy.

"I said that Roy to Tommy and Viv and they threatened to swat me."

"Well one of us could cause a diversion while the other gets the gen. I will toss you as to who will be the posthumous hero Derwent."

"No way I don't want to die young and in the bloom of my youth."

"Fred," announced Roy. "Drinks all round but make Derwent's the Sacrificial Cup."

"Does that mean I will be a sacrifice to the Nine Vestal Virgins then?"

"You should be so lucky," was the instant reply from Roy. "Fred, disqualify Derwent to be replaced by me so give me that Sacrificial Cup and don't you dare spill any of it."

Of course the bar erupted with laughter and many shouts of. "Put my name down for that cup Fred, why should the Warrant Officers get all the perks?" One character shouted "Name your price Fred," as another wanted the Flowing Cup to be auctioned. "Make it a Bingo prize," another shouted, amidst a roar of laughter.

"Now scenes like that make this bar duty a pleasure," smiled Fred, "and it is all down to you three crackpots, I think you deserve a drink on the house for that few minutes of daftness."

"Good old Fred," was the reply from the crackpots.

"That takes me back to my Astra Cinema days as a sprog," replied Fred. "There won't be an Astra cinema that has not resounded to the shout of 'Good Old Fred'. You may forget many things about your service life when you retire but that is something you will never forget."

"You have never spoken a truer word Fred," said Bill.

"Happy memories," said Roy.

"I'll drink to that," said Derwent.

"Not alone you won't," replied Roy, "get the drinks in and we will join you."

"Why, am I falling apart?"

"What are you talking about, am I falling apart?"

"You said you will join me....get it join me....falling apart"

"Get the drinks in you are doing my head in."

Bill and Fred were having a good laugh at the pair of them. "There is never a dull moment when you lot are in here. Tell you what I will get the drinks in."

That offer was received with broad grins from the crackpots with a shout of, "Good Old Fred."

"Oh don't start that off again," moaned Roy.

CHAPTER 40

The Passing Out Parade Day had finally arrived; at reveille all connected to the parade were out of beds quickly to prepare for the busy day awaiting them. In the student's accommodation there was a mad scramble to get to the ablutions the first there were goaded by others inpatient for their turn to hurry up and get their fingers out because the students had been given priority to attend an early breakfast ahead of the rest of the station. Under the watchful eyes of their NCOs the rooms had to pass his inspection before they could concentrate on getting themselves dressed in their best uniforms. Until parade time they would be checking each other for faults in their appearance with the NCOs having the final say.

The Station Warrant Officer's work party was checking the Parade Ground and surrounds for being litter free and clean and guiding vehicles carrying proud parents and friends of the students to designated parking areas.

The rest of the station personnel had been given permission to watch the parade as spectators, except those on essential duties.

Both flights had fell-in outside their respective Barrack Blocks waiting for the AOC to arrive and the order to March On. The NCOs having a good look at each individual to make sure everything was tickety boo and reminding them to sing the BlueBelles signature tune to themselves.

Station Warrant Officer George Miller on getting the nod from the saluting base shouted, "March On!"

"Quick March!" ordered Flight Sergeant Franks as he led the airmen onto the Parade Ground. At the far side they wheeled left, counting his steps Joe did a left turn and advanced six steps then began marking time while the flight carried on and at a given point they made a left turn as one and advanced behind Joe who led them forward coming to a halt at the required distance from the saluting base. As Joe about turned his flight automatically side-stepped four paces from the man on his right leaving a wide space between each man. The airwomen's flight followed carrying out the same unspoken commands and marched forward to fill the gaps left by the airmen. In unison they opened order for inspection then the combined flight took one step forward to take their dressings from the right. To complete the manoeuvre the front rank carried out the eyes front movement each one turning his or her eye to the front in succession. Joe about turned saluted the AOC and announced. "Parade Ready for Inspection SIR!"

As the AOC returned the salute there came spontaneous applause from the onlookers in appreciation for the display they had just witnessed. As the AOC and his retinue approached, the centre and rear ranks automatically stood at ease.

"Thank you Flight Sergeant for that wonderful display," said the AOC as he shook Joe by the hand. "I think Warrant Officer Barrett will have to be looking to his laurels now after witnessing that display."

"There will be no fear of that sir he encouraged me all along although I could run him a close second with a bit more practice." All the retinue had a good laugh at Joe's remark. The inspection then proceeded with Joe introducing both Sergeant Farrow and Sergeant (w) Dean. The AOC took his time having a word with each and every person on the parade bringing smiles to all their faces. When the AOC had returned to the saluting base Joe faced the flight who as one came to attention and closed order then automatically right dressed and Joe about turned to face the AOC who ordered the parade to stand easy which they did as one.

"Well ladies and gentleman," he began. "What a wonderful display you have treated all of us today." He was interrupted with loud applause. "I thought I had seen everything when I witnessed the BlueBelles at their best but Bai Jove you could give them a good run for their money. The point is you all enjoyed it, I could see it in your faces with every step and turn you took. Not only are you a credit to your instructors but to the Royal Air Force and not forgetting your parents and friends who must be very proud of you." There was more loud applause from the onlookers. He continued. "It is now my pleasure in announcing what must be one of the best results a man in my position could wish for. Ladies and gentlemen, each one of you has passed this course, we have had no failures." When the cheering had died down he continued. "That is the good part, the sad part is there will be no more courses in the foreseeable future, that means we can only find a training slot for six of you, two airmen and four airwomen who will receive an immediate promotion to Corporal and a place on the training staff here at RAF March. The shortage of recruits is unfortunately the reason for making this course to be the last and it is just impossible to find every one of you a recruit training post. You can be assured that Qualified Drill Instructor to Junior NCO level will be added to your personal records. Also you will be recalled to do a refresher course every six months because you will be on the stand-by list to replace any vacancies which come available here at RAF March. You will not be chosen alphabetically but on merit according to your pass rate. Now I have the honour to present some awards to various personnel. Warrant Officer Miller the British Empire Medal". George proudly marched forward to have the medal pinned to his chest. "Well done Mister Miller you have deserved it. Flight Sergeant Franks, the British Empire Medal." Joe proudly marched forward his face saying it all as the medal was pinned to his chest. "Congratulations Flight Sergeant you are doing the RAF a great service. Flight Sergeant (w) Page, My Commendation, Congratulations Sergeant and thank you for your dependability. Sergeant (w) Dean, My Commendation, thank you Sergeant and Congratulations. Corporal (w) Norma Peters, promotion to Sergeant, well done Sergeant you have certainly earned these" as he handed Sergeants chevrons to an astonished Norma. "Corporal Deacon, my Commendation Congratulations you have a good future in the RAF. Corporal (w) Springs my Commendation, thank you Corporal for the initiative and fine example you are showing. Now it is the turn of the students, unfortunately I cannot give every one of you an award. Sac Callum Beattie receives The Best Airman Student Certificate and his Corporal Chevrons. Sac (w) Helen Tracy receives the Best Airwoman Student Certificate and her Corporal Chevrons. Sac Tom Bolland, Sac (w) Angela Falls, Sac (w) Carol Liner, Sac (w) Audrey Little will receive their Corporal Chevrons. Congratulations and welcome to RAF March."

Cheers and tears followed the announcements.

Joe returned to the parade while the rest of the award recipients lined up on the right of the saluting base. The gaps left in the ranks had been quickly filled. Joe turned and faced the AOC saluted and announced. "Permission to March off SIR!"

"Permission granted."

Joe saluted and as he completed an about turn so did the flight then together they stepped off marching towards the rear of the Parade Ground then turning a sharp left. As they progressed Joe turned left and marched to the end of the square where he marked time waiting for the flight headed by Sergeant Farrow and Sgt (w) Dean as right guide and marker. As they closed on Joe he stepped off with everyone in step as they left wheeled to march pass the saluting base. Joe then ordered 'Eyes Right!' as he saluted the AOC then 'Eyes Front' as they cleared the base. When they had cleared the Parade Ground he halted them for the Station Commander to have a few words with them.

"Well done Flight Sergeant and Congratulations on your award and to all you students you gave a wonderful show of precision drill that could not be faulted in any way except to say it did not last long enough for us. You did your instructors and yourselves proud. On behalf of my Officers and Training Staff thank you for a great performance, RAF March is proud of you all."

"Can I stand them down now sir?" Joe asked.

"Indeed you can, enjoy your leave you have earned it."

The students appreciated Joe going along the ranks shaking each one by the hand with a personal thanks, goodbye and good luck, "Till we meet again, Parade! for our last time…Dis…Miss."

A student shouted "Three Cheers for the best Drill Instructor in the RAF. Everyone around the Parade Ground was startled by the outburst of loud cheering. When the students dispersed to see their families and friends The Wingco', Wings, Bill Barrett and Viv merged onto Joe to give their congratulations for his award and the great job he had done with the students.

"You lovely man said Viv giving him a kiss, where were you when we were training the BlueBelles?"

"Why did you not put on that show for my parade Flight Sergeant was I not high enough up the Senior Officer scale to warrant that show piece?" asked the Wingco'.

"Sorry sir but that was going to be just a one-off for the entire station to flavour just to show what a good Instructional Staff you have got."

"And don't we realise that Squadron Leader Cody?"

"We certainly do sir I have always maintained our training staff are definitely the best in the business."

"I should think so," the Wingco' replied, "at present we just happen to be the only ones in the business." That caused a burst of laughter from the rest of the party.

"Well you know what I mean," said Wings covering his confusion.

"If you will excuse me," said Viv, "I want to go and have a word with Sergeant Dean."

Bill Barrett gave Joe a good warm handshake, "well done Joe I was so proud of you out there no-one put a foot wrong and I was very impressed with the link-up between the two flights plus you had both airmen and airwomen working on the same wave length. Look, what do you say if we have a little celebration party in the mess tonight, I will contact our staff and they can bring their wives or partners, what do you say?"

"I am all for that Bill it should be a nice quiet little celebration."

"But of course," said Bill wearing a big grin. "Come on lets' go and have a word with George Miller."

They found George along with his wife surrounded by a multitude of well wishers ogling his Medal.

"Are you free George?" Bill asked.

"I will be after I have shook hands with Joe here because I am going to send my staff to him to teach them the rudiments of close order drill." His young admirers simply vanished into thin air. "That is the effect you have on them Joe they admire you training someone else but for them it is a no go area."

"That is because you as SWO and your predecessor here used the kid glove treatment and spoiled them, I don't know what this Air Force is coming to."

"George laughed, did you hear that Bill, who is he trying to kid?"

"When you two overgrown schoolboys have finished patting each other on the back I would like to go home for something to eat," retorted George's wife.

"Right you are dear," he said winking at Bill and Joe.

"Before you go, are you interested in a little celebration party to celebrate our award winners in the mess this evening?"

"What do you say dear?" asked George of his wife.

"That sounds to me like it should be a nice evening out provided you don't get carried away, yes we will come thank you Bill. Come on George lunch time I'm feeling peckish."

"She sounds like a bit of a martinet Bill."

"Don't be fooled by that Joe, she is one of the nicest women you will come across and don't think for one minute George is henpecked they are a couple of Darby and Joans, talking of which where is your dearly beloved today?"

"She has been at her mother's for the last couple of days, her mother had a bad fall so she has gone to do a bit of caring."

"Have you been eating in the Mess then?"

"Only for dinner it saves me the hassle of slaving over a hot stove at home."

"I am off now to help with the preparations and help Fred if he needs any in the bar. I'll see you later then Joe."

He made his way to the Mess to see his wife Tommy. "Is everything going to plan love?"

"Of course, the Chef is putting on a very nice buffet, I have organised stewards and got the services of the man who put on that nice disco at our wedding, all being well it should be a nice evening. Have you asked Wings? I am sure he would jump at the chance to attend."

"Good thinking, I had better get in touch with him, can I use your phone?" Tommy took him to her office where he rang Wings. "Sir, WO Barrett speaking, we are having a little celebration for our award winners this evening I would like to invite you, will you be free sir?"

"Thank you Warrant I would love to if there is nothing on similar lines in the Officers Mess, I will get in touch with you to confirm it or otherwise."

"The invitation is also extended to Squadron Leader Macfarlane if you would like to pass her the message sir."

"That is better still, I am sure she would be delighted in accepting, that would mean I would not be a wallflower," he said with a laugh.

"That will be the day when you would be a wallflower in the Sergeants Mess."

"Hopefully he will be coming Tommy he sounds quite excited about the prospect and it will be nice if Mac' comes along with him. I 'll go and have a look at Fred in the bar to see if he wants some help"

"You will be wasting your time dear; Fred has it all under control."

"Well is there anything I can do? I feel I am surplus to requirements."

"There is, you can get on the telephone and ask Mary Brown and her husband if they would like to come."

"Who the heck is Mary Brown?"

"Have you forgotten your favourite Warrant Officer already who has just recently changed her name....does Sam Brown ring a bell dear?"

"Oh heck, I will be in the proverbial if you tell her but being a loving and devoted wife you wouldn't....would you?"

"Don't edge your bets my love," she said giving him a kiss, "got to go now and give Chef a hand, let me know how you get on."

It was not long before he was back to tell her. "Mary will come but Sam has a village meeting to attend."

"Right, now phone Wings to tell Mac' Mary is coming because if she had got second thoughts that will change her mind."

That did the trick for when he phoned Wings almost immediately confirmation came to say she would be delighted to attend.

Word got around there was to be a celebration in the Mess consequently, most of the Sergeants Mess members and wives were more than eager to partake in the jollifications.

When Mary arrived she made straight for George Miller and smothered him with her congratulations. "You should have received the medal a long time ago you old rascal and I know what is coming next." In complete harmony between laughs they echoed those famous words, "Less of the old."

As they were chatting Bill Barrett brought in Wings and Mac.' who he had been waiting for at the entrance to the Mess to escort them in. When Mary saw Mac' she gave a little scream and they both embraced. After the congratulations and pleasantries Bill supplied them with drinks of their choice then Mary and Mac found a quiet a table as was possible then settled down when nostalgia took over they were oblivious to all that went on around them.

Wings joined the boys and between being coaxed onto the dance floor he managed to get a drink and a chat with his hosts and the celebrities.

Dot Dean had persuaded Norma Peters to attend the function with her and soon got her into the party mood as she received the many congratulations on her promotion and the many welcomes to the Mess. Joe Franks was having a ball, the WRAF members made sure he danced with each one. Norma Peters was thrilled to bits when Wings asked her for a dance.

"Is it always like this Dot when you have a function? Everyone is so friendly and they are really enjoying themselves."

"Yes, we try to make each function worth coming to and we have to thank Bill Barrett for lifting the Mess by the scruff of the neck and turning it from a pitiful place to what it is now. You would not believe what it was like, he got a committee together and they have done wonders in organising many functions and we have not had a bad one yet. Wait till you see Chef's buffet he puts a lovely one on, we will try to get in before the crush because it will be like a stampede. Come on I will take you to meet Tommy our Mess manager Flight Sergeant Barrett Bill's wife she organises all the backroom things I'll ask her if we can have peek at the buffet."

"Tommy greeted them with, Are you enjoying your first function Norma? Come on I will show you our Chef's artistic work, which will be demolished in ten minutes flat once the doors are opened. Look, I will open the doors and announce that the buffet is ready at precisely nine o'clock so make sure you both are well placed for me to give you the nod then shall we say, let the rest follow you in."

After viewing the spread they thanked her. "Isn't she nice Dot."

"She is indeed Tommy and Bill make an ideal couple they will do anything for anybody with no fuss."

"I know, she was lovely with me when I moved in this afternoon she even sent Jackie the receptionist to my room with a tray of tea and biscuits. It is like living in a different world in here, I am going to love it Dot."

♦ ♦ ♦

"I think the parade went down very well Eric," the AOC said, "I was very impressed with the display the students put on and it showed as they carried it out that they enjoyed every minute of it. W/O Barrett has got a good understudy in Flight Sergeant Franks."

"Indeed he has, when the school was set up Barrett put Franks solely in charge of it and never interfered. Apparently he knew that Franks was putting on a special display for you and that was the first time anyone outside of the school saw it, you can imagine their surprise when they witnessed a different parade to the one Franks put on for them. I don't think they will ever forget that, I saw their faces as they watched and it was a picture."

"So now we are back to square one Eric and it looks like it will be so for a long time to come but we have got the back up of instructors W/O Barrett fought for so we should have no more problems, I think you will be sitting on a cushy little number now for some time Eric."

"That is until W/O Barrett comes up with one of his brain waves Charles. Incidentally he has delegated Flight Sergeant Franks to be in command of the airmen staff and Flight Sergeant (w) Roper in charge of the airwomen staff."

"Leaving him to concentrate solely on improvements to the curriculum I suppose," said the AOC with a laugh. I could do with Barrett and his staff to take over mine then you and I could get a few days off to go fishing together Eric…if only!"

"If that was the case Charles I would rather keep my staff."

CHAPTER 41

Bill called Joe Franks and Margaret Roper to his office. "In a week's time our new staff will be returning from leave and the week after we will be receiving new recruits.

You two are going to be very busy because next week we will also be receiving two new flights replacing the ones who will be leaving having completed their basic training. What I want from you is a revised list of instructors incorporating Sergeant Peters and the five newly promoted Corporals and I would like them yesterday. You have also a little matter of accommodation for the Corporals who will be in excess to number of single rooms for NCOs."

"I understand that W/O Anderson has already sorted that out Bill."

"That is a good start Margaret, how about you Joe?"

"No problem that is already taken care of."

"There is nothing else I can suggest so I will let you get on with what you have to do but I would like to see your revised lists when you have completed them. One last thing, you are in charge out there and will be held responsible for its efficient running and I do not want anyone going over your heads to see me. When each team has to take their turn in the ops' room they then become my immediate responsibility. Have you got any questions or queries?"

"I would like an office for Margaret and me to share, obviously we cannot move in here with you, have you any suggestions Bill?"

"The only solution I can think of Joe is to get Tom Hardcastle over and ask his advice on partitioning this office, it is a good size and we could manage between us at a pinch. There is one drawback, because there are two of you I will draw the short straw and get the smaller of the two. "

Joe and Margaret laughed. "It is tough at the top," said Joe "but you must think of the well being of your staff if you want to run a happy ship."

"Look, you two clear off I don't want you here when Tom arrives and I don't want him listening to your ideas I know he has a soft spot for the ladies and I want a bit of elbow room and not ending up in a dog kennel."

"Come on Margaret let us get out of here before he starts snapping at our heels, who knows we may bump into Tom on his way here."

"If I pat his head it may calm him down," whispered Margaret.

"GET OUT of here," Bill yelled.

"You throw him a biscuit while I get the door open Margaret." They exited having a good laugh.

Bill reached for the phone and rang Tom Hardcastle. "Tom, Bill Barrett here, when you can spare the time can you come to my office and bring your tape measure? Thanks Tom I will be here then."

When he arrived Bill asked. "Do you want a brew Tom?"

"No thanks I was just finishing one off when you rang. Now what is your problem?"

Bill explained the situation adding. "This is the only solution I can come up with."

Tom did some measuring up and calculating. "It looks promising Bill; obviously we will have to take into account furniture...two desks and chairs. Could you manage with a smaller desk to give you a bit more room? You will be surprised at the difference it will make. You will need a communicating hatch and you will have an advantage over them befitting your status...you will have the only window but I can fit small glass partitions along the top which will stop them feeling claustrophobic. They will also need a private door. I think the three of you will be satisfied with the end product. I will just do some final measurements then I can get my staff cracking on it.

I will let you know when we are ready to turf you out while we fit it Bill."

"What about a couple of phones Tom will that be possible?"

"No problem, I can run two extensions from the original line you already have in this building, leave it with me I will see you run short of nowt'."

Three days later Bill got a call from Tom Hardcastle telling him to "Get your office paraphernalia moved out today the heavy gang will be moving in first thing tomorrow morning and stack your desks, chairs filing cabinets etc as far away from the centre of the room as possible."

Flight Sergeants Franks and Roper reported to Bill Barrett with the revised list of instructors.

"You took your time with them, what kept you?"

"You only asked for them yesterday," replied Margaret.

"Exactly, that is when I asked for them...yesterday."

"So we are in a playful mood today are we?" she asked "and what has brought that on? If it is a posting we will celebrate with you."

"Now if that was so Margaret you know you would miss me."

"Chance would be a fine thing," she replied with a smile.

"I would like to share my happy mood with you after all it does concern you and you have been bitching about it enough. Against my better judgement but also to keep you both under surveillance I have sacrificed half my office space to accommodate shall I say? Two ungrateful subordinates." He then told them what Tom Hardcastle was doing and what it would entail. "Now when you have finished patting each other on the back I want you to know I am not allowed to receive gifts...a pint in the Mess will suffice."

"That is great news," said a beaming Joe Franks, "so we may be installed by the end of the week."

"I want you to give me a hand this afternoon moving the fittings because Tom's gang are moving in tomorrow."

"Do you want me as well Bill?" asked Margaret.

"Of course it is for your benefit as well, besides you will be lifting the furniture with Joe while I tell you where to put it."

"I will tell you where you can…here she was interrupted by Joe.

"Of course we will help it is only right we should do so."

Bill smiled because he knew that Margaret was about to lambast him.

"Come on then let me have a look at your revised instructor's lists to see what sort of a mess you have made of them." He browsed through them shaking his head with an odd tut tut and hmm, he could sense Margaret was getting a little agitated. He threw them on the desk towards the two of them and said. "If that is the best you can do…he paused, looked at Margaret and as she was about to open her mouth to say something he continued…then you have done an excellent job," as he broke out in a huge grin.

"Bill Barrett you are an evil so and so," laughed Margaret "you really got me going with your ruddy wind up."

"Come here," Bill said then gave her a hug, and as he shook Joe's hand he said. "Now what would I do without you two stalwarts, thank you for your support and loyalty but don't forget I want you here this afternoon to help me get the office ready for Tom. By the way when or how are you going to tell your NCOs about the changes you are making?"

"Now you have approved of the changes we can get them in here after training to tell them, will you be there Bill?"

"Oh yes I want to note their reactions, if there are any. Come on Margaret I will walk with you to the Mess for lunch. Have you any news of when your wife is coming home Joe?"

"With a bit of luck she should be home sometime tomorrow thank goodness."

"Well let me know when she is due then we can manage without you, she will probably want you take her shopping."

"In that case she can wait until I get home at the usual time."

"Don't be mean Joe Franks," retorted Margaret, you should be welcoming her home with open arms."

"Not with a shopping bag in each of them."

After the three of them had sorted the office out ready for Tom and his staff they waited for the instructing staff to report in after training had finished for the day. When Bill, Joe and Margaret entered the ops' room the chatter stopped then Joe addressed them.

"You all are aware we have lost the job of training potential instructor-NCOs due to the insufficient numbers of recruits enlisting in the RAF…here he was interrupted.

"That means we will be on the merry go round again, when are we going to settle down with the same staff?"

Joe snapped back. "Do you think we enjoy changing the staff around? You can blame that on the circumstances. What would you suggest we do with new and inexperienced instructors give them a new flight of recruits and tell em' to get on with it? If that is your attitude you are no use to me and if anyone of you has an axe to grind you can see me tomorrow morning first thing. Now I am going to hand you some print-outs detailing the changes, I can see the excitement of anticipation on your faces but remember all objectors are to form an orderly queue tomorrow morning Flight Sergeant Roper will also be in attendance to receive any of her WRAF staff. I suggest you now knock off and read those print-outs after dinner I do not want to be accused of spoiling it for you."

"Don't you think you laid it on a bit thick Joe? After all it was only a question."

"Think about it Sergeant because you turned an informal talk into a formal one by not questioning but stating an objection. Like it or lump it these changes will come into operation when the new staff report back after their leave. In the meantime carry on as you are. Do you want to add anything before they leave Flight?"

"Only to remind everyone to treat the newcomers as you were treated when you first arrived."

After the staff had dispersed Bill said, "You handled that like a good un' Joe, I was watching their reactions and I reckon you have won the day I think someone is going to get a rollicking from his mates. I will bet you a pint you have no objectors knocking on your door tomorrow."

"No way am I going to take a bet on with your reputation."

"One good thing has come from that little exercise; you have showed them who the boss is. Now I can sleep peacefully in my bed knowing I have no more worries running this department."

"And I will have to see the MO. for some paracetamols and sleeping tablets."

"Didn't I hear you recently tell me that it was tough at the top Joe? Then welcome to the club. Come on lets get out of here I will walk with you to the Mess I have to pick Tommy up."

"Morning Bill not be long now before you are back in business, you have done a good job in giving us plenty of room to work in."

"Morning Tom, from the looks of the gear you have brought it resembles a DIY kit, everything painted and waiting to be put into place."

"I have got a good team Bill and they do a proper job, no cutting corners for them. By the way I was talking to Tim and Ann last night in the March Hare and they are worried about you and your little party not being to see them for ages, she says the old folk are giving her some agro and blaming her thinking she has barred you from the pub."

Bill laughed. "I can just imagine it coming from them, did you know they christened me Captain Bligh? Because they say I act like him."

"Ann told me you are a soft touch for them but they think the world of you all."

"Thanks for letting me know I will have a word with the rest of the family. Right Tom I will be off and let you get on with it."

♦♦♦

As he entered the ops' room he saw Joe and Margaret. "Got nothing to do?" He asked. "Joe you come with me it is time we had another check on the airmen's accommodation and I advise you Margaret to do the same with your airwomen and take Sergeant Dean with you. Come on Joe let's get cracking."

"I'll tell you what Bill you will find nothing wrong with Corporal Deacon's dormitories."

"Bill thought for a minute before replying. You are trying to catch me out aren't you? You crafty devil you know damn well his dormitories will stay empty until the new recruits arrive. We will still have a shufti at them and yes I will be very surprised if they are not spotless. We have a damned good NCO there Joe I hope it will be not too long before he gets his third stripe he deserves it."

On completion of their inspection Joe remarked. "I think I had better have a word with the Corporals and put a flea in their ears, the accommodation is definitely not up to my standard, they will get one warning and that should suffice because they know what will happen from past experiences if they do not toe my line."

"By the way Joe is your wife coming home today?"

"Aye but it will late on this afternoon so I don't need to dash home."

"Then shall we call a meeting of the living-in Corporals after training and read the riot act?"

"That is fine with me Bill we will stop off at each flight to tell them."

Sergeant Fell's flight was the first they came to. Joe asked permission if he could have a word with his Corporals.

"Corporals Harris and Lucas fall-in on me," he ordered. They marched smartly coming to a simultaneous halt. "Flight Sergeant Franks wants a word."

"Report to me in the ops' room after training that is all. Thanks Sergeant."

Joe repeated this order at each flight.

"They know what it is about Joe they will be sweating now wondering if it will be a repeat of Barrack Room daily inspections again."

"I thought they had learned their lesson from last time Bill but apparently not so it is time to put the 'you know what' up them once more."

On reaching the training offices they met Tom Hardcastle. "How's it going Tom hit any snags at all?" asked Bill.

"You are very lucky, everything is going like clockwork due to careful planning of course, it will be ready by knocking-off time. I will give you a preview before we leave and discuss any minor adjustments of which there will be none."

"We will not argue with you Tom or you will blow your whistle for the shop steward to come running. It will be alright so long as I have somewhere to hang my cap."

"Thanks Bill for reminding me, hat and coat racks I completely forgot all about them. Don't worry though you will have some fitted tomorrow."

"Thanks Tom I had better show my face in the ops' room to see if Margaret has returned."

"She is in the ops' room Bill she has been back for some time now."

"Nice to know you are keeping tabs on my staff Tom."

When Bill entered the ops' room he saw her in deep conversation with Joe. "What's up, trouble in t' mill Margaret?"

"Nothing much Bill, I was just telling Joe the Corporals need another good talking to and a reminder of the consequences. Mind you it is not too bad but there is a need for improvement... Joe tells me he is giving his Corporals a pep talk after training so I suggest I give the girls their pep talk before training in the morning that way Joe and I will not clash."

"That's fine Margaret in the meantime we can make ourselves busy and wait for the preview Tom Hardcastle has promised us. I suggest you now get in touch with Roy Shaw to find out if he has got the list of names yet of the next new lot of intakes for you."

"Bill" shouted Tom Hardcastle, "bring your office staff with you to come and see your 'des res'."

The first thing they saw was their names plates on their respective doors which brought smiles of approval, the four of them entered the double office.

"You have one large filing cabinet to join at which as you see is separating the two desks and on top of it is your shared telephone, because you do not qualify for one each. Is there anything I have not included which you think is a necessity? Your hat and coat hooks will be fitted tomorrow. Go on try your chairs out and see if you have enough leg room under the desks."

Joe and Margaret decided who was sitting at which desk then they sat and fidgeted.

"I would like a cushion for my chair," answered Margaret and a typewriter please."

"That is a good idea," said Joe, "I mean a cushion not a typewriter, apart from that Tom I would like to thank you, you and your staff have done a really good job for us haven't they Margaret.".

"Indeed they have and I am now waiting to receive an invitation to see his lordship's luxury suite next door."

"After the laughter had died down Bill said. "You sit your bums on those chairs while you can because you won't have much time for relaxing when your new flights arrive. Come on Tom let us go and christen my pad in the usual manner, have you brought the corkscrew?"

Bill was delighted with his new office. "I would not have believed you could have made so much space and the desk is big enough for my needs. Yes, I am going to be comfortable in here. Thanks Tom for all you have done for us," he said shaking his hand.

When Tom left Bill opened the hatch. "Come on, come and see how the upper- crust lives."

When they came round they knocked hard on the door entered had a good look round not saying a word to Bill.

"What do you think Margaret?" asked Joe.

"Hmm! I'm not keen on the curtains Joe and the bit of carpet seems out of place."

"Probably a surplus one from the airmen's Barrack Rooms. I've seen enough Margaret I think the standard is dropping."

"The next time you two enter my office you will leave your footwear outside the door, now get out peasants."

As they were leaving, laughing of course. Margaret asked. "Would you like a cup of tea Sir?"

"OUT" Yelled Bill in mock anger pointing his finger towards the door.

When the Corporals reported to the ops' room Joe with Bill staying in the background addressed them.

"It is obvious you know why you are here so I am not going to beat about the bush. Have you forgotten you are responsible for Barrack Room discipline or were you hoping that we had forgotten? The rules remain the same, your personal accommodation will now be set as an example for the airmen to follow and your privileges as NCOs will be restored if and when you toe my line. Fortunately we are blessed with one or two who are worth their salt as NCOs, to them I apologise if you think you are being tarred with the same brush, which is not the case. Dismiss."

"Well done Joe they certainly know where they stand, we will get no more trouble isn't that is what we said the last time? Right, let us make ourselves scares."

"Wait for me Bill Barrett," shouted Margaret as she came running out from her new office. I stayed behind to hear what Joe had to say then I can give my girls a similar warning."

"Fair enough Margaret, I would take young Norma Peters along with you for the experience, it will be different for her to be on the giving end instead of the receiving end. By the way did you get in touch with Roy Shaw?"

"I did and he has the names which he will give to me first thing in the morning having had it printed out prior to the stand down."

"Your new Corporals will be reporting in on Monday I suggest you detail Corporal Peters to take them to watch the procedure when the next batch of recruits arrive here from the station and explain to them what is going on."

As they entered the Mess Margaret said to Tommy who was waiting for Bill. "Here is your husband Tommy, escorted and officially handed over."

"Do you want me to sign for him Margaret?"

"No need for that, here is the key to his handcuffs but be careful Tommy he is ferocious."

"Clear off and go and get your face stuck in your dinner," he growled.

"Come Tiger," laughed Tommy, "we will go and do the same and it is your turn to wash up."

CHAPTER 42

There was pandemonium when Bill and company entered the March Hare pub. The locals were cheering and shaking their hands their faces lit up with huge smiles.

Ann Wilson came rushing out from her living quarters to see what the commotion was about and when she saw the reason she kissed and hugged each one of her friends.

"Oh we have all missed you it has been such a long time since we saw you and I have even been accused of barring you."

Tim her husband was just as enthusiastic in his welcome as he shook hands with the men and kisses for the ladies. "Just listen to that lot," he said nodding his head in the direction of the locals, "you would think they were at a football match."

"Roy said, "I will get the drinks in and whatever the locals want. Are you all ready for a drink?" he called to them.

"Yes please they answered in chorus." Then began talking quietly among themselves but loud enough for their voices to carry. "I told you we would get a drink as soon as they walked through that door."

"I said it would be that nice man who would buy us the first one."

"I thought it would have been Captain Bligh."

"Not him he is too busy chatting to the landlady."

"Yes and I'll bet he is the cause of them not coming to see us."

Of course the family were listening and finding it very difficult not to burst out laughing.

"It sounds like you are not the flavour of the month Bill," said Derwent.

"I will give them something to moan about in a bit," he replied.

Ann came and sat down with them and to get all the news from the camp.

"Barbara has just been awarded the AOC's Commendation," said a proud Roy.

"George Miller got the BEM along with Joe Franks who is now a Flight Sergeant I think you already know that," said Bill.

"Are you still holding your girlie evenings Tommy?"

"Only when she lets Bill play out," interrupted Roy

"We all enjoyed the last one," answered Tommy ignoring Roy's sarcasm, "didn't we girls?"

"It was lovely we had a great time, Tommy invited the other girls from the Mess and it was great I think they are hoping they will get another invite."

"There is no reason why we cannot make it a regular get together," suggested Tommy, "at least we will get to know each other more."

"What will you call yourselves?" asked Roy, "Ladies in Waiting?"

"Watch your step Roy Boy or it will be you who will be doing the waiting the next time you plead with me to go out with you."

"I was just teasing pet."

"Well I wasn't."

The rest of the group were smiling at the exchange between Roy and Barbara knowing what the pair of them are like.

"We had Tom Hardcastle in the other evening and he was telling us he had been doing a job for you Bill."

"Talking of which, said Bill handing Anne some money, "get him a couple of drinks in will you he did a cracking job and he is always very obliging."

"Have any of you booked any sunshine holidays yet?" asked Tim as he came to join them for a few minutes.

"Old misery guts has not mentioned it yet so it looks like we may be doing day trips if I am so lucky."

"Now Barbara you know that is not so, don't you remember on our last one when I said that I would not mind coming here again."

Everyone burst out laughing except Barbara.

"So when is AGAIN?" She asked putting emphasis on 'again'

"You will just have to give me more time to think about it I don't like having to make snap decisions."

"Well seeing it is almost twelve months since you almost made one I can see a light at the end of the tunnel, mind you it is only a pin head of a light so we must be near to a very hasty decision."

"There you go rushing me into something I am not ready for yet."

"If you are not ready well I certainly am, so get your thinking cap on you impetuous man or you will be receiving a post card from me saying, Glad you are not here."

The loud laughter from the group started the locals coughing loudly.

"Hey-up we are getting the dry cough syndrome," Bill said rising from his chair, "Watch this."

He went to the bar turned round and asked his group in a loud voice. "Have I got your order right?" He then rattled off the drinks they wanted.

"Yes, that's right shouted Ann and don't forget the cherry."

The locals had stopped coughing to hear the order and when Bill told Tim what the order was Tim asked. "Is that the lot Bill?"

"Sorry Tim, get yourself one, that will be all thank you."

When the locals heard that they began to cough again and rattle their empty glasses on the tables. On seeing that Bill was ignoring them they began their usual muttering between themselves.

"I told you that Captain Bligh stopped them other nice ladies and gentlemen from coming to see us."

"Did you notice he bought the landlord a drink? He can have a free drink anytime he wants."

"I think Captain Bligh is a bit of a creep, I wouldn't have a drink from him if he offered."

"Why don't you keep your trap shut do you want to spoil it for the rest of us?"

Said their spokesman, "I had better go and have a word with him he might have heard what you said."

With that he got up from his chair giving a cry of pain then hobbled painfully slow over to the bar. "Evenin' Bill how are you keeping? we haven't seen you for a while, are you busy up at t' camp?"

"Yes very busy so much so tonight is the first time I was able let this lot off the camp."

"Couldn't they come on their own without you?"

"They could but they could not afford it and I draw the line at them putting their drinks on the slate. As a matter of fact I have just asked Tim if he will refuse them if they ask him that is frowned upon by the RAF. It is a good job he agrees with me otherwise I would get the March Hare put out of bounds to everyone on the camp. Another thing, have you ever seen any of the ladies buy a round of drinks?"

"No".

"No and you never will, they have the same privileges as we do on camp so don't you think it only fair for them to stand us a round? We have to spend our money which as you know does not grow on trees entertaining them while they keep their purses safely locked away. Now that is enough of my troubles how are you and your friends keeping? I have noticed it is taking you all a long time to get rid of your coughs."

"It is the same with us, we have very little money to spend entertaining ourselves never mind anybody else, the only pleasure we have is to come here and hope to hear you and your friends enjoying yourselves. We do miss you when you are not here but are very thankful that when you do because the first thing you do is buy a drink for us old folk. It means a lot to us but in these hard times we just cannot afford to repay your kindness. We have even tried to copper up enough between us to do just that but it would mean us going short of food in our bellies. Anyway it is nice to see you back here, go back and enjoy the rest of the evening with your friends."

As he walked away Bill winked at Tim and said in a loud whisper. "I do feel sorry for those elderly folk Tim, fill their glasses up will you I think they deserve a drink."

Back at the table the locals asked. "How did you get on?"

The reply was a finger to his lips along with a wink and a grin.

"Well don't you take the biscuit Bill Barrett? Ann said shaking her head, "you do realise he took you for a ride?"

"Of course he did but don't you think that was worth a round of drinks? They may be elderly but there is nothing wrong with their faculties."

"Cheers Captain" was the cry from the locals as they lifted their glasses in salute.

"Have you noticed the coughing has now stopped Ann?"

When they were leaving Derwent went to the bar. "Put them a round in Tim I think they have earned it tonight."

The locals were profuse in their thanks. "Goodnight and God Bless, will we see you next week?"

"I think we might have to have a Kitty between us but we will try our best to get here" replied Bill putting on a brave smile for the locals benefit.

Making sure Bill and co' had gone the spokesman raised his glass and said quietly, there is one born every minute and in their case three."

"Keep you voice down," one of them said, "the landlady is pretending to clear the glasses and cleaning the tables but she is inching near to us to try and hear what we are saying."

In a loud voice the spokesman announced. "Thanks to our friends and benefactors for making our evening a very pleasant one, then whispered, "and to me for making it happen."

Ann addressed them with "You have done very well tonight for free drinks haven't you? You conniving scoundrels."

"Nobody forces them to treat us to the odd drink," the spokesman replied, "they do it because they are so kind and considerate to us old people not hard and bitter like some people are."

"You are right they are kind and generous and you jolly well make sure you take advantage of it. You seem to have conveniently forgotten what Bill has done for you lot and the other old age pensioners of the village. Not only are you spongers but you try to get as much out of them as you can then as soon as they leave you pat each other on the back in self admiration. You lot have no shame."

"That does it, come on let us get out of this dump," said the spokesman as he got to his feet. "We are not going to stay here to be insulted by her…at this point he was interrupted by Tim who asked. "What is going on here?"

"Don't you come poking your nose in you are as bad as her, we will get better treatment at the Rose and Crown."

"Then I suggest you go there for your drinks because you are all barred from here from now on, so get out of my establishment."

"You will be in for it when Bill gets to know how you have treated us."

"But they will be a lot better off financially not supporting you spongers…What brought that on Ann?" he asked after they had left.

"I over-heard rent a gob talking about how smart he had been getting them free drinks."

"Good riddance I say Ann, they have been a bit too clever this time and no way will I lift the ban. I will have a word with Jim at the Rose and Crown and put him in the picture, he will stand no nonsense from them."

"Thank goodness that is over Tim, come on let us clear up then go and celebrate with a brew. What do you fancy for your supper?"

CHAPTER 43

The new Corporals stood in front of Bill ready for him to sign their arrival chits,

"On behalf of my staff I want to welcome you as new members to my staff. You received top marks on the course but now your real learning is about to be put into practice under the guidance of Flight Sergeants Franks and Roper. You will find we have a very loyal staff who give me one hundred per cent and that is because we treat them fairly and I expect nothing different from each of you. Are you satisfied with your accommodation? The reason we have had to double you up with an experienced Corporal is because we have not enough single bunks for you all. The plus side is you will fall into our routine more quickly by listening to what your bunk partner tells you.

One last thing before you leave, while my staff are on duty they are not individuals they all belong to a team, remember that. Also if you do need advice be it personal or not do not be afraid to approach a senior member of staff for advice you will be surprised how helpful they can be. Right then let me sign your chitties then report next door for your instructions after you have finished arriving. Any questions?"

"No sir," was the response.

"Away you go then."

♦♦♦

On the afternoon of the arrival of the two flights of recruits Sergeant Fell with his two Corporals would be taking charge of the airmen while Sergeant (w) Dean and her two Corporals would be doing likewise with the airwomen.

Sergeant Farrow and Sergeant Peters with the new Corporals were to watch the handling of the recruits from de-bussing to the allocation of their designated accommodation.

"Remember how you were received although when you attended recruit training it would not be here at RAF March, so watch how we receive our recruits you will wish you had done your training here. Get any bad thoughts out of your mind because you will not see any bullying from our staff, but you may get an odd idiot from the recruits trying it on. That being so the offenders will be dishonourably discharged immediately. Your job will be to stop it before it has time to start, remember, your duties as NCOs does not stop at the end of the training day and if you come across anyone not complying with regulations if it is a minor offence you give a first time warning and anything you consider serious you come down on them like a ton of bricks and take disciplinary action. Now watch, listen and take note of the experts at work because that is what will be expected of you when you join your respective flights.

♦♦♦

Sergeant Graham of the Orderly Room tapped on the communicating hatch opening to Roy Shaw's office. "Can I come round and have a word with you sir?"

"Of course, come on round."

"Sit yourself down Chris and tell me what's on your mind."

"Actually it is a message from Ann Wilson at the March Hare. Me and Marion were in there Sunday night and Ann came over sat with us and said...I would like you to pass on what I am about to tell you to Bill, Roy and Derwent...Chris then told Roy what Ann had told him.

"Thanks Chris I will pass that on, they will be surprised but deep down I am not, obviously they saw a way to get a cheap night out with free drinks and took full advantage of us with their deception and false gratitude. I will tell Bill and Derwent at lunch I don't think it will put them off their food."

At lunch the usual talk was about things in general until Roy announced. "I have some very unpleasant news which was brought to me this morning which concerns us all including Tommy and Barbara. I suggest that instead of me telling you three now we can all have a nice quiet evening in the Quiet Room where I can satisfy your curiosity, it is only fair that the other two girls are present."

"Can't you give us a clue of what it is about Roy?" Asked Derwent.

"No, if I did you would want to know more and I am not prepared to do that so just curb your impatience until this evening. Shall we meet say at 8pm?"

At the time Roy specified they trooped into the Quiet Room leaving Bill and Derwent at the bar to order the drinks.

"What is the occasion are we celebrating?" asked Fred the barman.

"We don't know" replied Derwent "you could call it a mystery meeting."

"What is the mystery?"

"We don't know Fred it is a mystery to us."

"You are not holding out on me are you?"

"Now would we do that to our favourite barman?" asked Bill.

"Yes you would," snarled Fred, trying his best to put on a stern look, "and I am not falling for any of your bets either."

"If that is the way you want it, you are not our flavour of the month," replied Bill "and when do you finish your term of bar duty?"

"Chris Graham takes over on Monday."

"Brilliant," exclaimed Derwent, "it will be a pleasure to come in here then."

"Look, take your drinks and if I was not a gentleman I would tell you what to do with them."

Bill and Derwent picked up the drinks and left, laughing their heads off.

"Some bloody gentleman!" laughed Derwent. "Wait till we tell Roy."

"You have taken your time," remonstrated Roy. "Have you been having a quiet one out there?"

"No, we have been pulling Fred's leg. By the way did you know Chris is taking over from him on Monday?"

"Oh yes, even my staff are not excused that duty even though the station will suffer by his absence from the sharp end."

"Alright Roy you have made your point now tell us why you have summoned us all here?"

"Chris Graham my right hand man."

"Roy, will you get on with it and try to curb your enthusiasm over your wonderful staff."

"As I was saying before I was so rudely interrupted. Chris and Marion were in the March Hare on Sunday evening and Ann asked him to give us a message. Our so called local friends have been barred from the Pub on Tim's orders. Apparently Ann overheard them slagging us off for being in the 'one born every minute syndrome but in this case three. Harsh words were exchanged which resulted in when Tim asked what was going on they told him 'keep his nose out of it because you are as bad as her'. When Ann told them what we had done for the village old folk she added you have no shame. The spokesman jumped to his feet and said 'we are getting out of this dump because we will get better treatment at the Rose and Crown'. Tim reacted at once and told them to get out and barred the lot of them."

"It does not surprise me one bit I could see it coming," said Tommy, "they were getting to the point of nigh on demanding a drink. For all your good intentions you chaps brought it on yourselves. I am not decrying what you did but they were sharper than we thought and took us for a soft touch no wonder they thought the world of us suckers."

"Talk about biting the hand that feeds you they did a damned good job of that" added Barbara."

"I don't know what to say only that I feel gutted, I felt so sorry for them and believed every word of their sob stories, which one of us said 'you can't teach an old dog new tricks'? They proved that. Having said that I will miss the sly devils smiled Bill

"Well I won't for sure," retaliated Tommy.

"Nor me."

"Or me."

"Shall we now choose a more pleasant topic?"

"Yes," answered Derwent, get another round in Roy and to show no ill feeling I will come and help you carry em'."

"There are times Derwent Waters when I could…I don't know why we adopted you."

"I know interrupted Viv, "it was because of me so don't go slagging off my knight in shining armour, so watch your step Roy Shaw or it will be pistols at dawn.."

"That's my girl," shouted Derwent.

"Derwent, will you wipe that silly looking smirk off your face or I will not let you help me with the drinks."

"Sorry Roy, come on let's go while you are in a good mood."

"When they returned with the drinks Roy said to Bill. "What have you been telling Fred? He has been giving me earache wanting to know all about this mystery meeting"

"He thinks he might be missing out on a good story he could trade for other little gems of information you know what he is like for trading info' I think we can use this to our advantage, when he has got hold of a little snippet he will be eager to swap then."

"So Chris takes over the bar on Monday does he?" asked Tommy.

"Indeed he does, my staff are not exempt from the bar duty."

"Well do not spoil the boy with your silly crackpot ideas or you will have me to deal with besides Viv."

"Count me in with that girls," enthused Barbara, and take note of what Tommy says that means you Bill and you Derwent any untoward behaviour from you three and you will be grounded."

CHAPTER 44

Sergeant Millie Cooper was approached by one of her team Corporals namely Corporal Liner one of the newly promoted Corporals

"Who do I have to see to change my accommodation Sergeant?"

"Flight Sergeant Roper. Can you tell me the reason you want the change?"

"It is Corporal Wheeler who I share a room with who is making my life very difficult. She appears to hold a grudge against all the new Corporals and any mention of Sergeant Peters sends her in a rage."

"Leave it with me Carol go and re-join the flight."

So that is her little game Millie said to herself. I will keep my eye on you madam.

For the rest of the morning she watched Corporal Wheeler and realized she was not helping but hindering Corporal Liner.

At lunch time she saw Margaret Roper and asked if she could have a quiet word with her.

"Is it serious Millie?"

"I'm afraid so it concerns Corporal Wheeler."

"Look, after you have finished your lunch come to my room then you can tell me all about it."

After hearing Millie's story she said thank goodness you have come to tell me and you are right it is serious, very serious and if it is what I think it is our Corporal Wheeler is in serious trouble."

"It was only when Corporal Liner told me that I noticed Wheeler's behaviour towards Liner and her attitude to the recruits. I should have picked that up sooner Flight."

"Yes you should that is what we have been teaching in the Instructor School, but don't blame yourself because I know Wheeler of old and she can be nasty little bitch when the mood strikes her. You carry on as normal Millie but keep a closer watch on her I will go and report this to W/O Anderson."

"Come in." called Viv in reply to the knock on her office door. "Oh hello Margaret nice to see you, come and sit down. How do you like your new office albeit sharing it with Joe?"

"It is great; Joe and I are getting along famously and enjoy sharing it, besides I am learning a lot from him. Anyway Viv I am here to report on a serious breech of discipline concerning Cpl Wheeler." She then told Viv about the complaint she had received from Corporal Liner via Millie Cooper.

"That sounds to me that Wheeler has got the hump about Sergeant Peters being promoted over her head with her being a more senior Corporal."

"Those were my sentiments as soon as I heard the story Viv"

"That is something we do not want jealousy in the ranks it will cause so much unrest as it spreads especially coming from an NCO. I shall make sure that it is stopped dead in its tracks. What have you done about it so far Margaret?"

"I told Millie to carry on as normal for the time being but keeping Wheeler under close observation until I came to report the incident to you."

"Hmm! Come on Margaret we will strike while the iron is hot I will fill you in as we go and pay a visit to Sergeant Cooper's flight."

They strolled casually towards the flight in a nonchalant manner then stopped a little way off to watch the proceedings but not to cause any alarm.

"Looks like our presence has been noted Margaret everyone is on their best behaviour. Come on we will have a word with Millie."

When Millie saw them coming she called to Corporal Wheeler to take over the flight.

"Any further developments with Wheeler?" asked Viv.

She has been over bossy this morning and I am afraid Corporal Liner has borne the brunt of it. I asked her the reason she appeared to be picking on her and she replied.

"Because she is bloody thick that's why, she does not do what I tell her, whoever recommended her for promotion want their bloody head examining."

"I told her she was not there to tell her anything only to guide and advise her."

"She does what I tell her or you can get somebody else to play bloody nursemaid.

"I let it ride knowing the Flight Sergeant here was coming to see you Ma'am."

"Corporal Wheeler!" called Viv.

Wheeler walked over to her. "Yes Ma'am?"

"Corporal Wheeler, why did you not march over to me instead of sauntering?"

"Because I am not a recruit Ma'am and I will not be treated as one."

"You are supposed to show an example to the recruits you are training and from what I have just seen of your couldn't care less attitude which is bordering on insubordination I think you are a disgrace to your rank. I am relieving you of your instructional duties as of now. Go and wait for me outside my office and March there not slouch. Margaret go and give Sergeant Fields my compliments and tell her I want the loan of Corporal Banks to help out here until further notice as from now. You can tell her why; I will wait here until you return. Millie, you are getting Corporal Banks to replace Corporal Wheeler and Sergeant Fields will get a new Corporal."

When Margaret and Corporal Banks arrived Viv told Corporal Banks. "I am transferring you to Sergeant Cooper's flight as senior Corporal. When Corporal Wheeler vacates her bunk you will move in with Corporal Liner and take over Wheeler's duties. Have you any objections to that move and to share with Corporal Liner?"

"None at all Ma'am and I am looking forward to working with Sergeant Cooper."

"Sergeant Cooper I want a word with Corporal Liner please."

"Corporal Liner I want you now to go and clear your belongings from your bunk and move into the dormitory. This will be for only a short stay then you can move back into your bunk; Corporal Banks will be sharing it with you as well as being senior Corporal with this flight."

"Thank you Ma'am that is just wonderful thank you."

"Off you go and get out of that bunk as quick as you can....Are you satisfied with the arrangements Millie?"

"I most certainly am Ma'am thanks."

"Come on Margaret let us go and have a word with Sally Fields to put her in the picture, Wheeler can wait until I am ready to see her."

Eventually Viv and Margaret arrived at Viv's office and as they entered it Corporal Wheeler followed on behind them.

"Wait outside Corporal until I am ready to see you."

"I have been stood out there for a good hour already and...."

"You will do as you are told and if I get anymore lip from you madam you will stay there for another hour stood to attention. Now wait there until I call you in."

Viv then rang Squadron Leader Macfarlane and explained what had happened. I have her waiting outside my office Ma'am to give me an explanation of her actions."

"When you have finished with her Warrant bring her to me."

"Bring Wheeler in Margaret and let us hear what she has to say for herself."

"Corporal Wheeler I want an explanation as to what has brought on this despicable change of character where you appear to be waging a vendetta against the new Corporals and also Sergeant Peters."

"Sergeant Peters yes for being promoted when I am much senior to her, I hate her guts. The new Corporals are a waste of time and I resent playing nurse maid to them."

"Plus the fact Corporal you have become insubordinate to senior staff."

"So what do you want me to do, get down on my knees and plead forgiveness. No way, I know I am going to get kicked out of the service so what have I got to lose?"

"A promising career brought on by jealousy and a sick mind, you will accompany me and Flight Sergeant Roper to be interviewed by Squadron Leader Macfarlane."

"You can take me to be interviewed with who the hell you like it is not going to make any difference to my attitude and I could not care less, so come on then let us get it over with then I can get the hell out of here."

"I have Corporal Wheeler outside Ma'am and she is very belligerent and has set her mind on leaving the service."

"Thank you Warrant, bring her in and I think I can safely say she will get her wish granted."

Viv ushered Margaret and Corporal Wheeler in. Margaret saluted but Wheeler did not.

"Do you not salute a senior officer Corporal?"

"What's the point? I am getting kicked out anyway."

"That is by your own volition. What has got into you girl from being a good and well respected NCO then suddenly becoming just the opposite and now appear to be carrying a huge chip on your shoulder?"

"Well wouldn't you have a chip on your shoulder if you had been by-passed in the promotion stakes with a snotty-nosed little Corporal then to rub it in getting saddled with a brand new Corporal to play nursemaid to. You would not exactly call that the icing on the cake would you and you ask me where have I gone wrong. Look Ma'am, just give me my ticket, push me through the gates and forget all about me which will save all the hassle of me being passed from one body to another until finally one makes a decision."

"It is not as easy as that Corporal but in your case I could not agree more, the sooner you go through those gates it will be better for everyone on this station. No, I am afraid we have to stick by the Rules and Regulations that is why I am sending you to the Commanding Officer to straighten you out. Hopefully for your sake as well as ours and that will be the last we see of you."

"Thank you Ma'am, you deserve a salute for that."

"Take her outside Warrant and wait there with her."

She then used a direct line to the CO and explained everything in detail of what had transpired.

"I will get back to you Mac' after I have conversed with the AOC."

"An hour later the CO rang. "Bring her to see me Mac' it is the end of the road for her. We cannot charge her for any disciplinary action only for being unfit for further service."

Mac' laughed. "That is like sending a horse to the knackers' yard sir."

The CO laughingly replied with…exactly."

"Warrant officer Anderson!" Mac' shouted. Tell Flight Sergeant Roper to take Corporal Wheeler to see the Commanding Officer and you accompany me."

On the way to see the CO. Mac told Viv of the conversation she had with the CO.

They had a good laugh about the knackers' yard.

"I will tell that one to WO Barrett that is his type of humour and I can visualise him becoming your number one fan. Do you know what he will say Ma'am. Definitely a spin-off from Mary Butcher."

"That would be true Warrant because Mary gave me a legacy of her kind of humour. I will leave you here Warrant and go to join the CO.

Outside the CO's office Viv asked Corporal Wheeler. "Do not go in there with bared claws, the CO is a very nice man so please be courteous to him, he will not slag you off but you will find him very understanding."

The three of them marched in when called and saluted the CO.

"Corporal Wheeler it is a sad day for me to have you stood there having to answer to these accusations. Looking at your records I note your assessments are excellent and furthermore up until this rather unpleasant incident you were highly thought of by the training staff. I cannot understand why such a bright NCO should suddenly turn into a Jekyll and Hyde. Having said that, in retrospect the passing over of promotion can be blamed. Corporal Wheeler, there had to be a valid reason for that decision and the Air Officer Commanding in his wisdom made it. I understand your dearest wish now is to leave the Service and the AOC has granted you that wish. You will not leave us with a dishonourable discharge but your bad attitude and unacceptable behaviour which cannot be tolerated in our training programme leaves us with just one alternative and that is to discharge you as 'Unfit for further Service with the Royal Air Force'. Do you accept that Corporal Wheeler?"

"Yes sir and thank you for being so understanding."

Outside the office she broke into tears.

"Come here," said Viv taking her into a hug. "You are the first person to leave tear stains on my shoulder, Warrant Officer Butcher would be so proud of me." Which made the three of them laugh.

"Flight Sergeant Roper will take you to the orderly room to see about your clearance chit, then she will tell you about handing your kit into stores and how she wants your room leaving for the next occupant etc. if you hit any snags Flight you know where to find me."

At the orderly room Wheeler was told to collect her chit tomorrow at 09:00hrs.

"Never mind," said Margaret you can get your kit ready to be handed in to store but make sure your bunk is cleaned ready for the next occupant."

"What about Corporal Liner can't she do it?"

"Corporal Liner has moved into the dormitory sick to the teeth with your attitude, does that surprise you?"

"So who is taking over the bunk and replacing me on the flight then?"

"Corporal Banks and a new Corporal will replace her on Sergeant Fields' flight."

"You have it all planned out then."

"You have been with us long enough to know we do not sit back and wait for things to happen, it is called forward planning. A word of warning though now that you are being discharged don't think you can get away with causing any trouble. If you do you may spend your last days with the RAF doing detention, so just bear that in mind."

When Margaret returned to her office she immediately went to see Bill Barrett.

"I have had a call from W/O Anderson telling me we have lost a Corporal Why was I not informed immediately?"

"That is simple enough to answer. Have you forgotten you put me in charge of the airwomen? I carried the procedures expected of me with it being a WRAF matter and informed WO Anderson who took charge of the proceedings. This is the first chance I have had to put you in the picture because I have been with Corporal Wheeler sorting her out ever since we left the CO's office so what have I done wrong?"

"Nothing, I would not have expected you to have done it any other way."

"Then why ask me why you were not informed immediately in that manner? WO Anderson told you as soon as she could and did you ask her the same question?" You put me in charge of the WRAF and only to contact you if I could not handle a problem. Now does that responsibility still stand or are you having a change of mind?"

"Hey, hold on a minute Margaret I have never indicated having second thoughts far from it. I apologise if you thought I was blaming you for me not being informed. I was so frustrated it went completely out of my head that you would naturally go along the WRAF channel. Viv explained everything to me and told me a replacement was needed and replaced Wheeler with Corporal Banks that leaves Sergeant Fields taking the new Corporal Now it is getting complicated, who puts in the request for the replacement Corporal Myself or Viv.? I am going to ask Wings for some clarification, I do not like how it is going. Anyway, back to our discussion, are you satisfied with your lot Margaret?"

"Yes of course I am, every time something similar to this crops up we get complications."

"As Joe and I are fond of saying Margaret, it is tough at the top. If I am wanted I will be with Viv, I will try to get a meeting to sort out what can become a very confusing situation.

"You mean the right hand not knowing what the left hand is doing."

"Hello Bill, have you come to chew over the fat about Wheeler?"

"No only that it may be the cause of opening a can of worms."

"What do you mean?"

"Who is responsible for requesting a replacement for Wheeler, you or me?"

"I am of course because she is an airwoman."

"But I have always had that responsibility Viv."

"I am sorry Bill but not any more, you have the airmen I have the airwomen."

"In other words the trainees and staff are divided into two groups."

"Remember you have Wings and I have Mac."

"I have been taken over overnight and I did not see it coming."

"No Bill, what has happened is, the airmen and airwomen have automatically reverted to how it should be airmen and airwomen in separate units, you Bill had them all in one unit."

"I see the logic of what you say Viv but I must admit it is a hard blow to my system putting you and me on equal footing. Thinking about it my work load has been halved, it can't be bad. I will now have to get used to not bossing Margaret Roper around. Anyway Viv I am still at the end of the phone if I am needed. By the way have you applied for a replacement yet?"

"Yes, Margaret and I went through the list and picked the next candidate, she will get a surprise so soon after finishing the course I can just picture her reaction...she will be gobsmacked. What is the matter Bill you look disgruntled?"

"I know it is in order but right now I just cannot come to terms with it."

"What I suggest you do Bill is go and have a chat with your buddy...Wings after that perhaps you will feel better and if you are still feel down come and add to the tear stains I already have on my tunic."

"I might just do that, right now I feel I am being made redundant and surplus to requirements."

"You will never be that Bill, you built this training establishment so don't you think you should slacken the reins a little bit, after all you have placed Joe Franks as your second in command and Margaret Roper as mine and from my point of view they are doing a first class job. Another thing you sly devil you are grooming Joe Franks to take over from you as you did with me taking over from Mary. So if you get bored with life go and help Sam Brown in the market garden. What about that project the CO gave you for when a Training Establishment is re-opened?"

"You have become a hard woman Viv Anderson but thanks for putting my head the right way round. I will leave you and go and report to Sam Brown and collect a spade from him for my first lesson."

"Away with you, you daft ha'porth and don't forget the bucket to go with it."

CHAPTER 45

The two cars with Bill Barrett and company pulled into the March Hare car park. As they walked towards the pub entrance they were accosted by Ernie Moorhouse the spokesman for the local pensioners who had been barred from the March Hare.

"Can I have a word Bill?"

"What do you want from the three suckers this time?"

"Well we were wondering if you would put a good word in for us with the landlord and his missus to lift the ban"

"Now why would I do that after the conniving advantage you took of our generosity? It is the landlord's decision and we back him all the way, personally I would not give you a light in a dark corner."

With that he turned and walked away followed by a string of abuse and "You will be sorry you said that mister."

Inside the pub they were given the usual nice greeting as friends.

As Bill was relating the incident to Tim and Ann they heard the sound of breaking glass. Quick as a flash Derwent ran out to see someone running away but not fast enough for Derwent to grab hold of him and saw immediately who it was, Ernie Moorhouse.. He put an arm lock on him and marched him back to the pub. Outside, the rest of thee party were inspecting the broken windscreen of Bill' car.

"Go and phone Fred Armstrong Ann." Fred was the village policeman. "Bring this fool inside Derwent while we wait for Fred."

Ann went off and brought a car vacuum and other cleaning items to clear the car of broken glass which was soon cleared up with everyone mucking in.

"Can I have a drink to calm my nerves?" asked Ernie, "look at me I am trembling."

"You will do more than tremble when Fred gets here especially when he makes you spend the night in clink," said Tim, "and you are definitely not getting a drink."

When the village policeman arrived he was told what had happened.

"What have you got to say for yourself Mister Moorhouse?"

"It was this lot ganging up on me they would not let me go in the pub to apologise to the landlord and his good lady."

"So how do you explain the action of you throwing a brick through that car windscreen?"

Ernie laughed. "That wasn't me I didn't throw anything at Captain Bligh's car, it was some young kid who did it and I was chasing him to try and catch him but with me being so old and feeble he was too fast for me and that stupid sod there caught hold of me instead. I kept telling him it wasn't me but he took no damn notice because he had it in for me, he nearly broke my arm dragging me in here."

While he was telling his sob story it brought smiles all round.

"How did you know whose car it was that got damaged? It was parked between two other cars," asked the policeman.

"I reversed it in so that my wife would not have any trouble driving it straight out," informed Bill," tipping the policeman a wink.

"You did not, you drove it straight in because I had a job squeezing past the first car to get…".realizing his mistake he suddenly switched to… "At it to see the damage that young devil had done."

The policeman took Bill on one side. "Do you want to press charges sir?"

"Not really Officer but I do think he should be taught a lesson."

"Definitely, I agree entirely, what do you reckon?"

"Make him pay for a new windscreen and its fitting and not paying in pennies either he should be made to pay the full cost cash down. If he does not agree then send him before the magistrates and it will cost him a darned sight more."

"Right Mister Moorhouse, this gentleman will not press charges if you pay the entire cost of a new windscreen and its fittings in full and not on credit. If you refuse he will press charges and you know what that means, it will cost you a lot more."

"I am only a poor pensioner where am I going to find that kind of money?"

"You should have thought of that when you caused wilfully damaged to the car. So what are you going to do? Perhaps a night in the cells will help make up your mind."

"Alright, alright I will pay."

"Come on then I will escort you home and think yourself lucky you are not sleeping out tonight"

When things had settled down in the pub, Tim asked Bill how he and Tommy were getting back to camp."

"No problems there Tim I can get a taxi."

"You will not, I will drive you home, I have not had a drink so I will be safe. Drive your car round the back of the pub where it will be safe, I have a tarpaulin in the garage to cover it with. I will get in touch with Bert' who owns the garage in the village and we will take it from there. Now rejoin your party and don't worry about a thing."

Bill passed on to the party what Tim had told him.

"So Tim is running us home, that is very kind of him," said Tommy.

"I could ring that Ernie Moorhouse's scrawny neck, said Ann angrily. "That is him and his cronies barred for good after that, I will not have them in here again. By the way I haven't seen your Sgt Graham in here this last week or so Roy, is he on leave?"

"No, and you will not see him for a month because he is duty Sergeants Mess barman."

"So his lady friend will not get out for a month either, poor girl."

"From what I can gather I think they may be taking a leave together, I am half expecting him to sound me out about the hotel in Portugal if so they will have to save their pennies but we will just have to wait and see. Talking of holidays don't you and Tim ever think about having a week or two in the sun somewhere?"

"We have thought about it but that is as far as it has got. We could do with one because we are tied down here and it is not often we get out together. I will think about it and try to get Tim round to my way of thinking; well I can only try can't I?"

A few days later Bill received a message from the guardroom asking him to come and vouch for a Mister Wilson who is asking for you.

"Be right there in a few minutes." He then spoke through the hatch to tell Joe Franks where he would be if wanted.

He and Tim greeted each other with a handshake.

"I have brought your jalopy it is now roadworthy and fit to drive. It is parked outside the main gates I was not allowed to drive inside."

"Great, thanks Tim I will drive you back. Has Moorhouse paid up for the replacement?"

"Come on I will tell you the tale as we go along. Apparently Bert the mechanic went round to his house with the bill for the repairs. Ernie was not for coming to the door he had obviously seen it was Bert and he knew what he had come for. In the end he had to answer the door because Bert was not going to budge until he had handed over the bill. Anyway, when Ernie was told the cost he blew a gasket and refused to pay it. Bert did not argue but went to see Fred the policeman. To cut a long story short Ernie was taken to the police station and was given the ultimatum of paying up there and then or being arrested for criminal damage. That made him back down ending up with him being escorted to the bank where he withdrew the money and paid up in cash."

"I'll bet that hurt the old rogue," laughed Bill, "can't you see him going round with a begging bowl hoping to get enough to put food on the table and having a whip round to buy drinks to share amongst them, doesn't it bring tears to your eyes Tim?"

"It does that, tears of laughter. Anyway we have got rid of them for good."

"Well here we are, thanks again for all your help Tim, you and Ann are good friends. By the way, it is time you both had a break I think Ann is ready for a nice relaxing holiday, I can recommend that hotel we all went to in Portugal."

"I think you are right Bill, I'll have a chat with her, we do need a break."

"Will you have any difficulty getting a stand-in for the pub?"

"No, we have friends who will help us out that is no problem, the only problem will be…when. Will you be coming to see us on Saturday Bill?"

"I can't promise it depends on the women folk and you know what they are like Tim. Well I must be off and get back to the grind." He shook Tim's hand with, "thanks again Tim, love to Ann."

CHAPTER 46

The Station Commander called the Wingco', Wings and WO Barrett to his office.

"I have just returned from Command with a very interesting report. Apparently our fame as instructors of RAF recruits has spread to far distant lands. Consequently a Middle Eastern potentate is coming to pay us a visit to run his eye over our instructing methods with a view to us training his son before sending him to RAF Cranwell to qualify as an officer. I would like your views gentlemen on how you think we should approach this visit."

"Give him the red carpet treatment sir." offered the Wingco'.

"I would have the best trained flight with Instructors in their best uniforms giving a display on the Parade ground," said Wings.

"Well Mister Barrett what have you got to offer?" asked the CO.

"No preferential treatment sir, let him see the basics of how we progress with our training methods."

"I take it Mister Barrett you do not approve of the red carpet treatment for VIPs," responded the Wingco'."

"I did not infer that sir, that kind of treatment is necessary in certain cases. Each and every day our training methods are open to scrutiny, what could be called red carpet treatment without the red carpet. A slight exaggeration sir if you follow what I am trying to say."

The CO tried to disguise a chuckle with a cough.

"I am not disputing that Mister Barrett but suggesting that this very VIP person should be honoured with reverence according to his status."

"With respect sir, if he wanted his son to have preferential treatment he would not give RAF March a second thought but send him straight to RAF Cranwell. That indicates to me that he is making his son start right at the bottom as an ordinary erk which I applaud because here he will get educated at ground level and be able to stand on his own two feet to face the trauma of preferential treatment he is bound to get because of his father's status."

"Have you any comments to add from what you have just heard Squadron Leader?"

"Having been through Cranwell very much later than you two gentlemen and it must have changed dramatically over the years. With that in mind I find myself going along with Mister Barrett's summing up, I think the VIP will want to see us as we really are and not from the end of a red carpet."

"Wing Commander?"

"I hold my hand up to Mister Barrett I cannot argue with his summing up. Sir."

"Thank you gentlemen, I will do my own summing up then put it to the AOC and let you know the final decision."

"Excuse me sir, there maybe a problem regarding food unless of course he is westernised in that respect otherwise we will have a problem."

"You have a good point there Mister Barrett one well worth mentioning in my report."

Bill saluted and left.

"What do you think of our Mister Barrett's appraisal John?"

"That man never fails to amaze me sir, he has the knack to get to the roots of any problem almost immediately and nine times out of ten he makes sense with his solutions. Actually I am envious of his talents and trying to learn from them."

"Me too sir."

"Well you have a good head start on John here, so don't you think it is about time we were seeing some response from your close affinity with your mentor Bill?" responded the CO with a chuckle.

"Rome was not built in a day sir."

"True but RAF March's reputation came a good second, think about it Bill. Well gentlemen it now leaves me with a trip down to Command, I'll tell you something they serve a damn fine lunch there something I look forward to."

After leaving the CO's office Bill went to see Roy Shaw.

"Ah, the weary traveller has finally found his waterhole, two teas please," he shouted through the connecting hatch. "Sit yourself down William and just relax, your tea will be served immediately."

At that point an airman knocked on the office door and entered with the two teas.

"What do you want in exchange for this VIP treatment?" queried Bill.

"Speaking of VIPs I heard a little whisper we are about to be visited by one and knowing you are the Jack Horner with your finger in every pie who better could I get the info' from.?"

"So all my information is worth to you is a brew with not even one measly biscuit."

"Give me a name and you will get one, give me the reason for the visit and you will get two. "

"What do you want for a choccy bicky?"

"Your posting!"

"You are a tough 'cookie' Roy Shaw if you pardon the pun. I accept your offer up to a point."

"What do you mean 'up to a point'?"

"You'll see. Now here it is straight from the horses' mouth."

"No comment."

"A Middle Eastern potentate.

"Oh you do know some long words Bill."

"If you are going to continue interrupting me I will just settle for the brew and take my leave."

"Sorry old friend, carry on I am all ears."

"So I have noticed but too polite to say anything."

"Touché."

"This VIP whose name I do not know is coming to look at our training methods with a view to sending his son here for training before sending him to RAF Cranwell."

"And what was the outcome from your meeting?"

"Now that is a different story, you have got your two biscuits worth. Now I'll be off, thanks for the brew Roy."

"Hang on a minute Bill; don't you want to know the name of the new WRAF Corporal?"

"No!"

"Why not?"

"Nowt' to do with me, Viv is in charge of the airwomen, I am in charge of the airmen."

"Well come in the bar tonight and I will buy you a pint."

"Sorry old lad but Tommy won't let me play out tonight she has a job lined up for me."

"What's that?"

"Washing up!"

"Sod off Barrett you are doing my head in."

When he returned to his office Bill called through the connecting hatch inviting Joe Franks to come round for a chat.

"What is on your mind Bill?"

When he heard the full story he remarked, "So our fame is spreading, I am looking forward to taking that job on providing our methods are acceptable. Another thing Bill, six weeks is not going to be long enough for us to train him to reach a higher standard for us to make a good impression on the VIP. I suggest we get our heads together and sort this eventuality out."

"If you have nothing that can't wait for a little while because I have nothing pressing we can make a start now."

"That is fine by me so let us get our thinking caps on."

"The first six weeks are no problem but when the flight he will be in come to their passing out parade it will leave the lad high and dry. We cannot re-flight him because not only would he be embarrassed having to go through all the basics again but it would really brown him off and cause him to lose interest. So what do we do to give him that extra training? We have no staff to spare."

"Give me a minute or two Joe I have something running through my head about what you said about no spare staff." After scribbling on a jotter for a few minutes he looked at Joe with a smile. "I think I have got it Joe but don't think I am over-riding your authority you have the last say in the matter, if you accept it then it will be a joint decision."

"Fair enough Bill, what have you come up with?"

"After the lad's flight has passed out we do a little swap around with two of the corporals. I have chosen Corporal Deacon to give the lad the extra training under your supervision of course which will leave Jim Farrow with one inexperienced corporal. I then suggest you move Corporal Lucas from Alan Fell's flight to Jim Farrows'. Allan can manage with his remaining experienced corporal for a short period until we get back to normal. What do you think about that Joe?"

"I can see pitfalls there Bill. How are we going to induct him into a flight straight out of the blue? He will be at a disadvantage right from the word go, it will make him a loner and he will find it very hard to integrate. What uniform is he going to wear is he to appear as an RAF recruit? If so then I suggest he goes through documentation along with the other recruits but an allowance be made for him not taking the oath of allegiance. Kit him out as a recruit which can be returned to stores when he has qualified. Unless he confides in the other recruits no-one will be any the wiser. Our six weeks training should be enough for him to qualify if not he can be re-flighted for as long as is necessary. If the VIP wants his son to start his training at the bottom of the ladder without any preferential treatment that is going to be the best option and will save a lot of covering up and excuses.

"Joe," exclaimed Bill. "You have gone and kicked my effort right into touch with an almighty kick to come up with the answer, what are you trying to do make me redundant? That took some thinking out Joe well done you are not just a pretty face are you?"

"My wife would disagree with you on that score Bill."

The following day Bill was told to report to the Station Commander. Helen Fraser the CO's PA greeted Bill with. "The Magic Circle is now complete as Merlin the Magician makes his grand entrance," she said giggling.

"Come woman, announce me and don't trap my flowing robes in the door."

She suppressed her laughter enough to announce "Warrant Officer Barrett sir."

Bill saluted on entering observing that the Wingco' and Wings were present.

"Now that you are all here," began the CO. I am happy to inform you that the VIP will arrive here in four days time along with his son. Once he approves we will have to come up with some kind of schedule for his son. I do not suppose you will have had time to think of one yet but there is no time like the present gentleman, forward planning is called for. Yes Mister Barrett?"

"I have discussed that with Flight Sergeant Franks and he has put together what I think is the answer to a very tricky situation."

"Carry on then Mister Barrett we are all interested to hear of this wonderful plan."

"It is not a wonderful plan sir but is the answer we should be looking at and I think accepting." He began in detail to unfold the plan noting as he progressed more interest was shown on the faces of the three officers. On completion he asked if there were any doubts or questions to answer.

"I am looking for flaws," said the Wingco. "and I am blowed if I can see any."

"I think it answers all the questions we have been very doubtful about and I congratulate Flight Sergeant Franks for that," enthused Wings.

"Well Mister Barrett," spoke the CO, it appears and with some justification that you are indeed training you staff well, so much so your second in command has just stolen your thunder with an excellent solution to a very tricky situation. Flight Sergeant Franks is to be congratulated but it is what we will come to expect in future from a chip off the old block!"

"Thank you sir I would like to add a rider to that solution. You say the son will accompany his father here. I would suggest the son be kept in the background because most of the present trainees will probably still be here when the son arrives to do his training and there is a chance some of them could recognise him from his visit."

"That is a very good point which we will have to point out to the VIP when we explain our scheme to him. Anything else Mister Barrett?"

"Just one thing sir, the VIP may be impressed and tick our box if shown the BlueBelles film explaining what RAF March is renowned for."

"Jolly good idea Mister Barrett hopefully that should help make his mind up in our favour."

"Mister Barrett," spoke the Wingco', "will you ensure that all airmen's accommodations are laid out as per regulations and that includes the Corporals. Everything must be spick and span, my guess is he will want to see where his son will be billeted."

"Of course sir I have got that on my agenda."

"If that is all gentlemen I will now close this meeting," concluded the CO.

"I see from your face Merlin you cast your magic spell yet again," observed Helen Fraser, "tell me how you do it."

"Hypnosis and it works every time."

"Well stop staring at me like that and be off with you I am getting goose pimples."

"Ah ah, it is working on you at last."

"Go on, clear off you daft beggar before I get my little doll and pins out."

CHAPTER 47

RAF March had been smartened up and Station Warrant Officer George Miller had stationed himself outside the guardroom along with Flight Sergeant Tom Bridges of the RAF police waiting the arrival of the Air Officer Commanding escorting the VIP. As the car bearing the VIP's national pennant entered through the main gates Tom Bridges signalled to the Orderly Sergeant who was standing by the telephone in the guardroom. On receiving the signal he immediately rang through to the Officers Mess to inform the Station Commander of the VIP's arrival. The AOC returned the salute of George Miller and Tom Bridges while the VIP who was in his national dress acknowledged the salute with a half raised arm. The car carried on to the Officers Mess where the Station commander was waiting at the entrance to the Mess to greet and welcome the AOC and party. After the greetings and introductions the VIP and son were ushered into a private room to freshen up after the long car journey, stewards were at hand for any requests in the shape of refreshments. When they were ready the VIP requested a word with the AOC and Station Commander.

"I will put as you would say…my cards on the table. I do not wish to be overwhelmed with too many people as I make my tour, the only people I want with me are the officer in charge of the training and the drill expert to show me round and their methods of training. When that is completed I will come back to you gentlemen to give you my verdict and to formulate a plan of action. Is that agreeable to you?"

"But of course sir, Squadron Leader Cody will be your escort and he will introduce you to his staff." Wings was called for and introduced to the VIP and his son.

In the meantime Bill Barrett was informed to stand by to receive visitors. He promptly called through the hatch to tell Joe our visitors are on their way.

When the car pulled up Bill and Joe both presented the VIP with a very smart salute.

Wings introduced them adding. "These two are the backbone of our recruit training sir."

"I have heard of you Warrant Officer Barrett your training methods have become legendary even in my part of the world and it is my privilege to have met you in person. If I remember rightly you had a female leading your team in an all service victory."

"Yes sir and she is still with us here at RAF March now as a Warrant Officer and if you would like to meet her it can be arranged also you are invited to see a film of that famous victory."

"Thank you, nothing would give me greater pleasure. Now I want you by my side explaining in detail everything I need to know about your training methods."

"Before we start sir would you please not take offence if your son can keep in the background while we are with the trainees? The reason I ask is to keep his identity hidden, if or when he joins us for training some recruits may still be here when he does so and having to train as one of them his identity must be protected."

"I understand what you are saying and I appreciate your concern." He then turned to his son and told him to wear his dark glasses whilst they were viewing the airmen.

Bill told Joe to tell Margaret Roper to get in touch with Viv to meet them for the film show.

After a brief spell in the ops' room the tour began with Bill giving a detailed description of the training and answering the many questions. An inspection of one of the dormitories was next which the father and son found very interesting when they saw the daily layout and the poster showing a full kit lay-out, the communal ablutions, drying and ironing rooms.

"I am impressed, Warrant Officer Barrett. I can visualise your recruits leaving here with more confidence in themselves than when they arrived."

"Are you ready to see the film, sir? Everyone who has seen it has been amazed that young women recruits with only three weeks of service could produce drill to such a high standard."

As they approached where the film was to be shown, Bill saw Viv stood waiting.

"Sir, it is my privilege to introduce you to Warrant Officer Anderson, who led the BlueBelles Team to that famous victory."

Viv saluted smartly.

"It is a pleasure to meet you Warrant Officer Anderson, your fame, along with this man's, has spread even to my country and I am looking forward to seeing if it is really true what I have heard. I would like you to sit with me during the performance to explain any queries I may have. Lead the way Squadron Leader."

During the showing of the film the VIP sat enthralled. Not once did he ask a question and Viv was kept amused by watching and hearing his reactions, especially when the team swung into their specialist routine. At the end, his face was wreathed in smiles.

"That was an amazing performance but what were they singing as they made their triumphant exit?"

"That is the signature tune they adopted but with their own words sir. That song won us that victory because you will have noticed there was no military music to march to and we taught the girls to sing it only to themselves to help keep their rhythm and balance whilst marching. We called that our secret weapon sir."

"And it worked, Allah be praised."

As they left the building the VIP spoke to Wings.

"What an amazing experience, Squadron Leader You must have been very proud of them on the day."

"Unfortunately sir it was before my time here at RAF March but as the news spread the BlueBelles became the toast of the RAF and it was all due to our Warrant Officer Barrett."

"The VIP beckoned Bill and Viv to him and shook both their hands. Thank you very much, that film for me was as you say...the icing on the cake. It is people of your calibre that makes your Royal Air Force the envy of many. You both have done it a great service and you will be hearing from me soon."

They both thanked him and saluted.

"Come Squadron Leader let us go and 'de-brief' with your brass hats!"

"It looks like we made a hit Bill I must say he is a very nice man. Oh you should have seen and heard him during the film you would have thought he was our biggest fan."

"I think we all heard him but most of it was in his own language. I agree that he was impressed with the tour I would like to bet that film clinched it....I hope. I wonder what he meant when he said...you will be hearing from me soon."

"How he said it sounded to me as if he had made up his mind in our favour."

"I do hope so Viv, if it does happen that will be another star on our cards."

"Daft beggar."

Returning to the Officers Mess the VIP was asked if he would like to freshen up and have refreshments.

"Yes please" and told what he would like in the way of refreshments. "Then we will get down as you say to....the nitty-gritty."

When they had been refreshed the Station Commander led them into the Mess lounge which had been placed out of bounds to the rest of the Mess members.

The meeting comprised of....the AOC, Station Commander, Wingco' Hopwood and Wings.

"With your permission sir I will outline the plan we think will be more advantageous to your son if you decide RAF March is the one to start off your son's basic training. You have seen the environment in which he will be training and the manner of instructing he will receive but he will receive no preferential treatment. To protect his identity he will go through the same procedures as the other recruits, documentated and kitted out the only exception to the rule is, he will not swear allegiance. From there he will be transported here with the other recruits and this is where his training will begin for a six weeks period. That sir is our plan to protect the identity of your son. There is one other thing which we think is very important. Personal clothing, he must not wear designer clothing or anything to denote he is from a rich family. Find out what the ordinary boy in the street is wearing casual clothing is the answer and personal items such as watches etc nothing expensive that will give the game away. Yes Wing Commander?"

"Please may I make a suggestion?

The AOC looked across to the VIP, "Sir?

The response was a nod,

"Proceed Wing Commander."

"My advise is to make friends, join in with their moans and groans he will find plenty of those but he will find they bring the recruits together more in comradeship and in this day and age that is becoming a rare commodity. Lastly he must never lose his self respect."

"There you are sir," said the AOC as we say...the ball is now in your court."

"The VIP smiled, "I do enjoy these little sayings of your country they say so much with very few words. First I want to thank everyone concerned in this project for the warm welcome my son and I have received from you. We are both impressed with your training staff and their training methods. We were surprised with the dormitory accommodation but then realised it is part of your character building....no objections.

"Then we concluded with a film showing the expertise in training young ladies with just three weeks service to put on such a magnificent display of perfection in drill. Then to meet personally the two people responsible for their training was as you say....the icing on the cake," he said with a smile. One of those two would be in charge of my son's training if I chose RAF March for his training and that indeed would be a bonus. I think your plan for my son joining the recruits at the very beginning to hide his identity is sound common sense thank you for that consideration. I like the Wing Commander's suggestion my son becoming just another recruit, thank you Wing Commander that was well thought out. Now for my decision, right up to seeing that film I was pretty sure I was going to say yes but after seeing that film two people were responsible for me to make it a definite yes but there is a clause. I would like a copy of that film."

“Sir said the AOC, you will have one with pleasure and thank you for your decision,” he said. Each officer in turn then shook his hand and thanked him.

“By the way gentlemen when is your next intake due?”

“In two weeks time on a Wednesday sir,” answered Wings.

“Very well gentlemen thank you for your hospitality and may the blessings of your God be upon you.”

The officers walked them to their limousine and waved them off.

“There is one more duty to perform before we can star any celebrations Eric and that is to give Warrant Officer Barrett the good news in person, put a Tannoy message out for him to report to your office immediately.”

As they both made their way to the CO’s office they heard the Tannoy.

‘Attention Attention Warrant Officer Barrett is to report to the Station Commanders Office immediately, end of message’.

Bill was with Roy Shaw filling him in with all the details when they heard the Tannoy message.

“Looks like the decision has been made Roy and I will find out in a few minutes.”

“I hope it is the right one Bill, not only for the station but for you, good luck old friend you deserve it.”

He entered Helen Fraser’s office to be greeted with. “Hello Merlin so we meet again.”

“What are you doing with a Garlic bulb on your desk?” he asked

“That is to protect me from being hypnotised by you.”

“That smell will chase everyone away who dares to enter this office.”

“Come on they are waiting for you, have you got your wand? Warrant Officer Barrett sir,” she said as she ushered him in.

He saluted and was surprised to see his old friend the AOC there.

“Nice to see you once again Mister Barrett.”

“And you sir.”

“I think you know why we have sent for you.”

“To tell me of the decision sir.”

“Exactly. I don’t know how to tell you and what your reactions will be.”

Bill’s heart sank thinking where have we gone wrong.

“The VIP was very gracious in his summing up and he was very impressed with the BlueBelle film so much so he wants a copy of it. To cut a long story short because you want the verdict I can now tell you his answer was yes. I see that put the smile back on your face, forgive me teasing you Mister Barrett but it was the devil in me because it is such an honour for RAF March, Training Command and our training staff. We both wish to offer our thanks and congratulations because it was you who won the VIP over.” They both then shook Bill’s hand as they thanked him.

“Did he accept everything that was suggested sir?”

“Everything, the boy will arrive here two weeks on Wednesday with a new intake. Thank you again Mister Barrett for a job well done and give our thanks to Flight Sergeant Franks for the role he played.”

Bill saluted and at the door he turned and in the old routine asked. "No further comments sir?"
"Not this time Mister Barrett," he said with a smile.
"Are you staying overnight Charles?" asked Eric the Station Commander.
"I am, we have a lot to reminisce tonight plus having a quiet celebration drink."
"I thought you might there is a bed already made up for you."

CHAPTER 48

Bill made is way to see Roy Shaw to tell him the good news.
"Two teas with biscuits," Roy called through the hatch seeing the smiling face of his best friend, "and make them chocolate. Congratulations Bill you have pulled it off once again."
"How on earth did you find out it is not even on the grapevine yet."
"Your face gave it away Billy Boy remember I can read you like a book. Wait until the brew comes in then you can tell me all about it."
"Roy! You are getting all excited."
"I know don't you think it is something to get excited about?" Ah, here it comes." He thanked the young airman who brought it in. Chocolate Digestives your favourite, now get on with it."
Bill smiled to himself at the fuss Roy was making. "Thank you Roy I am partial to them."
"Never mind the bloody biscuits get on with it man."
Bill had to laugh to himself because it was a long time since he found Roy in such an excitable mood.
He began from being introduced to the VIP right through to his meeting with the AOC and Station Commander just a short while ago.
"Is that really what the AOC said that you were responsible for the result? Bill you deserve a knighthood for what you have achieved for RAF March."
"I will be satisfied with a Blue Peter Badge Roy."
"Not another, how many have you got now? You will be making the Duke of Edinburgh envious."
They both had a good laugh as they shook hands.
"The lad arrives a week on Wednesday along with the new intake, remember his identity is to be kept top secret. I will now go and report to Joe with the good news.
Thanks for the brew and the Choccy Bicky."
"I heard the Tannoy for you Bill and guessed it was to tell you the result."
"You guessed right Joe and it is in our favour we have won again. The AOC told me,' Tell Flight Sergeant Franks, thank you for his contribution to our success."
"That was very good of him Bill to recognise my bit I appreciate that."
"It was no bit Joe you gave them the main foundation to work on and believe me they had not a clue on how to start. The Wingco' wanted the Red

carpet treatment and Wings wanted a flight dressed up to the nines to give a demonstration on the parade ground. When I told them your idea they did not what to say it kicked their ideas right into touch as it did with mine. You have a lot to be proud of Joe and you can hold your head high I am glad I have you on my team. Do you fancy a little celebration in the Mess bar tonight?"

"That would be very nice I think we deserve one."

"Good I will tell the other crackpots and then Tommy because she will want to arrange a girlie night." He answered the ringing phone. "Thanks Marion I will be over straight away. Wings wants a word with me Joe no guesses to what it will be about."

"It can only be one thing Bill you will be getting a pat on the back, let me know if he wants to change anything."

"Will do Joe I can't see what he can change but you can never tell with our lords and masters."

"You can go straight in Bill he is expecting you."

"Come in Mister Barrett and sit yourself down. I asked you here to congratulate you and to thank you for bringing another success to RAF March."

"Excuse me sir but I thing Flight Sergeant Franks should be getting more praise than he is getting at the moment, after all it was his scheme which blew our efforts away and was the foundation of our success. Where was the personal thank you Flight Sergeant? The only one resembling that was from the AOC telling me to give Joe a thank you and well done."

"Hold it right there Mister Barrett, I will not have you criticising senior officers in that manner it is akin to insubordination, now leave my office before you say something you will regret saying later."

"I stand by my words and stand by my staff and yes I will leave your office sir," he then saluted and left.

He went straight to the orderly room to see his pal Roy Shaw who saw immediately that something was on Bill's mind.

"Two teas he called through the hatch. Come on Bill you have something on your mind, who has been upsetting you?"

"Myself more than anybody, I came in here with the thought of applying for a posting."

"YOU WHAT?" shouted Roy. "A bloody posting! YOU of all people? What has got into you? Are you cracking up or summat? Come on, tell me what is going on in that thick head of yours."

He told Roy what had transpired between himself and Wings.

"Oh no, you know damn well you can't talk to senior officers like that and expect to get off scot free. It is like you and Wings had swapped identities when he was acting up like a barm pot and you thought a posting would solve your little outburst. I know nobody is indispensible but you are not far short of that, this station will not close down and Joe Franks would slide into your position with no effort at all."

"You have got it all wrong Roy it was not like that I was so angry with myself I thought for a minute, get out Bill and let them get on with it they do not deserve the loyalty they get from the training staff. I realise I overstepped the mark with Wings but I had to say it. No doubt I will be summoned to see the Station Commander and we will just have to take it from there and if they wave the big fist….I am away, there is no doubt about it I will apply for a posting. By the way me and Joe are having a mini celebration tonight are you up for it?"

"What a stupid question you know damn well if I do not attend it will die in its feet."

"Good, let Derwent know will you? I'm off to tell Tommy she can have her girlie night."

Jackie the civilian receptionist was on duty. "Hello Bill you have come for a word with Tommy I take it. I will be only a minute. Very soon Tommy made an appearance and gave him his usual kiss must to the delight of Jackie who thought the world of them both."

"Don't tell me but you want to play out tonight with your pals….right?"

"Right! But that gives you the chance to have one of your girlie nights." Then he told her the reason for the celebration."

"Oh that is nice and I think you deserve to celebrate so I will celebrate with all the girls from the Mess they really enjoyed it the last time we had one. Come on Jackie we have some food preparation to see to lets go and have a word with chef. Don't look like that Mister Sergeants Mess Chairman it will be all above board and legit' because I do pay for the food and chef's time when he works after hours after all they will be only a few dainties."

"Okay I will leave you ladies to get on with it then."

The following day Bill received a phone call from Barbara Page who was PA to Wing Commander Hopwood to tell him the Wingco' would like to see him.

When she ushered and announced him Bill entered and saluted.

"Take a seat Mister Barrett."

"No thank you sir I would rather stand."

"Ah, so you know why I have sent for you."

"It was on the cards sir and I was prepared for it."

"Then I will not mince matters. The report I got from Squadron Leader Cody was something I did not expect coming from you. Is he correct in what you said to him?"

"I have no reason to doubt his word sir."

"Then can you explain this outburst which I find totally out of character?"

"Yes sir, it evolved round Flight Sgt Franks' submission of the scheme entailing that young man's identity and how he could join us without drawing attention to who he was and becoming just another recruit. As you well know that scheme kicked all our ideas bang into touch and was accepted unconditionally by all concerned. I was called to receive the personal thanks for my contribution by the AOC who in turn told *me* to thank Flight Sergeant Franks for his contribution. Without that I am sure the VIP would have turned his back on us. Thinking about it just preyed on my mind and I could not bottle it up any longer. Unfortunately the Squadron Leader was in the line of fire and had he not been I would have said the very same thing had it been you or the Station Commander sir. The Squadron Leader said it was akin to insubordination of senior officers then told me to leave before saying something I might regret later. If insubordination be it then I will stand firm to face any charges."

"Principles Mister Barrett, are to be applauded but do you know of anyone with principles who has ever won their battle? I know of no-one they all have bit the dust. I suggest I take this...shall I call it a misunderstanding no further? unless of course you decide otherwise. If you do I can only see you getting hurt and a very upsetting time for your staff plus us senior officers and I mean that sincerely."

"Thank you sir, I retract what I said now you have made me see that it was a damned stupid way of letting off steam. I will now go and apologise to Squadron Leader Cody"

"Well done Mister Barrett and I have completely forgotten about the incident."

Bill saluted and made his way to see Wings.

"Come in Mister Barrett I have been expecting you."

"I have come to....

"No Mister Barrett, I know what you want to say and it is totally unnecessary, we are on the same footing as we always have been...on the same team."

"Thank you sir."

"No! thank you Mister Barrett how many times have you been on the receiving end of my anger? This is the first time the roles have been reversed, you have trained me well Mister Barrett in all aspects and now I think I have grown up." He held out his hand and asked. "Friends?"

Bill shook it and replied. "Friends."

He saluted and left. Once outside he said to himself... is it my imagination or do I feel a lump in my throat.

CHAPTER 49

Corporals Deacon and Boland were at the local railway station to shepherd their new arrivals onto the RAF coaches as were (w) Corporals, Briggs and Falls ready to receive their new WRAF arrivals as they alighted from the train. Corporals Boland and Falls directed their respective charges to the coaches where Corporals Deacon and Briggs were waiting to check their names on the manifest they were issued with. When checked they were told to stack their kit bags at the rear of the coach then sit still. When the boarding was checked and all names tallied Corporal Deacon introduced himself and Corporal Boland to the airmen recruits.

"We are your drill instructors for the time you will be with us at RAF March. When we reach the station you will form up in threes and Sergeant

Farrow who is in charge of our flight will give you a welcome talk. Following that you will be taken to your living accommodation where you are allotted a bed space, your name will be on the small label attached to the door of your wardrobe. I will give you the information you will need to know of the Barrack Room rules and regulations. That is all for now, we are only ten to fifteen minutes from RAF March. Right driver take it away."

A similar scene was carried out on the bus carrying the WRAF.

On arrival the airmen were told to remain seated. "When your name is called by Corporal Boland collect your kit bag from him then fall in outside in three ranks."

When they had all de-bussed Sergeant Farrow addressed them.

"I am Sergeant Farrow and you are my flight for the next six weeks. Welcome to RAF March where it is hoped we can respect each other in comradeship. We want to train you to become a credit to the service besides being fully trained in drill which is an essential part of your service life. I will not keep you any longer for I am sure you are more than ready to off-load your webbing etc. Pay attention to what the Corporals tell you regarding Barrack Room discipline and remember he is there to help and guide you.

Carry on Corporal Deacon."

"As I call your name, fall in on me. When Corporal Boland calls your name, fall in on him. Do you understand?"

He received a half hearted reply.

"I said do you understand?"

"Yes Corporal," was the reply.

When they had been sorted out he told them. "This man here," pointing to the first man in line will find he is allotted the first bed on the left in number one dormitory, the rest of you follow on and if you keep yourselves in that order you will automatically come to your allotted bed space and I want this movement carried out in strict silence. Then you can start to unpack your gear, I will have a word with you when you have settled down. The same applies to you other people who are in number two dormitory of which Corporal Boland is in charge. Number one dormitory occupants follow me.

When the airwomen de-bussed they were made to form three ranks to hear a welcoming address from Sergeant (w) Dean.

"Good afternoon ladies, I am Sergeant Dean who is in charge of your flight while you are here to complete six weeks of recruit training. You have already met my two NCOs who will assist me in putting you through your paces. We pride ourselves on being good instructors and follow in the footsteps the two people who trained recruits like yourselves who had only been three weeks in the service to out-drill two teams of service women from the Royal Navy and the Army who were experienced service women and our girls The BlueBelles beat them out of sight. The film of that great victory is in our curriculum and you will be privileged to see it during your course.

The icing on the cake is, we have Warrant Officer Anderson in charge of your training, she was the one who led the BlueBelles to that famous victory you will be meeting her during your stay and hopefully she will sprinkle you with what is called the BlueBelle magic. The person responsible for the training of the Bluebelles is Warrant Officer Barrett who is in charge of the airmen's training you will also have the pleasure of meeting him. Now about your accommodation, you will be divided into two lots rooms one and two. I will now hand you over to your respective Corporals and please take heed to what they tell you."

"As I call your names out you will fall in on me in single file, the rest of you will fall in on Corporal Falls."

Eventually they were sorted out.

"Now some of you have already made friends and would like adjoining bed spaces, the ones who do not hold up you hands, six hands were raised. You six are allocated to room one and you will occupy the first three beds on the left and the first three beds on the right. Fill in the identity labels and place them on your wardrobe door. Are you clear on that point?"

"Yes Corporal," they answered.

"Good, then off you go, room one is on the left as you enter the building. Now you the remainder pair yourselves off in two files that means one of you at the front and your partner behind you at the rear and you have three minutes to carry that out."

The two Corporals watched the pushing and shoving with some amusement.

Corporal Briggs went down the line and divided them by placing an arm between two of the girls on the front rank stating. "From here to the left are in room one, file one will occupy beds four and five, file two beds six and seven and so on, do you all understand?"

"Yes Corporal." they answered.

"Don't forget your I.D. Labels, I will come and have a word with you later."

Corporal Falls asked her party, did you understand what Corporal Briggs was saying."

"Yes Corporal."

"Then carry out the same procedure except the first file will commence with bed one and two. Off you go then I will have words with you later."

"Bring your lads into my room Tom then we will put them in the picture with the rules and regulations."

As they filed in they were told to sit on the beds, these lads won't mind will you?"

There was a mixed answer of 'Yes and No'.

"Fair enough," stated Alfred Deacon, "if you would rather form up on the parade ground where we can make it formal that is fine with me."

A few arguments broke out until Alfred called for attention.

"Shall we have a vote then?

"YES! Bellowed the airmen"

"Hands up the ones who are keen to have a parade." There was no movement only deadly silence.

"Pity, when I was so looking forward to a nice little parade. Very well then SIT!" He laughed as they sat like a row of skittles being knocked down, the airmen joined in the laughter when they realised it was a wind-up.

"Right then let us get to the serious part of Barrack Room rules and regulations and what is required from you. What impressed you when you entered your respective dormitories?"

Many hands were raised. He pointed to the VIP's son. "What is your name?"

"Peter Bin Aziz Corporal."

"Tell me A/c (aircraftsman) Bin Aziz what your first impression was."

"Everything was neat and tidy, each bed space was in line with the rest as was the bedding and the floor was well polished."

"There you have it in a nutshell and that is how your dormitories will look until the end of training each day and there is a chart on your notice board to guide you. Each morning before work parade we Corporals will inspect you and your bed space. In the cleaning cupboard you should find ample floor pads for you to slide along the floor therefore saving a lot of hard polishing plus all the necessary items for cleaning. Here is a little tip, you will definitely need an iron for your pressing, you can either buy an individual one or chip in for the whole room to use. Headgear must be worn at all times when in your uniform outside your accommodation. Are there any questions you want to ask?"

"No?" If you do have any problems do not keep them to yourselves knock on my door or Corporal Boland's and we will give you or get you all the help you need. Tomorrow you will spend most of the day getting your kit ready to be inspected by Squadron Leader Cody on the following day. Now I want you to listen carefully and absorb what I am about to tell you. Bullying will not be tolerated at RAF March, anyone reported doing so will be dishonourably discharged from the service immediately and he will get no second chance. Such a discharge will also prevent you from joining any of the other services. Any questions?"

"Yes Corporal, my brother did his National Service in the RAF and he told me that in each billet a 'Senior Man' was picked to be in charge of the room as the Corporal's right hand man. Do you still have them?"

"We do not have them here thank goodness because we found Corporals would take advantage and let the Senior Man do all the dirty work for him. Also the post usually went to the airman's head and bullying became the norm in most cases except for his so called pals. Promotion which obviously we all want can make or break you if you do not handle it in the correct manner and that is what we try to teach you during your training course…how to become good NCOs and that is why all our instructors are hand picked. One other thing, no pin-ups, photographs yes but not on show during working hours. Has everyone found and moved in to his designated bed space?"

"Yes corporal," they all responded.

"Very well I think I am giving you earache so carry on settling in and we are pleased to have you in our flight. Oh yes one last thing, excuses will not be accepted for you not complying with the instructions on your notice board. carry on."

Over in the Waffery sorting out whose bed space was whose and causing tempers to flare up was brought to a stop when Corporal Briggs shouted "STOP! Now stand to attention where you are. This dormitory is like a mad-house now quietly and calmly sort yourselves out or I will stop proceedings and you will go to the bed space that I nominate and you will stay there for the duration of the course. I will be back in five minutes and if you have not sorted yourselves out by then I will sort you out, now get on with it."

She went to see how Corporal Falls was getting on with her brood. A similar scene met her so she beckoned Angela outside. "I'm sorry Jean but it is like St Trinians in there and I do not know how to cope with it."

"I will teach you Angela." She told her how she controlled her girls. "I want you to go in there showing your authority and make them do what I did; it is easy when you know how because they have to do as you tell them. Are you up to it?"

"I am and thanks, do you want to come and watch?"

"It would be my pleasure because you must be firm with them right from the start or they will run you ragged."

"STOP whatever you are doing, stand to attention and keep your lips buttoned. Until you prove otherwise you will now be known as the 'St Trinians shower'. For young girls your behaviour and language is disgusting, to say the least. You will now sort yourselves out quietly and calmly and if you have not done so in five minutes I will detail you to a bed space which you will occupy for the duration of the course. If you have not done so in that five minutes I will ground the lot of you which entails you staying in this room without the cinema or the NAAFI. Now get on with it and I do not want to hear a peep coming from this room."

Outside Jean hugged her. "Angela, that was great, you are better at it than me, you will find they will be eating out of your hand from now on. 'St Trinians shower' that is a pearler," she said, laughing. "When they have finished bring them into my room for their pep talk."

A similar address was given to the airwomen and bullying was at the top of the list.

"It still happens, only recently five airwomen were charged with bullying and within a few hours they were out through the gates with a railway warrant clutched in their hands. So if any of you have the inclination to throw your weight about, beware, for you will be for the chop. Rules and regulations for your accommodation, read the poster on your notice board and digest it, for it will be like that each morning and you will stand by your beds for inspection before the daily work parade. Tomorrow you will spend most of the day preparing your gear for a kit inspection to be carried out by Squadron Leader Macfarlane and if you have not got an iron to press your uniforms I suggest you get one, because you are certainly going to need one. Has anyone got any questions?"

"Where can we get an iron Corporal?"

The NAAFI shop sells them. I suggest you all club together and buy a couple because one will not be enough for the amount of laundering and pressing you girls will want to do. Anything else you want to know? Right then, there is one last thing you should remember, if anyone of you has a problem, be it a personal or service one, please come and see either Corporal Falls or myself, if we cannot solve it we will take you to someone who will. Is that understood?"

There were a few nods of the head and the odd quiet yes.

"I asked is that understood?"

"Yes Corporal," was the reply.

"Okay, but remember to wear your headgear when in uniform at all times outside your accommodation. Welcome to RAF March, carry on!"

♦♦♦

"We have a good flight there," Sergeant Farrow said to his two Corporals, "they are responding to our commands very well. Are you giving them a bit of homework between you, because they are very advanced in their training?"

"No we are not but you will never believe this, any queries about drill, etc, they do not come to us to sort them out, they go to Peter. Even on a Bull-night they will ask him to check their cleaning tasks and he quietly puts them right where it is needed. You know Sergeant, he reminds me a lot of W/O Barrett, he has similar mannerisms and his quiet voice carries a note of authority."

"I have noticed in his drill he stands out that little bit more than the rest. I wonder if he has had some previous experience. Anyway, it is good for the flight and makes our job much easier."

Prior to the passing out parade Peter was summoned to see the Commanding Officer.

"Well young man in a few days time you will be leaving us to join other would-be Officers at RAF Cranwell. Reading through your assessments you have made a very good impression with our teaching staff. They say that in your off duty you have given your fellow comrades help and guidance to make your flight the best that has passed out from here at RAF March. I can see a bright future for you and your Officer potential will take you right to the very top. You are a credit to your father and it has been a privilege to have you serve on this station." He shook his hand and wished him Good luck for the future.

CHAPTER 50

A few weeks after Peter Bin Aziz had passed out with his flight Bill Barrett received a letter from Peter's father.

Mister Barrett

Thank you for the training and treatment my son received from your staff and who has returned to me with a wiser and more mature character for which I am most grateful.

You may not be aware that my country has quite a formidable Air Force and being admirers of your Royal Air Force we are keen to emulate it as much as possible. To do this we have had experts seconded to us from your Service plus civilian experts. Most of these have their families here with them. Their children do not suffer from any lack of education that is paramount. Housing of the highest quality is provided with servants for every need.

Mister Barrett I want you to join us here to supervise the basic training of our young people who wish eventually to take up flying and to reach that standard they must commence at the very bottom rung of the ladder. That will be your job which I know will be the answer to our need for a well disciplined force.

We can discuss terms of agreement and whether you would prefer to come on Secondment to us or as a civilian. Either way would be no problem because I have had permission from your 'Brass Hats' at the MoD to approach you. Please take your time to reply because once as you say…'the ball starts to roll' it will take some time to conclude.

Mister Barrett we need you. Please reply through our Embassy.

Aziz Bin Faruq

"Here, read this love," he said, handing the letter to Tommy, his wife.

"Hmm, that looks promising," she said as she read it, "it is certainly worth thinking about. He obviously is impressed with you and he genuinely wants you on his staff. What do you think dear?"

"There is a lot to be taken into consideration. We leave all our friends behind and will we be better off going on secondment or as a civilian?"

"That will be explained at the interview and as a civilian you would not be tied down to the RAF after all we have only a few years before we are pensioned off, taking this job means we will see a bit of the world and come home pretty much well off without being tied to the RAF. I think it is a good challenge for you and for me the little housewife who would have servants at her beck and call like Lady Muck of the Manor that would take some getting used to. Also there appears to be quite a few Brits' there so they will have the social life well organised. At the moment I am all for it but as you say we will take it slowly."

"We will not rush into it but take it slowly weighing up the pros' and cons and we will keep this information to ourselves love. I have been thinking, he said he has permission from the MoD to approach me, I wonder if I will be hearing anything from the AOC?"

"He must be a person of some consequence and status for the MoD to sanction it Bill."

Days and weeks passed with no decision made by Bill and Tommy even though it was constantly in the backs of their minds along with the longing to tell their friends.

"Tommy," he said one evening after dinner, "I want to do it but I cannot decide how, by secondment or as a civilian and I have no-one to seek advice from. I want to know which of the two options will be more beneficial to us."

"Personally dear I would prefer us to go civilian that means you get the full salary plus your RAF pension. On secondment you will receive your RAF salary and the MoD gets the rest… thank you very much."

"You have made my mind up for me Tommy I will draft a note off to the embassy requesting an interview…got a stamp love?"

A week later a letter arrived stating a room has been booked at the Savoy Hotel for four nights all expenses paid for yourself and your wife. There you will be notified when you are to report to the embassy. A chauffeur with car will be at your disposal during your stay.

"Get a load of this Tommy." he said showing her the letter to read.

She screamed with joy as she flung her arms round him giving him a hug and a kiss. "Isn't that just wonderful?

Suddenly the scream of joy turned to a scream of horror…"I have nothing to wear, what am I going to do Bill?"

"No problem we will go into Leeds on Saturday and get you fixed up."

He got an extra hug for that.

He called to see Sergeant Marion Macken the PA to Wings.

"Is there any chance of getting a few minutes with Wings, Marion?"

She buzzed Wings. "Warrant Officer Barrett is here sir asking if you can spare a few minutes to see him."

"By all means Marion send him in."

"You can go straight in Bill."

"Ah, Mister Barrett, good to see you and what brings you here?"

"I would like to book seven days leave for me and my wife."

"Well seeing you very seldom take any leave how can I refuse. Can I ask if you are going anywhere special like a quick cruise round the Med'?"

"Nothing as exotic as that sir, no I feel I am in the need of a little break and we have decided to go to London and take in one or two West End shows."

"Excellent, they will cheer you up a bit I wish I was coming with you but playing gooseberry is not in my repertoire," he said with a laugh. Leave your leave dates with Marion and when you return we will have a dance night in the Sergeants Mess and you both can show us the dance routines you will have seen from the shows. Go and enjoy yourselves you both deserve it."

The day arrived when they began their adventure into the unknown. Tommy was both excited and nervous, the last two days had been frustrating for Bill watching Tommy pack and re-pack her two suitcases and having to reassure her countless of times that the clothes she was taking were appropriate and fashionable.

They arrived at the hotel early afternoon and were met at the entrance by the concierge's staff who took complete control by parking their car and waiting for word from the desk to which room the luggage was to be taken. After booking in they were escorted to their room by a member of staff who gave them a run down on all the electrical switches and what they controlled. On a table was a choice bottle of wine with two glasses and tit-bits along with a welcoming card. When he left the pair of them carried out their own investigating of the rooms and their contents. On a bedside locker they found two tickets for a West End show for the following evening.

"Well we may as well start our celebrating with a sip of wine don't you think Mrs Barrett."

"That would be very nice Mister Barrett let the celebrations commence."

The following morning Bill received a phone call from the front desk to inform him a letter had been delivered marked urgent and would he please collect it as soon as possible.

"Looks like things are moving Tommy I should think that will be a call to the embassy."

Sure enough it was, stating transport would pick them up at 2pm to take them to the embassy. On arrival they were shown into a room and asked to wait to be called. They had to wait only a few minutes before an official came.

"Will you come this way sir?"

Bill and Tommy rose to follow him.

"I am sorry madam but I am afraid you must remain here you are not allowed to take part in any official business unless you are specifically invited according to our custom. I will send someone in for you to order refreshments of your choice."

"Thank you I do understand."

Aziz bin Faruq rose from his chair to greet Bill. "Welcome Mister Barrett I am so glad you have come which means you are interested in my suggestion. Is that not so?" Please be seated and can I offer you any refreshments?

"Yes and no thank you sir."

Aziz laughed. "Your English sense of humour really does amuse me but let me answer myself. Yes you are interested in my suggestion and no you do not want refreshments." They laughed together.

"First Mister Barrett I want to thank you and your staff for the first class training and character building you gave my son he is forever singing your praises."

"He put his heart and soul into his training sir and I can safely say he has the makings to become a first class officer and you are going to be very proud of him."

"Thank you but shall we now get down to business? I have a draft made up which covers everything I hope, I want you to take it with you to read thoroughly, make notes of anything you wish to improve on or disapprove of. When you are satisfied give the document to the chauffeur in a sealed envelope then wait until you hear from me."

"Excuse me asking sir but will there be anything in the draft that will be of interest to my wife, such as the standard of living accommodation applicable to married families?"

"Mister Barrett I have had advisers helping with the draft and I am sure Mrs Barrett will be very pleased with what she will read."

"Thank you sir you are most kind and I am sure within the next few days we will see a happy ending."

They shook hands as an official entered the room.

"Take Mister Barrett to rejoin his wife and see them safely to their transport."

Arriving back at the hotel the driver introduced himself. "My name is Johnson sir and anytime you want me just ring the desk and ask for your transport, they have been briefed."

"Have you got a first name?" asked Tommy.

"It is Clarence, Madam but I would prefer you call me Johnson as you can well imagine."

"They all had a laugh and Bill said we understand Johnson," which left Tommy still giggling.

"If you are free for most of tomorrow would you like me to show you the sights? I will know if you are free if I do not get a call from the embassy."

"You are on Johnson that is a good idea thanks By the way will you take us to the West End Show this evening please?"

"No problem sir I know which it is and I will pick you up at 7:30 and I will be waiting for you when it closes."

Back in their room Bill asked. "Shall we go down for some lunch or we use the tea making facilities here or, I spy a fresh bottle of wine and nibbles?"

"We will go for lunch then we can study that draft."

"Come on then lets go I am feeling a bit peckish." After a wash and brush up off they went to enjoy a nice lunch.

"I don't know about you Bill but I could certainly get used to this way of living."

"Maybe you will get the chance when we read that draft, Aziz said you would be delighted with what you read and I am sure we are going to be in for a very nice surprise."

"If you have finished then let us go I am now dying to see what is in store for us more than ever." As they went up in the lift she squeezed his arm and whispered. "Isn't it exciting?"

Once in their room it did not take them many minutes to settle down to reading the draft. Very soon the silence was broken with "Oh my goodness just read that." "Yes but what about this?"

Finally Tommy who was very excited uttered. “We appear to have struck Eldorado Bill, reading from that we are going to go short of nothing and the salary is mind blowing. Bill we just cannot turn an offer like that down, it is something we dream about which never materializes not until now”

“I agree love, it is one chance in a lifetime and looking at it sensibly it is not going to be a bed of roses all the way, it will have it down side that is for sure and even Eldorado would not be immune from that. Now let us read through it again and again to find any hidden flaws which I am sure there won’t be and see if we can improve or change anything.”

After a couple of hours of concentration they could not come up with a single query and were satisfied with its entirety. He stated that in a note which he included with the draft. After contacting the desk he waited at the hotel entrance to give the envelope to Jackson.

“See you this evening sir,” Jackson said with a big grin as he drove off.

“Can you imagine the reactions of our little family when it comes the time to tell them Bill?”

“It is a good job I have taken plenty of photos’ to prove it or they would not believe us. When it has finally sunk in I am going to get some heavy flak from Roy and I am not looking forward to that one bit. I will need Barbara’s support to calm him down.”

“Yes it is going to be hard leaving them and very emotional too. We can face the music later, right now we are here to enjoy this occasion. What say you we have an early dinner then we can take it leisurely getting ready for the show?”

The evening was a huge success and the Musical Show went down a treat. In the car afterwards Tommy was humming the songs when she asked. “Have you seen the show Jackson?”

“Yes I got a couple of complimentary tickets from the Embassy for me and the wife.”

“You work for the embassy then.”

“Only on a temporary basis, I drive all the VIPs to and fro’ and take them sight seeing. I have a taxi firm that is how I got the job, they must be pleased with me because I have held the job for four years. Here is my card, anytime you are in London contact me and you will receive Royal treatment that means no charge.”

“Why thank you Jackson,” said Tommy, “that is very kind of you and we do appreciate it.”

“Would I be out of order asking what your business is?”

“It is no secret Jackson,” said Bill. We are both in the RAF, me I am Bill Barrett a Warrant Officer training recruits their basic drill. My wife Tommy is the Flight Sergeant Manager of the Sergeants Mess. I am being recruited by Aziz to supervise the training of his recruits.”

“Well would you Adam and Eve it,” exploded Jackson. I was an SWO during the war and am still an active member of the RAF Association. Now your name rings a bell with me. Correct me if I am wrong, the three Services all women drill teams was a walk over by the WRAF, you trained them, right.?"

"Right!"

"No wonder Aziz chose you for that job. He is a very shrewd man Mister Barrett...."

"Hold it here Jackson, my wife and I will be only too pleased if we speak on more friendly terms by you calling us Bill and Tommy. Her maiden name was Atkins hence the Tommy and when we return to camp I will personally send you a signed photograph of that winning team with mine and Viv Anderson's signature, she was the one who led those girls to victory."

"Wonderful and thank you I will bring my camera tomorrow and ask Tommy to take one of me with you, wait till I get home and tell the wife, she is an ex WRAF and still as keen as me, she will be over the moon. Well here we are and this is where I say goodnight leaving you a very happy man."

"What a nice man Bill."

Wednesday morning Bill lifted the receiver on the ringing phone.

"Good morning sir it is Jackson speaking from the front desk your transport is ready when you and your Ladyship are ready sir."

"We will be down in five minutes Jackson."

"Thank you sir," he smiled to himself when he saw the reaction from the receptionists hearing him mention Her Ladyship. He stayed near reception waiting for Bill and Tommy stepping from the lift. As they did so he went forward to meet them. Good morning sir, Ma'am."

"What's with this Lady...."

"Indeed sir if you will come this way," tipping Bill a wink.

Bill cottoned on Jackson was up to something. "Very well Jackson although it will be most inconvenient."

When they got into the car Bill asked, "What was all that about?"

"When I asked for your room number to phone you ears began to flap so I thought I would give them something to think about. You mark my words and see the difference in their approach and treatment of you, their faces said it all when I mentioned her ladyship."

"You are a wicked man Mister Jackson laughed Tommy, "but you are nice with it."

"I am going to take you a nice gentle run taking in the sights. If you wish to stop any where just give me the nod. True to his word he showed them sights of interest which very few tourists get the opportunity to see. "Do you fancy a nice cup of Rosy Lee?" He asked. "I know of a super little café off the beaten track which makes the best brew in London. Besides I would like a word with you Bill."

At the café he asked if they would like a cup or a mug.

"A mug please they said in unison."

"Typical RAF types" he said with a laugh.

When they settled down with the brews Bill asked. "What do you want to know?"

“It is a request actually Bill and I hope you will not think I am taking advantage.

After dropping you off last night I went to the RAFA club for a pint and to wind down. I got talking to the Club President and I told him I had met you, of course he knew about that great victory I think everyone in the RAFA remembers it with some pride. I thought he was going to burst a blood vessel. You can’t have a VIP like that on our doorstep Jackson without inviting him to our club we would be the envy of every RAFA club in London and beyond. Please Jackson ask him if he can spare us a couple of hours before he slips through our fingers and if he can give us a little chat about that victory. We can promise him a full house and it could help boost our membership.”

“What do you say Tommy?,” asked Bill.

“We have nothing planned and we would like to repay your hospitality. Do you want us to come tonight or tomorrow night Jackson? We have to book out Friday morning.”

“From our point of view tomorrow night would be best it would give us more time to organise the event and knowing our president it will be a great opportunity for him to put our club on the map. So can I tell him you will accept his invitation?”

“Of course you can it will be our pleasure.”

“Will you excuse me while I go and phone him?” Off he shot with a huge smile on his face.

“Well it is the only thing we could do in the circumstances love, we have nothing special lined up and I am sure we are going to be treated like Royalty if what Jackson has told us is right.”

“I am looking forward to it.” Tommy said with enthusiasm.

A good ten minutes later Jackson came back full of apologies. “Sorry about that I could not get off the phone he is so excited. and overwhelming with gratitude and from what he says the only absentees will be the Royal Family. Shall we carry on or do you want to head back to the hotel?”

“Carry on please.”

Arriving back at the hotel after a further two hours of sightseeing, they thanked Jackson for giving them an excellent tour. “Wait here for a few minutes I guess there will be a letter waiting for me at reception to report to the embassy because Azjz has only tomorrow to finalise the contract, shan’t be a minute.”

Sure enough he was handed a letter at reception stating he was to report to the embassy at 11am.

“I was right Jackson I have to report at 11am so we will see you when you call to pick us up and thanks again for today.”

“The letter states you are to accompany me love so it looks like you are going to meet Aziz after all.”

They were ushered into the same room as before and by the same member of staff.

After a short wait they were taken to meet Aziz.

"Good morning he greeted them with and this is your wife Mister Barrett, I am very pleased to meet you Mrs Barrett. I understand you have an unusual fore name tell me about it."

"When I was born I was given the name Jean and my family name is Atkins, when I joined the RAF I was given the nick-name of Tommy because during the First World War the British soldier was called Tommy Atkins as was G.I. Joe the name given to the American soldier. As I got used to being called Tommy by my friends and associates I began to love the name."

"Ah, I see the connection now…Tommy."

They all laughed at his usage of the name.

"So Mister Barrett you agree with what is in the draft, now are you ready to place your signature on a contract?"

"I am indeed sir."

"You can take my word for it that the contract is an identical cop of the draft you have read. What it does not tell you that once you sign wheels will be put into motion with the co-operation of your MoD and you will have nothing to do except offer your resignation to the RAF. Once you have been cleared you will then officially become a member of my staff and we will get in touch with you. You will be given three months to complete your personal commitments during which time you will be sent Identification cards and travel documents. Finally if you and Tommy," he said with a smile, will follow my secretary to have your photographs taken for your I.D. cards. Furthermore Mister Barrett you will be given a rank befitting of your status and I can assure you it will not be Tommy Atkins even though it is an honourable title."

They all had a good laugh over that remark.

The secretary appeared as though by magic. "My secretary will witness our signatures on both documents and my country's seal will be applied."

"There you are Mister Barrett," he said handing Bill his copy and shook hands. "I am sure you and Tommy," saying Tommy brought a smile and a twinkle in his eye, "will be very happy with us. Go now you have an appointment with our official photographer."

"Where to folk?" asked Jackson as they got in the car.

"Harrods please I have never been in there and I would like to while I have the chance."

"You can leave us there Jackson we will walk back to the hotel if it is not too far," said Bill.

"I will point you in the right direction when we get there it will only take you a few minutes' walk from Harrods. How did you get on with Aziz if you don't mind me asking Bill?"

"Alright, I signed the contract and hopefully I have made the right decision."

"There is one thing about Aziz Bill he is honest you have no worries in that department. Are you ready for tonight? I'll pick you up at 7:30 kick-off time is 8pm."

“Are you both ready for the fray?” Jackson asked as they clambered into the car, I can tell you that right now it is standing room only; it was debated if we should have hired Wembley Stadium. When the president gave the word it spread like wild fire even some RAFA big wigs have turned up, it is going to be a very interesting night my friend. Have you got your script?”

“That is something I do not need Jackson I have a good memory.”

“When we arrive I will introduce you to the President and the committee, protocol you know, then the President will take over and when the time comes he will introduce you to the audience with a short welcoming speech. Would you like to sit on stage with Bill, Tommy or sit with me and my wife?”

“I would love to sit with you and your wife Jackson I would feel more at home.”

“I was hoping for that because we would feel honoured and my wife is dying to meet you it will also put me in a more favourable position with the committee, we call that one-upmanship,” he said with a laugh. “Here we are and I see there is a look-out at the entrance to give warning of our approach. I will park up in the space specifically left for us it is only a couple of strides away.”

The President and committee were in the foyer ready to welcome them to the club.

Jackson introduced the President who was most profuse in thanking them for accepting his invitation to visit and to give a talk on one of our favourite subjects. He in turn introduced his committee members who were delighted to meet them.

“Please come into the committee room where we can offer you some light refreshments and have a little chat and I will run through the proceedings with you Mister Barrett. I will introduce you first of course then you take over. Will it be acceptable after your talk you could answer a few questions which I am sure will arise?”

“Of course I will be delighted to if I can come up with the right answer and if there are enough members left after my talk.” That brought a burst of laughter.

“Time we were making an appearance announced the President. Are you going on stage with your husband Mrs Barrett?”

“I’m afraid not I have promised our friends Mister and Mrs Jackson I would sit with them.”

When they entered the concert room they were astounded at the number of people who were applauding their entrance. Bill was more astounded when he heard a cry of ’Mister Barrett Sir!’ he looked towards the voice to see a young woman waving. “I don’t’ believe it, it is the Knock-Out Kid.” He waved back and mouthed I’ll see you later. “There are more of us,” she said as another show of hands went up.

“I don’t believe this,” he said to the President, “this has put the icing on the cake for me and the rest of you good people.”

On stage the President addressed the audience. “Ladies and gentlemen it is a great privilege to welcome our guest speaker a serving Warrant Officer with the RAF. You may not know what is so special about this man; he was solely responsible for personally training a flight of raw recruits of the WRAF with just three weeks service in to out drill the female Drill Teams of both the Royal Navy and Army in the Three Services Drill Championship. Ladies and gentleman it is my pleasure and privilege to present to you Warrant Officer William Barrett.”

After the tumultuous applause had died down Bill addressed them. “Thank you Mister President I do hope to live up to your expectations and I am known to my friends which includes all of you here as Bill. William is what I am called when I am on the receiving end of a rocket from my wife,” He said throwing a wink at Tommy who was laughing along with the rest. “Little did I know that I would be bowing down to the persuasive powers of our friend Mister Jackson when I came down to London, I suppose it is called in the trade business with pleasure and it is a pleasure for me and my wife to be here tonight. Making my way to the stage I got a wonderful surprise and greeting from a number of the original BlueBelle Team here in the audience, please will you all stand up and take a bow because you were the founder members.”

The ladies stood to receive a great round of applause as each blew a kiss to Bill. “One of those ladies is highly featured in my talk and also in my memory.

It all began at RAF Chatworth I was in charge of training the airmen and Warrant Officer Mary Butcher was in charge of training the airwomen.” He then told of how and why the BlueBelles were formed then had them rolling with laughter at some of the incidents that happened namely the Wibbly Wobblies, the girls version of their signature song, the stripping of Mister Teeny Weenie and the Knock-Out Kid during the battle of the sexes held in the NAAFI. We men will never understand our women folk because the Knock-Out Kid finished up marrying the guy she put in Sick Bay with a broken nose. They have now proudly produced a baby girl and named her Bluebell,”

this brought about a mixture of laughter and applause.

He then told how BlueBelles Team Two came about commencing at the MoD with a suspected drunken bet by the three Service Chiefs then came panic stations when our Chief realised what he had let himself in for knowing our girls would never have a chance against the might of the army especially. My name was mentioned linked to a flight of airwomen who beat a flight of airmen something which was not thought possible. Then things started to move the Chief grasped at the only straw available and the state he was in he would have grasped at anything. Even so he was convinced we did not stand a cat in hell’s chance of pulling it off. RAF March was chosen as the training establishment and top security was applied. The staff and airwomen who did not meet my criteria were posted off to the remaining two training establishments. I chose a young WRAF Sergeant to lead the trainees namely Viv Anderson and W.O. Officer Mary Butcher for discipline and motherly care of the young girls. We had our ups and downs but the young girls responded brilliantly, it was a joy to see the graceful movements they put into the routines. The time came to start them on a concentrated programme and they responded magnificently which was quite an achievement for young girls who were only in their third week of basic training, two of the girls I picked who showed potential were only in their second week of basic training.

I suddenly had a thought we were still at a disadvantage because the Army especially relied on marching bands. I went to my CO with the idea that the loud martial music would drown out the orders given because the female voice is not as strong as the male voice in that respect so if the band situation was dropped the competitors would be able to show their best. Can you get me an interview with the ACM sir? I promise it will convince him.

The next day I was stood before him explaining the situation. He was rather sceptical at first until I told him of my secret weapon. The other two services rely on a band to keep them in step and formation. Our girls do not because they are trained to sing to themselves their signature tune, their lips do not move and they cannot be heard and that is where we turn our disadvantage into our advantage. He was delighted with the idea and you can count on me to get those damned bands their marching orders I have a few friends in high places. As I was leaving he called after me…Barrett you are a crafty bugger. You know the rest Ladies and gentlemen those young girls were absolutely marvellous and for those who were fortunate to see it happen the memory will stay with them to their dying day. Before I close will the BlueBelle girls please come on stage?"

As they stepped up onto the stage they each received a hug and a kiss from Bill.

"Ladies and gentlemen there is one name that always springs to my mind when I hear the word BlueBelles and that is this lady here….The Knock-Out Kid, she and the rest of these ladies are the ones who deserve your applause."

They received a standing ovation from the audience.

The President came on stage, shook Bill by the hand and said to the audience. This man has done us proud this evening we all have been enthralled and entertained with his talk on the famous BlueBelles. It has been a great honour for this club because we are the only RAFA club to have had him for a guest speaker and most probably the last because I have been given to understand he will be leaving the RAF for speciality work overseas. The RAF owes this man a huge debt for the prestige he has given to the Service as we do for him entertaining us in the manner he has done. Thank you Bill Barrett Warrant Officer Extraordinaire."

The audience got to their feet as one to applaud this amazing man. It was quite a few minutes before the applause came to a stop.

"Thank you, you have been most kind and I have enjoined every minute speaking to you."

Driving them back to the hotel Jackson said. "Thanks for the plugs Bill you have no idea how popular I have become in that short space of time isn't that true love?" he said speaking to his wife who was riding with them.

"I wondered why people seemed over–friendly tonight, so that was the reason bosom friends of the Barretts," she said putting on a posh accent and giving the rest a laugh.

"You are going to become more popular soon when I send you an enlarged victory photo' of the BlueBelles plus a video of the event for your club but keep it quiet until you receive them."

"I don't know what to say Bill, I am speechless."

"I will give him a big kiss from both of us," said his wife as she leaned forward and gave him one."

"We feel very lucky to have met you dear Jackson," said Tommy we have enjoyed every minute of your company."

"Promise you will come to see us whenever you are in London won't you?" said Jackson's wife.

"It will be our pleasure," replied Tommy.

"Here we are at the Hotel Splendide Sir and your Ladyship." They all got out of the car to say their goodbyes with hugs and kisses.

"I almost forgot," said Jackson reaching into the glove compartment. "Here you are your photos' developed and printed and don't insult me by asking how much, they are very good too, I had them done privately."

"Thank you, you lovely man

"Have a safe journey and thank you for everything," said Jackson.

"You will be hearing from me soon," replied Bill.

CHAPTER 51

On their return home they were greeted with a vase of flowers along with a note that read. 'Welcome home-missed you-see you tomorrow'

"Ah Bill how sweet of them"

"But will that sweet turn sour when we tell them?"

"When are we going to do that?"

"We must submit our applications for discharge on Monday so it is pointless telling them after we have done that, I suggest we tell them tomorrow in the Quiet Room in the Mess, or would you prefer having them here to tell them?"

"I don't know I think we had better sleep on it.

The following morning Bill opened the door to see the other four members of their little family.

"Are we in time for elevenses," asked Roy or will we be interrupting something."

"Come on in nice to see you, put the kettle on Tommy," he shouted through to the kitchen.

Tommy came out to greet them. "Thank you so much for the lovely flowers, the milk and bread. Make yourselves comfortable while I sort out the brews. Coffee everyone?"

"Do you want a hand Tommy asked Viv and Barbara?"

"Not yet I'll give you a shout then you can carry the mugs in to the mugs."

"Watch what you are saying Tommy Barrett I for one assemble that remark."

"Don't you mean resemble Roy?" asked Derwent.

"Assemble, resemble the incineration was there," he replied.

"Insinuation Roy is the word you are looking for," came a shout from the kitchen.

"Hurry up with that coffee and let me drink it in peace."

When they were all sat down with their coffees Roy asked. Well get on with it.

Did you enjoy your little trip and do you both feel better for going?"

"It was marvellous, we really had a wonderful time didn't we Bill?"

"I wouldn't have missed it for anything very entertaining and satisfying."

"Where did you stay?" asked Barbara.

They both replied in unison "The Savoy."

Roy spluttered in his coffee.

"Take him in the kitchen and sponge him down and if you can find a bib put it round his neck," laughed Tommy.

"The only things I will put round his neck are my hands," retorted Barbara. "Come on Sloppy Joe lets get you cleaned up."

When calmness had been restored Viv asked. "You didn't really stop there did you?"

"We certainly did." replied Tommy, and we have photos' to prove it."

Out came the photos' showing them in all parts of the hotel especially in the room they had occupied. To say the foursome were impressed was putting it mildly.

"That must have cost a bomb," exclaimed Derwent.

"It certainly did," replied Tommy but there is a big story to tell about it which we are not prepared to tell you just yet."

"So when do you think you might condescend to tell us?" snorted Roy.

"We were thinking of telling you tonight in the Quiet Room but with that attitude of yours Roy Shaw you will be lucky if we tell you at all," Tommy retorted angrily, "and you will have to find out the hard way."

"Come on Roy you have overstayed your welcome it is time you kept your feet on the ground instead of in your mouth. I am sorry Tommy I don't want him to hurt you. Will we see you tonight in the Quiet Room then?"

"I doubt it Barbara I won't be in the mood now." She gave Barbara a kiss, don't worry it will pass over."

"He is not very tactful in what he says these days, I am sure he is getting worse.

He gives me the impression that he has something on his mind Viv," pointed out.

"I don't think I will ever understand the man," added Derwent. "I am not being unkind but I think he should see someone because I am sure at times he does not realise the effect his barbs have on people."

"I think the best thing that could happen to Roy is to marry Barbara, she has the best influence of anybody over Roy. I am suggesting that because there is going to come a time when even Barbara will say enough is enough and that would break him up."

"I think you have hit the nail right on the head agreed Viv but how are we going to get him to see the light?"

"I think that will be my job, Bill said, we both understand each other so I don't think it will be too difficult getting to him. The biggest problem is yet to come that is why we wanted a family meet tomorrow. It would not be fair for us to give you a preview without Roy and Barbara being present."

"We will let you know tomorrow what we decide," added Tommy."

"We understand don't we Derwent?" said Viv, "I would have been just as furious with Roy had he spoken to me like that. We will leave you in peace but don't let it spoil your homecoming....we missed you."

After they had left Tommy asked. "Any ideas about what we should do?"

"Yes, how about me ringing Nessie asking if we can go there for the weekend and we can discuss it on the way?"

"Good idea it will give Roy another headache when he cannot find us on the station."

In ten minutes he was back. 'Come by all means we have not seen my little brother for a long time,' she said.

It took them fifteen minutes to pack an overnight case then they were off. Once they had settled down to a nice steady cruising speed, they began the discussion.

"I think we should go ahead with what we originally planned...tell them the whole story in the Quiet Room," Bill said.

"I don't," said a still defiant Tommy still upset by Roy's attitude. I would like us to go to the Orderly Room ask for two application forms for discharge from the service.

That will shake him for starters and if he starts asking questions we tell him if he is so interested attend the meeting we originally planned."

"Hmm! I will go along with that love hopefully it will help shrink his ego a bit. I'll bet Barbara gave him some stick when she had got him alone."

"And our disappearance over the weekend will give him something to think about. Poor old Roy he has certainly opened a can of worms this time. Are we stopping somewhere for a bite to eat? You know we left without having a spot of lunch, I don't know about you but I am feeling peckish"

"We will stop at the next service station and I can ring Nessie and tell her when we should be arriving."

They arrived to receive a lovely welcome from Nessie. "I am sorry John is not here to greet you because is tied up with one of his elderly patients. Aren't you glad you did not marry a doctor Tommy it is so stressful on a marriage, mind you we have been married too long now to let it get us down. Take your case upstairs Bill me and Tommy can have a few minutes to ourselves in the kitchen making a brew."

"I will be back in a minute Nessie I must go and spend a penny."

It was not so long before John appeared, his eyes lit up when he saw Tommy, Come here and give me kiss," he said clutching her in a fond embrace, he had grown to become very fond of Tommy. "You are looking bonnier than ever married life obviously suits you."

"How are you? You old rascal."

"Much better for seeing you my dear but what brings you here? It must be something special because you usually tell us in advance."

"Yes, you are right John she replied we do have something very special to tell you and no it is not what you are thinking, unfortunately we are bit too late in life for that."

"Whatever it is it can wait until after dinner, do you want a brew love? She asked John."

"Yes please I could murder one."

"How would you like a Cottage Pie for dinner?"

"Ooo! I would just love one Nessie and can I help you make it?"

"Of course you can my dear it will add another string to your cooking skills especially doing it the country way instead of out of one of those so called Home Cooking Recipe Books that are flooding the market these days."

While the girls were busy in the kitchen John and Bill were chatting about the latest family news and the latest happenings at RAF March namely the big change over to the New Management team.

"How are you getting on there in the kitchen?" shouted Bill.

Back came the reply. "I'm on Jankers."

"Why what are you doing?"

"Spud bashing," was the response with a giggle.

"Serves you right for being a trouble maker."

"It takes one to know one," was the swift reply.

At dinner Tommy did the honours by serving the meal.

After tasting it Bill complimented Nessie. "You haven't lost your touch Nessie you improve on it each time you make it."

"I didn't make it Bill! Tommy did every bit of it I was just a looker-on."

Bill almost choked on his mouthful much to the amusement and satisfaction of the two women he said to John. "Well it is not bad don't you think so John?"

John could only nod he dare not open his mouth or the contents would have fallen out but his eyes said everything.

The women of course were in their element over Bill's faux pas.

"Nice wine John it tastes a bit special."

"Concede Bill you are digging a big hole for yourself."

Over coffee they discussed the family and the world in general the NHS being a favourite topic with John and Nessie and not for all the right reasons.

"Right," said Nessie, "we will get the table cleared and washed up then John and I will relax listening to this special topic you have in store for us, you two nip out in the garden and get some fresh air in your lungs, we will call you when we are ready, come on Tommy lets get cracking."

When they had settled down Bill commenced his story from when Aziz Bin-Farouq brought his son to RAF March to decide for himself if the training was as good as its reputation, fortunately for RAF March it was to his liking and so his son began his training at RAF March.

"A few weeks later I received this letter." He then read out its contents. "Tommy and I liked what we read and decided to accept a meeting with him." Bill then proceeded with his story in detail right up to leaving London.

"My goodness what a golden opportunity you had offered, you did jolly well right to accept it."

"Bill, that was a one chance in a lifetime and you had to grab it with both hands. I think you did the right thing there," added John. "You have a relatively short time left to serve in the RAF and this coming up is a safeguard for both your futures. Nessie I think we should crack open a bottle to toast these two to their future success and happiness."

The following day they said their goodbyes with 'don't forget to write' ringing in their ears.

♦♦♦

Monday morning saw Bill and Tommy entering the Orderly Room.

"Good morning," greeted Sergeant Chris' Graham. "What can I do for you good people?"

"We would like two application forms for our discharge from the Servjce."

His jaw dropped not believing what he had heard. "You are not winding me up Bill are you?"

"No."

"Then I had better call Roy to attend to you."

"No, just give us the forms please."

This he did and they left smiling knowing Roy would blow his top because he had not been informed and why they had ignored him.

"Come to my office Bill and we will fill them in where it is quiet."

She told Jackie the civilian receptionist. "If W/O Shaw rings tell him we are busy."

Jackie lifted the receiver on the ringing phone'. "Ah good morning Mister Shaw, no I am sorry but she says she does not want to be disturbed. No sir I am sorry I cannot do that I take my orders from her." She then replaced the receiver.

When the applications were filled in they both went to the Orderly Room to submit them. “Here they are Chris’ all signed sealed and delivered and we understand the Big White Chief is on the verge of blowing a gasket.”

“He has given me hell Bill I have never seen him like this before.”

“Would you please come into my office?” asked Roy speaking through the connecting hatch “and hand me those forms Sergeant Graham.” then closing the hatch door with a thud.

Bill winked at Chris’ and Tommy gave him a big smile, “thanks Chris” she said.

Bill knocked on Roy’s office door and they entered on command.

“You are not serious about this rubbish, shall I bin it? And what is all this about, as per MoD’s instructions?”

“It means exactly what it says.” “And you expect me to forward this to the Commanding Officer? He will think it is some kind of joke, he will…”

Bill interrupted him’

“He will have you court-martialled if you don’t.”

Roy spluttered, “You are not serious why did you not tell me about this before? We are supposed to be friends.”

Tommy joined in at that point.

“That is what we thought until you started your bloody antics Roy. You would have been told on Saturday night along with the rest of our family but you had to show off what a big clever man you are and talking down to me was the last straw I had to go away for the weekend to cool off. We are telling them tonight in the Quiet Room and you can please yourself whether you come along or not, I don’t know about Bill but I could not care less what you do.”

“I would like to apologise Tommy.”

“Don’t, because I am not interested anymore,” she snapped as she walked out.

“Don’t look at me like that Roy you have only yourself to blame,” Bill said as he followed Tommy out.

He paused to see Chris Graham. “Did you get all that?” he asked quietly.

Chris smiled as he nodded and stuck a thumb up.

Bill caught up with Tommy. “You certainly took the wind out of his sails and given him something to worry about.”

“If he makes a nuisance of himself tonight that is the end of our friendship I am getting sick and tired of that man.”

“There will be more people upset when the news gets around.”

“Let them, we have our future to think about and we are not honour bound to anyone. Anyway I will phone Viv and Barbara to tell them about the meeting.”

Bill had been in his office only a short time when he got a phone call from Helen Fraser the CO’s PA telling him to report to the CO in an hour’s time.

“Good morning Mister Barrett,” the Commanding Officer greeted Bill in return for his salute. “Sit yourself down because we have a lot to talk about.

I received a signal from MoD with instructions concerning your resignation from the RAF and to put it bluntly I was gob smacked as they say. It came from the highest authority there are to be no obstacles put in your way. This of course resulted form the visit of Mister Aziz and now my staff is being poached....a complete turn around eh' Mister Barrett from us doing the poaching. Never-the- less orders are orders but I would like to hear your version the information I received was very sparse and I am sure you can fill in all the gaps."

"It did begin with his inspection sir. He said 'You will be hearing from me soon.'

That puzzled me because I had not the foggiest idea of what he meant by that. I was soon to know when I received this letter from him." He then handed the letter to the CO. to read.

"My words Mister Barrett now that is the kind of letter anyone would have loved to receive. Please carry on from there Mister Barrett this is going to get very interesting."

Bill told the rest of his tale leaving nothing out.

"That is amazing and I cannot blame you one iota for accepting the contract, between you and me, you would have been a damn fool to have refused it. I would think the next stage will be a call for you from the AOC and you will have to repeat your tale once more. I will put Wing Commander Hopwood and Squadron Leader Cody in the picture it will lessen the hassle for you. You will of course retain your Married Quarter right up to the day you leave us unless you have alternative arrangements. We will have further discussions before you leave us, one being your recommendation for the one to step into your shoes."

"I have already sorted that out ready for your approval sir, all that will be needed will be a Corporal from the Reserve Pool."

"Give me their names now Mister Barrett then I can discuss them with the Wing Commander and Squadron Leader."

"Flight Sergeant Franks to Warrant Officer, Sergeant Fell to Flight Sergeant, Corporal Deacon to Sergeant and one Corporal from the Reserve Pool sir."

"I expected you would choose Franks that is no surprise because I have been given the information that you have been grooming him for some time ready to take over from you but it has come about earlier than was expected."

"He is a good man sir."

"Thank you Mister Barrett."

♦♦♦

The rest of the day was taken up by inspecting the progress of all the training flights along with Joe Franks and having a word with the Senior NCOs. In charge of the flights.

"Everything appears to be running smoothly Joe."

"Well did you think it might not be," replied Joe teasingly.

"No not for one minute but let us go and have a shufti at the accommodation, remember the old saying…when the cats away?"

"That does not apply while I am around," boasted Joe in fun.

They inspected each block and rooms, apart from one or two niggly little bits everything appeared quite good.

"I told you," Joe said, "I have kept my eye on the blocks to make sure they adhere to my standards. Are you satisfied SIR?"

Bill laughed then in mock overbearing manner he snapped. "Have you been to the opticians lately Flight Sergeant?"

"What are you on about Bill?"

"Block 2 Room one, go in and I will give you five minutes to see what is wrong."

Joe went in and he searched and better searched but could find nothing wrong.

"Times up," grinned Bill as he marched into the room. "So nothing escapes old Eagle Eyes. I go away for a few days and the accommodation reverts back to a shambles."

"Well I cannot see anything wrong is this a wind up Bill?"

"Not at all but I will tell you there is a joker in the Block. Alright I will put you out of your misery. Look at the footwear at the foot of each bed and tell me what you see."

Joe looked intently then burst out laughing. The footwear under each bed space had been switched, some had all right feet and some left feet and some with mixed sizes. How could I have not noticed that Bill? I have never seen that stunt pulled before if I knew who had done that I would shake his hand."

♦♦♦

That evening the six members of their little family met in the Quiet Room of the Sergeants Mess.

"We will get the drinks in before we start because it is going to be thirsty work talking," suggested Bill.

"I will come with you Bill," volunteered Derwent.

While they were waiting to be served at the bar Derwent said. "So you both are leaving the service then. That's all I know Bill, we only heard it from Barbara obviously Roy told her about your applications. She also said that Tommy was giving him a rough ride, I could see that coming eventually from any one of us."

"He is still our friend Derwent but of late as you have commented on it has been quite difficult not to lose patience with him, unfortunately Tommy had stood enough from him and he had better watch out tonight because if he starts acting up again Tommy will go straight for the jugular."

Derwent laughed. "And I don't blame her if she does."

Meanwhile in the Quiet Room there was an awkward silence until Roy said. "I want to apologise Tommy…but she cut him off.

"I told you this morning Don't, I am not interested in your apology."

"Don't you think you are being a little unfair Tommy," Barbara said, "he is trying to tell you how sorry he is."

"And I am also sorry Barbara but I will not turn the other cheek when someone talks down to me like Roy did, I am not the forgiving kind."

"I am sorry it has come to this after all we have been through together Tommy but there is no point in Roy or myself staying with your attitude."

"As you wish Barbara that is your choice."

They both left brushing past Bill and Derwent.

"Hey up Bill wasn't Barbara crying?"

"What has gone on?" asked Bill looking at Tommy.

"Barbara said I was being unfair for not accepting Roy's apology and decided both of them would leave."

Bill looked at Viv.

"That is exactly what happened Bill."

"That has certainly spoiled the evening," he replied.

"No it has not, you still have me and Derwent, that was just a blip can't we carry on as we intended besides we are dying to know all about your big adventure. The London trip has something to do with you both leaving the Service hasn't it? Come on don't keep us is suspense, unfold the mystery."

"Do you remember when Aziz thanked us after the cinema show saying 'you will be hearing from me'?"

"Yes I do, I thought at the time it was an odd thing for him to say."

"Well I did, until I received this letter. I would like you both to read it and it will tell you what our London trip was all about then I will fill you in with the details."

When they read it Viv gave a scream of delight, she then grabbed hold of Tommy and kissed her then did the same to Bill, Derwent followed up showing his delight.

"Oh how wonderful for you both, but before I count my chickens I am on the edge of my seat waiting for the icing on the cake. Isn't it just wonderful Derwent?"

"We have only read the letter but I am so envious of you and cannot wait to hear the rest. How about a top up before you start because I have a feeling it is going to be very thirsty work, it will be for me and I will only be listening."

Derwent and Bill went to the bar leaving Tommy and Viv having a good natter, Viv asking non-stop questions and Tommy trying her best to keep up with the answers.

"Oh Tommy, how I wish me and Derwent were coming with you, you will keep in touch with us won't you I could not bear it if we lost touch because you both mean such a lot to us." Tears started rolling down cheeks as they hugged each other.

"No way will we let our friendship slide Viv you have my word on that unless you get cheesed of about me prattling on about the luxury life we are living and you are the only one I can swank to even if you tell Derwent that bloody woman is at it again."

Their laughter blew away the tears causing Bill to say as he returned with the drinks. "I hope you are not laughing for joy to see the back of us."

"Now how did you guess? You must have heard me in the bar cheering. Now come and sit down we have waited long enough to hear the gory details. So take a good swig of your beer because you are not going to have time to take another one until you have finished the story."

"We followed the instructions and booked in at the hotel then things began to happen. He told them what followed in every detail and they were so engrossed listening to Bill none of them put a glass to their lips and neither Derwent or Viv interrupted him to ask questions until he announced "and they both lived happy ever after."

"That was something that we all dream about and wish it was happening to me, sorry Derwent I meant us."

"Something like that can only comes up once in a lifetime and when it happens to yourself you have just got to grab it with both hands. Please let Viv and I be the first on your list Bill if such an opportunity like that appears on the scene again."

They were so engrossed talking about it they did not realise that tempus fugit.

"Look at the time," said Tommy "I am missing my beauty sleep, come on let us get out of here and let the barman lock up."

At breakfast in the Sergeants Mess the next morning Derwent and Viv were sat in their usual places enjoying their breakfast and chatting about the previous evening. Roy collected his breakfast from the server and joined them at the table.

"Good morning Roy they chorused."

"Morning, how are you both did you have a pleasant evening?"

"Indeed we did it was very informative and interesting."

"Well?"

"Well what?" asked Viv.

"Well what was it all about?"

"Do you mean to say you expect us to tell you about it when you walked out in such a huff. If you think we are going to satisfy your curiosity you can think again Roy boy."

"Ah! So you are taking sides are you? Kick Roy when he's down."

"You have no cause to say that Roy but didn't Barbara take sides? As for kicking you when you are down it might knock some sense back into you. You have played the great almighty too long and it has backfired on you."

"She refused my apology twice so what do I have to do to make amends?"

"Don't push her give her time to come round, time is a good healer and before you realise it we will be one little happy family again."

"I hope you are right Viv and it is before they leave us. Thanks for that I feel better for it. But aren't you going to tell me about it?"

"No Roy, it is not our place to do so, under the present circumstances it is the prerogative of Bill and Tommy."

"Fair enough Viv I am only sorry I made a hash of things, me and my big mouth."

♦♦♦

Bill opened the connecting hatch and asked Joe Franks and Margaret Roper if they would come in into his office.

"What's up Bill?" Joe asked when they got seated. "Have we got an emergency on our hands because everything is running smoothly and when that happens something is bound to occur?"

"I wouldn't call it an emergency exactly Joe more of a shock to the system. Do you think we should have a brew before I start? It will take a little while to tell and you may be in a bit of a shock at the end."

"If we are in shock we will need the brew at the end said Margaret."

"Okay, Tommy and I are leaving the Service!"

"Oh my God," said a shocked Margaret, hang on I am going to make that brew now," as she dashed out of the office.

"That was a good excuse to cover up her emotion," said Joe.

When she returned with the brew Joe said. "That took along time Margaret."

"I thought I had better go and spend a penny in case we have a long session you know what his lordship is like once he starts."

Bill and Joe looked at each other both reading the other's thoughts.

"You were very wise Margaret." Said Bill it will take a little while to tell."

"It began with Mister Aziz and his inspection. To give you an idea of what I am about to tell you here is a letter I received from him."

"No wonder you are leaving the Service with an offer like that who wouldn't?"

"I think it is wonderful Bill you both must be excited over it's prospects and I'll bet Tommy is over the moon, lucky Tommy."

Bill then told them everything that happened in London.

"Once I have been cleared by MoD I will have three months grace before my master sends for me, which includes Tommy of course."

"I should jolly well think so too, there is no Punch without Judy," said Margaret indignantly.

"I don't know how you put up with this woman in such a confined space Joe it was bad enough when she was in here."

"We all have a cross to bear Bill; can I have the first refusal on your suite when you leave?"

"Please say yes Bill," pleaded Margaret and I will include you in our morning prayers."

"Hear that Joe, how can I refuse such a request coming straight from the heart?"

I will call the male training staff together in a day or two to tell them. Sorry Margaret I cannot do the same for your staff, you see I am only responsible for the airmen, Viv is responsible for the airwomen."

"Then why have you told me Bill?"

"Well I could not leave you out and tell just Joe besides Viv knows. So you and Joe can now chat about it in private."

"That is very kind of you Bill I appreciate it."

"So, when you leave is there going to be a big change round, do you think they will replace you?" Queried Joe.

"I'm afraid that is in the hands of the hierarchy at Command or even higher but if I do hear anything I will let you know, I must admit it could be a tricky problem they may even leave it as it is, who knows? My guess for what it is worth Wings will take a more active part."

CHAPTER 52

Over the next two weeks Bill had to report to Command for an interview with his old friend Air Commodore Wildeman then to MoD to be interviewed by the Air Vice Marshal.

There he received their good wishes and gratitude for all the good work he had done for Training Command and the Royal Air Force as a whole.

On returning to RAF March he found the letter he had been waiting for from Mister Aziz. It read;

Dear Mister Barrett,

The day has now arrived for you to become a member of my staff. You are now free to conclude your ties with your Royal Air Force. You should have been informed by your Commanding Officer that you are authorised to occupy your residence up to the day you have to report for your flight to your new place of residence.

From the first date of your new month you have three months to tie up and finalise your personal affairs.

Your new identity cards will be sent to you in due course along with the rest of your instructions.

Welcome to my staff Mister Barrett.

My Kindest Regards to 'Tommy'.

Aziz Bin Faruq.

Immediately he went to see Tommy.

He showed her the letter and told her to ring Helen Fraser asking for an interview of great importance with the Station Commander.

"You can come straight away," was the reply.

On entering they both saluted.

"Come and sit yourselves down. I know why you have come to see me it is about the letter stating you are no longer in the service of the Royal Air Force. Am I right?"

"Yes sir," Bill answered in surprise.

"In all probability our letters will be duplicated only mine is in the form of a signal from on high. May I see yours please? They are similar but mine are quite extraordinary orders which even I must follow to the letter. It appears our Mister Aziz is highly thought of by our Government and it makes one wonder if there is something bigger going on between the two parties. However, our problem is sorting you out with no hitches. In reality both of you are no longer serving members of H.M. Forces and we are now left minus one Warrant Officer and one (w) Flight Sergeant who I have been informed have to be replaced. All your recommendations Mister Barrett have been accepted but we need to have your replacement posted in Mrs Barrett. This is where the stipulations come in. You Mrs Barrett as a civilian are to hand over to your successor, .on completion you then retire from the Service. By the way please return you uniforms etc. to the clothing stores as from now and revert to wearing civilian clothes that includes yourself Mister Barrett."

"What about our I.D. card sir?"

"You both will hand them in to the Orderly Room where you will be issued with temporary civilian passes. Mister Barrett you will hand over to Warrant Officer Franks, he has been put in the picture of the procedure. Yes, all three will now be wearing their new ranks. The replacement (w) Flight Sergeant and the RAF Corporal are already on their way to join us, so in two or three day's time we will really be under new management.

Have you any questions you wish to ask?"

"Do we still have access to the Station's facilities sir?"

"But of course right up to the time you leave us."

"Thank you sir and for the last time we salute you whilst wearing uniforms."

"This is not our goodbye I will see you later."

"This is a right queer set up Bill," said Tommy as they made their way to their Married Quarter to change into civilian clothes. "There are going to be lots of questions asked by just everyone when they see us dressed in mufti."

"Can't be helped pet this is the way it has to be worked, we will be properly cheesed off by the end of the day roll on the hand over and let us settle down."

After packing all their Military equipment they stuffed them in the car boot and drove to the clothing stores and placed everything on the counter.

"Bring Warrant Officer Waters," Bill ordered a store man who was looking gob smacked at them.

Off he hurried to bring back Derwent who gave a big grin when he saw the kit dumped on the counter.

"Boot Sale or Charity Shop? So what is happening you are not on the move already? I thought you told us you had got three months grace before you left us."

"That is from my boss Mister Aziz, this is from the RAF, as from now we no longer belong to the Service but civilians with a temporary pass at least we will be when we hand in our I.D. card and complete a handing over."

"Warrant Officer Franks is already sporting his new promotion and so are the other two. Apparently they are dying to see you to give thanks to their fairy godfather."

"You will still see us around for we have permission to still use the Sergeants' Mess. Well come on then get your slaves to come and help you receive this stuff. If this is the way you treat civilians we are glad we are not one of your lot."

When everything was handed over and signed for Derwent asked. "What are your next moves Mister and Mrs Barrett?"

"The Orderly Room to receive our civilian passes and Roy will be so impatient waiting for us to appear I bet he is sending out scouts searching for us."

"Is there any sign of a reconciliation Tommy?"

Tommy just shrugged her shoulders as if to suggest, maybe or maybe not.

"Come on then love lets go and get it over with, we will see you later Derwent."

When they entered the Orderly Room Sergeant Graham spoke quietly. "Sorry…orders."

He spoke through the hatch. "Mister and Mrs Barrett are here sir."

Roy's face filled the connecting hatch immediately. "Will you please come round to my office?" he asked.

Bill looked at Chris' and cupped his ear. Chris nodded in return.

They entered Roy's office and placed their RAF I.D. cards on his desk.

"I understand you have a Civilian Temporary Pass for us both Warrant Officer Shaw," spoke Bill.

"Would you both like a brew?"

"We would like our passes please," replied Tommy.

"Right, well here they are," as he fished them from a drawer and handed them over.

They both scrutinised them and checked each others.

"They seem to be in order," informed Tommy. "Now we are fully fledged civilians." She then gave Bill a kiss and said. "Congratulations Mister Barrett."

"Bill returned the kiss with. "Congratulations to you too Mrs Barrett."

Roy watched with a puzzled look on his face.

"Well aren't you going to congratulate your best friend and his wife smiled Tommy? Come here you big daft lump," she said as she held out her arms to give Roy a kiss and a hug.

Roy grabbed hold and held her, being too choked to say a word.

"Come on what about me don't hog the man all to yourself." Said a grinning and happy Bill as the two best friends then embraced.

When Roy had settled himself down he spoke to Tommy. "Tommy I do really want to…."

Tommy interrupted him. "All I want from you Roy is a brew and a biscuit, everything else is history."

"Three teas with biscuits," he shouted through the hatch.

"Yes sir," shouted Chris as he moved away from the hatch in time not to get caught ear wigging.

While the brew was being made he whispered to the rest of the Orderly Room staff. "It looks like we will be getting back to normal from now on."

As soon as one of his staff had taken in the teas Chris took up his position again as near to the connecting hatch as was safe to do so.

For the next hour Bill and Tommy told everything that happened from receiving the letter from Mister Aziz.

"I must say I am impressed and it is a wonderful opportunity for you one that you could not refuse. There is no doubt about it you are going to do very well for yourselves your contract assures you on that and it is long enough for you to make a decision as to an extension or not. Yes, you have done the right thing because it is your own the future you have to look out for. Obviously it is not going to be the same here without you but we are all too close not to keep in touch. Now there is the matter of dining you two out and a new Mess Chairmen to vote in."

"I am not too sure about the dining out Roy because we are now civilians and not Service members," pointed out Tommy. "We cannot even sit in at a Sergeants Mess meeting now."

"I will see about that," Roy said showing his authority, "even if it means going to the top to receive special dispensation."

"Don't bother Roy just let it slide I think it would be too emotional for us to enjoy anyway," added Tommy.

"We will leave you for now Roy, I have to see Joe Franks and Tommy has to see her staff so we are going to be very busy for a little while as you can appreciate."

As soon as they left Roy rang Barbara to tell her the good news that he and Tommy had been reconciled.

She was delighted. "Tell me about it later love I am busy right now."

♦♦♦

Bill knocked on the door of his old office and entered on the command to come in. Warrant Officer Joe Franks jumped to his feet to greet Bill with a very warm handshake.

"I have been waiting for this old friend to thank you for what you have done for me; never in this wide world did I dream this could happen. I tell you it was an almighty shock when I was called to the Commanding Officer to be presented with this promotion. I will never forget all you have done for me Bill."

"You have deserved it Joe and you will make a good Warrant Officer."

"Alan Fell and young Alfred Deacon were also in shock when they got their promotion and we all know it was through you recommending us. Allan is next door sat at my old desk shall I call him in?"

"Yes by all means then I don't have to repeat my tale."

"Joe called through the hatch. "Can you come round Alan? And bring a brew for three with you?"

He nearly dropped the tray when he saw Bill sitting there. They shook hands and Alan couldn't thank Bill enough for getting him promoted. "I would rather see you in uniform than in civvies Bill, everyone on the staff is going to miss you."

"Of course none of us know the real tale of you leaving us," stated Joe.

"That is why I have come over to fill you in. By the way I will start handing over to you tomorrow. Right then here goes. It all started when I received this letter," which he handed over for them to read.

"Bloody Nora Bill," spluttered Joe, I think you would have been a right plonker to have turned that down. What do you say Alan?"

"I hope before my time is up in the RAF some kind soul will offer me a job like that." I'll bet your dining-out will be some do I can see it being wall to wall seating."

"Aye said Joe the seating will be at a premium because everybody will want to attend."

"I think you are going to be disappointed because we are now civilians not Service members and Rules and Regulation will not sanction it. Having said that, Tommy does not want one because it will be too emotional for us and all the friends we have made."

"That is understandable," voiced Joe, "but it also deprives all your friends from having a night to remember. So what are we going to do to make up for such a disappointment? I suggest we hold a farewell dance, Rules and Regulations cannot stop us from doing that then all it will take is for the females to persuade Tommy that is what all your friends want."

CHAPTER 53

"Do you know Bill, I feel like having a right good holiday because from all the hassle we have had since coming back from London I feel absolutely drained and we don't know when we will get the chance of one when we leave here."

"That would suit me fine love that would suit me fine, how about going to the travel agent and seeing what he can come up with right now?"

"Are you looking for a short break?" asked the agent.

"What can you find us for a six weeks cruise?" asked Bill.

"Phew, that would be very expensive indeed you would be talking of a few thousand pounds for that length of time for a cruise only. Can I suggest a different Caribbean cruise to the one you previously went on? Failing that I can only suggest the Med' where there are a variety of choices. You could fly to Australia stopping over a week or so in Singapore and Hong Kong either on your outward journey or return journey."

"Any thoughts love?"

"I think it is going to be a cruise I want to just relax with the minimum of disturbance and I doubt very much if I would get that cruising the Med'."

"So should we plump for the Caribbean then?"

"Yes, I think so the only snag is the length of the cruise it is not very long is it?"

"How about a two weeks stay either in Florida or one of the islands. You could start off in a hotel then finish off with your cruise which would cover five weeks," suggested the agent.

"Tell us the choices then please," said Tommy.

A three weeks Caribbean cruise and two weeks stay in a Florida hotel was finally settled on.

"Thank goodness for that," exclaimed Tommy on the way home. The five weeks are going to feel like heaven after what we have been through since coming back from London and the sooner we can get away from here on our return from holiday the better."

"We can always shorten it by staying with Nessie for a couple of weeks."

"Oooh! That would be lovely I can really relax there."

♦♦♦

On returning home they found a letter behind the door. "It is from Jackson, Tommy, thanking us for his autographed photograph, he says. 'The RAFA committee went bananas over the big photograph and the CD of the BlueBelles. The photograph has been framed and hung in a very prominent position and the CD has already drawn many RAFA members to our club to watch it. The committee have been asked by other RAFA clubs for the loan of it but they don't stand a chance it is locked away in the safe after every showing. It has made our club the favourite in the district to become a member of, so much so further membership has been forced to be put on hold. The committee were hoping you would have been able to come and officiate at an unveiling ceremony of the picture. I will make it my business to come and pick you up from the station when you and Tommy are to flee the country, I will get the gen and orders from the Embassy. See you both then. Joyce sends her love.'

When told about the cruise Roy and Derwent arranged that one would drive them to the airport and the other to collect them on their return.

"We will still have a hectic time on our return Bill. There will be Ann and Tim to visit and to tell the tale to, Mary and Sam and not forgetting George and Betty Miller and of course we will have to pay a special visit to Jackie and that visit will hurt me more than I can say because she will be heartbroken. I am determined to write to her as often as I can."

"I wonder if there will be a writing bureau in our furnishings because you are going to need one for all your correspondence."

"Good idea love, if I have not got one I know a man who will see that I do get one, she replied with a laugh."

♦♦♦

Roy and Barbara drove the holiday makers to Leeds Airport.

"Why are you taking five weeks off cruising?" Queried Roy.

"Because we do not know how long it will be before we get another break and we are making the most of this three months to do what we want and to go there in the right frame of mind and not tensed up like it has been here since we returned from London," answered Tommy. Most days we have felt really jiggered with all the questioning from almost everybody. Of course that was only to be expected especially from our closest friends but believe me Roy overall it has been traumatic. So when we return from this trip you should see a relaxed Bill and Tommy with that missing smile that has been absent lately."

"I can understand what you have been going through," added Barbara I know it has not been easy for you both because we have never had and never will have another scenario like this one. Words cannot express how much we are going to miss you both, not just us two or Viv and Derwent but everyone who has been fortunate enough to count you as their friends, I could give you a list of them a mile long."

"Come on it is time to go, you will be hearing from us of course. Will you put Ann and Tim in the picture if you go to the March Hare, we will fill them in with the details when we get back. Also see if you can wangle Joe Franks to move into our Married Quarter when we leave, it a better one than his."

"Have a safe journey there and back and above all relax and enjoy every minute," said Barbara as they all kissed and shook hands.

"I like this Premium Class travelling Bill because I am built for comfort," said Tommy as she settled down in her seat, "I wonder what the hotel in Miami is like."

"It should be good we paid enough for it," he retorted.

"Five whole weeks, I have never had a holiday for so long a time before do you think we will get bored?"

"Not unless you want to, if you get bored in Miami you can always make up for it on board ship and do a Wings by joining in the fun and games as he did."

"No way, the last time I played those types of fun and games I was wearing a gym slip I'll not mention my Halcyon Days."

CHAPTER 54

"Here they come, said an excited Viv, just look at those sun tans."

"You can tell they have not had a very energetic holiday" replied Derwent.

After the greetings and embraces Derwent grabbed hold of the trolley. "I don't know why I should push this weight after you have done now't but flop in the sun."

"I need to store my energy for what lies ahead besides why have a dog and do the barking myself? Come on get pushing and stop moaning."

When they were all aboard their transport the questions began to flow. The top of the list being, have you had a good time? Going through their repertoire lasted until they reached RAF March. Flowers and a welcome home card greeted them when they entered their Quarter.

“We will not stop,” Viv said “but will we see you tonight? Roy and Barbara are dying to see you. By the way we did a bit of shopping for you so you can have a meal and Sam Brown delivered your weekly order.”

“Thank you all so much for everything we will thank Roy and Barbara tonight, yes we will come to the Quiet Room same time as always and we would like to know all the news from here. Do you realise all you two have done is listen to our tale and we are now gasping for a brew, will you stay and have one with us then we can have a quiet chat?”

“Right, you are on I will make the brew while you two go and freshen up.”

“Things are beginning to change now”, Viv informed them. As far as the WRAF are concerned everything is fine, Mac’ is the best O.C we have had. Unfortunately it is not the same with the airmen, Wings now appears to be leaning on Joe a bit hard by nit picking and showing that he is the boss. He is now in complete control which he was not when you were here he was just the figure head.”

“Do you think that power crazy is rearing it’s ugly head Viv?”

“It would not surprise me in the least especially how he is treating Joe but you have trained him too well Bill he is standing his ground.”

“You know it is funny Viv but since we returned from London neither the Wingco’ nor Wings have called me in for an interview, now I think that is very strange.”

Tommy interrupted with. “Post is here and it is a package from the Embassy.”

“We will leave you now,” said Derwent.

“No stay where you are this should be interesting it should contain our I.D.s and my new rank.” Oh my God take a look at this Tommy.”

On the I.D. card it read…rank…Colonel.

Tommy screamed with delight as she flung her arms around him. Turning to Derwent and Viv she was bursting with excitement. “They have made my Bill a Colonel,” she managed to blurt out through the tears of joy running down her face.

Both Derwent and Viv congratulated Bill with hugs “That announcement is going to send some shock waves in the Officers Mess here.” said Derwent.

“There is a letter here referring to the rank, I will read it out.

‘*Dear Colonel Barrett,*

No doubt your rank will come as a shock to you but that is the status you will be held in here. I have informed your MoD to respect you and your rank of Colonel with immediate effect and any adverse criticism delivered to your person from your ex superiors would be dealt with very severely.

Enclosed is a sealed envelope to be opened by ‘Tommy’ I am sure will bring a sparkle to her eyes.

Aziz bin Faruq

Bill handed the envelope to a wondering Tommy.

On opening it she drew out a short note which read....this is the residence you will occupy. There were a dozen photographs of the house, its contents and surrounds which included a pool. The two women were speechless on the initial viewing but they soon made up for it with screams of delight. After looking at them a few times they decided to pass them over to the men one at a time with a commentary on each.

"Very impressive." Admitted Derwent. "I would like you to put our names first on the list for a holiday with you."

"Yes please," pleaded Viv.

"You will have to give us time to settle down first."

"Come on Derwent after all this excitement we had better go and let them do their unpacking. Thanks for sharing your excitement with us I will dream about that tonight. Don't forget tonight in the Quiet Room."

When they reached the Sergeants Mess Reception they were met by Roy Shaw. "As Mess chairman I invite you to the Sergeants Mess."

Bill and Tommy smiled. "Thank you Mister Chairman we are happy to accept your kind invitation."

As they entered they faced a room full of Mess Members and their wives who greeted them with loud applause.

"What is all this Roy?" Bill asked.

"This is our farewell dance in honour of you and Tommy. We could not get permission to officially dine you out but we came up with this social evening." He then shook Bill's hand and added very quietly..."Sir. Derwent let me into the secret, Bill, I am so proud of you!"

Bill addressed everyone. "Thank you, you are very kind and it is nice to see so many of our friends here tonight, please carry on it is going to be a long night so Tommy and I will have time to talk to you all....we hope."

"Come on we have a table reserved for our little group and we are favoured with a personal steward." Derwent, Viv and Barbara were already sat there waiting to greet them.

"Did you bring your photo's?" asked Viv

"We certainly did," replied Tommy, "but shall we have a little natter first we have had so little time together to talk of late."

"Excuse me butting in, but I suggest that the first thing would be to order our drinks I'm thirsty," pleaded Derwent.

The little natter inevitably concentrated on Bill and Tommy leaving. Many questions were asked and answered until Barbara announced. "Come on then Tommy I am dying to see your photos." On seeing them she gasped in disbelief. This is just for the two of you?"

"Not really, the servant's quarters are included."

"Servant's quarters? Roy, get a letter sent off quickly to Mister Aziz offering our services. We will definitely come and pay you a visit and it would be a lovely setting for a honeymoon. Where are you going Roy all of a sudden?"

"To the bar of course our glasses are empty." Off he scampered followed by a roar of laughter. At the bar the steward who was attending to the group took the order and said. "I will bring it in sir."

"Well get me a quick Scotch first I am in a state of shock."

"Are you feeling ill sir?"

"No, I have just had a fright and I want to calm my nerves before going back in there."

"It is a pity Mr and Mrs Barrett are leaving us, all our staff thinks the world of her and we are certainly going to miss her."

"And I wish I was going with them," replied Roy as he downed his Scotch."

He returned to the group followed by the steward carrying the drinks.

"You have been a long time," queried Barbara.

"I have just been having a friendly chat with the steward that's all."

They were suddenly interrupted by Wings. Sorry to interrupt your cosy little tête-à-tête but will someone tell me what is going on?"

"It is quite simple sir we are holding a private social evening for friends to say their farewells to the couple who are leaving us."

"Why was I not informed of this, have you conveniently forgotten that I am still the Sergeants Mess President?"

"As I have just said, this is a private gathering and with respect sir it has got sod all to do with you!"

"We will see about that and your attitude is bearing on insubordination, furthermore I notice a lack of respect by remaining seated when I walked in. I shall be taking further action against you four service personnel."

"Perhaps Colonel Barrett will have something to say about that Squadron Leader!" replied a smirking Roy.

"Him a Colonel, that is the funniest thing I have heard for a very long time. He will never be an officer as long as he has a hole in his ear." He snarled at Bill, "If you are accepted as an officer Barrett I will resign my commission."

"That will come much sooner than you think except you will not get the opportunity to resign. You have already put your foot in your mouth now put the other one in and keep quiet while I read you your demise."

"I am not going to stay here to listen to your drizzle."

"You will stay where you are Squadron Leader and that is an order."

He then read the letter from Mister Aziz while the rest of the group's faces were wreathed in 'stick that in your pipe and smoke it' grins.

"This is something I never thought could happen. Squadron Leader Cody you have finally shown your true colours. You played your game well and got what you set out to achieve....quick promotion, now you have met your Armageddon. I shall submit my report on your behaviour to Mister Aziz, and then I think your reign at RAF March will come to an end much sooner than later. Now my advice to you is to leave this Mess quietly and quickly."

A very dejected Wings left without saying a word.

Derwent and Roy shook him warmly by the hand. "That was brilliant Bill," said Derwent "I will never forget that as long as I live."

"Spoken like a true officer and gentleman, I am proud of you Bill," said Roy.

Barbara and Viv gave him a big hug and a kiss, "You were wonderful."

"Oooh, you were so masterful," grinned Tommy, "come here while I give you a great big smackaroo."

"Steward," called Roy, "bring a bottle of champagne please and tell the barman I will settle up with him later. We have to celebrate that episode."

The steward brought the champagne. "I have a message from the barman for you sir, 'Don't leave the country.'

"Toast time," announced Roy. To the loveliest couple and best friends one could wish to have. We wish them every success and happiness in their new venture and please never stay out of touch with us."

"Don't you think we should go and mingle with our friends?" questioned Tommy "that is why they came."

They moved from group to group thanking them for being so kind by coming to pay their respects.

Joe Franks asked if they had upset Wings. "He went through here with a face like thunder I thought it looks like somebody is in for a rollicking then he passed through here ashen faced without a word to anyone although a few did greet him. What did you do to him in there?"

"I did hear Joe that he has been giving you a hard time just lately.

"I can handle him Bill have no fear on that."

"So I understand Joe you remember that Latin phrase for not letting them grind you down."

"I certainly do and they won't."

"Keep this to yourself; you will have no further hassle from the little toe-rag he showed his true colours to me with insults about my person and new rank.

When I submit my report on his behaviour his feet won't touch the ground. He is a ripe candidate for Civvy Street."

"Thanks Bill once more you have got rid of the rotten apple in the barrel. By the way what is your new rank?"

"Colonel."

"Bloody Nora that is equivalent to Group Captain and here I am talking to you as an equal."

"Joe, we are still equal the rank will not change my outlook nor will I turn my back on old and trusted friends. Keep it to yourself until we have left RAF March there is only our little group besides yourself who know of this."

"Will you do me a favour Bill and let me buy you a drink? I have never bought one for a Colonel before especially when he is a damned good pal of mine."

They went to the bar all smiles and chatted away until Tommy came and broke them up with. "Roy wants to make a farewell speech."

"Ladies and gentlemen," began Roy. Thank you all for coming this evening to say your farewells to this lovely couple, not for a knees-up or a booze-up but for the respect you have for them. Most of us here have plenty to thank them for, for what they have done for this Mess and the personal help they have given us. Due to Rules and Regulations plus a spoke or two put in the wheel we were unable to give them the usual dining-out night, that is why we are here tonight and from your turn-out it has been an excellent substitute. Please shall we wish them well in their new venture in the usual way?"

The applause and shouts of 'Good Luck' lasted for a minute or two, until Bill lifted his arms in a gesture for enough.

"Thank you friends, that was heart warming for me and Tommy. I will make this short and sweet. In all my service I have never made as many friends as I have here in RAF March. We are very pleased we did not have a dining-out that may sound selfish because we know you wanted to send us packing in the time honoured manner but it was not to be. The occasion would have been too emotional for us and I did not want to lose my macho image. I would like to close by saying on behalf of Tommy and myself thank you for your friendship that is something we will always treasure. If anyone of you is in the vicinity of where we will be living you are quite welcome to pop in for 'A Barrett's Brew'."

He and Tommy were soon surrounded by well wishers who wanted to kiss and shake their hands in farewell.

♦♦♦

Mid morning on the following day Tommy answered a knock on the door. "Hello Chris' what brings you here?"

"I have a message Ma'am for the Colonel."

"Come in then you can give it to him in person. Bill," she called, Chris' is here with a message for you."

"Be right there, not be a moment. Hello Chris' nice to see you,"

"Good morning sir," he replied coming smartly to attention. "I have a message from…" here he was interrupted by Bill.

"You are in my house now so less of the formalities. Would you like a brew?"

Tommy did not wait for an answer but made her way to the kitchen saying it will only take a minute."

"Sit yourself down Chris' and let me have the message."

"The Station Commander requests you to attend his office at 14:00 hours today."

"Who gave you the message to deliver Chris'?"

"Helen Fraser rang WO Shaw telling him to send a senior NCO with the message."

"Thanks Chris' I was expecting that and the manner it was given adds more strings to my bow. WO Shaw will explain everything to you later, I am not exactly the flavour of the month and there will be a sigh of relief when I leave here."

"Are you still dating Marion Chris'?" asked Tommy.

"Oh yes we are what you called it in your days…courting."

"You have a very lovely girl there just make sure you take good care of her."

"If you will excuse me I must report back. Thank you for the brew."

When Bill walked into Helen Fraser's office she sprang to her feet.

Bill walked to her and kissed her on the cheek. "Remember me Helen? I am Bill Barrett and still your friend."

"Congratulations Bill I am so proud of you and you have got this lot in a right tizz wazz but watch out the daggers are drawn."

"Thanks for the warning Helen but I have come prepared with lots of arrows and I have got a great back-up team in you know who I mean."

"She pressed her buzzer, "Colonel Barrett is here sir."

"Show him in Helen."

"Come on Bill let's go, my money is on you, good luck."

"Colonel Barrett sir," she announced as she ushered Bill into the room."

"Come in Mister Barrett."

Bill saw that the Wingco' was present and did not reply but thought Hey-Up this is the start of the cold treatment by not offering me a seat and he has his back-up man present.

"I requested you come to see me because of a very disturbing report I received from Squadron Leader Cody."

"I received your request from a senior NCO who was detailed to deliver it. And I apologise for not having a person of similar rank to deliver my reply."

"Hmm. Can we then discus this incident that took place in the Sergeants Mess last evening?"

"There is nothing to discuss as far as I am concerned, you have your report and my report is in the mail addressed to the Embassy in London from where any action will take place concerning the incident."

"And what action do you think will take place if any?"

"That is entirely up to MoD."

"Sir"

"I beg your pardon," replied Bill.

"You jumped up nobody you will address me as SIR! And I want you off my station immediately."

"If you will bear with me for a moment please, you asked me into your office and treated me like something you had trod in. You had not even the courtesy to offer me a seat. You have belittled my rank which in fact is equal to your own, I have tried my best to carry out this interview in a civilised manner but it has been a one way exercise. I have a letter here which will explain my position which from your attitude is forcing me to allow you to read which is what I did not want to resort to." He then handed over the letter saying. "You are quite welcome to read it Wing Commander."

After reading it the Wingco' remarked. "It appears you have opened a can of worms Colonel."

"On the contrary Wing Commander, I was leaving this station quietly and without fuss albeit it could not come soon enough for some. It was your fellow officer who opened the can and unfortunately it is having a domino affect. You cannot place the blame at my feet the blame lies with your Squadron Leader's feet because that is where he shot."

"I would like to apologise to you…."

"Don't even try, how can I accept an apology after you turned on me and treated me like dirt?" He looked at the Wingco' and said. "Good luck to you Wing Commander Hopwood, you are a good officer one who can be respected."

"And to you also Colonel Barrett," was his reply.

Bill then turned on his heel and left. As he went into Helen's office on his way out she called him to her. Giving him a kiss she said, "That is for being you. The intercom was accidentally left on so I heard everything that was said, you were brilliant and how you kept so calm I do not know. Sadly this must be our goodbye I am going to miss you a lot but please take good care of yourself and Tommy." Before emotion could take over completely she hastily gave him a hug and a kiss. "Bye Bill."

"It looks like Barrett got the better of me there John," said the CO. to the Wingco'.

"He certainly did sir and without the ammunition he could have used. In my opinion he will make a damned fine officer and he acted like one."

"After my nasty outburst and treatment of him my position now will be in question and all because of that little shit Cody who just had to play the high and mighty. I was trying to save his neck but now that he has dropped me in the 'proverbial' there is no way is he going to get my backing. I would like to know what was in Barrett's report, whatever it was I am more inclined to believe him than Cody."

"Why don't we request Warrant Officer Shaw what really happened, he would be there without any doubt and he is an honest man."

"Good thinking John."

"Helen, ask Warrant Officer Shaw to come to my office."

When Roy was ushered in and saluted the CO greeted him with. "At ease Mister Shaw. I would like you to relate to us what really went on in the Sergeants Mess last evening to cause such an unfortunate incident. You will not be telling tales out of school you have my solemn promise on that, all we require is a true version."

"You will get a true version sir and you have my solemn word on that. He began with the sudden entrance of Wings and ended with his departure. You have my word sir that I would willingly testify on oath is what was said and happened."

"Thank you Mister Shaw you have cleared the mist surrounding the incident and I compliment you for your honesty."

Roy saluted and left the office. Going through Helen's office she called him to her and whispered. "Thanks Roy you were great."

"How on earth…."

She pointed to the intercom. "It must not have been turned off," she said with an imitation of an apology.

"You little minx, but I love you for it," he said giving her a kiss.

"Tell Bill it is panic stations in there."

"Thanks I certainly will."

"Well John what do you think of it now?"

"Deep down I have come to the conclusion that Colonel Barrett was right in his assessment of the ambitious Cody but it has taken a nasty incident like this for him to be found out. He is the bad apple in the barrel sir."

"All the evidence points to that and from the gist in that letter he has as the saying goes up here in the North …muckied his ticket. I am very concerned John as to whether I will be dragged down with him, after all my attitude was down and out disgraceful and he is duty bound to report it."

"It may not come to that sir."

"Well wouldn't you redress me if I treated you like dirt? Of course you would. I will just have to wait and see what happens if I am called to the Ministry its curtains.

After Bill had told Tommy the result of the interview she said. "Right that's it we are moving out. Now I am going out to see someone I will be back shortly, in the meantime start putting our things together."

Sure enough she was soon back. "Good news love, we can stay with Jackie, I gave her a quick account of what is going on and she is over the moon because we are staying with her. I now suggest we pack all our personal possessions then ferry them to Jackie's house, she has given me her key. We will stay here the night and will you go and see Tom Hardcastle to come tomorrow afternoon to take over the Quarter, then it is goodbye RAF March."

When the handing over was completed they went to see Roy and handed in their temporary I.D. Cards and exchanged the events of their respective interviews.

"If any mail comes for us Roy will you see that Jackie gets it please?" asked Tommy.

"Of course and we will tell Jackie when we want to meet you in the March Hare. The CO. will have kittens when he finds out you have taken him to his word by 'getting off his station' that is another nail in his coffin. You are going to put in a report of the treatment you got from him aren't you?"

"He most certainly is," assured Tommy, "he is not going to get away with treating my husband like dirt after all he has done for this station. The AOC will blow his top when he finds out what has gone on."

"Come on love let us go 'home' said Bill as he winked at Roy. Let us go and say goodbye to Chris' can you get Marion over Roy?"

They went next door to see Chris'. "We have moved out into the village Chris', Roy will fill you in with the details."

Marion the PA to Wings entered. "We sent for you to say our goodbyes Marion." Bill said. "Thank you for all the help you gave me." he then shook her by the hand and when he kissed her she broke into tears. Tommy hugged her to console her.

"I hope you are not going to break down Chris'." He said as he shook him warmly by the hand. "You two are a grand couple take good care of each other…we do."

"Bye Chris'." said Tommy as she hugged him and gave him a kiss and you two take notice of what Bill told you." They waved to the rest of the staff and with a final 'Goodbye' they left.

"I just want a word with George Miller to tell him we have been chucked off the site. Are you coming in with me?"

"No I will go on ahead in my car, don't be long."

George jumped up to attention when Bill entered.

"Don't be a bloody fool George it does not become you."

George grinned, "I never thought I would live to see the day when I would have to salute you."

"And neither did I but I can't do owt' about it, it goes with job."

"I heard you had a right bust up with your old pal Wings, is it hush-hush or can you confide in an old friend?"

Bill told him what happened and also about his interview with the Commandant. "That interview ended with him ordering me off the site. I know he is regretting that now but I was not waiting for him to have the chance to withdraw it, so I have handed back my Quarter and until I depart these shores we have been taken in by Jackie."

"After all you have done for this station and responsible for him and our ex-CO getting their promotion it beggars belief. What do you reckon will be the outcome?"

Bill handed him the letter. "Read this George it will give you some idea."

"Bloody brilliant I like it, justice will be done. I only wish I had been born under your star but I am proud of you." He grabbed Bill's hand and shook it warmly. "They say genuine friends stay that way for life, let's keep it that way Bill."

"There is no other way for us old friend and I am going to miss your help and guidance."

"Bill just one more thing. Less of the 'Old', now get out!"

Bill grinned, and as he turned at the door he muttered… "Bloody Station Warrant Officers I've .... em."

George just laughed after him, typical Barrett but I'm going to miss him.

♦♦♦

After settling in with Jackie they spent a few days with his sister Nessie in the Lake District where he enjoyed himself doing a bit of fishing in the lake and swapping yarns in the local pub with his fishermen friends.

Tommy busied herself collecting recipes from Nessie for future reference. "They will come in very handy when I have to invite the ex-pats to dinner I will give them something to think about when I give them a home cooked meal."

Their final farewell party was held in the March Hare pub for their friends who wished to attend. Sam and Mary Brown were delighted to attend yet sad they were losing two good friends. Mary was especially upset because she and Bill had been long serving friends in the service and she thought the world him, so did Ann the pub landlady, the three of them were the instigators of the BlueBelle Team and Ann had photographs of the teams proudly displayed behind the bar for everyone to see. The party ended with everyone joining in Auld Lang Syne and wishing Bill and Tommy well.

Departure Day arrived all too quickly, Jackie was storing all their effects they could not take with them and assured them her place would always be home to them when they returned to England. Roy, Derwent, Viv and Barbara arrived in the larger vehicle loaned to them again by Fred Fox their favourite Sergeant barman to ferry them to the airport. When they were loaded up it was a very tearful parting from Jackie their adopted Mum, Tommy insisting she would be in touch with her regularly. It was very quiet in the vehicle for a little while their four friends never spoke giving Tommy the time to get over leaving Jackie.

"Did you say you were being met at Gatwick?" Asked Roy.

"Yes by Jackson the chap who drives the VIPs for the Embassy. We are staying two nights at the Savoy Hotel. Tomorrow we have to check in at the Embassy for a last minute briefing and to check our paper work is in order. No doubt Jackson will whisk us off to his RAAF club."

"Here we are folk announced Derwent as he drove into the airport car park. Roy jumped out and quickly grabbed a trolley. After checking in they all went for a brew until, 'Go to the gate' sign showed up on the sign board.

Once more there were tearful farewells, handshakes and hugs. Promises of keeping in touch were demanded. "Remember," said Roy "we are and always will be....Family."

"Have a safe journey and God Bless."

They went through the departure gate with Bill's arm around a sobbing Tommy.

CHAPTER 55 ~ THE NEW MANAGEMENT TEAM

Squadron Leader Cody resigned from the Royal Air Force rather than face a court martial. His replacement was a Flight Lieutenant Arthur Ticker.

Group Captain Pilling was reduced in rank to Wing Commander and posted.

Wing Commander Hopwood was promoted to Group Captain and was made Commanding Officer of RAF March.

His replacement was a Wing Commander Charles Chaplain.

♦♦♦

Warrant Officer Anderson was awarded the MBE.